GODS AND GRAVES

KATIE MAY

EXPRESSO PUBLISHING, LLC

To my family, for believing in me. Most people would call me insane for trying to write this book in six days, but you supported me, kept me caffeinated, and encouraged me to take breaks when my fingers started to cramp. Love you all!

FOREWORD

This is a why choose/ reverse harem romance meaning the FMC won't have to choose between her love interests at the end. **It is a standalone.**

Tropes you can expect inside of this book:

- Instalust
- Greek mythology
- Possessive, protective love interests
- Touch her and die
- Slightly insane FMC
- Completely insane love interests
- "I have a real body!"
- Elite supernatural warriors who will do anything for their girl
- No OW drama

- NO MM
- Mixed-species harem

Here are a list of triggers:

- Violence
- Past sexual assault and abuse (some explicit flashbacks in chapter 42 that can be skipped)
- Death
- Neglectful parents

CHAPTER ONE

THEA

It starts with a tingle, followed by numerous vibrations that reverberate up and down the length of my arms. Then I begin to feel light-headed and nauseous, my stomach twisting into a thousand knots.

Finally, my dagger materializes in my hand and illuminates, the runes etched along its handle emanating a soft golden glow.

I groan and grip my head as I feel that familiar, incessant tugging sensation in the center of my chest.

Not now...

Not so soon after the last one...

Of course, no one hears me or listens to my plea.

No one ever does.

I'm speaking into a radio that has long since shattered.

The world around me dissipates one molecule at a time until I'm left in a sea of dazzling white light. I blink, and when I reopen my eyes, I'm no longer standing in my prison for the better part of an eternity.

I'm in a bedroom.

Where a vampire pounds into a succubus, sweat beading on his forehead from exertion and her hands gripping his shoulders.

"Yes, Jasper, yes!" The succubus writhes and moans on the bed, arching her back so her perky tits are practically in his face.

He lowers his head to suck on one of her nipples as his thrusts increase, the sound of skin slapping against skin filling the room.

I wonder which one of them it's going to be this time. Usually, it's obvious.

I have to say this is much more entertaining than some of my other...trips.

I'm not particularly attracted to either of them, but waves of blazing heat race through my veins, and my lower belly tightens. My core throbs as I watch the two lovers together. My nipples harden where they brush against the fabric of my shirt.

"Way to work it, Romeo," I deadpan, though neither of them turns towards me. They can't hear or see me, of course. No one alive can. "I love the enthusiasm. And way to be encouraging, Juliet. Ten out of ten performance."

The vampire—Jasper, *not* Romeo, my preferred nickname for men in these situations—begins to strum her clit as his fangs sink into the skin of her breast. She cries out in pleasure, raking her fingers through his unruly brown hair.

"Yes, baby. Yes," she coos, her lips curling upwards.

At first, I think her smile is because of the mind-numbing orgasm she obviously just had. Lucky bitch.

Then Jasper cries out—the sound anything but pleasurable—and trembles erratically. White foam erupts from his slightly parted lips, still stained red with her blood.

The woman's smile turns cold. Calculating. Malevolent.

Ahhh.

Interesting.

There's nothing more entertaining than a lover's spat, especially when it morphs into murder.

"You shouldn't have cheated on me, you lying bastard," she hisses, climbing off the bed with an intentional sway to her hips.

She tosses a strand of silky red hair over her shoulder and grabs a bathrobe off a hook on the door. She doesn't close it, however, which makes me wonder...what's the point of it? I can still see *every-*

thing, from her bloody tits to her mound of red pubic hair to her arousal drizzling down her thighs.

Have some damn modesty when you're murdering someone. Geez.

Meanwhile, Jasper claws at his throat, silent tears streaking through the blood and foam on his face.

I volley my gaze between the two of them then pantomime eating popcorn. I honestly have no idea what popcorn tastes like, but I like to imagine. Crunchy, probably. And I know most have a buttery flavor.

Now what does *butter* taste like?

My mouth waters at just the thought.

"How could you cheat on me with my own goddamn sister?" The succubus bares her teeth at the sobbing vampire.

"Yeah, you tell him, girlfriend!" I fist-pump the air then take another bite of my imaginary snack. "Cut off his lying, cheating dick and feed it to a shark. Of course, you'll have to buy a shark first, but...semantics."

"P-please." Jasper can barely get that one word out.

The poison in the succubus's blood is already coursing through his system. If I have to hazard a guess, I would say he only has a few minutes left to live.

Even as I think that, a white orb coagulates beside the bed, slowly taking form until it vaguely resembles a humanoid male. Then, the features become more defined—sharp nose, square jawline, bushy eyebrows.

On the bed, Jasper releases one last rattling exhale and then goes still.

Beside the bed, the ghost version of Jasper blinks erratically, his gaze dancing from his body, to his lover, and then finally landing on me. Shock and horror bleed into his monochromatic gray gaze.

"Who the fuck are you?" He doesn't sound scared yet, just confused.

I imagine it's a shock for him to be wrenched out of his body and thrown into the world of darkness and shadows. A lot of times, it takes the spirit a few minutes to even understand what happened in the first place.

"Jasper." I huff out a deep, heavy inhale, followed by a shortened exhale in a piss-poor attempt to mimic Darth Vader. "I am your father."

Another exaggerated breath.

His brows draw together, and I resist the urge to roll my eyes. No one ever understands my sense of humor—if you can even call it that. "Insanity" is another descriptor I've heard used once or twice.

The dagger in my hand begins to glow even brighter, and Jasper's eyes dip to the weapon in shock. Then that shock quickly morphs into toe-curling fear, his eyes widening and his skin losing color. Well, more color. I don't know why all the ghosts show up as some variation of white, black, and gray, but it's almost as if the second their souls leave their bodies, so does their color.

The pulling sensation—like someone wrapped a cord around my heart and is tugging relentlessly with both hands—becomes impossible to ignore. The air around me practically crackles with electricity. Raw, unencumbered power eats at my veins.

This is going to suck.

It always does, each new soul destroying a piece of me.

Literally.

"Please. No." Jasper shakes and cries, lifting his hands in the air as if he has a chance in hell of fending me off. "Take her! She's the bitch who killed me!"

He points at the succubus, who is still monologuing over her lover's corpse.

But my feet move of their own accord, and a drum pounds between my ears.

"Please! Please! No! No!" His crying ceases when I slam the dagger into his chest.

Almost immediately, tingles radiate up my arm in a way I imagine an electric shock would. I shake from the intensity of it, gritting my teeth to keep from screaming in pain.

Voices barrage me from every direction.

"We're back…"

"Did you think we would let you go?"

"We're watching. Always."

And a new one joins in with the others, the gravel cadence unmistakable.

Jasper.

"How could you let her live when she killed me?"

Thousands and thousands of voices all echo around me, a symphony of macabre dissonance I can't escape from. The walls begin to ooze a strange black liquid, and spiders skitter across the wood flooring. I have to remind myself repeatedly that these illusions are only in my head, but when a particularly large insect crawls onto my foot, I scream and kick.

I need to return.

Now.

Magic cocoons me like a warm cloak, and the bedroom fades away. I find myself standing in my eternal home, the dagger still clutched tightly in my trembling hand.

"Murderer..."

"Killer..."

"Death..."

Pain curls through my veins like liquid flames, overtaking my blood, burning me from the inside out.

God, is this what it's like to die?

Thank fuck I'm immortal. But I could do without the agony.

My legs give out, and I fall to my knees, agony thundering through me.

You can do this, Thea. You can do this.

Slowly, a sob catching in my throat, I begin to crawl towards the very center of my room, where a raised stone pedestal stands—a startling contrast to the other modern amenities in my glorified prison.

Almost there.

Just a little farther.

Keep going...

With a gasp, I lift my hand and set the dagger on the pedestal. Almost immediately, the voices cease, the pain dissipates, and the hallucinations stop.

But I know the reprieve will only last for a short while.

After all, I'm death's favorite reaper.

CHAPTER TWO

THEA

I have no memory of anything before this life—if you can even call it that. It's more of an *existence* than anything else.

I imagine that, at one point, I was alive. Human. Or maybe it's just wishful thinking. It would be nice to believe I had an existence outside of this stifling isolation. Maybe people who loved and cared for me. A family.

When I'm not called on a mission, I'm kept in this room, which changes constantly with time, with the exception of the pedestal.

My room is large and circular, with no windows or doors. There's a queen-sized bed that remains mostly untouched, since I don't need to sleep, and a wardrobe that holds everything from Victorian dresses to jeans and band shirts. A bookshelf rests against the far wall, and a couch and television are positioned opposite it.

There's also an easel with a canvas on it, as well as paint supplies, though I don't use them often. One would think that an eternity would make me an incredible artist, but that couldn't be further from the truth. I draw the way I imagine a rabid monkey would if it got repeatedly poked with a stick.

And, in the very center of the room, is the stone pedestal.

Runes adorn the siding, similar to the ones on my dagger. I have no idea what they mean or represent. All I know is that placing the dagger on top of the pedestal is the only way to stop the pain, the voices, the insanity.

Errr. Scratch the last one.

I'm pretty sure I'm past the point of no return in that department.

With a sigh, I flop onto the immaculately made bed and twist so I can see my best friend. My only friend.

"So...I had another murder today," I begin conversationally, absently fiddling with a strand of my golden hair. "I got to watch it happen."

Potty, of course, doesn't answer.

Prickly bitch.

"Apparently, Jasper was cheating on his girlfriend with her sister." I wait for a response that never comes. "I know, right? It's insane. I wish I had popcorn."

Potty the Cactus continues to regard me silently.

"Don't judge me," I scold the cactus. "You would find murders entertaining too if you were me. Now, if you're done being a judgmental prick in the mud, I'm going to nap."

I huff and close my eyes, resting my hands on my chest.

Of course, I can't actually sleep, but I like to pretend. It seems easy enough. The people I watch simply close their eyes and then drift away.

I wonder what dreaming is like.

After a solid minute of silence—which I swear is a record for me—I sit up and stretch out my muscles.

"That was a good nap," I tell Potty, but the cactus just gives me a "you're a dumbass" look.

Rude.

Ignoring her, I move towards my wardrobe, intent on reorganizing it for the one millionth time. Maybe I'll do it by length? No, I did that three weeks ago. Color *and* length? Era? Size?

My chest aches as I begin the painstaking task of organizing my clothes. I can't help but think of the lovers I just saw—even if it did end in death.

What would sex be like?

Love?

I don't have the option for either of them. Not only can I not touch a living being, but I also can't interact with the world of the dead besides reaping souls.

I don't know what it's like to be touched.

Don't get me wrong—I've gotten pretty skilled at doing it myself, but I know it's not the same.

Sometimes, I imagine hands caressing my skin, worshipping my flesh. Lips closing around my nipple while a tongue strokes my clit.

The throbbing between my legs intensifies, and a tiny whimper escapes me.

I want that. Badly.

So fucking badly.

However, that's not a possibility for someone like me. Not only am I trapped here on my off-time, but my interactions with the outside world are severely limited. I just woke up here one day centuries ago with no memory of my past and with the innate knowledge of what needs to be done.

Hell, I don't even have a name. Not really. Thea is the name I chose for myself.

My lust fizzles and fades as a crippling sadness takes its place.

But I'm used to these ping-ponging emotions by now. I usually have at least one grand epiphany every day.

My current one?

I'm stuck like this forever, so I better get used to it.

CHAPTER THREE

EVERETT

"Target just left. I repeat, the target just left," I say into my earpiece from where I crouch on a neighboring roof of the pub we're staking out.

"Roger that," Zaid says simply.

"Aye, aye, captain," adds Rafael exuberantly.

Krystian remains silent, but that's not necessarily a surprise. He may not be able to speak in his current position.

Our target—a wolf by the name of Dennis—stumbles just in front of the bar, his eyes glazed from intoxication and sweat coating his cheeks.

"How much did the fucker have to drink?" I ask no one in particular.

Krystian, who's currently in the bar, says, "About...five?"

"Five what? Five beers? Five shots? Five fruity fucking cocktails?"

A feminine giggle sounds through my earpiece, and I resist the urge to roll my eyes. Of course Krystian would be using the opportunity to flirt. It's not as if we're on a job or anything like that.

"Following him now," Zaid tells me, and below, a collection of shadows takes form and trails behind a stumbling, hiccupping Dennis.

Sometimes, I love my accelerated vision.

Other times, I fucking despise it.

Like right now, when I watch Dennis shove down his pants, grab his tiny cock, and aim it at the side of the building. A steady stream of piss gushes from it, and I wrinkle my nose in disgust.

"Is he peeing?" Amusement laces Rafe's tone, and the psychopath breaks into laughter. "Please tell me he peed on Zaid."

"Fuck off," Zaid grumbles, still in his shadow form a few feet away, out of range of the piss shower.

Smart thinking.

As a wraith, Zaid is able to alternate between his real body and this shadowy, incorporeal one. Makes him a fucking terrific spy. However, he can only hold this form for about an hour and usually only during the day, when the shadows are the most prominent.

"Krystian, get into position," I order.

There's another feminine giggle, a heavy sigh, and then what sounds like footsteps.

"I apologize, ladies. I have to head out," my elf teammate says formally, his British accent more pronounced than usual.

"Awww."

"Really? You just got here?"

"Maybe we can change your mind..."

Three? *Three* women? Fucker's only been in the bar for a half hour, at most, and spent most of that time watching Dennis and reporting his movements to us.

Of course, most women—human and supernatural alike—can't resist Krystian, with his white-blond hair, golden skin, and slightly pointed ears. His good looks draw them in, but his sunny personality keeps them hooked.

Krystian excuses himself from his adoring fans then steps outside. His gaze automatically drifts to me, high up on the roof next door, and he flips me off.

"You couldn't have given me a few more minutes?" he asks, amusement quirking up one corner of his lips.

"That's how long it takes you? No wonder women don't come back for seconds," I quip.

Krystian chuckles. "Oh, they come back for seconds. I just send them away."

"Can we focus, please?" Zaid asks in his soft, sibilant voice. "The sooner we get this done, the sooner we can return home."

Rafael mutters something about the compound not being home, but we all ignore him. The compound is the *only* home any of us know.

Especially since the world has changed so drastically from when we were first put to sleep, almost three or four centuries earlier.

When the truth of supernaturals came out to the humans, about four hundred years ago, the gods also revealed themselves. They vowed to be the protectors of the humans, saving them from rogue creatures that kill indiscriminately. Thus, the elite teams came to be. Each of them was chosen by a god with one purpose and one purpose alone—to protect those who can't protect themselves.

Centuries ago, I was born with a birthmark shaped like a sword and a shimmering haze surrounding me.

Ares chose me as one of his champions.

The other three were all born within minutes of me, and together, we trained and learned how to utilize our skills as supernaturals to protect the innocents. When we reached the age of twenty-five, we were put into a deep, catatonic sleep, which would only end when we were needed, since there's only ever one team active at a time.

We woke up two years ago, after Aphrodite's team was slaughtered by a feral giant.

"Target is in position." Zaid's voice cuts through my thoughts like the slash of a whip.

Immediately, I hop to my feet and take a running jump into the alley four stories below. I land in a crouch, my senses heightened, and meet up with Krystian. For once, his cocky smirk is no longer on his face.

"Let's get this over with," he tells me, reaching behind him.

A second later, a bow and arrow set materializes as if out of thin air—though I know it's actually a product of a powerful glamour.

We race the last few feet until we reach the destination we decided on earlier. It's a narrow street too big to be considered an alley, nestled between tall brick buildings. The smell of garbage assaults my senses from the rows of dumpsters lining the wall, and I inwardly curse my enhanced shifter senses.

Zaid solidifies beside us.

"He's there." He points to where Dennis is attempting to unlatch the gate at the end of the street in order to get home.

We've watched him long enough to know he takes this route every day when he returns home from the bar. He believes it's a shortcut, but the dumbass doesn't realize it actually adds five minutes to his walk.

Krystian notches an arrow, and it zips through the air and embeds itself in our target's leg.

He immediately cries out and falls to the ground, surprise and fear crowding his features as he turns in our direction.

"W-what? What's going on? Please. Don't hurt me. You can have all my money." The pathetic waste of space begins to throw handfuls of cash in our direction.

I bite back a snort.

"We don't want your damn money." Krystian's nose crinkles derisively, as if the mere idea we're petty thieves is laughable.

"You've been a naughty boy, Dennis." I tsk my tongue in mock disapproval.

"W-what are you talking about?" Dennis splutters. "How do you know my name?"

"Do you know what my arrows can do?" Krystian begins almost conversationally as he grabs one of said arrows and holds it in front of him. He reverently runs the pad of his thumb over the tip. "They're called light arrows. Have you heard of them?"

Dennis whimpers and scoots away, until his back is flush against the chain-link fence.

"They eat away at your skin. I would say you have, maybe, five more minutes until you're experiencing pain like you've never felt before." A wide, terrifying grin spreads on Krystian's face.

Sometimes, it's easy to forget that he's just as insane as the rest of us.

He hides his monster well—buries it beneath carefully curated smiles and flirty winks designed to lure you in.

"You're going to die for what you did to those women, Dennis," I tell him, folding my arms over my chest.

I don't feel an ounce of pity or guilt as I stare at the pathetic waste of space. He brought this on himself.

All of those human women he tore apart...

Dennis is the worst kind of monster because his acts were intentionally insidious. He *brought* those women to his house. He shifted into his wolf, knowing what his beast would do. He ate them alive, then he buried what was left of their bodies the next day.

"But I'll let you choose how you die." Krystian's grin widens, revealing the dimple in his right cheek that drives sane women crazy. "You can either let the arrows do their work, or..." He glances towards the far wall where Rafael has been watching the entire exchange silently. "You can let my friend end you."

Dennis starts sobbing harder, obviously knowing his death is inevitable.

He turns tear-filled eyes towards Rafael, snot pouring from his nose. "Please. Make it quick."

Krystian, Zaid, and I all wince.

They always choose Rafael.

And they always come to regret that decision.

"I'll make it as quick as you made your kills," Rafael says in a singsong voice, his normally stoic expression morphing into a demented, playful smile.

Then he pounces.

I quickly look away, my stomach muscles cramping. It's not because I'm disgusted by the display of violence or feel pity for Dennis.

It's because I hate that my teammate has turned into this...monster.

As a blood fae, Rafe has to drink blood more often than a vampire in order to utilize his powers. But the bloodlust has corroded away his mind—chipping away a piece at a time—until all he cares about is violence and death. He *revels* in tearing his victims apart. Listening to them scream. Having them beg for it all to end.

Krystian catches my gaze and nods at my unspoken question. "I put a glamour up. No one should be able to see or hear what's happening here."

"We're going to need a goddamn trash bag for all the body parts," Zaid huffs, frowning. "Again."

As Rafe rips Dennis apart one limb at a time, I can't help but think this is the only life we'll ever know. We're trapped in this routine, with no hope of escaping.

We get summoned.

We kill.

Then we repeat.

It's what we were trained for, but I can't help but wish for...more. What that "more" is evades me.

There's no use wishing for something that will never be.

We're stuck like this forever, so we better get used to it.

ZAID

It's surreal for me to think about how much has changed since we were first put to sleep—nearly four centuries earlier.

Phones. Cars. Internet. Televisions.

Hell, even the clothing is significantly different. I don't know if I'll ever get used to jeans.

It's eerily silent when we step into the compound, though I'm not surprised. At one point, there were hundreds and hundreds of supernatural teams training here. That all changed, though, when the gods and goddesses got involved. Everything is a competition between them, and our lives are no different.

As of now, there's only one elite team awake at a time, and we're in charge of policing the entire supernatural world.

Cold rage surges in my chest at the injustice of it all, though I force myself to breathe past it.

This is my purpose, after all. What I was born for.

But sometimes, I can't help but wish for more.

"Ares!" Everett throws his duffel bag on the ground as he steps farther into the room. "We're back."

The compound itself is massive, but it doesn't feel spacious. The walls, made of dark stone, stretch up high, their rough surface jagged and uneven in places, making it feel like the room was carved straight out of the mountain itself. The dim light from the overhead bulbs barely cuts through the gloom, leaving long shadows dancing across the floor.

The bunks are arranged in neat rows—over one hundred in total—though the majority are empty. Each bunk is just a simple iron frame with a thin mattress, the kind meant for functionality, not comfort. What's the point when we're barely ever here to begin with?

All of our beds are in opposite corners of the open room. We love each other like brothers, but being cooped up for days at a time... We need our space. Desperately.

"Ares!" Everett calls again.

"Hold your goddamn horses," a familiar gruff voice calls, and a second later, the god himself enters through a side door.

At first glance, you would think Ares is in his late

thirties, early forties. His eyes burn like twin coals, dark and smoldering with the fire of an unquenchable fury. He wears a pair of ripped jeans and a dark Henley, the outfit complete with a leather jacket that squeaks when he moves. His hair is wild, as dark as the night sky before a battle begins, and moves with the same restless energy that he does, caught in an invisible wind.

I can't help but both admire and fear Ares, our creator.

He's terrifying, but he's also the closest thing I have to a father.

I don't remember my life before I joined my brothers on our tenth birthday. Ares warned us that the deep sleep would leave holes in our memories, but sometimes... Sometimes, I get flashes of faces.

My birth family, I think.

"How did the mission go?" Ares's keen eyes travel over us, his lips twitching upwards when he notices Rafe covered in blood.

"Target neutralized," Everett says formally, standing with his hands clasped behind his back and his chin notched in the air.

"I see the target resisted," Ares says with a pointed look in Rafe's direction.

The tentative smirk from before transforms into a full-fledged smile. The crazy psychopath lives for this shit. His domain is the blood-soaked soil of the battle-field, the sound of weapons meeting flesh, the cries of dying warriors.

"We took care of him," Everett says, his voice and expression still carefully impassive.

"Good. Good." Ares taps a finger against his chin before seemingly coming to a conclusion. "Get some rest. You're being sent out in a few hours. Here's the case file."

"Yes, sir." Everett grabs the manilla envelope while I grit my teeth together.

We've only just got back from this mission—and before that one, five more. We haven't been able to sit still in fucking months.

This is your job, Zaid. What you were trained for.

As Ares exits the room, I move towards my bunk with a sigh. I'm too high-strung to sleep currently.

I hear the others moving around as well, and I can't help but think of the compound years and years and years ago.

Apparently, before the elite teams came to fruition, there were hundreds of supernaturals who trained here. Then, when the gods and goddesses decided to involve themselves, all of the select teams were chosen at once. We trained alongside Athena's warriors. Artemis's. Hades's. Zeus's. Aphrodite's. Hermes's. We were all put into a deep, catatonic sleep at the same time, with one team at a time being called to action.

Most of them are dead now.

The first elite team came from Zeus himself. They lasted twenty-seven years. Then, Hephaestus took over, but his warriors only survived eight months. Then it was Artemis's turn, then Apollo's, then Athena's, then Aphrodite's.

Now, it's our turn.

All we can do is fight supernaturals until we die.

And it's not only normal supernaturals, either. Sometimes, demons escape from the Underworld, and we have no choice but to put them down.

At least Ares seems to give a shit about us. He provides us with the materials we need to succeed. Perhaps it's merely because of his competitive nature—he's desperate for us to last longer than his ex's warriors—but it gives us an edge in combat.

Sitting upright in bed, I consider my bookshelf. It's been way too fucking long since I had the chance to simply sit and read a book. Before I can select a title, however, I become aware of eyes on me, the feeling accompanied by a prickling sensation.

"Did you need something, Krystian?" I ask, not bothering to turn from the shelf.

Krystian takes my question as an invitation to enter my personal space. He practically throws himself onto the foot of my bed. "If we're leaving in a few hours, it's going to be dark."

"Don't worry. We'll watch after him," I tell Krystian, knowing exactly what he's worried about.

Krystian dramatically wiggles, shaking my entire bed as he drags himself until his head is dangling over the side.

"I know. I know. I'm just... Ugh. I just don't remember this being such a big deal before we were put to sleep."

"I understand," I tell Krystian seriously.

Honestly, I don't know how the fuck I turned into the built-in therapist for all of my team members. Maybe it's because I'm a naturally quiet person, preferring to watch and study from the shadows. Either way, they all come to me when they need advice or if they simply want to vent.

"I know it can't be easy on you."

"Just make sure he doesn't do anything stupid, okay?" Krystian sits up and spears me with an uncharacteristically serious expression. "Promise?"

"Of course."

He asks me this almost every night, and I always have to reassure him. I understand why he's nervous—what he goes through is unnerving as fuck—but he has no reason to be fearful.

"I wonder what we're hunting down this time

around." Krystian blows out a breath, stirring a strand of white-gold hair in the process. "I hope it's a demon."

"Why a demon?" I absently bring a hand to my side, remembering the feel of claws raking across my skin.

Fucking demon.

"Because they're mindless idiots and don't beg for mercy when we kill them," Krystian answers simply.

I frown, unable to disagree with him.

Sometimes, our victims' cries make me feel a little bit like the monsters we hunt and kill.

"You can't feel guilty for what we do," I tell Krystian firmly. "We only hunt down the worst of the worst. They don't deserve to live after what they did."

"Yeah. Maybe." Krystian doesn't speak right away, and I almost think he fell asleep. I'm seconds from kicking him off my bed and onto the ground when he sits upright with a sigh. "Just...keep an eye on Krys tonight, yeah? You know how he can be when he's on a mission."

"Everything will be fine," I tell Krystian, wishing I could believe it myself.

When did "fine" start losing its meaning?

How can we be "fine" when we're prisoners to a war we don't even understand?

Sometimes, I feel like we're nothing but pawns on a game board the gods designed themselves. They move us around like we're stringless puppets and don't hesitate to beat us down when it serves their purpose.

Krystian leaves, no doubt to bother Everett until nightfall, and I finally decide on a book.

Settling back against the pillows, I dive into a world where the good guys have a choice in whether or not they take down the bad guys.

CHAPTER FIVE

THEA

"Lisa, you bitch! How could you cheat on José with José's twin brother? And José! How could you impregnate Lisa's mother?" I scream at the television screen—some sappy Spanish soap opera centering around a dysfunctional, and a slightly incestuous, family.

It's been an entire hour since I've been called away to reap a soul. My last one was a ninety-five-year-old woman on death's bed. I'd been gentle with her, offering her my hand and pulling her into my embrace. I didn't want her to see the dagger, so I quite literally stabbed her in the back.

"José! Don't do it! Don't you dare do it!" I jump up and down on the couch.

Well, float up and down on the couch. I don't need to sit if I don't want to. Actually, I don't really know how it works. I float normally and can drift through walls, ceilings, and floors. However, this room, and the items in it, are different.

For one, I can't leave. The walls are completely solid.

For two, I can actually touch the furniture in my prison. Lie on the bed. Recline on the couch. Flick through the channels on the television. Hold a paintbrush.

Yet, if I choose to, I can float in the area or pass through the television.

Whatever magic keeps me contained here is fucking outrageous.

"José! I swear to fuck—" I begin, then curse when, on the screen, José pulls a beautiful woman into a passionate embrace.

Anna, Lisa's sister.

So now José—the horny fuck—has slept with every woman in the family.

"You're going to regret this decision," I tell José seriously, as if he can actually hear and respond.

Sometimes, I like to imagine the characters can.

And sometimes, they actually do. This usually occurs after I reaped multiple souls back-to-back and haven't had time to return the dagger to the pedestal. My hallucinations will create a life-sized José and Lisa and Anna and Mary and Fernando.

A sudden pain bursts through my chest, setting every nerve ending aflame, and I gasp.

Fuck.

Not again.

The dagger flies off the pedestal and into my waiting hand, the runes already aglow with that strange, heady magic.

"Wait!" I beg to whomever is listening. "Let me finish this episode. I need to know if Lisa is going to take him back!"

Of course, no one listens to my desperate pleas. No one ever does.

Bright light seeps across my vision, like a fresh ink blob getting doused in water. The world around me changes and distorts.

Tall, spindly trees poke through the forest floor, and a blazing sun bears down, with wispy, feather-like clouds cloaking the lower half.

"Who's the lucky contestant today?" I murmur, pivoting on my heel to take in my surroundings.

Forest...

Daytime...

And no people.

No one.

Nada.

Nothing.

I huff and fold my arms over my chest, tapping one of my feet impatiently.

"Hello!" I call out. "Can someone die already, please? I have a soap opera to get back to."

Predictably, there's no response, and my irritation grows.

Why can't the person already be dead?

Why am I always forced to watch it happen?

Pounding footsteps precede the appearance of a huge beast.

A wolf?

No, not a wolf.

A hellhound.

The creature's massive form wears a cloak of coal-black fur that ripples with an unnatural, molten sheen —as though its very hide is imbued with the essence of fire. Its eyes—two burning orbs of crimson—glow with an intense, demonic light. Its elongated snout twists unnaturally, baring yellow teeth as sharp and jagged as broken glass and dripping with saliva that sizzles when it touches the ground.

The beast is large and terrifying and intimidating and—

"You're fucking adorable," I coo, placing my hands on my knees to stare at it better. "Who's a good hell-hound? *You're* a good hellhound. Yes, you are. Yes, you *are*."

Hellhounds are mindless beasts created when hell's fire bubbles to the surface. They hunt indiscriminately and burn their victims alive.

Adorable.

The creature paws at the ground, and a low, guttural growl reverberates from deep within its chest.

Is this the creature I'm reaping? I've never done it with animals before, only humans and supernaturals. I wonder if the creature's victim is nearby. Maybe that's who I'm—

An arrow sails through the air and embeds itself into the hellhound's side. The monster releases a howl of rage and anger, whirling around to face the attacker.

"Mamma Mia," I murmur, ogling the man stepping from between two trees. "Who are you, and where have you been all my life?"

I've seen hundreds of thousands, if not millions, of men in my time on this earth, and none compare to him. Just his presence ignites all of my nerves and makes my nipples pebble.

Blond hair, the strangest shade of white-gold, frames an angelic face plucked from heaven itself. He's muscular, but not in a way that's overwhelming or excessive. A white T-shirt clings to his physique in a way that shouldn't be legal. The slightly pointed ears let me know he's an elf.

"Over here!" the elf calls, his arrow still trained on the snarling beast.

Holy crap.

Is that a British accent I detect?

I begin to subtly fan myself, even as an uneasy feeling slashes at me.

Is he the person I'm here to reap?

For some inexplicable reason, ice-cold fingers of dread creep down my spine.

I don't want to stab him, dammit. He's too sexy to die.

Another man races out of the forest holding an onyx sword—one of the only substances capable of permanently killing a hellhound.

"Good grief. Did I just intrude on a sexy man convention? And how do I get an invitation to attend every year?" A frisson of electricity curls in my chest as I study the newest man.

Sandy-blond hair, though it could actually be a shade of light brown. Hazel eyes. Broad shoulders. Thick, corded biceps. Tapered waist.

I find myself licking my lips repeatedly and force myself to stop.

Too creepy, Thea.

Knock it off.

"Let's take him down." The muscular man steps forward, his sword raised.

"Um... I wouldn't do that if I were you," I interject, but of course, they don't hear me. "I think you're forgetting that hellhounds usually—" Three other beasts emerge from the forest, their heads lowered and growls rumbling through their chests. "They travel in packs, dumbass."

Everyone knows that.

It's in the Hellhound 101 guidebook.

The elf curses and swivels until his arrow is aimed at a different hellhound, this one approaching from the right.

"Fuck! Zaid, we need you," he calls.

I nearly shit my pants—metaphorically, of course, because I don't actually need to poop—when the shadows beside me combine to form a third man.

This one's smaller than the other two, but he's no less attractive. Pitch-black hair falls slightly in front of his face, which is pale and sharp, with high cheekbones and a strong jawline. He holds a sort of unassuming beauty that captivates me more than any of the others. It's...unusual. *He's* unusual.

I can't put my finger on what it is about him. Maybe it's the fact that his features aren't perfectly proportionate like the elf's are. Maybe it's the tiny scar on the other side of his jaw. Maybe it's the strange color of his eyes—not blue but not quite gray either.

Butterflies spin drunkenly in my stomach.

"You're a wraith, aren't you?" I move until I'm only an inch away from his face, standing on my tiptoes to study him better. "Want to be my shadow daddy?"

The wraith—Zaid, apparently—lifts his hands in the air, and two whips of shadows slash at the nearest hellhounds, forcing them back. More and more shadows appear and begin wrapping around the creatures, holding them still.

In front of me, the sandy-haired supernatural lunges at the closest hellhound, his sword raised.

The elf fires arrow after arrow at the hellhound advancing on him. Each place the arrow touches causes the skin to sizzle and crack.

The last two hellhounds are still contained by Zaid's shadows. I wonder how long he plans to do that. Is he going to join in the fight or—?

"WHOOO!!" The voice comes from above me— far, far above me.

I jerk my chin up to stare at the tallest tree, where a figure balances precariously on the highest branch. Then, to my absolute horror, he jumps.

"Um...okay, then," I say, blinking.

The man lands on one of the hellhound's backs with a deranged cackle.

"Dude, do you know you have blood on you?" I ask the newcomer, gesturing vaguely towards my own face.

Actually, he's drenched in blood. It coats his shoulder-length black hair, streaked with red and blue, his tan skin, and his clothing. When he smiles, I notice some of his teeth are sharper than the others.

A vampire, maybe?

No. Not a vamp.

A blood fae.

I can tell by his hair. Those red and blue strands? They're natural, not dyed. Only fae have hair like that.

A blood fae, a wraith, a shifter, and an elf.

It sounds like the start of a bad joke.

The fae begins to stab the hellhound repeatedly with his dagger. Only when the creature falls still does he jump to his feet and move to the next victim. God, even the way he walks is terrifying. He moves like a predator that suggests he's not trapped with the hell-hounds—they're trapped with him.

It's kind of hot, if I'm being honest.

Warmth radiates through me as I watch the four men fight. They're strong. Powerful. Lethal.

And one—or all of them—is going to die.

The reminder cools my raging libido like a bucket of ice water. A tremor works its way through me, and panic claws at my gut.

Which one will it be?

As I watch, the shifter gets slightly too close to a hellhound's paw and risks losing his head.

I yelp and call out, "Be careful, okay? Don't stand

too close to their damn paws. It's common sense to not put your head in the path of a deadly object, yeah?"

The shifter ducks at just the right moment, then he slams his sword up, spearing the creature's chest. The hellhound's molten eyes widen then glaze over. Its body goes still.

"Woo!" I cheer, pumping my fist. "Three down. One to go."

I turn my attention towards the final creature, still engaged in a battle with the elf. The creature's skin is sizzling and deteriorating before my very eyes, yet it doesn't stop its relentless advance.

"Come on. You got this, elf boy. You can do this," I encourage from the sidelines, praying the fire in my chest cremates the lump in my throat.

It's hard to breathe.

The elf fires off one more arrow, then he dives out of the way of the hellhound's attack.

But the monster doesn't slow down as it continues to race forward, its head lowered and nostrils flared.

Is it coming for...me?

No, not me.

The wraith beside me.

A scream catches in my throat just as the hellhound tackles the wraith to the ground, its talons digging into his skin.

"No!" I scream, desperate to do something, anything.

Without thinking, I slam my dagger into the hellhound's flank, and the great beast goes still. A tiny whimper escapes it just before it falls on its side, dead.

Oh...*fuck.*

Fuck. Fuck. Fuck.

Did I do that?

I stare at my dagger in disbelief.

How is that possible? My dagger can't pierce the flesh of living creatures. Is it because the hellhound isn't actually living? Is it because it's a part of hell? Is it—

A voice reaches me then, his gravel tone scraping across my skin. "Who the fuck are you?"

I whirl, only to immediately pause when I see a sword aimed at my head.

Wait, what?

I flick my gaze to the right and then the left, but... nope. There's no one standing directly behind me or beside me.

"Um...you talking to me?" I ask, expecting him to ignore the question entirely.

They always do.

"Who the fuck else would I be talking to?" The shifter takes another step closer, and the tip of his sword slices at my skin.

Holy shit, that hurt.

That hurt.

I can feel pain—and not the usual agony I experience daily reaping souls, where it feels as if all of my internal organs are being rearranged and then stomped on. No, this is different.

I can *feel*.

The sword against my neck. The grass under my bare feet. The wind battering my cheeks.

Then I do probably the most idiotic thing imaginable.

I begin to laugh.

CHAPTER SIX

KRYSTIAN

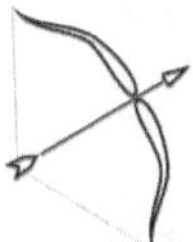

The first thing I notice is that the girl is beautiful. Otherworldly so.

Her face is small, almost delicate, though her lips are full and pouty. Kissable. Bitable.

Wavy, golden hair cascades around her shoulders like moonlight and sunlight woven together. Blue eyes, framed by thick lashes, peer back at me, wide and guileless and full of disbelief.

She wears, of all things, a dress. A goddamn ball gown. The bodice clings to her ample breasts, the fabric adorned with hundreds upon hundreds of tiny, intricate jewels. The skirt is short in the front, revealing the full extent of her tan legs, and long in the back. It extends behind her like a gossamer train.

One second, the area she now stands in was empty.

The next, she appeared, seemingly out of thin air, with a dagger in her hand.

A dagger she used to save my brother.

Who the fuck is she?

Why is she following us?

Did she have something to do with the hellhounds and their attacks?

"Who. Are. You?" Everett repeats, digging the sword into her skin hard enough to draw blood.

I wince instinctively, despite knowing she's a threat. It's hard for me to see a woman in pain. Call me old-fashioned.

I may be a womanizer, but I'm a *respectful* womanizer.

The crazy chick begins to laugh, tears streaming down her cheeks as she holds her stomach.

"Oh my god. What is happening?" she breathes out through peals of laughter.

She seems entirely unconcerned that Everett has a sword at her throat and Zaid has snuck up behind her.

Rafe and I stand slightly apart, though I haven't lowered my bow yet. She's hot as sin, but they're usually the most dangerous. Certainly the craziest.

Rafe simply tilts his bloody head to one side, staring at her with unblinking eyes.

Then, abruptly, the woman drops to the ground and begins to pluck at the tufts of grass.

"Oh my god! Grass! This is what grass feels like!" she exclaims, a wide, beguiling smile on her face.

It somehow transforms her from simply beautiful to...ethereal. Stunning. Breathtaking.

Fuck.

"Here! Feel!" She holds a blade in Zaid's direction, who simply gapes at her, unsure of what to say or do.

I understand his dilemma. On one hand, she saved his life. On the other...

"Who the fuck are you?" Everett repeats, exasperation tinging his tone.

"Thea." Still sitting, she extends a hand for the surly shifter to shake.

He doesn't.

But I, unlike my neanderthal brother, have manners.

"Pleasure to meet you, Ms. Thea," I say, leaning over her proffered hand to press my lips against her skin.

"So that's what a kiss feels like," she murmurs, her gaze fixed on where my lips touched her.

A flush crawls up her neck and seeps into her cheeks.

Has this stunning woman never been kissed before?

I feel my cock stir to attention at the prospect of her being untouched. Innocent.

"Thea." Everett says her name like it's a curse word, though if Thea hears the derision in his voice, she doesn't show it.

She simply turns to him and smiles, waiting for him to continue his interrogation.

"What are you doing here? Were you following us? Did you send those hellhounds after all those people?"

The smile fades from her face, and her nose crinkles in a way I almost find...adorable.

Ugh.

What the fuck is wrong with me?

"Um. I'm here because I was doing a job, same as you, apparently. No, I wasn't following you. Not really. I only stalked you for, like, five minutes, tops. And finally, no. I did not send those hellhounds after anyone. That would lead to more work for me."

"She's telling the truth," Rafe says quietly, his head still canted at an odd angle as he studies her.

As a member of the fae community, Rafe is incapable of telling a lie. And as a blood fae, he can detect whether or not anyone else is lying. He says their blood has a "tell"...whatever that means. I think he's full of shit, but I wouldn't dare call him out on it. The last person who challenged Rafael ended up in thirty-seven different pieces.

I don't necessarily like the way Rafe is staring at the girl now.

That unwavering intensity... I've only seen it a few times before.

And every time, the person who captured his attention ended up dead.

"If you weren't following us, then why are you here?" Everett demands, his jaw twitching.

"I told you." Thea stares at him like he's daft. "I'm working."

"Were you hunting the hellhound?" I ask, and when she turns to me, I flash her an encouraging smile.

"Errr. Yes?" She phrases it as a question.

"Lie," Rafe deadpans.

Thea huffs out a breath, blowing at a piece of blonde hair that has fallen across her face.

"Okay, fine. I was hunting you guys." She waves her hand in the air dismissively, but I go very, very still.

She was...hunting us?

I don't want to think that someone as tiny as her is a threat, but I can't deny her words or the severity of them.

"You just said you weren't stalking us," Everett growls, digging the sword into her throat once more.

"I wasn't. I only just arrived." She sounds defensive.

"All of this is the truth," Rafe tells us, his tone carefully impassive.

Dozens of questions flood my mind, each one more confusing than the last.

"We don't want to hurt you, lovely Thea," I tell her with another charming smile—though the effect is probably lost on her, considering I still have an arrow trained at her chest. "Just tell us the truth."

"I'm telling you the truth." She plucks at another blade of grass and holds it in the air to examine it, twisting it to and fro. "I only just arrived, but I came for you guys. Or, at least, one of you. Don't know which one for sure, though I'm ninety-nine percent sure it was for your handsome wraith."

She lifts her free hand...which I now see holds a strange dagger etched in runes.

"Drop your goddamn weapon!" Everett barks.

At the same moment, I pull back the string of my bow.

Please don't make me shoot you.

Please, please don't make me shoot you.

"You asked me for the truth!" Thea points out, sounding exasperated. "I was sent here to collect one of your souls. I don't know what happened, or how long it'll last, but somehow, I ended up corporeal."

My heart hammers in my chest like a caged animal.

"Wait." I slowly lower the bow so it's no longer aimed at her. "Are you saying...?"

"I'm a reaper," she explains with an eye roll, as if that fact should've been obvious. "And I was supposed to reap one of you. Probably the wraith, but somehow, I saved his life instead. Now...can one of you buy me popcorn? Please?"

CHAPTER SEVEN

THEA

est. Day. Ever.

If I would've known stabbing a hell-hound would lead to this, I would've done it ages ago. Not that I know what "this" is or how long it'll last, but for now...

I inhale deeply, taking in the unfamiliar smells of the forest. Pine, I think it's called. And something else, something distinctly earthy.

And who would've thought being slightly stabbed with a sword would make my skin feel like it's burning?

Eeep.

I jump to my feet—god, the grass feels amazing beneath them—and turn towards the wraith. I did save his life, after all. The least he can do is buy me some popcorn.

And maybe give me some orgasms, but we'll get there with time.

Baby steps.

"Sooo. About that popcorn?" I fold my hands together and gaze up at him innocently, pushing my lips out.

He blinks, seeming at a loss for words, and I call that a win. I think I like making him speechless.

"Come on! Chop, chop! Let's go. Who knows how long this will last? What if it's permanent? Oh my god." I squeal and clap my hands together.

Next to me, the wraith winces, reaching a hand out to cover one of his ears.

"You're a reaper?" The shifter stares at me incredulously.

If I had to guess, I would say he's the leader of this little group. If I want to get my popcorn, he's the one I'll have to impress.

"Pretty sure." I shrug, already bored of this conversation.

Above me, a bird flies by, cawing, and I turn my head to watch it, transfixed. What would a feather feel like? Soft, I imagine.

"How can you be 'pretty sure'?" Irritation laces the shifter's tone.

"I don't know." I shrug again. "I just...arrived in my

little prison room and started reaping souls. I'm pretty sure that means I'm a reaper."

He exchanges a glance with first the elf, then the blood fae, and then finally the wraith. Confusion draws his brows together.

"Is that normal for a reaper?" he asks, and at first, I think he's talking to me.

But the wraith is the one who answers. "I've never researched them before, but from what I gathered over the years, they're born and trained by their families until they eventually take over. I don't even think they're immortal, though they do have longer-than-normal lifespans."

Huh. Interesting.

But not as interesting as my popcorn is going to be.

Look, I may not know a lot, but I do know my one purpose in life is to reap souls. If that doesn't make me a reaper, then what else am I? I wonder if I'm some elite super reaper. Ohhh, like an assistant manager to the other reapers, though I've never done anything even remotely "manager-like" in all my centuries of existence.

"What are we going to do with her?" The shifter thrusts a hand in my direction.

Are those tattoos on his skin?

"Ohhh. Pretty," I murmur, instinctively reaching for him.

I've always wondered what a tattoo would feel like. Is it different from normal skin? Coarse? Rough? Soft?

Just before my finger can make contact with the angel wings, the shifter pulls away from me with a snarl.

"Don't fucking touch me."

"Don't fucking touch me," I growl, mimicking his tone. Then, a thought occurs to me. "What are your names?"

The shifter folds his arms over his chest and scowls, obviously not in the mood to talk, but the elf takes a step closer.

"I'm Krystian, love. That brooding, angry asshole is Everett. The wraith is Zaid. And the blood-soaked psycho is Rafe."

Zaid smiles timidly, though he doesn't make a move towards me. Everett continues to scowl. And Rafe? He just watches me, his head tilted to the side, blood sliding down his face and neck in steady streams.

I wave at him.

He blinks.

I wave again, a little more vigorously, and finally, he lifts a hand and wiggles his fingers.

"God, the movies made it sound like making friends would be hard, but it's not, is it? I already have four amazing besties." I clap my hands together enthusiastically.

"Friends?" Krystian draws his brows together.

"Besties?" Everett growls, then he bends to grab my dagger, still embedded in the hellhound's side. He cries out in pain and drops the weapon, shaking out his fingers. "What the fuck?! It burned me!"

"Maybe you shouldn't touch what doesn't belong to you." I awkwardly reach for the dagger and slide it into my thigh sheath.

"What the hell is that thing?" Everett demands, still staring at his fingers like they betrayed him.

"It's her version of a scythe," Zaid answers, appearing stunned. He forks his fingers through his dark hair, ruffling the strands. "Fuck, this is insane."

"It fucking burned me!" Everett repeats.

"It didn't want you to touch it," Rafe deadpans.

Krystian takes a tentative step forward. "Why don't we bring her back to the hotel for now? Just until we have more information."

"Someone keep an eye on her at all times," Everett grunts out, still glaring at me.

"Oh. A hotel? I've never been to a hotel before. How far away is it? Does it have a pool? A hot tub? Let's go!" I begin to skip ahead of them, but before I can make it more than a few steps, someone grabs the veil of my dress and gives it a tug.

"Wrong way," Rafe says, still staring at me with unnerving intensity.

I give him a two-finger salute and then hurry in the opposite direction, jumping over the dead hellhound bodies.

This is fucking awesome.

THIS IS *NOT* FUCKING AWESOME.

"How much longer?" I whine, dragging my feet.

My bruised, bloody feet.

Apparently, walking barefoot through a forest is a big no-no.

"Why the fuck aren't you wearing shoes?" Everett snarls.

He has only just seemed to realize my current predicament, his eyes intent on the blood staining my soles as I hold one up after the other to inspect them.

"Because I was incorporeal and never had to worry about shit like this," I snap back.

Apparently, pain makes me crabby. Who would've thought?

"Here." Krystian moves in front of me and kneels down.

I stare at his back in disbelief.

What the fuck does he want me to do?

Wipe my blood off on his shirt?

Before I can voice my question out loud, I feel hands on my waist, hoisting me in the air. The tan, bloody hands tell me they belong to Rafe.

A second later, I'm on Krystian's back, my legs dangling. I instinctively squeeze his throat in a death grip.

"Can't. Breathe," Krystian rasps.

"Sorry." I loosen my grip.

Krystian rises, and I realize that he's giving me a piggyback ride so my poor, abused feet won't have to touch the ground.

My pulse thrashes sickeningly.

"So..." I begin conversationally, resting my chin on Krystian's shoulder. "You're an elf?"

Krystian chuckles, and I decide I like the sound. It's...calm. Comforting. Warm.

"How can you tell?" he asks sarcastically, wiggling his pointed ears.

"You're a light elf, correct?" I continue.

I can't help but wonder what he would do if I licked the shell of his ear. I'm not an idiot. I know that can be seen as...inappropriate, but the desire to do so is nearly overwhelming.

My question, for some reason, makes Krystian stagger. I tighten my grip on him, but he regains his footing before we both become intimately familiar with the forest floor.

"Something like that," he answers evasively, and I don't press.

My knowledge of the world only stems from what I gathered during my reaping jobs and through books and movies. Light elves and dark elves have been at war for centuries. Light elves derive their power from the sun, while the latter utilizes the moon. Besides that little snippet of information, I don't know much about them.

"So, how long have you been working with this group?" I ask, desperate to keep the conversation going.

Who knows how long I have before I poof out of existence once more?

Krystian seems relieved at the subject change, the knots in his shoulders loosening.

"Do you want the literal answer or the figurative one?" He slides his gaze towards me, his eyes twinkling.

"Um...both?"

"Well, we met hundreds of years ago, after we were all born marked as a member of Ares's team. We trained until we were in our twenties, then we were put into a deep sleep until we were needed. We woke up only two or so years ago."

"Two years, three months, twenty-seven days," Rafe deadpans from farther back.

"Wait..." I remember hearing about that. All of the gods and goddesses chose an "elite team" that they trained in an elusive, secret compound. Only one team is ever active at a time, and the second that team is killed off, a new one takes its place. "You're Ares's team?"

"The one and only." He chuckles, though the sound is strained, lacking any genuine warmth or amusement.

"Enough small talk. We need to get a move on if we hope to make it back to the hotel before dark," Everett snaps with a pointed look in Krystian's direction.

Once again, the muscles beneath my fingers turn taut, though Krystian doesn't snap back.

The five of us walk the rest of the way in silence, and the entire time, I brace myself for my body to fizzle and fade away. For my dagger to heat where it rests in its thigh holster—because I refused to leave without it and no one but me can carry it. For the voices in my head to scream at me incessantly. For the tug in my chest to intensify.

It never comes.

And I can't help but wonder...

Am I free?

Or is this another gilded cage I have no hope of escaping from?

CHAPTER EIGHT

THEA

We walk for hours.

Well, *they* walk. I simply hold on to Krystian for dear life.

"Why didn't you guys take a car or something?" I grumble, fiddling with the collar of Krystian's shirt.

I like the feel of the fabric sliding against my fingers.

"Because you can't drive a goddamn car through the forest," Everett snaps.

He doesn't seem to like me much.

"And we were following the hellhound," Zaid adds. He, too, isn't walking. At some point, his legs morphed into shadows, and he simply floats above the forest floor. "We had to be stealthy."

"Does Everett even know the meaning of that word?" I ask seriously, regarding the large, sexy shifter.

He's a mountain of muscle, and each footstep he takes makes the ground shake and tremble.

Everett tosses me a dirty look over his shoulder and then turns away with a scoff.

"Tough crowd," I whisper in Krystian's ear.

The elf shivers.

"So...when you're not hunting monsters, what do you like to do in your spare time?" I ask, flicking my gaze from face to face.

When no one immediately answers, my smile fades.

Oookay. Awkward.

Then Zaid clears his throat and flashes me a timid smile, one that makes him appear boyish and innocent. I decide I like him the best. He's the nicest.

"I have a collection of books I love to read, though I haven't had the chance in a while." Color crawls up his neck and settles in his cheeks.

"Oh my god!" I squeal and tighten my grip on Krystian instinctively, my arms digging into his neck.

He sputters and stumbles, and I release my choke-hold. Oops.

"You like to read? I *love* to read! What are some of your favorites? Are you in a book club? I've always wanted to join a book club, but...you know...there's a lack of opportunities where I'm from."

Zaid absently scratches at the back of his neck, still seeming embarrassed.

But why would he be? Books are amazing.

"Errr. Thrillers, mostly."

"And romance." Krystian turns his head to stare at me, waggling his eyebrows. "He loves a good smutty romance."

"I don't blame him," I respond seriously. "Some of the best plots and character development I've read were from romance books."

Zaid's lips begin to twitch at the corners, and he ducks his head.

"She's right, you know."

Of course I am.

Zaid and I will totally have to set a time where we can discuss all things books. I have a shelf in my bedroom that changes constantly—new books coming and going faster than I can read them. I don't know if the magic in the room is responding to my mood somehow or if there's something else at play.

"So Zaid likes to read. What about the rest of you?" I lower my chin so it can fit snugly on Krystian's shoulder. "Let me guess. You like archery?"

Krystian's chuckle reverberates through me, and liquid heat infuses my veins.

"I wouldn't say that, love. Am I good at it? Yes. Do

I like it?" He shrugs, the movement shifting me. "Not necessarily."

"So what do you like?"

He stops walking and cants his head to the side, considering. The fingers gripping my thighs flex and twitch.

"Huh. I don't think anyone has ever asked me that before." A note of wonder enters his voice.

"Well, I'm asking now. What do you like?"

A smile scrawls over his face. "Video games."

"Video games." I blink at him.

The man is basically a live-action video game—complete with the kick-ass bow and arrow set.

"I don't play them often, but it's fun. Relaxing. I like being able to kill monsters, knowing I won't die myself. You get do-overs in video games. Resets. Saves. Not so much in real life."

An unfamiliar emotion sits in my stomach like a poisoned blade. I can't put a name on what it is. Pity, maybe? No, that doesn't sound right.

Sympathy?

No...

Empathy.

Yes, that's it.

I'm empathetic. I can understand exactly what it's like to be trapped in a role you don't want to play.

"Well, maybe if I'm still around, we can play a game together?" I ask tentatively, suddenly feeling shy.

Krystian's answering smile causes the nerves swirling in my belly to dissipate, replaced by a baking, pervasive heat.

"It's a date," he says.

Everett scoffs and shakes his head.

"Well? What about you, big guy? What do you like to do in your spare time?" I ask him, raising my voice to make sure he hears me.

He glares at me over his shoulder, his eyes like shards of ice, sharp enough to do irreparable damage. Of course he doesn't answer, simply stalks farther ahead like he wishes to escape me and my questions.

Rude.

"Rafael? What about you?" I turn towards the last member of the team—and the most mysterious one.

So far, he hasn't said more than a few words at a time, but I can feel his gaze on me like a physical caress, pulling me under in a riptide I can't escape. Each sweep of his eyes causes my heart to smash against my ribs and goose bumps to pebble on my arms. It's unnerving and terrifying and exciting in a way I can't articulate.

"I like to kill things," he whispers.

His voice is deep and raspy, almost husky.

I chuckle. "I mean, besides killing things. What do you like to do?"

"I told you. Kill things." Through the blood smeared on his face, his brown eyes penetrate my defenses.

I suddenly feel uncomfortable—too hot, too itchy—and I wiggle slightly. Krystian slaps my thigh lightly in warning.

"Stop moving," he reprimands.

"Sorry." I wince.

We finally break through the tree line and onto an empty street. In the distance, I can see the lights of a nearby town and hear the honking of horns.

After what feels like hours later—but Krystian assures me it's only ten minutes—we arrive at a dilapidated motel that has seen better days.

"I thought you said you guys were staying in a hotel?" I arch an eyebrow in Everett's direction.

"We are." He stares at me like I'm a turd who gained arms, legs, and abruptly developed a sentient mind.

"This is a motel," I point out. "Hotels have doors to the rooms on the inside. Motels have them on the outside."

Everett seriously looks as if he's going to strangle me.

"Same fucking thing," he grits out.

"Actually—"

One of Krystian's hands leaves my thigh and moves to my mouth, covering it.

"Let's not poke him any further than we have to, okay?" Despite his words, laughter rings in his voice, the sound having the acrobats in my stomach doing backflips instead of mere somersaults.

Everett leads us to two rooms side by side. He claps his hands together and spins to face us.

"All right. Let's clean up, then maybe get some food, okay?" He purposely doesn't look in my direction —making it clear I'm not invited on their little outing.

Whatever. I don't mind crashing.

"Yeah. *Someone has a little blood on him*," I stage-whisper, jerking my chin towards a blood-drenched Rafael.

The fae doesn't even blink.

Everett grinds his molars together. Then, without another word, he storms inside the room closest to him. Rafael regards me for a second longer—my heart stuttering with warning at the possessive, predatorial gleam in his gaze—before he follows after Everett.

Leaving me alone with a shy wraith and a grinning elf.

"Well." I playfully squeeze Krystian's ear. "Aren't you going to invite me into your room?"

Zaid and Krystian exchange a glance, before the

former sighs and digs in his back pocket for a key card. Krystian pushes the door open with me still clinging to his back.

The room—like the rest of the motel—is rundown. Two queen-sized beds are separated by a tiny night-stand holding a remote control, a phone, and what appears to be a channel brochure. A television is mounted on the far wall with a dresser underneath it. A floral armchair rests in the corner of the room, numerous holes adorning its surface. There's a door opposite the entrance that no doubt leads to a bathroom.

"You know…" I muse as Krystian lowers me to the ground. "Usually, guys buy a woman dinner before bringing her back to their room."

Zaid snorts as he moves to lie on one of the beds. Krystian makes a beeline towards the bathroom.

"Most guys don't have girls quite literally appearing out of thin air in front of them." He's silent for a moment, his gaze contemplative, before he sits up. "I never thanked you. For saving my life, I mean."

I wave away his thanks. "Honestly, I'm just surprised it worked. It never has before."

"You tried to save people before?" His brows draw together, creating an adorable furrow in the center of his forehead.

"At first," I confess, fiddling with the hem of my

pink dress, admiring the way it sparkles in the artificial light. "But after three hundred or so reaped souls, I realized there was no point in even trying. Nothing I did or said changed anything."

"So why did you try with me?" Zaid's earnest eyes make my heart flutter.

"I...I don't know. I guess I just didn't want you to die."

"But why me?" he presses, scooting across the bed until he's directly in front of me, his thighs boxing me in.

He reaches for my hands, his touch soft. This... This is what I imagine feathers would feel like.

He's close. Too close.

The air feels thick, and I suddenly can't breathe. And since air seems to be a necessity now that I'm corporeal, that's bad. Really, really bad. I don't know what to say. What to do.

Fortunately, I'm saved from responding by the door to the bathroom opening and Krystian stepping back out. In his hands is a pile of clothes.

"These might fit you," he tells me, dropping them onto the empty bed. He then seems to notice how quiet the room has become—and how unnaturally close I am to Zaid. "Am I interrupting something?"

I jerk away from the wraith like I've been electrocuted.

"N-no!" I stutter out, at the exact moment Zaid says, "Yes."

Traitor.

Krystian smirks before his smile fades, all traces of humor and levity stripped away.

"I thought you could change into some pants and a shirt. Don't get me wrong. The dress you're wearing is hot as fuck, but it's a little old-fashioned. And it can be a little revealing at certain angles."

"A little revealing?" I frown and drop my gaze.

The dress is significantly shorter in the front than the back, but the train should've covered all of the important bits. Unless someone was staring at me from the side when I was on Krystian's back—

"Zaid!" I squeal, whirling on him.

His face turns beet red.

"I'm going to the bathroom!" He practically launches himself off the bed.

Krystian chuckles again. "I also grabbed you a pair of shoes. They're going to be too big on you, but they'll work for now. If we need to, we can stop at the store tomorrow morning."

My chest feels compressed, my ribs too tiny to contain my heart and lungs.

"Why are you being so nice to me?" I whisper.

"Because you saved my brother," Krystian answers simply—and maybe to him, that's all there is to it.

"We'll protect you, Thea. Even Everett, though he'll fight you tooth and nail before admitting it."

Unexpected tears burn my eyes. "I... I... Thank you. I mean it. I want to make sure you know how much I appreciate you—all of you. Especially if I were to disappear again."

God, I hope that doesn't happen—at least not anytime soon. There's no pain. No hallucinations. No incessant tuggings in my chest. No isolation.

A muscle in his cheek flutters. "We'll make sure that doesn't happen. Now..." He claps his hands together and focuses back on the clothes. "Get changed. We need to get some food in you before you wither away on us."

CHAPTER NINE

THEA

"I look ridiculous," I bemoan, studying myself in the motel's mirror.

The pants Krystian let me borrow are four sizes too big and have to be secured around my waist with a belt. The shirt is just as large, practically dwarfing my petite frame. I'm wearing seven pairs of socks—not all of them clean—and even that isn't enough to keep the tennis shoes on my feet.

Krystian presses his lips together to keep from laughing. "You look...nice."

I flip him off.

We reconvene with the other two—Rafael has showered and changed into a leather jacket and blue jeans, while Everett is still dressed in the clothes he wore before—and walk down the street to a diner.

It's surprisingly busy for this time of day, though

we only have to wait a few minutes before getting a seat.

The air smells of burnt coffee and hot grease, a comforting perfume that I can't help but inhale greedily. I could smell things in my incorporeal form, but not very well. Every scent was diluted, sometimes impossible for me to detect. But this... This is something else entirely.

Red booths line the windows, their seats cracked and mended with duct tape. The Formica countertops have been scrubbed clean but bear the soft, permanent dull of a thousand elbows and hot plates.

A single waitress with a name tag that reads Darla moves between the tables with a wearied grace of someone who has done this for years, refilling cups without asking and smiling at familiar faces. From the jukebox in the corner, an unfamiliar song plays, the music warbling slightly as the machine clings to life.

I excessively rub my hands against the booth, my smile growing.

Everett, who is sitting across from me, scowls. "What the fuck are you doing?"

"Have you felt the texture of this booth? It's like...silk."

"Vinyl," Zaid corrects, his blush sharpening when I glance in his direction. "What you're feeling is called vinyl."

"It's amazing." The two of us share a secret smile, but the moment is interrupted by the arrival of the waitress.

Her eyes widen when she takes in my guys—errr, *the* guys. She licks her lower lip and begins to twirl a bouncing red curl around her finger.

"Hello, darlings. Haven't seen you guys here before." She leans forward slightly to offer a better view of her cleavage.

"We're just passing through." Krystian smiles tightly, and I have a feeling the waitress is swooning at his British accent.

I know I am.

Trying to ignore the grating sensation I feel all the way in my teeth, I point to the menus in her hands.

"Can we get some menus, please?" I'm not even sure I'll be capable of eating, but I'm determined to try.

You only live once, after all.

Well, you only come back to a living body one time, after all.

"Oh." She seems flustered, the guys' presence addling her brain.

She passes each of the guys a menu before handing one to me last. She once again leans far enough over the table that I see the lacy edge of her bra.

"Here you go."

The fury inside of me lights like a match.

Ugh. Is this what jealousy feels like?

I hate it.

"Thank you." I take the menu from her, scowling when our hands accidentally brush.

"I'll be back to take your orders." She hesitates a second longer, her gaze sweeping over the table once more, before she sashays away.

Only when she's gone do I huff and fold my arms over my chest. "Can you believe that woman?"

The *audacity* of flirting with the four guys when they're obviously here with me.

"You don't like it when people flirt?" Krystian's mouth curves, and my gaze tracks the movement.

"It's rude." I scowl.

Everett snorts. "You seem like the type that enjoys the attention."

"Huh?" That one sound comes out on a whoosh of air.

"Thea," Zaid begins softly. "You do realize she was flirting with *you*, right?"

"With me?" My voice comes out high-pitched.

"Anyone with working eyes would flirt with you," Krystian points out with an eye roll.

Wait...what?

"But...but... I thought she was..." I gape at the four of them—Rafael and Everett sitting across from me,

Krystian beside me, and Zaid at a seat pulled up to the edge of the table.

"I can kill her if you feel uncomfortable," Rafael suggests, his voice monotone.

Kill her?

"Of course not!" My lips curve into a wide smile. "I've never had someone flirt with me before. OMG! This is amazing!"

"Did she really just say OMG?" Everett asks Zaid, sounding incredulous.

"Let her have it," Zaid responds.

The waitress returns a few minutes later, her cheeks still red and her chest heaving. On closer inspection, she appears to be in her late twenties. She's pretty, I suppose, with reddish-orange hair coiled in tight, corkscrew curls and freckles on her nose and cheeks. I'm not particularly interested in women, but when in Rome, do what the Romans do. Or whatever.

I hold the woman's gaze and sensually lick my lips.

Krystian begins to choke on his water.

"Darla, is it?" I purr, leaning slightly on the table. The oversized shirt does very little to help my figure, but it's the thought that counts. "I think we should rearrange the alphabet to put U and I together."

Zaid blushes, Everett turns his face to keep from laughing out loud, and Krystian facepalms himself.

Rafael? He simply glares at the innocent human wait-ress, who seems at a loss for words.

"What the fuck are you doing, love?" Krystian asks.

"Flirting. Duh."

His white eyebrows climb up his hairline. "Are you interested in Darla?"

I find it kind of rude that we're talking about her when she's standing right there, but I answer Krystian regardless.

"Not really. But flirting's fun. And I think I'm pretty good at it."

"You're not," Everett snaps.

He seems grumpier than usual.

Zaid turns to the flustered waitress and says, "We'll have one of everything on the menu, please and thank you." When he notices my gobsmacked expression, he explains, "Supernaturals need more calories than the average human."

As Darla hurries away to put our order in, I call out, "Text me! Actually, text Krystian. I don't have a phone, but he probably does."

Krystian chuckles and drapes an arm over the back of the booth—and consequently my shoulders.

He leans in close to whisper against my ear, "Are you trying to set me up on a date, love?"

Immediately, a vicious pain burns through my chest, and a growl escapes me.

"No," I hiss.

"No?"

"No dates for you. No dates for any of you." I say this to the rest of the men who are staring at me, a range of emotions on their faces. "Not when I'm around. It's just rude."

"Rude?" Everett gawks in disbelief.

"Everybody knows there can only be one woman per friend group. Duh." I'm totally lying, but hopefully they don't know that.

By the looks on their faces, they totally do.

"You're a vicious little thing, aren't you?" Krystian's fingers lower to absently fiddle with a few loose strands of my hair.

"I would be less vicious if I were in clothes that actually fit me." Quickly, I try to change the conversation.

Before I can come up with something, however, Everett speaks.

"So what did you mean before? When you claimed you were a reaper?"

"Exactly what I meant." I shrug. "I'm a reaper."

"How do you know?" he presses.

"How do you know you're a shifter?" I counter, then I turn towards Rafael. "How do you know you're a blood fae?" I look at Krystian next. "Or you're an elf?" I face Zaid. "Or you're a wraith?"

"And you said when you're not reaping souls, you're kept in a prison?" Zaid asks gently.

It's evident he's taking over the interrogation. I don't mind, though. Anything is better than being yelled at by Everett.

"I don't really know what to tell you guys. I woke up in a room with no windows or doors. No way for me to escape. Sporadically, my chest will begin to ache, and I'll be transported to a death scene. I'll reap the soul then return to my room. I've never been able to communicate or touch the living world before." A pang lights along my heart, more vicious than ever before.

I really, really don't want to go back to that existence.

The guys exchange eloquent glances with each other.

"That's... That's not normal," Zaid confesses, and I don't know if he's speaking to me or the others.

"No, it isn't," Everett agrees with a growl.

"Do we talk to Ares about this?" Krystian asks.

Ares? As in...the God of War?

"What would he know about it?" Everett scoffs. "We'd be better off talking to Hades."

"You want to talk to the god who imprisoned Thea for who knows what reason?" Zaid deadpans, giving Everett a cold stare. "How the fuck would that help us? He'll probably just send her away again."

Panic rakes down my spine, and I tighten my grip on the table, my knuckles bleaching white.

"Please." I can barely get the word out past my numb lips. "I don't want to go back there. Please."

Zaid's expression softens. "You won't."

"But if she was locked away, then it was probably for a reason—" Everett cuts off with a pained hiss, his gaze darting to his hand.

Which now has a butter knife protruding from it.

"She won't go back there," Rafael tells Everett, each word soft and concise.

Violence swirls in his brown gaze—the color so dark it almost appears obsidian.

"Motherfucker." Everett reaches for the blade.

Before he can grab it, however, the waitress returns to our table with plate after plate of food that four other staff members have to help her carry. Quickly, Everett lowers his hand so it's out of sight.

"Here is...one of everything," the waitress says, dropping down the first plate.

We end up having to slide a second table over to fit all of the dishes.

When she's done, she stands back and regards the feast. "Did y'all want anything to drink?"

"Chocolate milkshake, please," I blurt. "And a coke. And a hot chocolate. And a water. And a glass of milk. And a—"

"Four chocolate shakes for the table, please," Krystian interjects smoothly. When I stare at him, betrayed, he says, "Too much sweetness will make you sick, love."

"All right," Darla agrees with a nod. "Anything else I can get for you?"

The last is directed at me, punctuated by a flutter of her lashes.

"Do you have any popcorn?" I smile widely at her, and she blinks, seemingly dazed.

"Umm..."

"Of course they don't have fucking popcorn," Everett snaps, reaching for a burger.

"We'll get you popcorn after dinner," Zaid reassures me.

If I were closer, I would totally kiss him.

The waitress leaves, and the guys divvy up the meals while Everett wraps his hand in a cloth napkin, though the bleeding has already stopped and the wound has started to heal.

Rafael slides a plate in front of me, then he adds a variety of items onto it—tiny slices of chicken, what appears to be a fried dish, a pancake, some pasta, half of a sandwich, and a salad.

"For you," he tells me gruffly, and my heart soars, a trill of sensation lighting along my spine.

"You don't have to eat it all," Zaid says. "If you don't like something, you can just leave it."

"One of us will eat it if you don't," Krystian adds.

I nod, though the food in front of me already consumes my attention. I have no idea where to even start.

Krystian, noticing my dilemma, waves his fork at the pancake.

"Start there. That'll be your breakfast. Then move on to the cheese curds, sandwich, and salad. That'll be your lunch. End with the pasta and chicken to represent dinner."

I beam at him. "You're not just a pretty face, you know that?"

"Oh, I totally am just a pretty face." He winks and leans in even closer until I can feel his breath against my cheek. Shivers ripple down my spine at his proximity. "But I have other talents as well."

I don't know how to respond to that, so I shift slightly on the seat—desperate to alleviate the ache between my legs—and then cut into the pancake. Just before I can take a bite, however, Everett leans across the table.

At first, I think the bastard is trying to steal my food, and I contemplate stabbing him like Rafe did, but he merely pours a strange brown liquid over the pancake.

At my look of disbelief, he grumbles, "Syrup makes it taste better."

Oh.

Hesitantly, I bring the bite to my lips. It certainly smells incredible—now even more so with the syrup on it.

I realize all of the guys are watching me, their food forgotten in front of them.

"Go on," Krystian encourages.

At my hesitant look, Zaid nods once, a smile tipping up his lips. "Trust us."

I take a bite.

CHAPTER TEN

KRYSTIAN

This woman is going to goddamn kill me.

"This is soooo good," Thea practically squeals, then she moans yet again.

The sound travels straight to my cock.

Zaid shifts uncomfortably in his seat at the head of the table. Obviously, my brother is dealing with the same problem I am.

"You seriously never had food before?" he asks, but not in an asshole, accusatory way like Everett would.

He sounds genuinely curious.

"Never." Thea's already digging into her next dish, a beatific smile on her otherworldly face. "You guys seriously get to eat this stuff all the time?"

"Next time, have Everett cook for you," I tell her, trying my damndest to ignore my visceral reaction to those tantalizing moans she continues to make. "He's the best chef I know."

Thea whips her head in Everett's direction, curiosity alighting in her eyes while syrup drips down her chin. And goddammit, all I can think about is my cum taking the syrup's place.

"Really?"

Everett grumbles something inarticulate, but I notice he doesn't outright refuse to. For him, that's progress.

Hell, it's practically a declaration of marriage in Everett speak.

Now that we're satisfied Thea is eating—and obviously loving the food—the four of us begin to scarf down our own meals. It's silent for a few minutes, the only sound the clanging of silverware. At some point, Darla returns with our milkshakes.

I'm ninety-nine percent positive Thea actually orgasms when she takes her first sip. Her blue eyes roll into the back of her head, and her entire body begins to convulse. Darla, who's still standing by the table, appears flushed, her damn nipples poking through the fabric of her uniform.

I don't consider myself a possessive or jealous person, but having her so close to Thea when she's like this...

I tighten my grip on my knife.

"You can go now," Everett snaps at the waitress, his eyes frosty.

I wonder if his thought process went down the same direction as mine.

Or if he can sense how close Rafe is to the edge, hovering precariously at the tip, madness clouding his brown eyes.

Darla stutters out an apology, then she retreats to the kitchen.

God, what the fuck is wrong with me?

Normally, I would find it hot as fuck. I mean, what's better than watching two girls please each other and then having them turn all of that attention onto me? But the thought of anyone laying a single fucking hand on Thea makes me see red.

The reaper continues to "enjoy" her milkshake, oblivious to the direction of my thoughts.

Zaid clears his throat and subtly readjusts himself in his jeans. "We should discuss our next steps." He waits until we're all staring at him before continuing. "Someone obviously knows something about Thea. We just need to figure out who to ask without information getting back to the wrong person."

"Athena?" I suggest, thinking of the calculating, aloof Goddess of Wisdom.

If anyone would know anything about Thea's situation, it would be her.

"She's been MIA for over one hundred years now," Everett points out. "Ever since the team she selected died."

Rumor has it Athena started a relationship with her warriors, which ended when they all passed away on one failed mission. She hasn't been seen since.

"There's only one other person I can think of asking," Zaid begins hesitantly. "Someone who knows everything about everyone."

We all groan—except for Thea, who volleys her gaze between us, confused.

"Who are you talking about?" She uses a napkin to wipe away pasta sauce that has gotten stuck to her lips.

"Aphrodite," I answer, internally cringing.

"You mean the Goddess of Love and Beauty?" Thea's frown deepens.

"The one and only." Everett blows out a breath and reclines back in the booth.

Aphrodite is also Ares's ex, though their relationship ended horribly. I don't know all the details, but apparently, the God of War fell in love with another woman centuries ago. He became so obsessed with the new girl that he stopped giving Aphrodite attention. She was absolutely furious, but her anger only grew when her own team of warriors passed away and we took their place.

It's her mission in life to destroy us. And how does she go about doing that?

Attempting to seduce us.

She knows, as well as we do, that if she were to succeed, Ares would murder us. They may not be together, but Ares is still insanely possessive of her.

Once, when we arrived at the compound, it was to the sight of a naked Aphrodite splayed out on Rafe's bed, one of her hands fondling her tit and pinching her nipple while the other played with her pussy.

I jacked off to that imagery for weeks.

Now, my cock doesn't even stir at the memory of the Goddess of Beauty pleasuring herself.

What the fuck?

How can I get a boner from listening to Thea moan but not feel anything when I think about the most beautiful woman alive in the throes of passion?

Well, second most beautiful.

I'm not sure even Aphrodite can compare to Thea.

For experiment's sake, I close my eyes and think of Aphrodite the last time I saw her.

She lay on the cot, her long hair cascading around her in a curtain of silk. Her large, perfect breasts were peaked from the chill, her pink nipples hard. She squeezed the tight nub and threw her head back, crying out.

She gasped, continuing to twist and flick her nipple. "Yes!"

Her other hand crept over her toned stomach, through her perfectly trimmed pubic hair, and finally to her spread pussy lips. She rubbed her finger through her folds, then she added a second.

"Oh, fuck. Yes. *Yes.*" She began to stroke herself even faster, her back arching and her tits bouncing enticingly.

Then she came around her fingers, her pussy convulsing, liquid gushing down her tan thighs.

At the time, I was hard as steel and had to quickly leave the room before I did something I regretted—like getting her on all fours and fucking her.

Now? I feel absolutely nothing. Not even a stirring of lust.

I think of Thea instead, sitting beside me in a hideous oversized T-shirt and pants that do nothing to accentuate her figure. Her lips sucking on the straw of her shake as moan after moan escapes her.

My cock strains against the denim of my jeans.

"Dude." Zaid nudges me, and I force myself to reopen my eyes, to rejoin the world of the living. "What the fuck was that? You zoned out for a second."

"Nothing," I say quickly.

Too quickly.

But the last thing I want him to know is that I was thinking of Thea's goddamn moans.

What the fuck is happening to me?

Is it because she's attractive? There's no denying she's the sexiest woman I've ever laid eyes on before, but it's more than that. It's...*her*. Her smile. Her laughter. Her joyful innocence.

Am I crushing on a woman I only just met? I want to say no—the mere idea is preposterous—but my body calls me out on the blatant lie.

Something about Thea consumes me.

"So we get a hold of Aphrodite," Everett reiterates, frowning. "Then what?"

"Then we ask her what she knows about me," Thea interjects. "If what you guys are saying is true, then what's happening to me isn't normal."

"It's not." Zaid shakes his head. "I did some more research at the motel when you were changing. There's never been any case like you described."

"So I'm the only reaper in existence trapped in a prison?" Thea absently reaches for a fry on Rafael's plate.

Surprisingly, he doesn't stop her. He actually pushes his plate closer so she doesn't have to strain herself.

That alone is fucking strange. Rafael once stabbed

me in the shoulder when I tried to steal a bite of his pizza.

"What happens if I return to my prison before we can figure out why that is?" Thea queries.

A pang lights along my sternum, and sick panic wells up in me.

She mentioned it before in passing, but now that I'm actually thinking about it...

"That won't happen," I tell her resolutely.

She arches an eyebrow. "How can you be so certain?"

"Because we won't allow it to," Zaid adds.

Rafael simply nods.

"And even if it does, we'll find a way to bring you back." That declaration, surprisingly, comes from Everett, who's focused intently on his empty plate, as if embarrassed to meet Thea's prodding gaze. "You protected my teammate. Now we'll protect you. You have my word."

Then Thea does the worst thing she could possibly do around four hardened warriors.

She begins to bawl.

CHAPTER ELEVEN

THEA

"Why the fuck are you crying?" Krystian sounds horrified.

"I just..." I sniffle, the tears coming faster and faster. "I just never had anyone care about me before. You four are the best friends a girl could ever have."

Overcome by the enormity of my emotions, I reach for Krystian—who's closest—and hug him tightly.

He awkwardly begins to pat my back. "There. There."

"People are looking," Everett hisses, sounding slightly frantic.

When I move to pull away from Krystian, he simply tightens his grip on me, his arms like iron bands.

"Shhh. I got you, love. I got you." He rocks me slightly as my tears stain his shirt.

Once I'm certain I'm no longer a blubbering, inarticulate mess, I pat his shoulder. "I'm okay now, Krystian. You can let me go now."

At first, I think he's going to refuse, but after a few seconds, he releases me with a reluctant sigh.

I settle back in the booth, wiping at the tears beneath my eyes with the pads of my fingers.

"Sorry, guys." I chuckle mirthlessly. "I'm not used to this."

"Having friends?" Zaid inquires softly.

"Having hormones."

A throat clears at the foot of the table, directly behind Zaid, and I lift my head to see Darla standing there. In her hands is a piece of chocolate cake.

"For you," she says shyly, sliding it my way. Concern etches lines into her forehead. "Are you okay, hon?"

"She's fine," Everett barks.

One of his hands forms a fist on the table.

"She's okay," Zaid reassures her. "She's just..." His lips twist. "Hormonal."

That seems to be enough explanation, because Darla hurries away without any follow-up questions.

"I'm really, really stuffed," I murmur, digging my fork into the fluffy cake layered in icing.

"Then why are you eating the cake?" Krystian asks, amused.

"Because I like food."

I close my lips around the fork, and holy fuck. Lust streaks through me, and heat floods my body in an addictive, all-consuming rush. My eyelids begin to flutter as a moan catches in my throat.

"Oh god." Pleasure consumes me—a tide that rises and ebbs, gathering strength until it devours the shoreline. "This is fucking delicious."

I moan again as I take another bite. I don't want a single piece to go to waste. If that means licking each prong of the fork, then so be it.

I continue to devour the cake—unable to stop the moans that escape me—as the guys watch me silently, their eyes heated. At first, I think they're jealous that I got a piece of cake and they didn't, but then I realize it's not the dessert they desire.

It's me.

Need throbs lower in my belly as I take in all four of their expressions. The space between us feels as precarious as kindling and just as ready to burn. I'm a flame personified, blistering hot.

"Was that good, love?" Krystian asks.

His voice is husky, sounding like it's been scraped over coals.

All I can manage is a whimpered, "Hmmm."

Rafael leans across the table, his hand extended, and I hold my breath. His finger catches on the edge of my lip, gliding across it like roughened silk, before he pulls away. Chocolate balances on the tip of his finger, and as I watch, transfixed, he brings it to his own mouth. His tongue flicks out to catch every last drop of chocolate.

"Delicious," he agrees raspily.

My ribs squeeze my heart like a vise.

Everett clears his throat, a muscle in his jaw fluttering. "We should get back to the hotel."

"Motel," I correct automatically.

He ignores me. "It's almost dark."

That one sentence garners a reaction from every man at the table—but none more than Krystian. He stiffens, the lust draining from his eyes until it's replaced by something akin to terror.

"How much time do we have?"

"Relax," Everett says. "We still have an hour."

"What's going on?" I flick my gaze between the four of them. "Are you guys afraid of the dark or something?"

"Or something," Krystian mumbles, appearing uncharacteristically subdued.

Discordant notes scream like alarm bells in my head.

"And are you going to tell me...?" I stare at him pointedly, but he, too, ignores me.

Instead of answering, he flags down the waitress and asks for a bill.

When she returns a few minutes later, she hands it to me, and I notice a number scrawled at the top.

Before I can take a closer look, Rafael rips it from my hands and passes it to Everett, who already has a credit card out. When he catches my look, he rolls his eyes.

"Ares pays well," he explains.

As soon as the waitress returns with a slip for him to sign, we head out of the diner. The motel looms before us, tall and foreboding.

"Come on. We need to go faster," Krystian urges, flicking his gaze towards the descending sun.

"You can go on without us," Zaid tells Krystian. "We'll be right behind you."

Krystian hesitates, his gaze flicking towards me, before he shakes his head, his jaw setting determinedly.

"No, I'll be fine. It's fine." He once again glances at the darkening sky.

"What the hell is going on? What will happen when it turns dark?" I ask, exasperated.

"Nothing," Krystian says quickly.

Too quickly.

"None of your damn business," Everett grumbles.

Zaid, who's walking beside me, smiles reassuringly. "We'll explain later."

Each step he takes has his hand brushing against my own. I wonder what it would be like to just...grab it. Hold it. I've never held anyone's hand before.

So I do.

The calluses on his palm create a unique type of friction that makes my stomach flutter.

Zaid glances at our interlocked fingers, surprise alighting in his eyes. When I smile at him, swinging our hands between us, he returns it, a blush creeping up his cheeks.

We arrive at the motel, and I make a beeline towards Krystian and Zaid's room. Zaid drags me back, appearing apologetic.

"I'm sorry, sweetheart, but you'll need to stay with Everett and Rafael tonight."

"What? Why?" No offense to Everett and Rafael, but I trust Krystian and Zaid significantly more.

And they're actually nice to me.

Not that Rafael isn't nice, per se, but he's a little... scary. Adorably scary, but scary all the same.

Krystian is already slipping into the room, slamming the door shut behind him.

"It's not a big deal." Zaid gives my hand a squeeze and then releases it.

I instantly miss his touch, the prickling heat that invades my body.

"I'll see you in the morning, sweetheart." He waves

and slips into the bedroom after Krystian, making sure not to allow even a sliver of light to appear.

What the fuck?

"That was weird, right?" I say to Everett and Rafael. "Really weird."

"I can get you your own room," Everett says in lieu of an explanation.

He turns towards the lobby—a separate building on the opposite side of the parking lot—but Rafael pulls him back.

"She stays with us," the blood fae says coldly.

Everett's jaw clenches. "What?"

"She stays with us." Rafael places a hand on my shoulder and guides me into the room—a mirror image of Krystian and Zaid's.

Rafael gestures for me to take the bed farthest away from the door, then he claims the one next to it.

Everett remains standing, his arms folded over his chest and his customary scowl firmly in place.

"Where the fuck am I supposed to sleep?" he demands, volleying his gaze between the two of us.

Before I can offer him my bed—I'm not sure I'll actually be capable of sleeping—Everett stomps to a closet.

"Fine. I'll sleep on the floor."

"But..." I begin, gesticulating wildly towards the bed. "You can sleep here, and I can take the floor—"

"I'll take the damn floor!" Everett snaps, throwing pillows and extra blankets down. "Now, go take a shower or whatever the fuck you want to do before bed. Lights will be out in an hour because we need to leave early tomorrow."

He focuses on the task at hand, and I return my attention to Rafael with wide eyes.

"He's so bossy," I whisper.

"I heard that," Everett says.

Rafael chuckles, the sound dark and foreboding.

But I suppose I can use the time now to check off another thing on my bucket list.

A hot, steaming shower.

CHAPTER TWELVE

RAFAEL

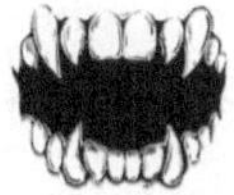

The reaper intrigues me.

Entices me.

Excites me.

When she's around, I feel things I've never experienced before.

Any emotion aside from bloodlust is new and foreign to me.

I'm not sure I've ever been attracted to anyone before—male or female. When Aphrodite put on her little show for me and my brothers, I didn't feel even an inkling of lust.

Only annoyance that the bitch was making a mess of my bedsheets.

But now, with Thea, I can't think of anything else.

I want to know every thought in her pretty head.

Every desire.

Every wish and fear and hope.

My need for her is borderline obsessive.

I bite down on my lower lip as the sound of the shower starts up.

Fuck, I'm hard as steel. All I can think about is her standing beneath the spray of water, soap bubbling on her golden skin as she cleans herself.

Everett glances towards the bathroom with a pained expression, his cock tenting his loose basketball pants.

"Fuck." He scrubs a hand through his sandy hair. "I'm going to do a perimeter sweep. Can you watch her?"

I wonder if he would ask such a thing if he knew my thoughts. Every one of them is dark and depraved, and they're all centered around her.

But of course, he doesn't suspect the true extent of my obsession. How could he, when I've never behaved like this with anyone before?

I can tell Krystian and Zaid are wary of me and my intentions, and they would be right to worry.

I'm goddamn insane, and everything about Thea —from her scent, to her voice, to her lilting laugh, to her sweet giggles—makes me lose my mind even more.

Why her?

Is it because she's beautiful?

Is it because her story calls to the fucked-up, broken part of me?

I know what it's like to feel trapped and isolated. To feel alone and misunderstood.

My little bird has been trapped in a cage for an eternity, and now that she's free, I want to trap her again.

To me.

Once she's mine, I'll never let her go.

A cry erupts from the bathroom, and I'm moving before my brain can catch up, kicking the door open.

I freeze, every coherent thought—and there are not a lot to begin with—leaving me.

Fuck.

Thea stands in the shower, the curtain wide open, as if she didn't know she was supposed to shut it ahead of time. Water seeps onto the floor in a steady stream, flooding the room.

Fire scorches my throat as I take in the beauty standing before me.

She's naked. Of course she is. Who would take a shower fully clothed?

I know I should look away, should grant her privacy, but I'm not like my brothers. I can't peel my eyes off the perfection of her flesh.

Her breasts are perky, each one easily a handful, her nipples a light, dusky pink and currently beaded.

As I watch, transfixed, she pinches her nipple and cries out again.

Her free hand plays with her perfect pussy, her fingers disappearing into her folds.

She hasn't seemed to have noticed me yet, so I take the moment to study her unencumbered.

Perfection.

She's fucking perfection.

Mine.

She's mine.

A growl rattles my chest, and her hands freeze. She snaps her head up.

"Rafael?" She doesn't look embarrassed at being caught touching herself. Confusion creases her brows and draws down her lips. "What...?"

"Keep playing with your pretty pussy, little bird," I growl, my lust blossoming, tinged with desperation.

Impulse demands I charge forward. Replace her hands with mine—or my cock.

But I stand perfectly still, my hands fisted by my sides.

"W-what?" She cocks her head to the side.

"Play. With. Your. Pussy."

She swallows, and one of her fingers swirls through her folds in a way I can tell she likes. Her chest flushes, and her eyelids flutter.

"Add another finger," I instruct, my gaze riveted to the show she's unintentionally putting on.

Does she have any idea how sexy she is? How perfect?

A whimper catches in her throat as a second finger joins the first, the two of them scissoring in her tight cunt.

"Leave your hand in your pussy, but play with your tits." My nails dig into my palms with the restraint it takes not to cup myself, not to stroke my throbbing cock in tandem to her fingers pistoning in and out of her pussy.

Thea grips her nipple between her thumb and pointer finger and begins to tug and twist at it.

"Yes, just like that." I lick my lips. "Does that feel good, little bird?"

"Yes," she pants out, her eyes snapping open, tears filling them. "So fucking good."

"Did you masturbate often before you arrived here?" I keep my tone impassive. Conversational, almost.

Only someone who knows me well could hear the heat underneath it.

"It doesn't..." She breaks off, a gasp escaping her.

"Yes?" I arch an eyebrow, encouraging her to continue.

"It doesn't... I mean, it didn't feel as good then as it does now."

A smile curls up my lips.

"Is it because I'm watching?" I ask. "You're such a good little slut, putting on a show for me."

She cries out, tightening her grip on her puckered nipple. Fuck, I want to taste it, want to flick it with my tongue. Then I want to kiss down her belly until I can reach the ambrosia between her legs.

A tight rubber band constricts around my chest, hellbent on suffocating me.

Not yet.

She's not ready for that yet.

Not ready for *me*.

"Strum your clit, little bird. Yes. Just like that. Such a good little slut. Do you want to come?"

"Yes. Please, Rafe. Please." Tears continually cascade down her cheeks, and the use of my nickname leaving her plump, kissable lips causes my heart to stutter.

"Good girl. Come for me, Thea. Come all over your hand."

Thea shakes and convulses, then she comes with a scream I wouldn't be surprised my brothers could hear in the room next door. She throws her head against the tiled wall, trembling from the aftershocks, and I can't help but think she looks like a goddess. She deserves to be on a throne somewhere, worshipped and revered.

She's a beautiful poison, deadly and enticing. Unhealthily intoxicating. I can't get enough of her, even knowing it'll kill me.

She'll kill me.

While she comes down from her high, I slip out of the bathroom. I need a second to collect myself, to get my thoughts in some semblance of a working order.

What I did was stupid. Dangerous. Idiotic.

If I wasn't obsessed before, I certainly am now.

Thea is mine.

And no one will take her away from me.

CHAPTER THIRTEEN

THEA

Showers are amazing.

Having a sexy blood fae watch you in one? Even more amazing.

I towel off then throw back on the oversized T-shirt Krystian loaned me and grab my dagger off the counter. I don't have any undergarments—why would I need them in a world where I never got dirtied or peed or pooped or had my period?—then return to the room.

Rafael is lying on his bed, flicking through the channels on the television. I don't see Everett anywhere, and relief floods me. It's not that I'm against Everett knowing what I got up to with Rafe, but...I have a feeling he would judge me.

And I'm fragile, dammit.

I bite my lip as I wait for Rafael to say something,

anything. Hell, I would even take a head nod of acknowledgment or a fist bump.

Instead, he keeps his gaze fixed firmly on the TV, though I know he's not actually watching anything. He's flipping through the channels way too fast.

I shuffle from foot to foot as I place my dagger on the bedside table, then I clear my throat.

"So..." I begin awkwardly, wringing my hands together. "Are we going to talk about what just happened? You know the..."

I pantomime thrusting my fingers upwards because I can't say the words out loud. I'm real classy like that.

Rafe's fingers flex around the remote control, but he still doesn't respond.

"The silent treatment." I purse my lips. "Way to make a girl feel special."

Rafael finally swivels his head to stare directly at me, and the intensity in his eyes nearly takes my breath away. A boulder wedges itself in my throat.

"What do you want me to say, little bird?" His voice is low and raspy, scraping across my skin in a way that's almost painful. It sounds as if he doesn't speak often, which makes me hold on to each word he says like the gift I believe it is. "That I'm hard as fuck thinking about those sexy moans you made? That I can't help but imagine how tight your pussy would be as I fuck you? That when I close my eyes, all I can see is your perfect body and tight nipples and wet cunt?"

A pulsing ache erupts in my center.

Did I whimper? I think I whimpered.

Fuck.

"You're really bad at giving the silent treatment," I whisper, moving towards the makeshift bed on the floor.

He smirks and returns his attention to the television. "Go to sleep."

It's an order.

"Sir, yes, sir." I offer him a mocking salute, then I plop on the floor.

Rafe's eyes narrow. "What are you doing?"

"Going to sleep." I give him a "duh" look and then fluff the pillow behind me.

"You sleep on the bed." Anger flavors his words.

"Everett is already cranky. Can you imagine how evil he'll be if he doesn't get his beauty rest?" I snort and then shake my head. "Not happening. Not on my watch. I'll be fine here. Besides, I don't even know if I'll be able to sleep."

I fall onto my back and rest my hands on my chest. The floor is uncomfortable but not too horrible with the blankets beneath me to soften it.

Silence stretches between the two of us, broken only by the quiet television.

I break it first.

"I really don't want to fade away again." It's a whispered confession, tugged from deep in my chest. A blistering burn crawls up my throat and crowds my eyes. "Now that I know what it's like to be alive...I can't go back to the way things were. I *can't*."

"That won't happen," Rafe vows solemnly.

"You can't promise me that." I turn on the makeshift bed until I'm lying on my side, my hands under my cheek. "No one can."

"I will." With my back to him, I can't see his expression, but I can feel his gaze on my flesh, white-hot and burning, eliciting shocks of skittish sensation.

The intensity of his promise brings unexpected tears to my eyes.

I've been alive for...well, it feels like forever.

No one has ever promised to take care of me before.

Do I expect Rafe to uphold his promise? Not at all. He barely knows me.

But it's nice to know he cares enough—at least right now—to make a vow in the first place.

"You guys never gave me popcorn," I murmur drowsily.

Rafe chuckles darkly. "Later, my little bird."

And then I do something I've never done before.

I sleep.

I WAKE to strong arms around me, holding me against a broad chest. The scent of cedar tickles my senses.

Everett.

I grumble something inarticulate—probably a "what are you doing?"—and Everett shushes me.

"Go back to sleep."

A second later, I'm dropped onto a warm, soft bed, and blankets are draped over my shoulders.

Then I drift away again.

I DON'T KNOW what wakes me first—the feeling of eyes on my skin that tells me I'm being watched, or the heavy breathing of the men in the room.

Blinking wearily, I struggle to orient myself.

"W-what?" I sit upright in bed, rubbing at my eyes with the palms of my hands.

My first thought is—this isn't a dream.

I'm still in a motel with Rafael and Everett, though at some point, I've been moved from the floor to the bed. Rafael sleeps soundly on the bed opposite me, while Everett is sprawled on the floor, tiny snores emitting from him.

My second thought? Someone is in the room with us.

Tension floods my body instantly, and chills careen down my spine.

Rafe and Everett continue to sleep, completely oblivious to the intruder.

Or...

Or they've been spelled.

Fuck. Fuck. Fuck.

Ice trickles into my veins, and I reach for my dagger I placed on the bedside table, gripping it tightly.

The silhouette in the doorway steps forward, and I let out a breath of relief when I see it's Krystian.

"Holy fuck. You scared the shit out of me." I place a hand against my chest as he continues to study me, unaware of the contortions my heart is putting my head through. "Why are you just standing there? And what's up with Rafe and Everett?"

They seem like the type that would jump out of bed, alert, at the slightest provocation.

"I need to talk to you," Krystian says in a low voice. "It's urgent."

My pulse spikes like a spooked rabbit as I throw

back the covers and hurry towards him on bare feet. "What's going on? Are we under attack?"

Moonlight flickers across his face like sentient white vines.

My feet still.

This is Krystian...but it's not.

This close, I can see that his eyes are black as pitch. Inky veins extend from his eyes and branch across his face, pulsating beneath his pale skin. Even his hair seems to have changed. It's still white, but instead of golden undertones, there appears to be blue streaks layered in the strands.

Krystian's smile widens, unveiling perfectly white teeth. "I wondered what Krystian was keeping from me. I didn't expect it to be a beautiful woman. Hello, dear. You can call me Krys."

CHAPTER FOURTEEN

THEA

I take an automatic step backwards, fear causing my heart to pound even faster. I flick my gaze towards first Rafael and then Everett, but they remain asleep.

"Don't worry." Krys rolls his dark eyes, a wry smirk tugging up his lips. "I just put a glamour on the room. They can't see or hear us, currently." He takes a step back and gestures for me to follow him out of the room. "Let's have a talk, shall we?"

I grind my teeth together but do as he says—mainly because I don't know if he's a threat to the oblivious sleeping men.

Who is this man?

Krystian's...evil twin brother?

"I can see the wheels in your head spinning." Krys

leans against a stone pillar, kicking out his legs and folding his arms over his chest. "Ask your questions."

"Who the fuck are you?" I demand.

The wind is biting and cold, instantly eliciting goose bumps on my bare arms and legs. I mimic Krys's posture, but mainly to ward off the chill, the dagger still clutched tightly in my hand.

"I'm Krystian," he answers simply, shrugging a single shoulder. "Whom I'm assuming you've met."

"You just said your name is Krys," I point out.

"Krystian decided we need separate names." Annoyance crowds his features.

"I'm...so confused," I confess.

"I'm the same person." He pushes off the pillar to take a step towards me.

This time, I don't counter it with one back.

"I'm Krystian, but I'm a better version of him, one that doesn't allow inhibitions to stop me." His lips curve. "I'm assuming you heard the difference between a light elf and a dark elf, correct?"

I think through my limited knowledge of the various supernaturals.

"Light elves get their powers from the sun. They're usually peaceful and kind and empathetic and all of that, right? Dark elves' powers derive from the moon. They're more likely to give in to their dark urges, and they lack... How did you describe it? Inhibition. They lack inhibition."

I stare at him as something occurs to me with startling clarity.

"I can see your mind putting two and two together." Krys's smile broadens. "I was born at the exact second day turned to night. As such, I exhibit traits of both a dark elf and a light elf." He executes a dramatic bow, bending at the waist. "I'm still Krystian, but at night, there's nothing holding me back. Nothing stopping me. I don't feel guilt or pity or empathy or any of the other emotions that may hinder my counterpart.

"Krystian is terrified of me, though I have no idea why." He laughs, the sound mirthless. "I believe his fear is what causes the disconnect between us. I have no idea what happens during the day; he has no idea what occurs at night. We're practically Jekyll and Hyde at this point."

"But you're the same person," I clarify, studying him carefully.

"I think I'm the more fun version, but essentially, yes." He extends a hand, and I notice the inky veins extend to the tips of his fingers. "Now, come with me."

"Why?" I eye him suspiciously.

"Because I'm going to kidnap you, obviously." His ovoid eyes glitter.

"Most kidnappers don't announce it ahead of time," I point out.

"I'm not like most kidnappers." His mouth molds into a smile, and I can't decide if it's charming, devious, or a combination of the two. "You trust Krystian, correct? You must, if you're willingly staying in a room with his teammates. If you trust Krystian, then you can trust me. I'm still him."

"You literally just said you're kidnapping me," I argue. "And I'm not dressed for an outing."

I gesture towards my bare legs. He doesn't need to know I have literally nothing else on besides the T-shirt.

"I think you look perfect," he says, the pale strands of his hair kissing the angles of his face.

"Fine," I huff. "Let me change quickly."

Without waiting for him to respond, I hurry back into my room, where Rafe and Everett are still sleeping.

Quickly, I pull on a pair of pants and then secure them with a belt. Next comes the socks and shoes. Finally, I slide my dagger into the waistband of the jeans.

I debate, briefly, about finding a way to wake up the others, but curiosity takes precedent.

Despite everything, I believe Krys's story. He truly

is Krystian—or at least, a version of him that's tainted by darkness.

And because of that, I don't believe he'll hurt me.

Actually, I *know* he won't.

The innate knowledge bolsters my resolve, and I hurry outside before I can change my mind.

Krys is leaning against a car I didn't notice earlier. Has it always been there, or did he steal it?

"Where are we going?" I ask as I slide into the passenger seat.

"Kidnappers don't tell their victims the location," Krys points out, smirking.

"Kidnappers also don't give their victims a choice," I snark back.

And it was a choice. If I would've said no or chose to stay behind, Krys would've allowed me to.

How do I know that?

The knowledge comes to me easily, innately, but there's no rhyme or reason behind it.

Is it simply because I trust Krystian, a man I barely know?

Or is there something else at play in all of this?

Questions swirl in my head, one after the other.

With a laugh, Krys puts the car into reverse and squeals away. I hold on to the seat for dear life.

What the fuck am I getting myself into?

And why am I so excited?

CHAPTER FIFTEEN

THEA

Krys is, surprisingly, a good singer. His smooth, rich baritone floods the car as we swerve down street after street.

"So where, exactly, are we going?" I ask for the one billionth time.

And of course, he doesn't answer. Instead, he throws his head back and sings at the top of his lungs—some eighties rock song that is making a reemergence due to the internet and social media apps.

"It's rude not to give your kidnapping victim more information," I point out.

He chuckles and finally goes quiet, though I can't decide if that's good or bad. I actually really like his singing.

"Are you going to keep pestering me until I tell you

the truth?" He slides his gaze towards me before refocusing on the road once again.

"Yes." I nod seriously. "I can be very annoying with proper motivation."

"Wow. I never would've imagined," he deadpans.

I hit his shoulder.

"But fine. I'll tell you." Krys steers the car into the parking lot of a small, isolated building that has seen better days.

Graffiti covers the brick walls, and the shutters have been drawn tight over the windows, allowing no light in or out. Hundreds of motorcycles line the entrance—though a dozen or more of them topple over when Krys purposely parks his car on top of them.

"Um. You just hit a motorcycle...or two." Or twelve.

Krys chuckles darkly and throws open the door, scratching a thirteenth motorcycle beside our car.

"Oh, did I?" He blinks his eyes at me innocently.

Hurrying to follow after him, I open my own passenger door and cringe when it dings the side of a bike parked beside us. At first, I think I got away with doing minimum damage, but to my horror, the bike sways precariously before toppling on its side...and hitting the motorcycle beside it.

What happens next can only be described as the domino effect. Bike after bike falls with a deafening crash as I stand there, gawking, my face flushed and chest heaving.

Krys materializes beside me and slings an arm over my shoulder. "That's my girl."

"That was totally an accident," I blurt, cringing.

Krys throws his head back in laughter. "Sure it was, shortstack."

He begins to guide me towards the entrance, but I dig my heels in, not wanting to meet the owners of the bikes I just destroyed.

"Krys, I think we need to go."

"Nonsense." He waves away my worries with a literal flick of his wrist. "This is where we're supposed to be."

"But..." I bite down on my lower lip hard enough to draw blood.

Before I can conjure up another argument, Krys kicks the door to the bar open—literally kicks it. The wood cracks and shatters, swinging on rusty hinges.

Almost immediately, one hundred faces whip in our direction, teeth bared.

Oh...

Oh fuck.

They're all some type of supernatural.

Gorgons and fae and elves and shifters and vampires and demons and werewolves and witches.

"Krys." I tug on his shirt sleeve, suddenly desperate to get out of here.

The hairs on the back of my neck stand straight up, and goose bumps pebble on my skin.

Every alarm bell in my head screams "DANGER" over and over again.

"Don't worry, shortstack." Krys gives my arm a commiserating pat before stepping away. Then, his voice louder, he calls out, "Which one of you ass-sucking bitches owes me money?"

Yup.

We're dead.

Wait.

Can I even die?

I'm certain I'm about to find out.

"You shouldn't have come here, Krys." The man who speaks is large and broad and hairy. His eyes glimmer malevolently as he takes a step closer. "I warned you what would happen if you showed up unannounced."

Krys laughs, though this one is dry and acerbic. "And I warned you what would happen if you crossed me."

Krys reaches for his back—the way Krystian did during the battle with the hellhounds—and a bow materializes out of seemingly thin air. He notches a pitch-black arrow and aims it at the man's chest.

Krystian's arrows are white, I realize belatedly.

Of course, it's hard to focus on anything but the shock rooting my feet to the ground.

"Krys," I whisper, fear sluicing in my stomach.

"Stay behind me," Krys warns, his tone grave.

Then he lets loose the arrow.

It hits the man square in the chest, causing him to fall back with a cry. Almost immediately, black squiggly lines erupt from the puncture wound and extend in all directions. Screams escape the man's mouth as his flesh sizzles, turning the color of pitch.

"What the...?" I gawk in disbelief.

"Poisoned arrows," Krys explains, flashing me a wink over his shoulder. "Not as cool as Krystian's flesh-eating ones but just as effective."

A few things happen very, very quickly.

First, the man collapses, his torso and arms completely black, his gaze distant and unseeing, though his chest continues to rise and fall steadily.

Second, someone screams.

Third, one hundred pissed off supernaturals charge at us.

Krys shoots off arrow after arrow, each one hitting its target with expert efficiency.

"Holy fuck." I back away until I'm flush against the wall, my stomach in knots.

Krys simply laughs, spins out of the way of an

approaching vampire, and shoots off another arrow. He seems to have an infinite supply.

With Krys preoccupied with the supernaturals attacking him from the front, he misses the shifter sneaking up behind him, glee lighting up his grotesque, scarred face. The shifter lifts his hand, and the knife he holds catches in the artificial lighting, already stained with blood.

"No!" I scream, lunging forward before my brain can catch up with my body.

The shifter moves at the last second, and instead of hitting his heart like I intended, my dagger lands in his shoulder. He whirls around instantly, his fangs bared and dripping with saliva. I wince, tugging my dagger free.

"Um...oops?" I flash him a sweet smile.

The bastard backhands me across the face, sending me flying.

Pain ricochets through me, and tears burn my eyes.

It occurs to me then that I never felt pain before. Not really. The stones and twigs that scraped my feet in the forest are nothing compared to this. Even Everett's sword against my throat didn't hurt this badly.

The shifter advances on me, danger and violence emanating from his golden eyes, and a sliver of fear embeds itself in my heart.

All of the people I've stabbed over the years have been incorporeal souls with no way of fighting back. I'm skilled with my dagger, but can I fight off a two-hundred-pound shifter?

I'll certainly try.

Tightening my grip on my blade, I stagger to my feet, trying to ignore the pain reverberating from my bruised cheek.

Before I can even take a step forward, someone moves in front of me, his body vibrating with barely contained fury.

Krys.

"You dare to hurt her?" His words are sharp—the fatal swipe of a blade.

All of the amusement and levity he displayed only moments before has dissipated, replaced by stone-cold anger.

Fear seeps into the shifter's eyes, though he attempts to regain his bravado, going so far as to puff out his chest. "The bitch attacked me first."

The sound Krys releases then could best be described as a growl.

"I was going to kill you for hurting her. But because you called her a bitch?" He advances on the shifter. "It's going to be slow and agonizing."

It's only then I realize that every other supernatural in the bar—all one hundred-plus men and women

—are lying on the ground, writhing in agony, black veins erupting from the various arrows protruding from their bodies. Only the shifter remains.

Krys moves like liquid itself, each movement fluid and deadly. He's replaced his bow with a katana that he uses to cut off both of the shifter's arms.

The shifter screams and drops to his knees.

The next five minutes are...brutal.

Horrifying.

Disgusting.

And oddly sexy, in a very, very demented way.

I need therapy.

Krys dismembers the shifter one limb at a time, but he doesn't allow him to die. I don't know if magic is involved or the shifter's naturally advanced healing keeps his heart pumping, but the man is conscious during every minute of his torture.

"You never should've laid your hands on her," Krys says darkly, his sword raised and prepared to cut off the final body part—his head.

"No!" I scream, charging forward instinctively.

Krys pauses and turns towards me, his brows furrowed. "If this is too much for you, you can wait outside."

Despite his softened voice, his eyes are still deadened. Cold. Cutting. They glow with a malevolent darkness I don't think I've ever seen in Krystian before, though I suppose I don't know him well enough to tell for sure.

"It's not that." My stomach twists painfully. "It's just... I don't want him to die."

He stares at me in disbelief. "What?"

"I mean, I don't want to be around him when he dies," I say quickly. "I don't know what will happen to me if I'm around a soul."

For all I know, that will be the catalyst capable of pulling me back to the other plane of existence.

I'm not sure how much Krys knows about my origins—he claims he isn't aware of anything that happens during the day, yet he didn't bat an eye at my appearance nor ask for my name—but I'm hoping he'll hear the pleading in my voice.

I can't go back to that existence.

I won't.

I'd rather die.

Understanding lights in Krys's eyes, and he slowly drops the sword back to his side.

The shifter sobs in relief.

"You're living tonight only because my goddess is merciful," Krys says seriously. Then a wicked smile tugs at his lips. "But tomorrow night? I'll hunt you down and kill you. If, of course, you don't die from your injuries before then."

"No! Please! No!" The shifter trembles and

attempts to back away—though it's hard without any of his limbs.

He resembles a fucked-up snake.

"You talk too much." Krys lunges towards the shifter, grabs his tongue, and slices it off with his katana.

I arch my eyebrows, even as my heart flutters.

I've never had anyone defend my honor before. I know I should be disturbed by the display of violence, but I'm not. Maybe it's because I've been around death my entire life, but I've grown desensitized to it. It barely fazes me.

Krys casually wipes the blood off his sword with the shifter's shirt, then he straightens. He places the sword in an invisible holster on his back, and that weapon, like the bow and arrow set, disappears.

"Come on, shortstack. Let's get out of here. The poison should be killing off these idiots in just a few minutes."

He places his hand on the small of my back and guides me towards the exit.

A thought occurs to me.

"Wait." I dig my feet in, forcing him to slow down. "What about your money?"

"Huh?" He stares at me in confusion.

"You said they owed you money." That's why he went on a killing spree in the first place.

"Oh." He chuckles. "Funnily enough, they actually didn't owe me money. My mistake. Now, let's get you back to the motel before the others realize you're gone."

CHAPTER SIXTEEN

Thea is gone.

And so is Krys.

"They couldn't have gone far," Everett growls, pacing.

He rakes his fingers through his sandy-colored hair, causing it to stand straight up.

Rafe sits on the bed, a dagger in one hand as he cuts the palm of the other. Blood wells, dark red and glittering with magic, and he closes his eyes, concentrating. I know he's attempting to perform a very complicated tracking spell. The problem is, this spell only works when the caster has an intimate relationship with the person they're trying to find, whether that's romantic or platonic.

And considering Rafe has only known her for one

day? And that he has the emotional capacity of a damn cabbage?

"I'll see if I can pick up their scent," Everett says abruptly, and his eyes flutter shut.

I know he's about to shift, but the last thing we need is his monster loose in the motel.

Everett and his beast are a lot like Krystian and Krys. They're the same person, but one is contained by societal norms and empathy. The other? They only have two modes—fuck or fight—and there's no guarantee which one it'll be.

"Don't." Rafe's eyes snap open, and blood floats in the air, a trail of it leading out the door. "I have it."

My brows shoot up at that, but I don't bother to question it. All that matters is finding Thea...before Krystian—or Krys, as Krystian likes to call him—does something he regrets.

I don't think he would intentionally hurt her, but Krys is careless with people's feelings and well-being. He doesn't think before he acts. If shit hits the fan, he won't hesitate to leave Thea behind in order to save himself.

It makes him immensely dangerous on missions.

The three of us stalk out of the motel room and into the parking lot—directly to an approaching car.

"Who's fucking car is that?" Everett bites out, his hands forming fists by his sides.

"Who knows?" I strain my eyes to see better, but as a wraith, I don't have enhanced senses like the others.

All I can make out are two blurry silhouettes.

"It's them," Everett tells us, and relief floods me instantly, the force of it taking me by surprise.

I didn't realize how attached I've become to the five-foot-nothing spitfire until she was gone and I was left fearing the worst.

It's terrifying to care about someone who isn't a member of my team—someone whose past is too nebulous to define and shrouded in mystery. Her entire story raises a thousand different questions.

What, exactly, is she? She claims she's a reaper, and that may be true, but why is her upbringing different from the others?

Why is she trapped?

How is she here now?

How long will this last?

To the east, the sun rises above the horizon, reaching out with spindly arms to paint the surroundings in red and orange.

As soon as the car pulls to a stop, Thea pops out, dressed in that hideously oversized shirt that belongs to Krystian and pants that may have been mine at one point. She smiles brightly when she sees us, unaware of the panic her disappearance caused.

She waves and skips forward. "You guys are up early!"

Rafe is in front of her instantly, his hands on her shoulders as he takes in the bruises darkening her cheek.

Rage like I've never felt before barrages me, pulling me into a tidal wave I can't hope to escape from.

"Who. Did. This. To. You?" Rafe growls out, each word crisp and concise.

At the same moment, Krystian stumbles out of the car, appearing confused and disoriented.

"W-what?" He blinks at us. "Where am I? How did I...?" He finally seems to notice Thea and Rafe, and all of the color drains from his face. He swallows convulsively. "Please tell me I didn't do that to you."

His voice is practically a whisper.

"You?" Thea draws her brows together. "No. Of course not. You took care of the one who did."

"What the fuck were you thinking?" Everett bellows, storming up to Krystian and grabbing him by the collar of his shirt.

"It wasn't me!" Krystian insists, frantic. "I would never put her in harm's way. Never."

"Obviously you fucking would!" Spit flies from Everett's mouth as he hauls the other man into the air.

Krystian pales even more.

None of us like to bring up the truth—that Krystian

and Krys are the same person, driven by the same desires and motivations. Krys acts on everything Krystian will never consciously do, whether that's accept odd jobs as a mercenary or murder someone who harmed him or fuck a pretty girl who gave him googly eyes. Krys represents every one of Krystian's darkest desires.

The light elf doesn't fight back against the shifter as he turns desperate, beseeching eyes Thea's way.

"I'm so fucking sorry."

"Why would you be sorry?" She blinks, seemingly at a loss for words. "It was my own idiotic fault for jumping into the fray when you told me to stay back. But in my defense, I did save you from getting stabbed."

"Fray?" Rafe growls out, still studying Thea's bruised cheek intently.

"Stabbed?" I parrot.

"What the fuck did you two do?" Everett exclaims, finally releasing Krystian.

The elf drops to the ground on all fours, his head lowered in shame.

Thea steps away from Rafe and folds her arms over her chest. "I'll tell you...if you apologize to Krystian."

"What?" all of us exclaim at once—including Krystian, who finally lifts his head to spear Thea with an unreadable look.

"You heard me." One of her feet begins to tap impatiently. "I went with Krys willingly. He told me to stay back, but I chose to involve myself in the fight. If I'd listened to him, I never would've gotten hurt. And as soon as he saw me go down, he ran in front of me and tortured the guy who hurt me."

I blink at her, unable to believe what I'm hearing.

Apparently, I'm not the only one.

"Krys protected you?" Krystian sounds incredulous.

"Of course he did." Thea arches an eyebrow. "He's you, isn't he? And you would protect me, right?"

Krystian opens and shuts his mouth repeatedly, but apparently, he has no rebuttal.

"But your fucking face," Rafe growls out, once again reaching for her. His fingers graze her mottled skin, and when she winces, he drops his arm back to his side. Whirling towards me, he snaps out, "Fix it!"

"Let's get some ice on that," I tell Thea gently, guiding her towards my room.

Guilt gnaws at my stomach like fire ants. It was my job to watch Krys, and I failed. Yes, he created an illusion that made me believe he was still in the room with me, but I should've seen through it, through *him*.

Everett hurries to the ice machine and returns a few minutes later with a bag, handing it to me. I gently rest it against Thea's face, cringing sympathetically when she winces.

"I know it hurts," I say soothingly. "But we need to get the swelling down."

"Stupid shifter." She pouts, and I shouldn't find it as adorable as I do.

"So what exactly happened, sweetheart?" I reposition the ice on her face then hold it there.

I have no idea what healing abilities a reaper has, but I guess none. If she did, she would've healed by now, or at least started to.

Everett, Rafe, and Krystian are all listening intently, but I keep her attention on me, pretending we're in a world of our own.

"It's as I said. Krys came to my room, and we left together. He brought me to this seedy bar, where we accidentally destroyed a bunch of motorcycles."

Everett—who owns a bike—winces at that, but Thea doesn't notice, her eyes intent on mine.

"And then?" I press, desperate to know how she got this injury...and if the person who did it to her is still breathing.

"And then Krys stormed inside and demanded his money back," Thea explains.

Krystian frowns. "His money?"

"That's what he said, but I think he was full of shit," she confesses, her tone flippant as if this isn't the part of the story she wants to focus on. "Anyway, all of the supernaturals attacked him at once, and he shot arrow after arrow at them. It was really freaking cool, if I'm being honest. Sexy, even."

A tiny blush stains her cheeks at her impromptu confession. Krystian, I notice, stands a little straighter, absently brushing at a strand of his unruly blond hair.

"I saw a shifter sneaking up on Krys from behind, so I intervened. Stabbed the fucker in the shoulder. He turned around, backhanded me, and then Krys dismembered him."

She sounds oddly...blasé over the fact that Krys tortured a guy in front of her.

Then again, nothing seems to perturb her. In some aspects, she's as sweet and innocent as a newborn baby. In others, she's hardened and fierce, a warrior goddess in her own right.

"He's dead?" Rafe asks darkly.

Thea shakes her head. "No." At our looks of disbelief, she hurries to elaborate. "I was afraid the arrival of a soul would force me back to the world of the dead, you know? Didn't want to risk it."

The air turns somber.

"She's right," Everett says gruffly, breaking the silence. "We can't risk sending her back. That means no killing around her."

"No killing *around* her?" Rafe asks.

"Correct."

Rafe focuses on Thea. "Do you remember the bar you were at?"

"Ummm. Yeah. It was called Lacey's Jugs or something along those lines. About twenty minutes in a car."

"I'll be back," Rafe says darkly, stalking out of the room and towards the borrowed—stolen—car.

Thea watches him leave with a quizzical expression, but I quickly reclaim her attention before she can ask questions.

"And you're okay, right? Besides your face, of course." I didn't see any other injuries on her, though it's hard to tell with her clothes so baggy.

"I promise I'm fine." She tries to smile, though I can tell it causes her pain. "I'll be good as new by tomorrow."

I don't have the heart to tell her it'll take at least a week to heal.

"And I don't blame you, Krystian," she adds, glancing at the sullen elf. "You know that, don't you?"

Krystian lowers his eyes to his feet, seemingly unable to meet her penetrating gaze.

"Krystian..." Her voice is a growl.

"You never should've been there in the first place," Krystian finally explodes, snapping his head up to stare at her. "If I was still in control..."

He can't seem to find the words to finish that sentence.

"You want to know the biggest difference between the two of you?" Thea asks, canting her head to the side. She doesn't wait for Krystian to respond before continuing. "You both look after and protect me, but Krys doesn't treat me as breakable. I think you know, at least subconsciously, that a tiny punch to the face won't get rid of me that easily."

An uneasy silence permeates the air as we all process her dogmatic proclamation.

A punch may not have gotten rid of Thea...but that only begs the question—what will?

How can we protect her from threats we can't even begin to comprehend?

We need to find Aphrodite, and fast. If anyone will have answers, it'll be her.

I just pray we won't be too late.

CHAPTER SEVENTEEN

THEA

Krystian and Everett both excuse themselves, leaving me alone with Zaid.

He repositions the ice pack on my face after about ten minutes, and I wince as a shooting pain reverberates through me.

"Sorry." He blanches. "I know it hurts."

"Just a smidge." I place my thumb and pointer finger a millimeter apart, trying to smile.

"Here. Hold this for a second."

I take the ice pack from Zaid, and he moves to a suitcase on the floor in the room. He reappears a second later with two orange pills in his hand.

"Ibuprofen," he explains when he catches my dumbfounded look. "It should help with the pain and swelling. Hopefully, we can stop on the way to Aphrodite and find someone to heal you."

"There are supernaturals who can do that?" I take the pills from him and throw them back, forgoing water.

I know a lot about the world, but there's still so much for me to learn.

"Certain species are more gifted than others, yes." His fingers tentatively caress my mottled cheek, eliciting a fresh round of goose bumps. "Fuck, I hate that this happened to you."

"I'm not too upset." I capture his wrist, but instead of pushing him away, I pull him closer, nuzzling against his palm. "It means that I'm still here. That I'm alive."

His gaze momentarily flicks to my lips, which have instinctively parted. Is he going to kiss me? Do I want him to?

The answer to that last question is—yes. One thousand times yes.

My breath abandons me as I lean towards him. The air between us feels both stifled and charged, like waves of electricity are slicing through the air. All of the tiny hairs on my arms stand at attention.

"You're so beautiful," Zaid whispers, his tone low and reverent.

I lean in even closer, my stomach moving in riotous swirls, and he lowers his head.

"We're back!" Krystian doesn't bother knocking as he pushes open the door, a wide, beguiling smile on his handsome face. The smile remains in place, even as his eyes flick between the two of us. "What's going on here?"

Zaid backs away hastily, his cheeks bright red, and I pretend the blanket beneath me is immensely interesting.

"You horny dog," Krystian continues, his shit-eating grin widening.

"Shut up," Zaid mumbles.

Everett, who's standing slightly behind Krystian, rolls his eyes and shoulders his way through.

He drops a plastic bag onto the bed beside me.

"Clothes," he grunts out.

"Clothes?" I arch an eyebrow.

They were only gone for about fifteen minutes. How did they have time to go clothes shopping?

"And food," exclaims Krystian cheerfully.

I'm glad to see that his usual humor and lightheartedness have returned. I hated seeing him so...melancholic and depressed. It made me want to run over to him, shake his shoulders, and tell him that I didn't blame him for what happened. I actually had fun with Krys, despite my injury. And the bloodshed.

Krystian hands me a to-go box, a heavenly smell emitting from it. I pop open the lid, and my mouth nearly waters when I see a stack of fluffy pancakes and a side of syrup.

"Oh my god. I think I'm in love," I moan.

"She's talking to the food, right?" Krystian asks.

"Definitely," Zaid says.

"Yes," agrees Everett.

I ignore them as I dig into my breakfast.

"Where's Rafe?" I ask around a mouthful of buttery pancakes.

Everett crinkles his nose in distaste. "Chew with your mouth shut."

"Excuse me if I don't know the proper way to eat," I snap, taking another bite. "I haven't eaten anything in, like, four hundred years."

Krystian watches me with amusement. "I can't be the only one who thinks this is sexy."

"Sexy?" Everett whirls towards Krystian.

"Those cute little noises she makes? The way she licks syrup off her lips? Fuck yeah, it's sexy. I'm hard as a rock." Krystian glances pointedly down at his basketball shorts, which are currently tented.

I giggle and lower my head, unsure if I should be proud, embarrassed, or a combination of the two. To know that these strong, proud, sexy men find me attractive...

Yeah, it's a heady, intoxicating sensation, and one I could get used to.

The men watch me eat, not even bothering to pretend they're doing anything else. Everett tries to appear disgusted, releasing the occasional grunt and eye roll, but there's an incandescent heat in his gaze that blazes through me in a sweeping inferno.

Once I finish every last bite—going so far as to lick the takeaway box—I fall back on the bed, feeling satisfied in a way I've only felt a few times before. And... stuffed. My stomach feels bloated, and whenever I move, nausea curdles in my gut.

"Ugh. I ate too much. Is this what it feels like to fall into a food coma?" I flop around dramatically.

Krystian chuckles and pats my ankle. "Hang in there, love. You'll survive."

"I hate food," I whine.

"No, you don't," Zaid counters with a snort.

He's right.

I really, really don't.

"Go get dressed," Everett instructs, nudging the bag of clothes closer to me. "We need to leave as soon as Rafe returns."

I swivel my head to stare up at the brooding giant, pushing my lips out in a pout. "You're not going to let me whine and complain, are you?"

Everett simply folds his arms over his chest and scowls.

I take that as a no.

Sighing, I throw myself off the bed, grab the clothes bag without looking at it, and head to the connecting bathroom. Once inside, I lock the door and dump out the contents Everett bought me.

I expect to see either extremely frilly, obscene clothing I wouldn't be caught dead in...or a hideous outfit a grandma would wear.

The clothes are, surprisingly, cute. Modern. Stylish.

And in my size.

I slide on a pair of hot-pink panties, trying not to blush at the prospect of Everett—freaking Everett—picking them out for me. The jeans go on next, and I can't help but think they fit like a dream, molding to my curves. There are a couple of different shirts, as if he wasn't sure which one I would prefer, and a bra.

A bra that fits me perfectly.

What the fuck? How did he know my bra size? *I* don't even know my bra size.

I choose the pink shirt, then I dig through the rest of the bag and pull out a hairbrush, some hair ties, a toothbrush, and toothpaste.

I never had to do any of this stuff before. I was always just...clean, with perfect teeth and perfect hair. I didn't even have to brush it if I didn't want to; the strands cascaded in perfect waves down my back.

That's certainly not the case now. I'm sporting a serious case of "rat's nest" on the top of my head.

After a few minutes of painstakingly combing out all of the snarls and then brushing my teeth, I deem myself presentable. There's nothing I can do about the black and blue bruise on my face, however.

I enter the room to see the rest of the guys finishing up their own breakfasts.

"How did you know my bra size?" I ask Everett bluntly, dropping my dirty clothes on the bed.

Krystian chokes on his bite of eggs, and Zaid's face turns crimson.

Everett simply arches an eyebrow, unamused. "Excuse me?"

"Is that, like, your superpower?" I query. "Can you look at any woman and be able to tell her exact bra size?" I gesture towards the open window, where an eighty-year-old woman is staggering along the sidewalk. "What about her? Can you tell me her bra size?"

"Yes, Ev. Tell us her bra size." Krystian's lips twitch up in amusement.

Everett rolls his eyes and ignores us both, focusing back on his food.

I realize that, out of all the guys, I know him the least—which is saying something, because I barely know the others.

It's obvious that Everett is a shifter, but what type eludes me.

A wolf? Dragon? Tiger?

Everett freezes with a forkful of eggs halfway to his mouth.

"What?" he demands, glaring up at me. "Why are you looking at me like that?"

"Just trying to figure out what you are," I confess, shrugging.

"And how's that working for you?" He snorts derisively and refocuses on his food.

I contemplate him carefully, taking in the broad expanse of his shoulders, the scruff on his jawline, and the tattoos coloring his skin. "You're a dragon, aren't you?"

"No." Everett doesn't even look my way again.

"You're totally a dragon."

"I'm not." He shakes his head and takes another bite of his food.

"You are." I turn towards Krystian and Zaid, who are watching the exchange with amusement. "He's a dragon, isn't he?"

Krystian winks. "I don't shift and tell."

"You don't shift at all," Zaid points out, but I notice that he doesn't confirm or deny my theory either.

The guys finish their meals in silence then spend only a few minutes packing up. I hold on to my bag of supplies, feeling inexplicable warmth in my chest whenever I glance in Everett's direction.

He bought this for me.

Despite his feelings for me, and his obvious distrust, he still went out of the way to purchase these items, knowing I needed them.

My heart swells, and before I can stop myself, I hurry to Everett's side.

"Thank you," I whisper, keeping my voice low so the words are just between the two of us.

I expect him to blow me off or ignore me, the way he usually does, but instead, he appears uncomfortable and grunts out, "You're welcome."

We exit the room, and I'm surprised to find Rafe leaning against the "borrowed" car, something clenched tightly in his hand.

"Rafe? Where have you been?" I wonder, skipping towards him.

He extends the object for me to see.

My brows shoot upwards, and my heart picks up speed, ricocheting against my rib cage.

It's...a bouquet.

A bouquet of severed fingers, all of them contained with what appears to be a piece of intestine.

"Is that...?" I can barely breathe past the stone wedged in my throat.

"The men who hurt you," Rafe explains gruffly, thrusting the makeshift bouquet closer to me.

Tears burn my eyes.

"Dude," Krystian breathes in horror.

"What the fuck were you thinking?" Everett bellows.

I ignore them and take the proffered digits with a wide, beaming smile. "I love them."

Silence.

And then...

"You...love them?" Zaid ventures hesitantly.

"Thank you. Thank you. Thank you." I bounce on the balls of my feet as I study each finger individually.

White, black, brown...and all coated in a layer of red.

"You get her nice clothes, and she asks if you have the power of detecting bra sizes. You get her severed fingers, and she practically swoons," Everett mutters to himself, his tone acerbic and bitter.

"You're a little messed up, aren't you, love?" Krystian says lightly.

He doesn't sound perturbed by the prospect, though. If anything, the heat in his eyes builds until it's a blazing inferno that sets me aflame.

"She's perfect," Rafe counters gruffly.

I preen.

Apparently, we're going to travel by portal.

By freaking portal.

Of course, I knew it was a thing, but to know it's an actual thing and not just a thing that's a thing... Well, I'm not sure I want to do the thing, because the thing is freaking portal traveling.

I'm just an itty-bitty, teeny-weeny bit nervous.

"It doesn't hurt," Zaid assures me for the one billionth time, his tone calm and placating—a direct contrast to the turmoil in my head.

"Why don't you guys go on ahead. I'll stay here. Hold down the fort, so to speak." I flick my gaze towards Rafe, who's currently using blood magic to open said portal.

Red drips from a wound on his palm in a steady

stream, landing on the grass at his feet. A shimmering, garnet portal has erupted from the ground and hovers slightly in the air, roughly the size of Everett, if not bigger.

"I won't hurt you," Rafe promises in that gravelly, raspy voice of his that never fails to twist my stomach into knots. "Never."

"But..." I take an automatic step away, only to ram into Krystian's hard chest.

He immediately wraps his arms around me.

"Come on, love. It'll be fine." He lifts me off the ground and begins to walk us both forward, my legs swaying like a pendulum.

"No, wait!" I beg as we step through the light.

I wait for...pain.

Agony.

For my insides to be artfully rearranged or maybe even my skin to peel off.

None of that happens.

One second, I'm standing behind the motel with the guys. The next, I'm in what appears to be an apartment complex or a hotel, the lobby decorated in sleek leather couches and glass tables.

"That wasn't so bad, was it?" Krystian whispers in my ear, and a thrill shoots through me at his proximity.

Even if I'm pissed as fuck he dragged me through the portal without my consent.

I wiggle, demanding to be let down, and Krystian complies with another chuckle.

I whirl on him. "You asshole! What if I had died?"

"You wouldn't have died." He rolls his eyes like I'm being absurd.

"You don't know that."

"We portal travel everywhere, and I'm still in one piece," he points out, gesturing down the length of his body.

His rather impressive body...

Focus, Thea! You're mad at him!

"You... You..." I wag a finger in his face but can't think of a threat strong enough to encapsulate my anger.

Instead, I storm away with a huff, moving until I'm leaning against a far wall.

The others have already arrived through the magical portal, and they're all watching me with various expressions that range from wary to amused. The former is Zaid. The latter is, of course, Everett. Asshole.

The wraith takes a tentative step forward, holding his hands in the air placatingly. "We're sorry we brought you through the portal without your permission." He levels a glare in Krystian's direction, but the light elf simply smirks and shrugs, unrepentant. "It won't happen again."

"I forgive Zaid and only Zaid," I tell them primly, thrusting my chin in the air.

"I didn't push you through the portal," Rafe points out, shoving his hands into the pockets of his hoodie.

"Fine. I forgive Rafe too."

"What about me?" Everett scowls. "I didn't do anything."

"You laughed," I remind him.

"I did not fucking laugh."

"You totally did." I narrow my eyes at him suspiciously. "And...and you're doing it right now! See?! You're totally smiling!"

Everett works to compress his lips into a straight line.

"He can't help but smile," Krystian points out. "You're just too freaking adorable."

That wipes the smile straight off Everett's face.

"She's not adorable," he growls out.

"She totally is," Krystian counters.

"Enough of this." Zaid moves to step between us all, effortlessly garnering our attention. "Do we have a plan? We can't just barge into Aphrodite's apartment and demand she tell us what she knows about Thea. For all we know, she had a part to play in it."

"We need to hide Thea," Rafe murmurs, contemplative.

"Wait...hide me? Like, put a blanket over my head?" I ask.

Everett stares at me like I'm dumb, which...fair.

"I'll put a glamour on you, love," Krystian says. "I won't be able to hold it for long—at least, not one powerful enough to hide you from a goddess—but it should last for an hour or so. She won't be able to hear or see you."

Trepidation claws down my spine. "I won't, like, fade away, will I?"

"No, sweetheart," Zaid assures me quickly. "You'll still be here. We'll still be able to see and hear you. She just won't be able to."

"But she *will* be able to touch you, so make sure you're not standing in her way," Krystian adds.

"And then what?" Everett folds his arms over his chest and scowls. "We ask about Thea?"

"We pretend that we heard some new gossip about a reaper held hostage by Hades," Zaid corrects. "You know Aphrodite won't be able to resist."

The guys all nod, and a solemn aura permeates the air.

We're doing this.

We're actually doing this.

We're going to meet with a goddess, and hopefully, get some answers.

If not...

Well, I don't want to think about that.

I won't fade away again.

I refuse.

I'm not surprised Aphrodite chose to set up camp in a swanky, upscale apartment complex in downtown New York City.

The lobby shimmers like the inside of a champagne flute—tall ceilings wrapped in velvet gray and gilded with brushed brass trim that catches the early morning light. A chandelier of fractured crystal spirals down from above, suspended in midair. At the far end, a concierge desk—minimalist marble and matte black steel—stands abandoned, a collection of brochures on its surface.

Potted fiddle-leaf figs flank the lounge area, which holds a collection of leather armchairs, glass tables, and a stone fireplace. The scent of sandalwood and oranges drifts through the air, and jazz music blares from hidden speakers.

There's not a single fucking person to be seen.

Not one.

Rumor has it Aphrodite bought the entire building, kicked out all of the tenants, and turned the rooms into sex dungeons.

"So...the Goddess of Beauty," Thea begins as we move to the elevator.

According to Krystian, the glamour is already in place, making her invisible to anyone who isn't us. Unfortunately, she's still able to talk.

And talk she does.

"She's, like, really pretty, isn't she? Super pretty?"

The elevator opens with a ping. Inside, the paneling is dark walnut, inlaid with pearled numerals that glow softly under the recessed lighting. Who the fuck needs a fancy elevator?

Thea doesn't wait for any of us to answer her questions as she continues on, her voice growing high-pitched and frantic. "Of course she's pretty. She's the Goddess of Beauty. Do you guys think she's pretty?"

Trap, an inner voice in my head screams. *It's a trap.*

None of us answer as the elevator comes to a stop on the very top floor—the penthouse.

Of course Aphrodite is pretty, but I would be an idiot if I confess that out loud.

Thea's prettier.

I won't admit that to her, though. The last thing I need is her head getting even bigger than it already is.

The elevator opens directly into the penthouse with a soft, pneumatic sigh.

"Woah," Thea breathes, stepping slightly in front of us, her head twisting this way and that to take in the sights.

Sunlight filters through the floor-to-ceiling windows like silk, tracing over every available surface—obsidian countertops, mirrored pillars, and floors of dark-stained oak.

At first glance, the apartment is luxury incarnate. It's all modern furniture in monochromatic colors. Artworks that border between obscene and sensual. A fireplace carved into the walls, with flames eating at the tempered glass.

The only door leads to what appears to be a bathroom. A four-poster bed sits in the center of the large room like an altar, dressed in charcoal silk and flanked by obsidian columns that aren't just ornamental.

Discreet hooks line the ceilings, one of them still boasting rope. A wall opposite the bed has a shelf full of every sex toy imaginable—butt plugs, anal beads, dildos of all shapes and sizes, cuffs, paddles, whips... All of them are arranged with a surgeon's precision.

A scent—clean, spiced, and unmistakably carnal—hangs in the air.

"Holy fuck. Aphrodite is freaky," Thea exclaims, moving towards the wall of toys.

She holds up a leather mask for inspection.

"Put that down," Krystian whisper-hisses.

Thea drops it immediately...and then moves to the paddles, standing on her tiptoes to grab one off the wall.

"Oh! Look!" She pantomimes spanking the air, her lips pursed in fierce concentration.

It's...cute.

She's cute.

How irritating.

"Is she even here?" Zaid murmurs to no one in particular.

"Is that who I think it is?" a somewhat familiar voice coos, high-pitched and lilting. A second later, the bathroom door opens, and Aphrodite steps into the room, smiling sensually. "My boys! What a pleasure."

I clear my throat and very purposely look away.

Because Aphrodite? She's wearing virtually nothing.

I catch a glimpse of a black thong and stickers on her nipples, her reddish-brown hair piled in a loose bun at the top of her head.

"Aphrodite," Zaid says formally. He, too, isn't looking directly at her, making sure to keep his gaze trained just above her head. "It's a pleasure."

"I hate her," Thea deadpans, finally moving away from the sex toys to stand behind the goddess. "I really, truly hate her. It's hate at first sight."

Krystian brings his fist to his lips to hide his smirk.

"I think I know why you're here," Aphrodite purrs, sashaying forward.

She reaches for one nipple sticker and tosses it aside, then she grabs at the other.

"Is that a nipple piercing?!" Thea's voice goes shrill.

Instinctively, I dip my gaze to the goddess's breasts, noticing that there is, in fact, a metal barb cutting through her pink nipple. That must be new. It certainly wasn't there the last time she attempted to seduce us.

"Don't fucking look!" Thea sounds horrified.

I immediately turn away, and that only pisses me off.

Who is she to tell me what to do? To tell me who I can and can't look at? I barely fucking know her, and we're certainly not in a relationship.

So, ignoring the erratic thumping of my heart, I force myself to look at the goddess, to take in all of her supple curves and defined lines. Her large breasts, slightly flushed. Her nipple piercings. The black thong that leaves very little to the imagination, accentuating her pubic hairs and slit.

I feel...nothing.

How goddamn concerning.

"I will poke out your eyes and then feed them to my cactus, so help me God," Thea threatens, moving until she's blocking the goddess from my view.

Her tiny hands are curled into fists as she glares up at me.

That act of defiance...

The way her cheeks burn with righteous indignation and anger...

All of that honey-blonde hair cascading around her...

Fuck, she's beautiful.

My cock stirs the way it didn't before with Aphrodite. I just pray Thea doesn't notice—or she assumes my reaction has something to do with the goddess before me.

Wait...did she say cactus?

She's so fucking weird.

"We're not here for that," Zaid says with a restrained chuckle, trying to be diplomatic. "You know Ares will castrate us if we touch you."

Thea places a hand on her hip and cocks it to the side. "That's the only reason you don't want to touch her?"

We ignore her, obviously, and keep our attention fixed on the goddess. Well, I try the best I can, but it's hard with Thea jumping up and down, repeatedly trying to block Aphrodite from view.

I can't help but notice her breasts jiggle each time she jumps. I wonder what she looks like wearing the bra I picked out for her. Fuck.

Stop. Thinking. Of. Her.

"You sure?" Aphrodite giggles and absently traces a hand down her chest, flicking at the bar in her nipple. "Because you boys look awfully excited."

"You better be happy to see me and not her," Thea warns.

I instinctually scowl at her—then remember she's invisible and stands at Aphrodite's boob level, so it looks like I'm scowling at the goddess's tits.

Goddamn reaper.

"We really don't want to piss off Ares," Zaid tries again, forcefully ripping his gaze from Thea to give the goddess his full attention. "You know how he is."

Aphrodite scoffs and moves towards the bed. Thea has to practically dive to not be run over by the raging goddess.

All of us look away as Aphrodite bends over to grab something off the bed. Everyone, that is, except for Thea.

"Dude! She's wearing a butt plug!" Thea points at Aphrodite's ass, then she lowers slightly and squints to see better.

"Oh my god," Krystian murmurs, gawking.

Thea remains oblivious. "Yup. Definitely a butt plug. It looks like it's vibrating. Ohhh. That's on my bucket list. I've always wanted to try one."

Now, all I can envision is a naked Thea with a plug shoved up her perfect ass.

Goddammit.

I blame the pheromones in the air, exacerbating my lust.

Aphrodite straightens and wraps a silky bathrobe around her. It's practically transparent, leaving very little to the imagination.

"Do you think I care about Ares's precious feelings?" The goddess's lips curl. "He certainly didn't care about mine when he was fucking his lover."

We've all heard the story dozens of times before.

Hundreds of years ago, Ares started an affair with a woman he met—a woman who wasn't Aphrodite. Ares became obsessed with his new lover and broke things off with Aphrodite, and she became infuriated. Ares begged for Aphrodite to come back to him years later, and they've been hate-fucking ever since.

"You might not care, but we do," Krystian says with a chuckle, holding his hands up in the air placatingly. "He's a scary asshole on a good day."

I can't even imagine what he would do if he thought we were moving in on his girl.

"If you're not here to fuck me, then what do you want? I'm awfully busy." Aphrodite sniffs and perches on the edge of the bed, reaching for a bottle of lotion. "I have an orgy scheduled to take place in just under an hour. So unless you want to join..."

"An orgy?" Thea perks up.

"No," Rafe growls, that one word directed at Thea, though Aphrodite nods as though he was responding to her.

Yeah, no fucking way will we allow Thea to partake in an orgy with a bunch of random-ass humans and supernaturals. Just the thought of anyone touching her makes me want to slam my fist through a face.

Not that I care.

She can do whatever the fuck she wants.

Just as long as it doesn't involve other men or women, obviously.

"We just wanted to get the details on the latest gossip." Krystian waggles his eyebrows.

Aphrodite perks up. "Gossip?"

Hook, line, and sinker.

"Something about Hades's favorite reaper..." Zaid scratches absently at his chin, gauging her reaction carefully.

But he doesn't have my enhanced senses, so he doesn't hear the way her heartbeat picks up speed. He doesn't see the sweat that dots her forehead.

"What are you talking about?" She sniffs and refocuses on her task at hand—sensually rubbing lotion into her thighs and calves.

I scowl and continue watching her, studying every micro expression, every twitch of her lips and tightening of her eyes.

"Just a rumor we heard," Krystian says, moving to claim an armchair closest to the bed. He rests his elbows on his knees and leans forward. "It made us curious."

"None of us know a lot about the Big Three," Zaid takes over, speaking of the three most powerful gods in existence.

Hades, Zeus, and Poseidon.

Three brothers who rule different aspects of the world and everyone in it.

Zeus has domain over the sky, Poseidon controls the ocean, and Hades? He rules the realm of the undead.

And, more than likely, Thea's prison.

"I always thought Hades was obsessed with Persephone, so to hear that he kidnapped a reaper..." Krystian gives a slow shake of his head. "What's the story there?"

Everyone knows that Hades isn't above kidnapping to get what he wants. It's how Persephone came to live down in the underworld, at least for half of a year. Hades is desperately in love with her, but she can't stand him. Rumor has it she's in a relationship with Artemis, a fact that infuriates the God of the Dead.

"I honestly don't know what you're talking about," Aphrodite says primly.

That bead of sweat I noticed earlier cascades down her nose and lands on her thigh.

"Maybe I misunderstood." Krystian waves away our previous inquiry. "But did you hear about Apollo?"

Aphrodite perks up at that. "What did he do this time?"

"Well, apparently he was caught balls deep in a satyr and..." Krystian drones on about random gossip that I can't tell if it's true or made up.

I suppose it doesn't matter. Aphrodite eats it all up with rapt fascination.

I tune their conversation out and focus on Thea, who's frowning at the floor. I know she's desperate for answers, and I can't help but feel a pang of guilt for not finding her any.

"That's where Athena went?" Krystian's sharp exclamation draws my attention back to him.

"Poor girl." Aphrodite sniffs delicately. "She was heartbroken when she lost her team. I don't blame her for hiding away."

Zaid's fingers begin to tap against his thigh, as they

always do when he's anxious or planning something. My guess is on the latter.

Krystian and Aphrodite talk for a few more minutes until I have enough.

Taking a step forward—and capturing both of their attention—I say, "Thank you, Aphrodite. But we need to get going."

"Oh." Her face falls.

"You know how Ares can be," Zaid says lightly, trying to alleviate the mood. "He always has a job for us."

That's true. The only reason we're not being pulled away for a mission is because Ares doesn't know we completed the hellhound one. I... I didn't tell him.

For the first time in my life, I disobeyed orders.

"You can always stay..." Aphrodite reaches for Krystian, her perfectly manicured nails trailing down his arm.

Thea is there in a second, her teeth bared and eyes sparking with a savage lethality.

"Paws off, sister. Now," she threatens, and I realize the crazy bitch is actually holding her dagger in the air, like she plans to stab Aphrodite in the chest.

Krystian quickly detaches himself from the goddess and moves to his feet, backing away.

"No can do. I have to go." He smiles charmingly to show he means no offense.

Aphrodite huffs. "Krys would've stayed."

Krystian blanches.

Thea takes a threatening step towards the goddess, her arm raised.

"It was lovely catching up," Zaid says quickly, subtly positioning himself between the enraged reaper and the clueless goddess. "We'll have to do it again sometime."

Aphrodite perks up at that, even as Thea snaps, "Over my dead body."

Rafe smiles adoringly in Thea's direction—the sight unnerving as fuck to see—then moves towards the elevator.

The rest of us follow, though Zaid has to practically push Thea to get her moving.

Just before the metal doors close, Aphrodite rushes forward, placing her hand in the box.

"Wait," she blurts.

"Yes?" I grunt, already done with this entire fucking day.

We got jack shit from Aphrodite, despite the fact she obviously knows something, and no leads on what to do next.

"Just..." She glances in both directions, then leans forward, keeping her voice a hushed murmur. "Just don't discuss certain...rumors around the other gods and goddesses, okay?"

Krystian's brows clench together. "Huh?"

Aphrodite's solemn expression clears, replaced by her usual sensual cheer. She waves, the barest movement of her fingers, and says, "Goodbye, boys. Hope to see you again soon."

"Not happening," Thea huffs.

We say our goodbyes—well, Krystian and Zaid do; Rafe and I simply glare straight ahead—then take the elevator back to the lobby.

None of us speak until we're out of the apartment complex and standing on the bustling New York street.

"She definitely knew more than what she was saying," Zaid points out.

"No shit," I grumble, still irritated we didn't get any information out of her.

But what the fuck could we do? Torture a damn goddess? Yeah. I can't see that going over well with the others.

"We *did* get something," Krystian interjects.

"What's that?" Thea frowns at him.

"Athena's location." Krystian's smile broadens. "I doubt she had anything to do with what happened to Thea, but she's the Goddess of Wisdom. She should have the answers we need."

"Athena hasn't been seen in over a century," I point out. "And anytime someone tries to meet with her, they end up dead."

"I guess we just have to press our luck." Krystian shrugs nonchalantly, already moving towards a side alley where Rafe can open a portal.

"Where is she?" Thea queries, dancing along beside us. She seems in a much better mood now that we're away from Aphrodite. "I wasn't really paying attention. I was too focused on her butt plug."

Krystian doesn't respond right away, and I can tell he's thinking about his next words carefully.

"I think we can get her to help us once we get to her."

"*If* we can get to her," Zaid mumbles, kicking at a loose piece of trash.

"Where the fuck is she?" I demand, throwing my hands up in the air.

Krystian turns to stare at us, his features grave. "The Labyrinth. According to Aphrodite, she's hiding out somewhere in the Labyrinth."

CHAPTER TWENTY

THEA

"What the fuck is the Labyrinth, and why do you all look like you need to take a shit?" I demand, frowning.

Zaid ruffles his black hair. "Years ago, King Minos commissioned an architect named Daedalus to design a maze capable of keeping the Minotaur contained."

"*The* Minotaur?" I parrot, realizing that Zaid isn't just talking about any old minotaur.

"The original monster," Krystian supplies. "He was going on a killing spree, but no one knew how to stop him. This was before the gods intervened, by the way, so the humans and supernaturals were on their own."

"The Labyrinth was the only thing that could contain the beast," Everett takes over, his voice subdued. "Athena knew that, so she sent a vision to King Minos."

"Years later, Theseus entered the Labyrinth and killed the monster," adds Zaid. "The maze remained empty for years until the gods and goddesses came to earth."

"Athena decided she was going to take over the Labyrinth herself," Krystian explains. "She wanted a way to test her devout followers and see if they really walk the path of wisdom. The entire Labyrinth is nothing but a series of tests, riddles, and traps, designed for only the brightest of minds to solve."

"Well, we're fucked," I lament.

I normally consider myself a pretty optimistic person, but I know myself and the guys. We're not exactly the top brass here, if you know what I mean. Except for maybe Zaid.

"I'll do some research on it today," Zaid says, proving my point that he's our only hope.

"Can't Rafe just portal us to the center of the Labyrinth?" I turn pleading eyes on the blood fae, who watches me impassively.

"No," he answers simply.

"Magical wards surround the entire area," Krystian explains.

"Of course they do," I grumble.

Why can't any of this be easy?

"And we're sure that Athena is our only option?" Everett directs the question at Zaid, who considers it for a long moment.

The wraith nods. "Unfortunately."

"Then I suppose we have no choice." Everett pinches the bridge of his nose as if attempting to fend off an encroaching headache. "We'll head to one of our safe houses and come up with a plan. We'll leave first thing tomorrow."

Panic prickles my skin, though I try to keep my expression clear.

I know we need time to dissect all of this new information and come up with a plan, but...tomorrow? We need to wait until tomorrow? A part of me fears I won't have that long, that any second, that incessant tugging will erupt in my chest and transport me back into my prison cell.

I scratch at the inside of my wrist, tension flaring inside of me.

The others remain oblivious to my internal turmoil as they finalize the plan, and a second later, a portal appears.

This time, I don't hesitate to walk through—especially now that I know my insides won't be rearranged.

We materialize in a tiny bungalow.

Sunlight pours through wide-paned windows,

casting golden lines across the polished hardwood floors.

The living room is cozy, anchored by a brick fireplace darkened with age, its mantel cluttered with framed photos of the sea. Built-in bookshelves flank the hearth, and I wonder how many of these books belong to Zaid. I imagine most of them.

An archway leads to a dining nook, where a modest oak table sits beneath a hanging light. Beyond that, I can make out a compact kitchen, designed for functionality over extravagance. The vintage countertops and cabinets are painted the color of early spring leaves, chipped slightly at the edges.

Down a short hallway in the living room, doors lead to five different rooms. Probably four bedrooms and a bathroom.

It's cute and cozy and the exact opposite I would've expected from the guys.

"You live here?" I ask, gawking.

Krystian chuckles. "Only been here a few times in my life." He studies the tiny house too, as if seeing it through fresh eyes. "We spend most of the time in the compound or on the road. But we wanted a few safe houses where we could get away from everything."

"This place is safe, warded, and most importantly, hidden from Ares," Everett says.

The guys' suitcases—and my bag of supplies—are

already here. Huh. I never even realized they were gone, though I suppose we didn't travel with them to Aphrodite's apartment.

"You guys are constantly busy, aren't you?" I muse, moving my fingers over the mantel of the fireplace, surprised when they come back dust-free.

Either there's a spell on the home keeping it clean or they hired someone to dust and vacuum while they're away.

Krystian's laugh is dark and humorless. "Our job is to take down monsters and wayward supes. We don't get a lot of time off."

"We don't get *any* time off," Rafe corrects, already stalking down the hallway towards one of the rooms.

"Why don't the gods have more teams working at once?" I ask, the question nagging at me. "If they're worried about saving human lives, then wouldn't it make sense to have a bunch of teams?"

Everett snorts like he finds my question cute and heads towards the kitchen.

Zaid smiles sadly. "Centuries ago, that used to be the case. There were hundreds, if not thousands, of teams working."

"Then the higher powers got competitive," Krystian fills in, a tight smile on his handsome face. "It became less about protecting the humans and more about one-upping each other."

A painful ache erupts in my chest. "And you have no say in the matter? You can't refuse or ask for help?"

"It's not so bad," Krystian says, trying to remain positive, though I can see the tension in his neck and shoulders. "The pay's good."

"It's just not fair," I insist.

Why should their entire existence revolve around hunting monsters and defending humans? Why does that burden need to fall on them and them alone?

"Life isn't fair," Everett calls from the kitchen, where he's poring over the contents of the fridge. Someone must've filled it recently—or else the food was magicked to not go bad—because Everett grabs out a bag of tomatoes, some cheese, and a few other ingredients I can't decipher. "I'm making spaghetti with homemade meat sauce."

"Thank fuck. I'm starving." Krystian dramatically grabs at his stomach, his tongue lolling.

Apparently, our conversation is over.

"Is there a bathroom I can use?" I question.

"Down the hall to the right," Zaid says, pointing.

I thank him and then skip in the direction he indicated. Once I reach the door, I knock, just to make sure Rafe isn't using it, before ducking inside.

It's cute and tiny, everything colored in white and blue.

"Fuck, I have to pee," I mutter, reaching for my jeans.

That's one of the only things I hate about having a real body—excrements.

What's the point of eating food if you're just going to get rid of it a few hours later?

My fingers snag on where I keep my dagger tucked snugly in the waistband of my pants. Only...I don't feel the cool metal of the blade or the jewel-encrusted hilt.

Holy fuck.

Did I lose my dagger? Where is it?

I try to remember when I last had it, but I come up blank. I'm ninety percent certain I shoved it in my pants after threatening Aphrodite with it.

I pull my pants down the entire way and twist in the mirror.

"What the...?" My brows draw together, and I reach for the edge of my panties, pulling them down slightly to see better.

Tattooed onto my skin is the dagger.

Fuck. Fuck. Fuck. Fuck.

I run my fingers over the intricate design, but it feels like skin. Just skin.

"This isn't good," I whimper. "This isn't good at all."

I move through the house in a perpetual daze, my mind spinning and questions tumbling over one another.

What the fuck happened to the dagger?

Why is it embedded in my skin?

How did it happen?

What will happen to me?

I walk into the dining room, the scent of garlic and simmering meat sauce immediately filling my senses.

Everett stands at the counter, dishing up the spaghetti with his usual efficiency. His broad shoulders tense slightly when he notices me enter. I'm not sure if it's because he's pissed that I've interrupted his perfect routine or because I'm the one walking in, but I try not to let it faze me.

I have more important things to worry about.

Instinctively, I touch my side, directly over the intricate dagger tattoo.

"Dinner's served," he says, his voice rough, as always.

He doesn't look my way as he slides a plate in front of me, the pasta already covered in a bright-red sauce. The garlic bread is golden, crisp, and tempting. My mouth waters, and all thoughts of daggers flee.

Everett watches me intently, studying my every move, something unspoken hovering between us.

He doesn't like me, but he goes out of his way to take care of me—like making sure I'm fed and buying me clothes. His silent, unacknowledged kindness brings an unexpected lump to my throat.

"Looks delicious." I force a smile, taking a seat at the table.

His eyes narrow suspiciously, but before he can comment, Krystian races into the dining room, his eyes alight with mischief.

"Holy crap. I was seconds away from eating my own hand." He grins at me and winks. "Or Thea, though I'm not sure she's ready for that."

"Um, is this topic up for discussion?" I ask innocently, twirling spaghetti around my fork.

"Of course," Krystian replies at the same moment Everett bites out, "No."

Zaid and Rafe enter as well and claim seats on

either side of Krystian, leaving the space beside me for Everett.

Zaid smiles tentatively. "I swear Everett would be a gourmet chef if he didn't have to hunt down monsters."

Everett rolls his eyes, but... Is that a blush staining his cheeks?

I squint, certain I'm imagining things, and Everett glowers at me. "Eat your damn food, and stop staring at me like a damn creeper."

Rafe peers down at his plate with an intensity that's borderline unnerving. It's like he's mentally dissecting the meal. Or maybe planning something—like shoving the noodles up Everett's asshole, something I would pay to see.

His eyes meet mine for a brief second, and a cold shiver races down my spine.

"Eat your food, little bird," he orders, his voice taking on a dangerous edge.

I nod quickly, pushing my fork through the pasta once more. The tension in the air is thick, and I find myself caught between two extremes—Everett's silent care and Rafe's unsettling energy.

Zaid and Krystian are definitely much less intense than the other two.

"You okay?" Zaid asks softly, his eyes glimmering with concern.

I wonder what made him think that, then I realize it's because I haven't taken a single bite of my food.

For the first time since I've arrived on earth, I'm not hungry. My stomach is in too many knots.

"Just thinking about what Aphrodite said," I fib, waving my fork in the air for emphasis.

He gives a small nod, not pressing, but his eyes linger on me. I can tell he doesn't quite believe me, but he doesn't know what to ask next.

The conversation drifts, Krystian pulling it back to something lighthearted, talking about some ridiculous prank he pulled on Rafe the week before. Rafe, of course, isn't amused, but there's a slight curve to his lips that I catch when he thinks no one is looking. Zaid listens intently, while Everett simply scarfs down his food like a man possessed.

I can't help but think how quickly my world has changed. Just a day ago, I was trapped in that damn room with no hope of ever escaping. Now, I'm here, surrounded by four men who are so vastly different from each other, yet each one pulls me in some way.

Krystian's carefree nature is a balm to my tattered soul, while Krys's intensity reminds me that I'm more than anyone can comprehend. Rafe's madness is magnetic, though I'm not sure I'm strong enough to survive the pull towards him. Zaid is the safe harbor I never knew I needed, but Everett... Everett is something else entirely. His gruff exterior belies a certain protectiveness I don't know how to interpret. It's not as if he's giving me any clarity, either.

Krystian continues talking, his voice cheerful, and for a moment, I allow myself to envision a future where I'm not a tool of death. Where I'm not a prisoner. Where I'm not isolated from the rest of the world. But in the back of my mind, there's this constant nagging reminding me that nothing good lasts.

Either they're going to get sick of me—a silly girl who doesn't know what she is or where she came from—or I'm going to be ripped away from them.

I brush at the dagger tattoo yet again.

As the evening wears on, laughter fills the room—easy and familiar—but my thoughts are a jumbled mess.

Rafe calls me "little bird," and maybe that's all I'm meant to be.

Caged and isolated.

Perhaps there's a reason I was locked away in the first place.

And maybe once that reason comes to light, the guys will wish they never helped me to begin with.

CHAPTER TWENTY-TWO

THEA

"Hey. You asleep?" Krystian leans against the doorframe of the bedroom they allowed me to borrow.

I toss him a droll look over my shoulder. "Yes, because I sleep standing up all the time."

Krystian snickers. "Hey, in my defense, you're a weird little creature. Who knows with you?"

I flip him off and turn back to the clothes laid out on my bed. Everett must've also grabbed me pajamas, though I don't know if I want to wear the teal silk set or the nightgown.

Krystian steps forward to see what I'm looking at. "Oh. Go with the teal. It'll look great on you."

Smirking, I grab the nightgown instead and move towards the connecting bathroom.

Krystian follows me, seemingly unperturbed when I slam the door in his face.

"So...it's going to be night soon," Krystian begins, his voice slightly muffled due to the door.

"I'm not afraid of your dark side, Krystian," I tell him as I throw off my clothes and slip on the nightdress.

The fabric is cool against my overheated flesh, billowing around my thighs. I'm fortunate it hides my dagger tattoo from view.

"You may not be, but I am," Krystian confesses after a long moment of silence.

I freeze at that, considering, then pull open the door, one eyebrow arched.

He's gripping the doorframe, his head lowered, strands of silky white-blond hair obscuring his features from view. Tension lines his shoulders and neck.

"Why?" I ask softly, wanting him to look at me.

Needing him to.

He doesn't.

"There's a lot you don't understand, love." Krystian heaves out a tired breath, that one noise laced with years of wariness and unencumbered pain.

"Krys is you, isn't he? Your dark desires and urges?" I finally lower my head in order to meet his eyes. "Do you not trust yourself?"

Those blue orbs blink repeatedly. He seems unsure of how to respond.

"It's not that." He lifts his head and shakily runs a hand through his hair, ruffling the strands. "It's just...I don't know what I do at night. Sometimes, I'll wake up covered in blood with no memory of how I got there. Or in the bed of a woman with no knowledge—"

He cuts himself off quickly at my sharp look.

The last thing I want to hear about is him—or Krys, for that matter—in the bed of another woman.

"Krys seems to believe that your distrust of him is what causes the disconnect between you two. It's why you don't remember what happens during the night, and vice versa." Though I'm beginning to believe that Krys isn't as oblivious as Krystian believes him to be.

"Do you know who also has no inhibitions?" He doesn't wait for me to respond, forging ahead with an uncharacteristically serious expression. "Psychopaths."

"You think Krys is the psychopathic version of yourself?"

"I know he is." He licks his upper lip. "I don't want to hurt you, Thea. I would never forgive myself if I did something to you."

A choked, strangled sound escapes him, as if the mere prospect is too awful to even comprehend.

"I don't believe you will," I tell him sincerely.

"I would never," Krystian agrees. "But Krys—"

"Is you."

"Is a psychopath," he counters.

Frustration builds in my chest.

"You don't believe that." I shake my head adamantly and take a single step closer to him.

"I don't?" He cocks an eyebrow.

"If you did, you wouldn't be here, when you know you're about to transform." I allow my gaze to roam over his perfectly sculpted face, every inch chiseled by the gods themselves.

"I still have time," he whispers, his breath stuttering.

"How much time?" I hesitantly reach for him, cupping the back of his neck.

My fingers tangle in his shiny blond hair.

"Thea..." My name on his lips is a plea, a warning, and a benediction all at once.

Lust streaks through me, and a pulse of need erupts in my center.

"Kiss me, Krystian," I plead.

He swallows. "Thea, please."

"Kiss me."

Because if I fade away right here and now, I want to know what his lips feel like against my own.

Krystian shudders in my embrace, and I can feel the last of his resistance snapping. Shattering. Deteriorating like tissue paper in water.

Krystian doesn't just kiss me. He *devours* me. Each press of his mouth against my own makes me think he's trying to suck out my soul. And as he kisses me, something dark and incurable cements itself deep inside my bones.

This man... He's mine.

All sides of him—the good and the bad, the part he loves and the part he fears.

It's only been two days, yet I feel like it's been an eternity. My soul knows him, calls for him, and each swipe of his tongue against my own tells me he feels it as well.

I melt against him, groaning hoarsely, tingles racing up and down my spine.

Do all kisses feel like this? Or just his?

Krystian pulls away, breathing heavily. "Fuck, love. Fuck."

"Don't stop," I beg, planting kisses across his neck until I reach his jaw.

I have to push myself up onto my tiptoes now that he's no longer leaning.

"If I don't stop, then we'll do a lot more than just kissing." He tries to chuckle, but the noise is raspy with barely suppressed need.

"And that's a bad thing?" I flick my tongue out and trace his lips—his full upper, followed by his thinner lower, and then finally the seam.

He groans and opens his mouth, kissing me like he wants to punish me for teasing him.

His hands move to the straps of my nightgown, and another strangled moan escapes him.

"Fuck, you look so goddamn sexy in this. I'm fucking losing my mind."

"I thought you preferred the teal set?" I ask, sucking on a spot on his neck.

He seems to like it, if his gyrating hips are any indication.

"I lied."

He grabs the straps of my nightgown, forcing them down my arms.

"Holy fuck." His eyes widen as he stares at my naked body, now dressed in only a pair of panties—this pair black.

Then he's kissing me again, his hands roaming my body, tracing every dip and curve. His fingers brush over my puckered nipple, and a shiver of delight rolls through me.

"You're so sexy, love. So fucking sexy. You put every goddess to shame." He begins to kiss down my throat, my shoulders, my breasts, stopping when he reaches my neglected nipple.

He pulls it into his mouth, his tongue flicking out to play with it.

I gasp and grab at his hair, holding him still.

He releases my breast and steps away, his chest heaving and his face flushed.

"I can't... I can't stop. Fuck. Tell me to stop, Thea. Tell me to go away."

"I want you to fuck me, Krystian," I tell him, pulling down my panties and kicking them aside.

He swears raggedly, his gaze glued to my revealed pussy. "Love..."

"Please, Krystian." I squeeze my tits, pinching my nipples.

His gaze drops to them automatically, and his breathing grows choppy.

With an almost blistering speed, he throws his shirt aside, then he kicks off his pants and boxer briefs.

Leaving him gloriously, deliciously naked.

Fuck, he's gorgeous. I could stare at him all day and never tire of it. He's not as muscular as Everett, but his body is lean and defined, his waist tapered. His cock brushes against his stomach—long but not necessarily thick.

I don't know if I reach for him or he reaches for me. All I know is that we lunge for each other, the momentum sending us flying back onto the bed. I land on top of him, our lips fused together, our bodies flush.

I pull away to reach for his cock, loving the feel of it in my hand. I don't know what I expected, but it certainly wasn't this—velvety softness combined with steel.

"Fuck, yes. Baby, just like that. Fuck."

I line the head of his cock up with my slit, already dripping for him. I don't really know what I'm doing, but this feels good, so I continue doing it. Each drag of his erect cock against my pussy causes goose bumps to pebble on my arms.

I gasp, my eyes fluttering shut. "Fuck."

Krystian swears—the noise rough and strangled—and then flips us so I'm on my back and he's hovering over me. His blue eyes ensnare my own, making it impossible for me to look away.

"What are you doing to me?" he asks, his swollen cock sliding through my slick entrance.

"What are we doing to each other?" I counter, tears prickling my eyes.

Because this isn't just a one-way street.

I have feelings for him—strong, inexplicable feelings that scare me.

He lines himself up and thrusts inside of me. I throw my head back and cry out, the feeling of being stretched indescribable.

"You feel fucking amazing around my cock, love. Fuck." He pulls out and then slams back into me, his hips hitting my own.

There's no hesitation. No easing me into this. It's

like his body knows exactly what I need, and he's willing to give it.

I wrap my legs around his hips and arch my back, taking him even deeper.

"Your pussy is so tight, love. So goddamn tight. I don't know how long I can last," he pants, his hips thrusting steadily.

Lifting my head, I trap his lips in another heated kiss, nipping and sucking on his lower lip.

"You feel like you were made for me, like your pussy was made for my cock," he rasps, pumping harder into me.

And it occurs to me then that I should've felt pain at his rough intrusion. There should've been blood.

But it's as he said—it feels as if my body was made for him.

"Fuck me hard, Krystian. Give me everything." I drag my fingernails down his back.

"It's already yours."

Those possessive, heated words send a shockwave straight to my core, which tightens around his cock instinctively. Krystian's hips stutter, inarticulate curses and praises leaving his lips, and I grip him tighter.

"Yes, yes, yes!" I scream as my pussy pulsates around his length.

With a hoarse cry, he buries himself to the hilt, his hips jerking erratically before stilling. He collapses half on top of me, his head buried in the crook of my shoulder.

"Holy fuck," he breathes, his lips brushing against my skin with each exhale.

I run my hand across his back, holding him to me.

I can't seem to catch my breath. To think. To do anything but touch him and stare mindlessly at the ceiling.

"Is it... Is it always like that?" I whisper.

"Not for me," he responds simply, and then he stills, his nose still pressed against my skin. "Thea?"

"Yes?" I ask.

"Did you always have that tattoo on your thigh?"

I open my mouth, close it, and then open it again. But before I can respond, Krystian shakes, his hands curling around me in a way that's almost painful. I freeze and slowly lower my head.

Pitch-black eyes peer back at me.

Krys grins—the smile hungry and possessive, making goose bumps blaze across my body.

His hard cock brushes against my side as he rolls overtop of me.

"Hello, my love." Blond hair, streaked with black and blue, falls across his face. "How do you feel about round two?"

CHAPTER TWENTY-THREE

KRYS

I don't think anything will compare to staring down at Thea's flushed, post-orgasmic face.

Fuck, just thinking about what I did to her earlier—what Krystian did—makes my cock harden.

My sunny counterpart doesn't think I'm aware of what goes on during the day, but that just isn't true.

I know everything, including how fast we've fallen for this intoxicating woman.

Krystian is afraid to confess the truth to her, to admit how much he needs her, but I'm not.

Thea is mine.

I've claimed her, and there's no going back for me. She has imprinted herself into the foundation of my very soul, weaving herself in such a manner I have no hope of untangling her. Not that I want to.

There's no fear in her eyes when she stares up at me. No trepidation or unease or distrust. She knows I'll never hurt her, that I'm just one side of a coin, and my existence revolves around her now.

I lower my lips to hers, nibbling on her bottom lip hard enough to draw blood.

I don't want to be gentle. Not like Krystian was.

I need to consume her. Make her mine. Burrow myself so far inside of her that she can never remove me.

"I'm not going to be gentle, shortstack," I warn her.

An impish smile tugs at her lips. "Then maybe you shouldn't lead."

Before I can comment, she rolls us so she's on top and I'm beneath her. I can't say I mind the new position.

I grip her hips and smirk. "You want to ride me, love?"

Instead of answering with words, she reaches behind her and lines my cock up with her entrance. She slowly slides herself onto my length, and we both moan. I arch my hips up and shove all the way in, not giving her a chance to adjust to the intrusion. She doesn't need me to.

She's fucking mine. Her body was made for me.

"Holy fuck!" She places her palms on my chest and

rides me, her tits bouncing in a way that makes me lose my fucking mind.

I'll kill for this girl.

Die for her.

The sound of slapping skin fills the room, intermingled with our moans and gasps.

"Yes, Krys, yes. Fuck. Yes. Your cock. Fuck." She's so close to her next release that she's not thinking coherently.

The sight of her sweat-drenched skin, matted blonde hair, and glazed eyes nearly undoes me.

I grip her hips tightly as she leans over me, burying her face in my neck. My cock reaches a new position inside of her, which makes her cries grow even louder. I imagine every single one of my brothers can hear her right now—and are wishing they are the one with her instead.

"Come for me, Thea. Come on my cock." I swear as my cock spasms inside of her, and Thea explodes with a scream, throwing her head back.

Cum drips down her thighs, but she doesn't seem to notice as she lowers herself on top of me.

"Fuck, Krys," she whimpers, wrapping her arms around me.

I'm damn near feral for this girl. The things I want to do to her...

But no. She's not ready for that yet.

Next time, though.

My cock stiffens at just the thought of my handprints on her rounded ass.

"You're mine, Thea," I tell her, both as a promise and a warning. "You're not leaving me. I won't let you. I'll fucking tie you to the bed if that's what I need to do."

She doesn't look scared by my proclamation. If anything, her lips curl up, dark satisfaction in her blue eyes.

"Is that so?"

"That doesn't scare you?" I question, brushing at a strand of her sweat-soaked hair.

But I already know the answer.

"Would it scare you if I said I felt the exact same?" The confession is almost whispered, like she's afraid of speaking those words out loud and being rejected.

I kiss her desperately, hungrily, pulling at her bottom lip with my teeth.

Fucking hell, I love the way she looks when she's flushed and freshly fucked.

"You're not afraid of me," I muse, running my fingers down her cheek.

"Of course not." A wide yawn cracks open her jaw, and her eyelids begin to droop. "You're Krystian."

My heart thumps faster.

It's the first time anyone has referred to me by that

name. Everyone wants to believe I'm some separate entity, but that's not true.

I'm Krystian.

And I'm also hers.

I'm made up of darkness and violence and death, but all of those facets of myself belong to her. She wields me. I'm her weapon to do with as she pleases.

"Go to sleep, my love. You're tired." I press a kiss to her forehead.

"Will you stay with me?" Her lashes flutter open, vulnerability flashing in those blue depths.

"Until you fall asleep," I promise.

She seems satisfied by that answer and yawns again, her lids drooping.

"Goodnight, Krystian." Her voice slurs.

"Goodnight."

I EXIT the bedroom an hour later to three jealous, possessive glares.

Everett balls his hands into fists, the muscles in his jaw working overtime.

"If you took advantage of her, so help me god..." He takes a threatening step forward.

Anger flares deep in my chest. "I would never do such a thing."

Even with no inhibitions, I would never, ever hurt someone that way, least of all Thea.

"We all heard her cries of pleasure," Rafe deadpans, his brown eyes hard. "She definitely wanted what he was giving her."

Zaid scrubs a hand through his dark hair, muttering something that sounds suspiciously like, "Lucky bastard," under his breath.

I bite down on my smug grin.

But there's a reason I'm here right now and not snuggled with my shortstack.

I glance at Rafe and quirk an eyebrow. "Fancy going on a trip with me?"

A dark, malevolent grin unfurls on his lips, giving him a devilish appearance. It's rare the blood fae smiles, but when he does, it's always when death or torture is involved. The bastard makes me look sane.

"I thought you'd never ask." Rafe takes a step towards me.

"Wait." Zaid holds up both hands, his expression pinched. "Are you sure this is a good idea?"

"Not at all," I respond honestly, my grin widening. "Which makes it the best idea."

Everett scowls and crosses his arms, but he doesn't

protest. He knows, as well as I do, that it's our only option.

"Just…be careful, okay?" Zaid chews on his lower lip.

"Never." I smirk, then allow the smile to fall off my face. "Take care of her."

"Always," Zaid vows.

Everett simply mutters, "Yeah, sure, whatever."

For him, that's a battle cry. He may not want to admit it to even himself, but the surly bastard will protect our little reaper with his life. Somehow, she has wiggled her way past all of our defenses, burrowing so deep under our skin that we have no hope of removing her.

Rafe nods seriously then unsheathes a blade. He brings it to his palm, creating a deep wound, and blood spills. A portal sputters to life, materializing in the center of the living room.

Zaid and Everett step back as I move towards the portal.

"Adíos," I say, saluting them.

Then I step through the portal…directly into an orgy.

Revulsion crinkles my nose as I take in the numerous writhing, moaning bodies.

Rafe appears directly behind me, and the portal snaps shut.

"Disgusting," Rafe murmurs, though his voice doesn't change inflection, remaining completely impassive.

Nobody bats an eye at the portal or our sudden arrival. I imagine we're not the first supernaturals to arrive here.

"This way," I tell Rafe, moving carefully through the bodies.

In front of me, a vampire is getting her tits sucked by a human and a fairy. A shifter fucks her from behind as she moans and cries. Next to them, a warlock sucks the cock of a werewolf.

"Krys." The vampire reaches for me, her nails digging into my arm. "Come join."

At one point, I might've taken her up on the offer, but that was before.

"No thanks, darling." I offer her a tight smile. "I'm a taken man."

Her lips purse in an exaggerated pout. "I don't see anyone else here."

Her manicured finger trails down my bicep.

"Hands off," Rafe growls, grabbing her wrist.

She sucks in a sharp gasp, pain flaring in her eyes. Rafe stares at her silently, and though I can't read his expression, whatever the vampire sees makes her skitter away, her metaphorical tail between her legs.

"She's lucky she didn't touch me," Rafe says darkly, continuing his way through the throng of naked bodies.

At that exact moment, a warlock reaches for Rafe desperately.

Rafe breaks the man's fingers, though his screams are lost in the cries of pleasure.

I smirk at the bloodthirsty psycho.

"I like the way you work," I tell him.

"He touched what doesn't belong to him," Rafe says seriously.

I suppose I'm not the only one completely under Thea's spell.

In the distance, I hear Aphrodite moan and then cry out. We turn to see the goddess surrounded by five men and three women, all naked and touching her and caressing her. Aphrodite pulls one of the women into a kiss, fondling her breasts, while one of the men kisses up and down her neck.

"She's distracted." I pull my gaze away, feeling bored and desperate to return to Thea.

I want to crawl into bed and wrap my arms around her before she wakes up.

The two of us take the elevator up to the penthouse —the same one we just left.

There are two guards stationed there, but we dispatch them within seconds.

"Search everywhere," I instruct Rafe, already

moving towards the bed—and doing my damndest to ignore the crusty condoms, lacy bras, and wet strap-ons littering the surface.

Between the two of us, we open every drawer, check under every surface, sift through every article of clothing, study every sex toy for clues.

The bitch is hiding something.

"Found something," Rafe interjects quietly.

I move towards him and peer over his shoulder.

At first, I think I'm looking at a sketchbook, but then I realize that the designs on the page are tattoos. Intermixed with the sketches are photographs of skin with the designs.

"Aphrodite has a tattoo book?" My brows lift in disbelief.

I try to remember if I ever saw any on the goddess before.

Rafe continues to study the book intently, and I finally find what has captured his attention.

There, in the far corner of the page, is the sketch of a very familiar rune.

The same rune on Thea's dagger.

It almost appears to be two swooping lines with an arch overtop of it and a dot below it. Unlike the other sketches, there are no accompanying photographs.

"It could just be a coincidence," I murmur as Rafe flips to the front of the book.

He grunts but doesn't agree or disagree. I'm beginning to believe nothing to do with Thea is a coincidence. I don't know if it's divine intervention or fate or the product of meddling gods...but a coincidence? Definitely not.

"Wait. Stop." I jab a finger down. "Look."

Written in cursive script are the words—*Property of Athena.*

CHAPTER TWENTY-FOUR

THEA

"So where, exactly, is this Labyrinth?" I ask the following morning as we all sit around the dining room table for breakfast.

Everett created chocolate chip pancakes—yes, fucking, please—and fluffy scrambled eggs.

I reach for another pancake at the same moment Krystian does, and our fingers touch. Heat engulfs my cheeks, and I quickly duck my head, especially when a sensual, mischievous smirk decorates his face.

I don't know how to act with Krystian now that we had sex. I'm not sure if this changes things between us.

I know I want it to.

"Go ahead, love," Krystian purrs, pulling back his hand.

He nods towards the pancake.

When I simply gawk at him, memories of our time

together playing on a loop in my head, Everett blows out a breath, grabs the pancake, and drops it on my plate.

I dig in with ruthless abandon.

"We can portal to the entrance of it," Zaid explains, carefully cutting his pancakes into perfect squares. "But from there, we're on our own."

A frog jumps from the ground onto Zaid's shoulder, and I freeze, a forkful of pancake halfway to my mouth. I wait for him to acknowledge the green amphibian, to bat it away or scream, but he continues eating, a thoughtful expression crossing his face.

What the fuck?

I wait for someone—anyone—to acknowledge the frog's arrival, but no one does.

"What should we expect?" Everett asks gruffly, pushing back his empty plate and reclining in his seat.

"I tried to do all the research I could," Zaid tells him. "But unfortunately, there's not a lot of information to go on. Most people who entered the Labyrinth—"

"—never made it out," Rafe finishes, absently twirling his butter knife. "How interesting."

I swallow down the razor blade lodged in my throat.

"Maybe we should just search for a new lead," I say quickly.

The last thing I want is for anyone to get hurt trying to help me—especially one of these men. The mere thought makes a fist squeeze my heart.

The frog hops off Zaid's shoulder and moves across the table towards Everett.

No one acknowledges it.

"There's actually something we want you to consider," Zaid tells me earnestly, placing his arms on the table and leaning forward.

His grayish-blue eyes ensnare my own, holding me captive. I can't look away.

"Yes?"

"You could potentially stay behind," he says, and then hurries to continue before I can protest. "You'll be safe here. No one but one of us can get past the wards. We'll be back before you know it—"

"No way in hell!" I snap, scowling. "You just said that this mission will be dangerous."

"Which is why you should stay behind," Everett points out stoutly.

"You'll need me," I protest. "I refuse to remain here while you guys risk your lives for me. This is *my* problem. Now, I would completely understand if you guys want to remain behind while *I* go on my own—"

"No way in hell," Krystian growls adamantly.

"Not happening," Everett scoffs.

"No, sweetheart," adds Zaid.

Rafe simply says, "No."

"Then we're doing it together." I flick my gaze between the four of them, allowing them all to see how serious I am.

I refuse to back down. If they think I'll allow them to go on their own, then they have another think coming.

And yes, it's *think*, not thing. I'm literate, bitches.

The frog hops up and down in front of Everett, its long tongue extending.

Everett ignores it and turns to me.

Umm...

"If you're going, then you need to listen to every-thing I say. If I say jump, you fucking jump. Don't ask me how high. We won't have time for that shit. This isn't just to protect you but the rest of the team as well. Do you understand?" He levels me with a dark, pene-trating look.

I nod wordlessly.

Everett's job on this team is to protect the others. He's the leader—whether officially or unofficially, I don't know. I have to trust that he'll do what's best for all of us.

And...I *do* trust him. Despite his cantankerous, combative nature, I know he'll never hurt me or put me in harm's way. He's an asshole, but sometimes, that's the only way to get people to listen. You can either have everyone love you or keep everyone safe. He chose the latter. I can respect that, and him, even if I don't entirely understand it.

Everett's mouth molds into a frown, but he seems satisfied with my answer.

The frog moves onto his hand and climbs up his arm.

Finally, I can't take it anymore.

I point a finger at the frog and exclaim, "Is anyone going to do something about that?"

"About Everett?" Krystian chuckles. "He's beyond saving."

"Fuck off," the shifter grumbles, flipping him the finger.

"No." I absently brush at a disarranged strand of hair that has fallen into my face. "The frog."

Zaid frowns. "The frog?"

"The frog on his arm." I give them a "duh" look.

The guys exchange a look.

"What frog?" Krystian's brows draw together.

"Sweetheart, there is no frog." Zaid offers me a soft smile.

A strange feeling arrows through me as I watch the frog jump off Everett's arm and hop across the table.

"Do you guys really not see it?" I ask, my voice turning high-pitched.

My heart begins to pound even faster, battering my rib cage.

"No," Rafe says simply.

I swallow then lower my hands to the dagger tattooed on my waist. I've been saved from explaining it all morning. For all Krystian knows, I've had it my entire life. But now...

I'm running out of time.

My breathing turns thready, and nerves pinball around in my stomach. Sweat coats my hands, and I wipe them repeatedly on my jeans.

"Breathe for me, sweetheart. Breathe." Zaid's in front of me, his hands on my thighs.

When did he move? Why can't I breathe? Why does the air seem to be made of fire that I'm dragging into my lungs?

"We need to hurry," I whisper, gripping his hands tightly.

The silence turns fraught with tension.

"What's going on?" Everett barks, standing.

The other two move to crowd around me, but instead of feeling suffocated or claustrophobic, a sense of peace, of security, floods my veins. They'll protect me. I know they will. They promised.

I stand, nearly sending a crouched Zaid toppling backwards, and begin to pull down my jeans.

"What the fuck?" Krystian's eyes widen and then heat.

Rafe licks his lips.

But they all freeze when they spot the strange tattoo etched on my skin.

Zaid, who's closest to the marking, leans forward, his eyes narrowed suspiciously.

"What's that?"

"My dagger," I respond, my voice tight.

"Do you mean a tattoo of your dagger?" An acrimonious tension ripples through Everett, causing his muscles to strain.

"No. It's *my* dagger." I absently trace the design. "I had it in the waistband of my pants, but now..."

"Now it's melded into your skin." Zaid's face pales in horror.

My breath quickens, panic coursing through me. "Whenever I reap a soul, the dagger...does stuff to me. Bad stuff. I see things that aren't there. I hear voices. I lose my goddamn mind. It only stops when I place the dagger on a pedestal in my room."

"But you didn't reap any souls," Krystian points out, trying to remain positive.

"If I lose my mind again..." I swallow, feeling like I've shoved an entire sword down my throat.

There will be no escape, no relief. I won't be able

to simply place the dagger on the pedestal and get my mind back.

My ribs seem to press against my lungs. I can barely suck down a full breath.

"We won't let that happen," Zaid assures me, straightening from his crouched position to grab my hands. "We'll figure this out, Thea. I promise."

And for the first time since I met these men...

I don't believe them.

CHAPTER TWENTY-FIVE

THEA

Apparently, the Labyrinth's entrance is in Edinburgh, Scotland.

We enter through an unassuming door on a bustling street, descend a steep staircase, and weave through a series of underground homes and streets.

"This is normally a tourist destination," Zaid explains to me, a taut smile on his face. They've all been doing that lately—staring at me as if I'm seconds from cracking. "Hundreds of years ago, this used to be above ground, hence why there are so many streets and houses."

"And none of the tourists or guides stumbled upon the entrance to the Labyrinth?" I arch my eyebrows in disbelief.

"It's not that easy to get into." He chuckles, though the sound is forced.

They don't need to walk on eggshells around me, but whenever I tell them as much, they assure me they're not.

Liars.

"Here." Zaid stops in front of a plain brick wall, artificial gold lights flickering off its wet surface.

"Here?"

"Here," Rafe says, stepping forward.

He grabs his dagger out of a sheath, cuts his palm, and then places his hand against the wall.

We all wait with bated breath.

I don't know what I expect to happen, but when nothing does, my shoulders slump.

If this is a bust, then we'll be back to square one.

Zaid shifts his weight. "Maybe we need to—"

The wall crumbles away, the bricks seeming to deteriorate into thin air. Where there was once part of a building now stands a seemingly dark abyss.

Every knot in my stomach tightens simultaneously.

"Is this...?" I squint, hoping to see something— anything—in the oppressive darkness.

"The entrance of the Labyrinth," Rafe answers darkly, giving his dagger an expert twirl in the air and catching the handle.

"Oh. Fun." I scratch absently at the inside of my wrist.

The guys position themselves so they're surrounding me—Everett and Rafe taking the lead, with Krystian and Zaid behind me—and then we move as one.

The darkness is unnerving and absolute. The farther away we get from the door, the darker it seems to become, until I can barely make out the men in front of me. The only indication they're still here are the occasional grunts and curses.

Instinctively, I reach forward, my hand brushing the soft cotton of Everett's shirt. I expect him to push me away, but instead, he grabs my hand in his, interlocking our fingers together.

I push out a breath of relief.

"Flashlights aren't working," Zaid says from behind me.

"Phones aren't either," Rafe grunts out.

"So we're just supposed to walk in absolute darkness?" I ask.

The second the question leaves my lips, though, hundreds of lights flicker on, one after another.

Torches.

Fire twists and dances high above us, illuminating the pathway—the graying stone walls, dripping with an undefinable liquid, and compacted dirt walkways.

"So...how do we know when we're nearing a puzzle?" I query. "And how do we even know which direction to go?"

The pathway up ahead splits into three directions.

"We don't," Everett answers, and I realize, somewhat belatedly, that he's still holding my hand.

Is it because he doesn't notice? Or because he wants to?

My heart pounds dauntingly against my rib cage, and unease curls up my spine like red creeping thyme.

We reach the first fork in the tunnel, and Zaid steps around us, his head cocked to the side.

"I'm not going to be able to hold the form for long," Zaid tells us, confusing the shit out of me. "You know how hard it is when I'm not outside during the daytime." He pauses, frowns, and then adds, "But the flames should be enough—if they don't go out."

Huh?

I must've spoken it out loud, because Zaid turns towards me, an unexpectedly serious expression on his face.

"I'll be back in a few minutes."

Then, to my utter shock, he coalesces into shadows, disappearing from view.

I jerk forward, but Everett, who still has a tight grip on my hand, pulls me to a stop.

"He'll be fine," he assures me, his tone gruff. "He's

just checking each pathway to figure out which way we need to go."

The next few minutes are the longest of my life, which is saying something. Fear grips my throat in an impenetrable chokehold. I can't help but think of the worst-case scenario. What if the flames sputter out? What if a monster attacks Zaid in his shadow form? What if he can't find his way back? What if—

The shadows deepen in front of us and then solidify, Zaid's body taking form followed by his face and inky hair. Lines of tension create furrows between his brows, and sweat drips down his cheeks. He places his hands on his knees and takes a couple of harrowed breaths, as if he ran a marathon.

"Sorry," he pants out. "It's hard to hold the form in these conditions."

I strain to go to him, to comfort him, but Everett's grip on my hand remains firm. All I can do is stare, biting on my lower lip hard enough to draw blood.

"This way," Zaid says at last, pointing down the right pathway. "The center one leads to a dead end, and the left ends at a pit of spikes."

Krystian reaches into his backpack and digs out a water bottle, extending it for Zaid to take. The wraith does so gratefully and swallows it down.

Everett's hold loosens, and I take the opportunity to lunge forward and study Zaid intently.

"Are you okay?" I ask somewhat desperately, pushing up on my tiptoes to cup his cheeks.

His warm eyes meet my own, and he gently places his hands over mine. "I'm okay." A tentative smile pulls up his lips. "I know my limitations."

That may be true, but I'm beginning to believe all of these guys will break these so-called "limitations" if it means saving me.

I don't want that.

At all.

The five of us move down the right pathway. I remain beside Zaid, my shoulder brushing his with every step we take. I study him out of the corner of my eye, making sure he won't keel over and die. I have no idea how long these side effects will last.

"I'm fine, sweetheart," Zaid assures me for the one millionth time. "I promise."

"Rafe?" I glance over my shoulder at the blood fae, who has fallen slightly behind.

"Truth," Rafe answers simply.

The tightness in my chest loosens.

Zaid gives my hand a squeeze, though he doesn't speak again. He doesn't need to. Just his hand in mine is enough. It's a revelation and a homecoming all in one.

"This place is fucking creepy," Krystian laments,

his head swiveling in all directions as he searches for threats.

Everett snorts. "It's a maze designed by a madman and hijacked by a goddess. It's not supposed to feel like a summer vacation."

Krystian doesn't bother to look over his shoulder as he flips the shifter off.

We press deeper into the tunnel, and the world shifts. There's a pulse underfoot, like a heartbeat. Then—

A roar splits the air, high and metallic, and the floor shudders beneath us. From the dark, it charges: a monstrosity of brass and iron.

The Minotaur.

No...not *the* Minotaur.

A mechanical one.

Its horns gleam under the flickering torchlight, its eyes glowing blood-red.

I've never seen anything like this before. It stands nearly ten feet tall, its body forged from riveted bronze plates and brass joints that hiss and vent steam with every movement.

Each hoof slams against the ground with the force of a battering ram, cracking the ancient flagstones beneath. Its torso is vaguely humanoid—massive, broad, and covered in armor etched with arcane glyphs —but its head is unmistakable.

The brutal, crowned skull of a bull, complete with curved iron horns sharp enough to gut a normal human.

Those twin glowing eyes lock onto us, the molten red glare a physical burn against my skin. From its snout, steam billows in rhythmic bursts.

In place of hands, it has gauntleted fists equipped with blades. Six curling metallic claws jut out like steel fingers ready to slice us into macabre confetti.

"You've got to be kidding me," I breathe.

Athena is truly a twisted bitch if she chose to recreate and upgrade a dead monster.

"Back," Everett growls, extending his arm out to stop me mid-step.

Zaid automatically positions me behind him, his body rippling with tension.

Krystian reaches for his bow and notches an arrow. He aims it at the creature's chest, pulls the string back, and—

The arrow bounces off the minotaur's flank and lands on the ground.

"Well, that didn't go as planned," Krystian muses.

The minotaur throws his head back and roars. Then, it charges.

When it moves, it's faster than it should be—certainly faster than it looks, considering it's made of heavy metal.

The creature's limbs whir with deadly precision, its mechanical nostrils flaring.

Rafe takes a step forward, his palm already bleeding. He throws his hands out, and bloody whips encircle the creature, stopping it in mid-lunge.

Zaid vanishes in a ripple of darkness and reappears behind the beast, a blade in his hand.

The minotaur struggles against the bindings containing him, twisting his head to and fro, and rusty gears spin in his neck.

"Zaid!" I scream, causing the creature's head to whip in my direction. "The neck! Go for the neck!"

Zaid's eyes sharpen on the creature, and I can tell he sees the gears too.

With a roar, the wraith lunges at the creature and brings his arm down in a swooping arc. The dagger embeds itself deep in the minotaur's neck, and sparks fly. The creature swipes its claws in both directions, desperate, but Zaid's dagger has done its job. The gears slow and then stop entirely.

The creature—the minotaur rebirthed—falls forward with an audible thunk, loose pieces of machinery spilling from him. Instead of blood, oil pools around it, dark and cloying.

The damn thing smells. Not like rot, not like a sweaty beast. But like scorched iron, ozone, and engine grease, as if it were born from fire and wrath.

"It seems as if we just passed Athena's first trial," Zaid says, breathing heavily.

He wipes away sweat with the back of his hand.

"Usually the first one is the easiest," Krystian points out.

"*That* was the easiest trial?" I blink at him in disbelief.

"We took the creature out pretty quickly, did we not?" Krystian smirks cockily.

"You know what? You're right." I puff out my chest, emulating a confidence and optimism I don't truly feel. "We totally got this."

Famous last words.

CHAPTER TWENTY-SIX

THEA

We walk for a few minutes longer in relative silence.

I find myself lingering at the back of the group, beside Rafe, whose flinty gaze never settles on one thing for more than a second. He's constantly on guard, tension thrumming through his corded muscles.

"Sooo..." I begin, peeking at him coyly. "I don't know a lot about you."

He whips his head towards me, his eyes widening.

"Okay," he rasps out, focusing straight ahead once more.

Okay?

Okay?!

"Do you have any family?" I ask, quickening my pace to match his long strides.

"No."

"No?"

"We're, technically, over four hundred years old, love," Krystian interjects from the front of the group. "Yes, some of our family members are still alive, but a lot aren't."

Every supernatural has a different aging process. Some—like elves—are immortal. Others age slowly, while certain types live and die like humans.

I squint at Everett, the only shifter I personally know.

"How are you still alive?" I blurt.

I know shifters can live long lives, but they're not immortal. At least, I don't think they are.

"Real tactful," Krystian says with a snort of amusement.

I shrug, unrepentant.

"Because I'm a member of Ares's team," Everett answers, his head on a constant swivel as he searches for threats.

"So being on his team makes you immortal?" I ask.

"We won't die of natural causes or old age, but a bullet to the heart or a fatal stab wound? Yeah, that'll do the trick," Krystian says.

Huh.

"I wonder if I'll die from a stab wound," I muse, contemplative.

I honestly have no idea what can and can't kill me the way I am now. For all I know, I'm immortal like the rest of them. Maybe a fatal wound will send me back to where I started, trapped in a room with only a cactus to talk to.

"Hopefully we'll never have to find out," Zaid replies gravely, and murmurs of affirmation ripple through the guys.

I'm saved from responding by the tunnel opening up, leading to a barren, circular room. Two statues stand in the center of the room, each guarding a separate path. One is a figure of bronze—a cloaked man with a bowed head, tarnished green by time. The other is marble—a veiled woman standing gracefully, her fingers resting on the frill of her skirt, her white surface cracked.

"What the...?" Krystian's bow appears in his hands, and he notches back an arrow, aiming it at the statue's chest.

"Hold on." Zaid holds up a hand and moves forward until he's able to read an inscription carved into the wall. "*One speaks the truth. One speaks lies. But wisdom is not in asking, but in knowing how to ask.*"

A soft groan echoes from within the metal of the bronze statue. A slow, deliberate shift begins—his fingers twitching, joints creaking with the sound of rust grinding against time, his bowed head lifting slightly. The patina on his cloak cracks like old bark, revealing glints of burnished copper beneath.

Next to him, the marble woman stirs. Her chest rises imperceptibly, as if drawing her first breath in ages. The delicate folds of her dress, once immobile, begin to ripple as though stirred by wind. Her hand, pale and smooth, lifts inch by inch, a faint trail of dust falling from her fingers. The veil over her face flutters, and from beneath it, faint light glimmers where her eyes should be.

"This ain't good," I say, pointing out the obvious.

The statues are silent, though I can feel their gazes on us. A shiver ripples down my spine.

"We need to ask them questions," Zaid explains, a frown tugging at his lips. "It's the only way to figure out which path to take."

"What did the inscription mean?" Krystian waves his hand vaguely towards the words on the wall.

"Exactly what it says. One statue will tell nothing but lies; the other will only tell the truth." Zaid scratches absently at his chin. "But usually there's a limit to how many questions we can ask."

"You've seen this before?" I stare at him in disbelief.

Zaid shakes his head. "No...but I've heard about this before. It's a popular trial of Athena."

"Okay, this is easy." I step around Rafe, a bright smile on my face.

"Thea..." Everett's voice is a low growl.

I wave him away. "I got this." Turning to the statues, I wave. "Hello. Which pathway do we need to take to get to the center of the maze and Athena?"

The marble woman shifts her veiled face towards me, the sound of rock grinding against rock permeating the air.

"The door to the left is the one you would want to take. But be careful—we are not the only threats you'll need to face." Her voice is soft and lyrical, a startling contrast to her appearance.

The bronze statue shifts slightly. "The door to the right leads to the center of the maze. Athena will be waiting there."

His voice is raspy though not harsh.

"If I were to ask the other statue which door to take, what would they say?" I ask, popping my hip out and feeling immensely satisfied with my own cleverness.

Zaid turns to smile at me, pride glimmering in his dark eyes.

Yeah. Take that, Everett. Suck it. I'm so fucking smart.

"They would tell you to take the right passageway,

because they lie," the woman statue says. "Thus, you must take the left."

The bronze statue exclaims, "They would say to take the right door. But of course, you already knew that."

I whirl towards the others, smiling brightly. It takes considerable effort not to fist pump the air and scream, "I told you so," to Everett at the top of my lungs. As it is, when I see begrudging respect in his eyes, heat rushes through my veins.

"Left passageway it is, then," Krystian says, moving in that direction.

But I remain where I am as something occurs to me.

"Will we find the answers we seek once we reach the center of the maze?" I ask tentatively, keeping my attention fixed on the marble statue.

"You will find answers, but they may not be the ones you're looking for," she answers.

"You will receive no answers and only be left with more questions," the bronze statue says.

Then, there's a loud creaking sound, and I watch in riveted fascination as the statutes resume their previous positions. The bronze statue's head lowers, and the marble statue once again grabs at her skirts.

They don't move again.

"Woah," I breathe, struck by the sheer brilliance of Athena's creation.

"Come on, sweetheart." Zaid's fingers interlock with my own, and he pulls me towards the passageway. "We need to get moving."

I take a deep breath, bolstering myself, and then shoot one last glance over my shoulder at the statues. I can't help but think that their existence is...sad. Their entire purpose revolves around Athena and this maze. Do they have feelings? Wants? Desires? Or are they simply pawns in this game?

Maybe I can't stop thinking about them because I relate to them. I, too, am a tool for someone else to use. Until I met the guys, I was virtually the same as them—frozen, only coming to life when I was needed.

I turn away from the statues, albeit reluctantly, and hurry after the others, Zaid's hand still curled around my own.

I just hope my story ends better than theirs did in mine.

CHAPTER TWENTY-SEVEN

RAFAEL

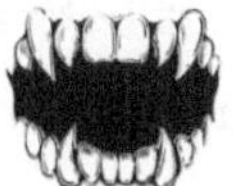

Nobody has ever asked me about my past before, about my family. Granted, the only people I can stand spending time with are the guys—and they already know everything about me—but it's the thought that counts.

A part of me wants to tell Thea everything. Wants to describe my childhood with a single mom who worked herself to the bone and three younger siblings. My mom died just over one hundred years ago, but my siblings are still alive. Most of them have kids of their own.

I keep watch over them from time to time. Protect them when necessary. Hurt anyone who dares to harm them.

But I've never shown my face—not once.

Would my younger siblings even recognize their

brother after all these years? They have wrinkles adorning their skin and gray in their hair. I'm still... young. And I'll remain as such until something kills me.

I always thought I would be the first of my team to go. Everett calls me reckless, unhinged, psychotic. Maybe that's all true, but before Thea, I didn't have a reason to care about my life or the lives of others. I simply went through the motions, half-heartedly attempting to survive.

Now...

Now I have a reason to fight. To live. To wake up in the morning. And that reason is a five-foot woman with golden hair, a beatific smile, and a laugh that makes the ice around my heart thaw.

Thea is mine.

I think I knew it from the first moment I saw her—when she materialized out of thin air with a battle cry that reverberated through my bones. And I was absolutely certain of that truth when I watched her fall apart in the shower, two of her tiny fingers deep in her pussy.

I've never felt this way about anyone before. I didn't even think it was possible for me to feel this deeply for someone.

I would be the first to admit I don't entirely understand emotions. Sympathy, empathy... What's the difference? I learned how to mimic what others were doing, hoping no one would glance at me too closely and notice anything's amiss. Then, I gave up on pretending. Why did I care what people thought about me?

That isn't to say I've never cared about anyone before. I love my family, in my own way, and my teammates.

But Thea...

The girl is so fucking cute. I loved her triumphant smile when she "tricked" the statues into revealing the truth. She seems to have forgotten that I have the ability to detect when someone is lying or not.

But I let her have her moment.

I would let her have anything, if she asked.

What is it about her? How can I have fallen so quickly for someone I barely know? Is it fate? Something else? I don't believe in love at first sight, but how else can I explain the almost desperate need I possess to look after her? To own her? To care for her, the way I've never cared for anyone before?

My pulse quickens the second we step into a chamber at the end of the passageway. The air is thick with something—something wrong.

I whip my head around just in time to see Zaid position Thea protectively behind him.

"Hello, my friends," a voice croaks from in front of us. "I've been waiting for you."

A woman steps forward, her frail hands resting on a cane. Her hair is as white as freshly fallen snow, and her skin resembles cracked porcelain. She's blind—I can tell from her milky-white eyes—but there's something in the way she holds herself, an awareness that goes beyond sight.

We stop a few paces away from her, and my gaze flickers to the golden plaque above her head. My throat tightens as I read the words carved in the stone: *The wise speak when they know and listen when they don't.*

What the fuck?

What vague bullshit is this?

I glance at Zaid, but he's staring at the woman with a furrowed brow, confusion evident on his face.

Thea attempts to take a step forward, but Zaid pulls her back. She tries again, and when it's apparent there's no escaping Zaid's iron-like grip, she huffs out a breath and smiles at the woman instead.

"Hello! You don't look too scary, do you? My name is—"

"You're Thea," the woman says simply, removing one hand from the top of the cane in a sweeping gesture. "And the four dashing men with you are Rafael, Everett, Krystian, and Zaid."

Everett growls and takes a threatening step towards her. "How the fuck do you know that?"

"Because I know everything, young shifter." A toothy grin curves up her lips. "I am the Oracle of Delphi, and I can answer any questions your heart may desire."

"An oracle?" Thea breathes from behind me. "Like, someone who can see the future?"

The oracle's sharp but blind eyes land on my little bird, and my hackles lift.

"I know you have a lot of questions, my dear. Ask away. I may be of some assistance to you."

"Wait! Don't!" Zaid shouts, and I realize he has his hand over Thea's mouth, keeping her from speaking. She struggles futilely in his grip, but he doesn't loosen, his desperate eyes flicking from face to face. "The inscription... The wise speak when they know and listen when they don't."

"So we need to listen to the oracle?" Everett surmises, frowning.

Zaid shakes his head adamantly. "I think the trick here is *not* listening to the oracle. Showing restraint. If we were to start asking her questions, we would receive misleading answers that could guide us down a route we can't return from."

Thea finally wiggles away from Zaid and turns to

glare at him. "Okay, first, your hand smells good. I kind of wanted to bite it."

Um...okay?

Fuck, I love it when my little bird gets feisty. It makes me hard.

"Second, this may be the only way of getting answers. Who knows *what* Athena will tell us...or if she will even tell us anything worthwhile? The oracle has answers, answers we need."

"Oracles are known for being vague intentionally," Krystian points out, raking a hand through his white-gold hair. "I think I need to take Zaid's side on this one. It'll be best if we just ignore her and continue on our way."

"You have to remember that this is a test, Thea," Zaid says gently, beseeching her with his eyes to listen and understand. "Everything about this maze is designed to test our intelligence and strength."

"I'm not an idiot, Zaid," Thea snaps.

Zaid seems taken aback by her sharp tone. "I know you're not."

"You guys are all forgetting that this is about me. I should be allowed to make decisions concerning myself." She jabs a finger at her chest for emphasis.

"There's no 'you' anymore," Everett growls, moving to stand directly behind Thea, so close that his chest brushes against her back with every exhale.

"The second we agreed to help you—the second we made you an honorary member of our team—that 'you' turned into an 'us.' We make decisions together."

All of us stand in stunned silence, unable to believe the words leaving Everett's mouth. My brows crawl upwards in disbelief.

My, my... It seems as if our gruff, growly shifter has a heart after all. I always knew Thea would wear down his defenses. I just didn't expect it to happen so quickly.

When Everett sees us gawking at him, he bares his teeth. "Fuck off."

"So we take a vote?" Krystian asks, his gaze flicking towards the grinning oracle.

"All those who want to ask the oracle questions, raise your hands," Zaid says.

Thea's hand automatically lifts, and after a moment, mine does too.

She's right. For all we know, Athena will give us no answers. But if this oracle can tell us something, anything, about Thea's origins and how she's able to remain in a physical form...

Zaid's lips purse when he sees my hand up, but he doesn't call me out. Instead, he says, "And all those in favor of continuing along?"

Krystian, Everett, and Zaid all raise their hands.

Thea frowns, appearing discouraged, and Krystian quickly moves towards her.

"It'll be okay, love. Athena will have answers. I know she will."

"Are you sure about that?" The oracle tilts her head to the side, strands of white hair reflecting off the flickering torches. "Or will you just receive more questions? Don't you want to know where you came from? Who you are?" The creature's white gaze flicks towards me. "I can see the wheels in your head turning, Rafael. What questions do you have for me?"

I bite down on my lip hard enough to draw blood, that one move filling my magic reserves and making power spark in my fingertips.

This whole damn Labyrinth feels like it's leading somewhere dangerous, and I can't stand the thought of Thea falling into whatever trap Athena has set out for us.

The oracle's head tilts, like she's sensing my thoughts, and her lips twitch into a barely there smile. The sight makes my stomach twist.

"Rafe, don't," Zaid warns.

"Harm will come to her, Rafael," the oracle continues, nodding towards a door behind her. "Come into my room, dear. Let me tell you your future. Let me tell you how to save her."

Harm will come to her.

Harm will come to her.

I turn to look at Thea, my heart hammering in my chest, and the world narrows down to just her. She's the one who keeps me tethered to this world, to sanity. I won't let something happen to her. I can't.

Before I can move, I hear Everett's voice—low, firm, a warning. "Rafe."

I don't want to listen. I can't. I need to know what the oracle is talking about. It's the only way I can protect my little bird.

Maybe this is a trap. Maybe I'll be trapped in this damn maze forever.

Does it even matter, if it means Thea is safe?

Zaid's hand catches my arm with unexpected strength, pulling me back. I haven't even realized I started walking in the oracle's direction.

"Rafe, let it go," he says, his tone gentle but urgent. "Trust me. Please. We're not supposed to ask questions. Just ignore her and move on."

I try to pull away, my teeth gritted, my pulse pounding in my ears.

She's going to get hurt, and it'll be all my fault.

Everett grabs my other arm, his fingers digging into my skin. "Rafe! Don't!"

Thea steps forward—my beautiful, broken bird, free for the first time—and her voice trembles. "Rafe...

I...I changed my mind. I don't want to hear what the oracle has to say. Let's just go."

And for a moment, I feel the weight of her plea. It presses down on me, making it hard to breathe.

She's scared, scared for me, and the thought makes my heart pick up speed.

But it's not enough.

Thea's going to die if I don't do something.

I jerk against their hold, my pulse thrumming.

"Rafe!" Everett bellows as I tear him away with a flick of my wrist.

"Good boy," the oracle coos, extending a ghastly pale hand for me to take.

A growl rises in my throat, and I shoot my arm out. Blood-red whips slash at the oracle as she cries and screams.

"Holy crap!" Thea screams, stumbling a few steps away, her mouth agape.

A startling silence settles over us all. All I can hear is my own erratic breathing and the pounding of my heart.

The air in the room shifts. It thickens, like a fog rolling in, suffocating and dense. It presses against my skin. The oppressive silence suddenly breaks, replaced by a low, rattling noise.

The oracle's frail form trembles, the cane she's been holding twisting and bending as if it's alive. Her skin, so pale and delicate before, begins to crack and split. The jagged lines spread like a spider's web across her face and body.

Her once serene smile turns into something far darker and sinister—her lips stretching impossibly wide, the corners of her mouth splitting like a cracked vase, exposing rows of needle-like teeth, black and gleaming.

A low growl builds in her throat.

Her eyes train on me, but they're not white anymore. They're black pits, endless voids, capable of sucking in the light around her. Her head jerks, the motion too quick, too unnatural. The cracks in her skin widen, and something—a shape—begins to bulge beneath her flesh, shifting like something is crawling underneath the surface.

Her limbs elongate, the bones snapping and twisting in grotesque angles. Her skin stretches and morphs into something monstrous—pale and slick like an eel. She looms over us, her body towering high above, her form now a hulking, grotesque shape.

The creature's mouth opens wide—impossibly wide—and her jagged teeth resemble shards of glass. Her hands, no longer frail, stretch towards us with claws that are long, sharp, and dripping with some sort of dark substance. Every time it puddles on the ground, it hisses and sputters.

Fuck.

A cold smile unfurls on my lips.

This bitch wants a fight? Then a fight she'll get.

Zaid, his wraith form flickering, is the first to react.

He raises his hands, and shadowy tendrils shoot from his palms, curling around the air like smoke and grabbing at the creature's form.

The monster roars and twists, her body contorting in ways that shouldn't be possible. The tendrils snap like twigs.

She throws her head back and screams, and that sound—god, that fucking sound—digs into my skull, making it feel like my thoughts are being dragged from me.

I don't wait for her to get her bearings as a deep, primal rage rises inside of me.

I grab my dagger and slice at my palm, allowing my blood to well. Then, I shoot projectile after projectile at her, though I'm not sure what good that's doing. She barely seems to react.

Krystian's bowstring hums as he fires a shot, his arrow flying through the air with expert precision. It hits the oracle-monster in the shoulder with a sickening thud, though the creature barely even flinches. Her eyes—those hollow, void-black pits—focus on him, and with a flick of her wrist, she sends him flying across the room like a rag doll.

He crashes into the wall, but before his bow can shatter on impact, it disappears and then materializes in his hands once more.

"Not today, Satan. Not today," he mutters under his breath, grabbing another flesh-eating arrow from his quiver and nocking it into place.

He pulls the string back, his eyes narrowed in determination.

Already, I can see the first one is doing its work. The skin surrounding the puncture wound is sizzling and hissing as the poison eats away at the oracle's flesh.

"Wait!" Zaid yells abruptly, moving to stand in front of Krystian and stopping him from letting his arrow loose.

"What the fuck, Zaid?" Everett roars, his eyes glinting with the appearance of his beast—a beast he won't let free, unless there's no other alternative.

"We can't kill it!" Zaid insists.

"Why the fuck not?" Everett demands.

In answer, Zaid flicks his gaze towards Thea, who stands slightly behind us, holding a borrowed dagger in her hand. Zaid's, if I had to guess.

It occurs to me then what Zaid's saying.

If we kill the oracle—a beast who is alive—then Thea might...

She might leave us.

The minotaur was crafted out of machinery, but this beast... This beast has flesh and a heart and blood.

"Don't be an idiot!" Thea screams as the oracle staggers and roars, swiping a clawed hand at us. But her movements are sluggish, the poison eating away at her skin. "I didn't disappear when we killed the hellhounds, did I?"

"The hellhounds were already dead when you turned corporeal!" Krystian points out, lowering his bow. "And who's to say that the one you killed isn't what caused your dagger to...merge with your flesh?"

His gaze dips to the waistband of her jeans, where, underneath all of her clothes, is the reminder of her looming deadline.

"If we don't kill it, it'll kill us!" Thea insists.

"Not if I can help it," I growl.

Then I charge, moving faster than I ever thought possible, thoughts of my little bird spurring me on. My blood surges with the heat of rage and desperation.

The oracle-monster looks at me, that demented grin stretching wider and wider.

She swings her poison-tipped claw at me, but I'm faster, ducking low and then spinning to the side until I can come up behind her.

But I can't get close enough to strike. Not yet.

And I think I know exactly where to aim this time around.

Krystian's arrow hits again, this time in her knee, and she stumbles.

That's all the opening I need.

The blood in my palm solidifies until it forms a blade, and I jump on her back, clinging to her neck with all my might. I slam the blade down into her right eye.

Again and again and again and again.

A black substance oozes from the wound and hits my skin, causing it to burn. The pain is like nothing I've ever felt before, and instinctively, I cry out, releasing my grip on the creature's neck. I fall to the ground with a pained shout.

"Rafe!" Thea screams, racing for me.

Zaid reaches for her, but Thea's faster.

She swings her borrowed dagger at the monster's stomach—the only part of the beast she can reach—and the monster staggers back. The oracle cries out and falls, slamming against the door she was attempting to lead me through only moments earlier.

The wood shatters, revealing hundreds—if not thousands—of corpses. Yellow bones litter the entire room.

Zaid was right.

If we were to ask her questions, we would've ended up just like them.

"Thea!" Krystian roars, shooting arrow after arrow at the beast in an attempt to distract her.

But the oracle doesn't peel her pitch-black gaze from the approaching reaper.

The strangest thing begins to happen.

Thea's skin begins to glow—an unearthly luminescent sheen that makes it appear as if she's been dipped in sparkles. The dagger in her hand transforms before my very eyes. While before it was an unassuming, somewhat blunt dagger, it's now sharp and covered in ancient runes.

The dagger Thea arrived with.

The dagger that has somehow melded with her body.

"Thea!" I stagger to my feet and race for her.

No. No. No. No.

Thea doesn't seem to hear any of us. It's as if she's in a trance.

She lifts her arm in the air...and then brings it down, hitting the creature in the heart.

And while our attacks did nothing to stop the grotesque monster, Thea's has the opposite effect.

The oracle-monster screeches, her form twisting and distorting as the entire room reacts to her demise. The walls begin to shake violently, and the floor crumbles beneath us. The creature's massive body starts to unravel like twine, her form breaking down into nothing but tendrils of darkness that dissolve in the air.

The room pulses once, twice, three times, then—everything stops.

The oracle is gone. The walls and floor have stopped trembling. The air, once heavy and suffocating, feels lighter.

And Thea stands in the center of the room, the dagger in her hand normal once more.

"Little bird," I whisper, taking a step towards her.

She whirls on me, desperation painted across her face, and drops the dagger to the ground. She begins to scratch erratically at her skin, her gaze flicking this way and that.

"We're out of time," she whimpers, a pained cry leaving her. "They're here. The voices...the hallucinations... They're all here."

CHAPTER TWENTY-EIGHT

We walk down another narrow passage, the walls damp and slick. I fucking hate it here—how the walls seem to close in on me, how quiet it is, how stiff the air has become. The beast inside of me growls, desperate to break free, even knowing he's too damn big to fit.

I hate everything about this place, but I'll endure it a thousand times over if it means saving Thea.

Thea.

Even thinking her name has an emotion gnawing at the edges of my thoughts, crawling in the pit of my stomach.

Protect.

Possess.

She's walking a little slower than usual, though Zaid and Krystian both easily keep pace with her. Her hands are fidgeting at her sides, twitching, like she's trying to hold herself together but losing the fight. Or maybe she's reaching for a dagger that's no longer there.

We all unanimously agreed that Thea will no longer get any weapons. Not until we can figure out what happened back there with the oracle.

She begins to mutter to herself, barely above a whisper, and my black heart cracks just a little.

"No, please. Don't..." She places her hands over her ears and rocks slightly. "Stop it. Leave me alone."

Her gaze flickers from side to side as tears form in her eyes.

"Thea?" Zaid says gently, reaching for her hand the way he has done countless times before.

"DON'T TOUCH ME!" she screams, stumbling away until her back is flush against the cave wall.

Her gaze fixes on something in the shadows ahead, her pupils dilated. Her lips move again, but this time, I can't detect a word she's saying.

"Love..." Krystian tries, his features pained.

Her breath quickens with fear, and the sound makes my heart rate spike. My instincts demand I rush towards her, pull her into my arms, and assure her she's safe, but I hold myself back. If she won't even let Krystian and Zaid near her, then she sure as fuck isn't going to allow me to touch her.

Rafe moves beside me, his jaw clenched so tightly I wouldn't be surprised if he chipped a tooth. His hands curl and uncurl into fists repeatedly by his sides.

"When I find out who did this to her..." He allows the threat to hang unspoken in the air.

Darkness—madness—percolates in his dark-brown eyes.

"They'll die," I agree easily.

And I won't make it a quick death, either.

"Please don't touch me. Please." Thea curls into a ball and begins to sob.

And I make a vow right then and there that the person behind this will pay for each and every one of those heartbreaking cries. I already planned to torture the fucker, but I'll take my time. Make it last for weeks, if not months. I am immortal, after all. I have nothing but time.

Thea's head whips up abruptly, and she focuses on something just over Zaid's shoulder, something I can't see.

"Do you see that?" Her voice borders on desperation.

"There's nothing there, sweetheart." Zaid smooths back her golden hair.

"No. No. No. There's something there." The tears cascade faster and faster. "It's coming towards me. Get it away! Get it away!"

She kicks at the air and then screams, focusing on her leg as if she sees something crawling up it.

"Thea! Baby! There is nothing on you! I promise!" Krystian grips her cheeks and forces her gaze to his. "You know I would never lie to you."

"How can you say that?" she sobs, wrenching her head away. "I can feel it on my skin. No...under my skin. Oh god."

Her fingernails rake against the inside of her wrist. Then she starts to pull at her skin, drawing blood.

"Fuck! No!" Zaid pulls her hand away. "Stop hurting yourself!"

"I need to get it out! Please, Zaid. Let me get it out. It hurts. It hurts so bad." More blood oozes from the wound, steadily dripping onto the floor beneath her.

Rafe, his features carefully impassive, steps forward and removes his backpack. He grabs gauze and tape and kneels before the trembling reaper.

"I can't lie," he whispers, his voice as blank as his expression. "So listen to me carefully—there is *nothing* on you. Nothing inside of you. You're safe, Thea. You're with us."

Thea sniffles and glances at him. No, not at him. Over him. She's lost, gone somewhere that none of us can follow.

And that fucking terrifies me.

Rafe begins to address her bloody wound, his touch

unexpectedly gentle. I've never seen the psychotic asshole behave like this. He treats her like she's something precious, something he wishes to treasure until his dying days.

A lump forms in my throat.

Thea may be here with us, but she's not *with* us anymore. Not really. And until we can figure out how to save her, she'll be stuck like this.

Trapped within her own mind.

I'm moving before I can think better of it and kneeling before her. Krystian shoots me a warning look, his eyes wide with panic, and Zaid simply sniffles and looks away. Rafe refuses to even acknowledge my presence, his gaze intent on her wrist.

"Listen to me, Thea, or so help me..."

Her gaze moves almost mechanically to mine. She's shaking, her body trembling like a leaf in a storm, and her breath hitches slightly. But she doesn't pull her gaze away.

"I know I can be an asshole, but haven't I always looked after you? I did it then, and I'll do it now. I gave you my promise, and I intend to keep it. You're safe, Thea. You're with people who...care about you. So tell those voices in your head to fuck right off and come back to me. Please."

For a split second, she's there—the girl I've come to know, admire, and despise. The reaper. The one who I can't stand because she makes me feel too much.

But then her gaze shifts again, flaring with that hollowed-out look, and I can practically feel her pull away. She's lost in a world only she can see, and there's nothing we can do to stop it.

"Come on, Thea," I say, my voice breaking against the weight of everything I'm holding back. "You're not alone, okay? You're not alone."

Her eyes don't focus. They flicker—distant and lost.

"I'm alone. They tell me I'm alone. So, so alone," she whispers, barely audible. "Alone, alone, alone, alone."

I swallow hard, willing myself not to panic. This is Thea, for fuck's sake. I can't give up on her. I won't. She's the same woman I've been silently protecting, the one I've been pushing away since she first batted those long lashes at me.

"Can you walk, baby?" I ask gently, helping her to her feet.

The term of endearment slips out before I can think better of it. Fortunately, no one pays me any attention.

Thea nods mutely, a tiny bit of coherence flaring to life in her eyes. "Yes."

"Let's go," I say, giving Krystian and Zaid a pointed look.

They'll look after Thea, while Rafe and I will look after them.

We move down a series of pathways until we reach another chamber.

A loom stands at the very center like an ancient monolithic relic, pulsing with an eerie light that bends the shadows around it. It's not like any loom I've ever seen. This isn't something you'd find in a workshop, tucked away behind a curtain to collect dust.

No, this thing is alive in a way that makes my skin crawl, like it's been here long before we arrived and will be here long after we're gone.

It's massive—taller than even me, with threads of glowing light weaving throughout the air in intricate patterns that almost seem to shift as I watch them.

The frame of the loom itself is made of polished obsidian, smooth and glossy. At first, the threads don't seem to have any rhyme or reason. They're just delicate strands of glowing light, crossing and weaving together at random.

But when I look closer, I realize they form a kind of tapestry—a tapestry that moves, the images blurring before my very eyes. It's unsettling. There's a rhythm to it, but it's a rhythm that doesn't make any sense.

"What the fuck is this?" I demand, whirling towards my brothers and the reaper.

But they're no longer there.

"What the hell?" I bellow, realizing I'm alone.

Where the fuck did they go? Is it Thea? Did something happen?

Impulse demands I turn around. Find them.

But I can't move.

The loom won't let me.

I feel it in my bones when I stare at it. A cold, metallic taste spreads through my mouth.

Each thread pulses slightly, almost as if they're alive, and weaves together intricate images. So fast it's hard for me to make sense of them. Fragments of memories—flashes of people, places, and faces that I recognize but can't put a name to. It's like the loom is weaving through time itself.

And the sound...

It's a strange melody, like weaving the threads together is also weaving the air around us. A soft, aching hum permeates the air and vibrates in my chest. It's unnerving and pulls at something deep inside of me, at a place I try to ignore. It's as though the loom is singing to me, calling me to see it. To see everything.

"What do you want me to see?" I demand, curling my hands into fists. "Hurry the fuck up!"

A delicate, soft thread of light slides forward, wrapping itself around my wrist. Panic sets in, and I try to pull back, but the thread doesn't loosen. And as I'm trapped in its hold, the world around me shifts, turning inwards.

Suddenly, I'm no longer standing in this cold, winding maze.

I'm back at home—my childhood home.

"Again," my father instructs, nodding towards the wooden practice sword I dropped.

Ever since I've been marked by Ares, my father has been training me to fight. To survive.

I don't officially start training until I reach puberty, but that hasn't stopped my father. In his mind, there's no reason for me to have a childhood, not when my future is already so certain.

I parry each blow he delivers my way, sweat beading on my temples. But then Dad sweeps his sword towards my legs, and there's nothing I can do but accept the hit. I fall onto my ass, staring up at the blue sky.

Father stands over me, his eyes heavy and full of disappointment. "Ares obviously made a mistake with you, Everett. If you can't handle an old man, then how are you supposed to save our world from the monsters?"

His words are sharp. Scathing. I flinch, the hurt slicing deeper than I care to admit. But as an adult, I realize that it's always been like that with us. He has never, not once, looked at me with pride. He saw me as weak and undeserving of my title.

The bastard's still alive—he's the only immortal shifter I know—but he's never reached out. Not once. For all he knows, I'm dead.

Pain arrows through my chest, making it hard to breathe.

The loom encircling my wrist flashes, and the scene changes.

Now I'm a young boy, arriving at the compound.

"There's my soldier." The man who speaks is tall, dark, and terrifying.

The malevolent glint in his eyes suggests he's someone who has been alive a long, long time and has grown nonchalant.

He slaps a hand down on my shoulder hard enough to rattle my teeth.

"Come, boy. Let me introduce you to your team-mates." He leads me into a room full of bunks and children, all of whom stare at me curiously, likely wondering if I'm a member of their team.

Ares leads me towards a corner in the back, where three little boys stare up at me. The tallest has tawny skin and black hair, streaked with red and blue, that flops haphazardly over his forehead. His eyes are cold, almost glacial, and his lips are pressed in a perfectly straight line. Beside him is a grinning boy with white-blond hair and a single dimple. The third boy has black hair, pale skin, and a timid smile.

I don't have a lot of memories of my time in the compound, due to the deep sleep the gods put us in. But I do remember this meeting—and the feeling of completeness that filled me when I stared at the boys.

My team.

The thread flashes again.

Now I'm older, a man in the middle of battle. Blood covers my hands—some of it mine, most of it not.

I look around at the fallen bodies, each one a consequence of my choices. I'm a killing machine. That's all I'm good for. I have a singular purpose in this life, and it's to slaughter as many supernaturals and monsters as possible.

I've felt numb for so long, and this battle is a testament of that.

But now...

Everything has changed.

I've never allowed myself to get close to another person. My brothers are the only exception. I always thought I didn't need another person to protect. I already have my team, and that's enough. But now I'm tangled up in all of this shit—in her—and there's no escaping the web she wove.

I thought pushing her away would make everything easier. Hell, I thought it was the smart thing to do. If I kept my distance, I wouldn't have to feel this thing gnawing at the edges of my chest every time she's close. If I kept my distance, I wouldn't have to watch her crack open and break off pieces of herself for the world to take. But now, as I stand here in the middle of a bloody battlefield, something is different.

I'm different.

She's the only person who has ever tried to get past my walls, and I pushed her away like a damn fool. I can admit I was afraid—still am. Afraid of what would happen if she really saw me. Afraid of what it would mean to need her. Afraid of what would happen if I were to lose her.

The vision shifts around me and then cuts out. I'm once again in Athena's Labyrinth, standing in front of the loom. The thread around my wrist loosens and then retreats, returning to the intricate tapestry before me.

My brothers and Thea surround me, and the threads around their wrists untangle as well. They sag forward, seeming relieved.

"Thea!!" Krystian shouts, turning towards her.

She blinks, seemingly in a daze.

"Did everyone else...?" Zaid scratches at his cheek absently.

"Get transported into visions of the past? Yes," I say, keeping my gaze intent on Thea.

I can't look away.

Maybe that was the purpose of the loom—for us to look at our past and present and learn from our mistakes. To realize personal truths about ourselves.

Mine?

I'm done hiding. Done pushing her away.

I want Thea—have since I met her, if I'm being completely honest.

And now I'm going to do everything within my power to save her. Then I'll prove to her once and for all that I'm deserving of her time and affection.

I won't let her go.

Not now. Not ever.

CHAPTER TWENTY-NINE

THEA

The cave walls are made of faces, and they're all screaming at me.

"Murderer."

"Killer."

"Reaper."

"Die."

"Die."

"Die."

I place my hands over my ears in an attempt to block out the cacophony of voices, all blending together until it sounds like a single discordant note.

On the ground before me, snakes slither and hiss, snapping at my heels. I squeak and jump in the air, instinctively reaching for Zaid.

The wraith wraps his arms around me protectively,

but he isn't looking at the snakes...which means they're not really there.

"Thea. It's okay. You're okay."

His calming voice doesn't soothe me, however. Not the way it usually does.

I'm not sure anything will at this point.

I nod shakily, my gaze fixing on something over his shoulder.

A monster.

A monster constructed entirely of blood, with elongated fangs and glowing eyes. It advances on me with a lethal gait, malevolent menace twisting up his lips. He extends a clawed hand, the talons sharper than his teeth, and a scream lodges in my throat.

Not real.

Not real.

Not real.

But when he swipes his claws at me, I swear I feel the pain of the assault on my cheek, which begins to throb and ache. Blood wells. Or at least, I think it does. No one else seems to notice the red liquid cascading down my cheek.

"You killed me."

"You're a monster."

"Die, reaper. Die."

"Why won't you just let me leave?"

"Why are you keeping us trapped here?"

"Why?"

"Why?"

"Why?"

"Why?"

The voices are loud—too loud. I can't hear anything else. Not my guys trying to comfort me. Not my own thoughts. Not even the erratic pounding of my heart slamming against my rib cage.

I drop to my knees, agony ripping through me. I tear at the strands of my hair, which seem to wither beneath my hands. Oh god. The snakes. They're in my hair. They're in my fucking hair.

I pull and tug and scream, belatedly aware of multiple bodies surrounding me. Stopping me. Someone grabs my wrist, pulling my hand away from my hair. A different voice screams my name, begging me to stop.

They say this is just in my head, but it certainly doesn't feel like it. The snakes... They're crawling all over me. Tightening around my neck. I can't breathe. Can't breathe. Can't breathe.

"What's the meaning of this?" An unfamiliar feminine voice cuts through the dissonance in my head like the slash of a whip.

I blink through my tears, surprised to see a beautiful face peering back at me, framed by dark hair. Surrounding her are five silhouettes, their forms hazy and indistinct. Ghosts, maybe. Or perhaps hallucinations.

Or...fuck...maybe they're real, and it's impossible for me to distinguish reality from fiction.

"Get the fuck away from her!" That voice... It's Everett's.

But I've never heard him sound so desperate before. So fearful.

"Do you want me to help or not?" The woman kneels down in front of me, her face consuming the entirety of my vision.

She bites her lip as she considers me, her eyes emanating a strange, eerie light. Her gaze hardens on my hip, hidden by my shirt and jeans, and she reaches for my clothes abruptly, revealing the strange tattoo.

Someone growls.

Someone else curses.

The woman? She simply blinks, shock and horror mingling on her features.

"Fuck," she whispers, her glowing hand hovering over the tattoo.

"What the hell are you doing?" Krystian demands.

"Saving her life," the woman responds simply.

The voices grow louder and louder, practically screaming at me. Blood drizzles from my ears.

"Make it stop," I beg—though I don't know who I'm even talking to.

For all I know, this woman doesn't exist either.

And then, mercifully, it does stop.

I have a second to see the woman's taut frown... then everything goes black.

CHAPTER THIRTY

THEA

I dream I'm the star of a Spanish soap opera.

José has just confessed his undying love to me, and Anna and Lisa have chosen to duel me for his hand in marriage. I'm standing in a jousting ring, holding my abnormally large sword, as the two women hurl daggers at me with their eyes. José watches from the sidelines, and for some reason, he's dressed as a duck with a top hat. No idea why.

I charge at the women with a battle cry, and then—

"Thea."

Awareness returns to me slowly, groggily. I blink, momentarily forgetting where I am and how I came to be here. I'm not in my room-slash-prison any longer, but I'm also not in the guys' safe house. And I'm certainly not dueling two women to win over a man I've never met before.

What...?

I blink again and attempt to take in my surroundings.

I'm lying on a couch, my head in Rafe's lap and my feet in Everett's. Everett's, of all people.

I must still be dreaming.

Or maybe this is another hallucination.

But...it's quiet. Abnormally so.

All I can hear is the rhythmic roar of cascading water echoing off stone walls, a low, constant thunder that pulses in my chest.

Cold, damp air clings to my skin, carrying with it the earthy scent of moss and stone.

The cave I'm in is vast, its ceiling arching high above like the vault of a cathedral, lost in shifting shadows. Jagged stalactites hang like the teeth of some sleeping beast, while the smooth, glistening floor glows faintly with reflections of luminescent fungi and stray shafts of sun filtering through the cracks far above.

A waterfall dominates the space—a white churning torrent spilling from a crevice in the rock and falling into a black pool that seems bottomless. Mist rises in veils around it, catching the light in tiny prisms.

An underground waterfall?

But that isn't the strangest thing. No, what really makes my eyes widen is the uncanny fusion of raw nature and sleek modernity.

While there's a tiny bit of natural light spilling from high above, there's also electric lighting recessed into the cave walls. A minimalistic kitchen is tucked into an alcove carved by nature, outfitted with matte-black appliances that gleam against the textured rock. A smart panel glows beside it, its touch-screen interface incongruous yet strangely at home.

Against one wall is a bed that seems to be built into the stone ledge, covered in soft linens and woolen throws. Recessed shelves hold books and small plants—ferns and mosses that thrive in the humid air. The bathroom, located behind a frosted-glass partition partially opened, features a large shower and claw-footed tub, along with a porcelain sink and toilet.

"Thank fuck you're awake." Krystian's voice drags my attention away from my surroundings and back to the matter at hand. "When you fell..."

He trails off with a choked sound.

"What happened?" I furrow my brows together as I try to remember. "Where are we? How did we end up here?"

"You're in the center of the Labyrinth," a somewhat familiar voice exclaims. A second later, a beautiful woman steps forward, her keen eyes unnerving. "Welcome to my home."

"You're Athena," I breathe, trailing my gaze over

the woman in surprise. "You're the Goddess of Wisdom."

I don't know how I expected her to look—maybe nerdy-ish, with glasses and a turtleneck sweater—but definitely not like this.

Her dark hair hangs loose around her shoulders in tight curls. She wears a white shirt, skinny jeans, and a leather jacket. Tattoos poke through the collar of her shirt, climbing up her neck. She looks badass and fierce and terrifying—someone you would see in a biker's bar, not in a classroom.

"You've passed my tests." Her voice is carefully indifferent, her cold eyes giving nothing away. "Congrats. It's not often I have visitors here."

"What happened? What did you do to me?" I drop my hand to my hip, where the skin there almost seems to burn.

Something akin to sympathy paves its way across Athena's face. "I did what I could for now."

"What do you mean 'for now'?" Everett growls, his hands tightening around my ankles. "I thought you said you cured her!"

"I never said that," Athena points out. "I simply said that I helped her and that I'll explain more when she wakes up."

"She's awake. Start talking," Krystian grumbles, folding his arms over his chest.

He and Zaid stand slightly in front of the couch I'm on, their glares fixed on Athena.

Athena smiles, and it's absolutely breathtaking. Aphrodite may be the Goddess of Beauty, but Athena? She could give her a run for her money.

"It's funny how love works, isn't it?" Her smile slips slightly, replaced by something softer. Sadder. Her gaze flicks towards a framed photo beside the bed. "One second, you're strangers, and the next, you're willing to talk back to a god for them."

Love?

I shift uncomfortably, the mere mention of the L-word making my skin crawl.

"Please. Just tell me what's going on. What happened? How did you cure me? Do you know who I am?"

Athena moves to claim an armchair opposite me, her movements fluid and graceful. She folds her hands primly in her lap.

"I've never seen you before today," she answers.

"Truth," Rafe rumbles, and I remember he has the ability to detect lies.

Athena's smirk returns. "You don't need to use your powers on me, fae. I have no reason to lie."

"I don't trust you," he answers simply, unabashedly.

"I suppose it makes sense why you're cautious."

She tilts her head to the side, a strand of curly hair catching in the light. "But you have nothing to fear from me. None of you do."

"Then give us some damn answers," Krystian snaps, and my eyebrows shoot up at the vitriol in his tone.

At first, I think he transitioned into Krys while I was unconscious, but when I turn towards the elf, I see that his eyes are still a light, calming blue.

"I did what I could to help young Thea for the time being," Athena begins, seeming to choose her words carefully. "But it's like trying to use a bandage to stop a dam."

"I don't understand," I whisper, my brows drawing together.

"That tattoo..." Athena nods towards my hip. "Where did you get it?"

I hesitate, choosing my next move carefully. Do I tell her the truth or lie?

But we came all this way for her help, and the only way to get it is by telling her the truth.

"I don't know how much the guys told you..." I flick my gaze to Rafe's impassive face, then Everett's scowling one, before finally focusing on Zaid and Kristen, who still stand side by side.

"They've told me nothing," Athena says, obviously amused by that prospect. "They simply snapped at me, threatened me a few times, and then guarded your unconscious body like hellhounds. It's...admirable."

Once again, sadness flickers across her face, there and gone too quickly for me to be sure I saw it correctly.

"Well..." Quickly, I tell her the entire story. About how I have no memory of my life outside of that strange room and the incessant tugging in my chest forcing me to reap souls. The insanity that always barrages me, followed by the pain. I explain how the only way to stop it all is to place the dagger on the pedestal in the room.

At that, Athena demands for me to describe the runes, so I do.

Then I explain how I was brought to the guys and defied the natural order of things by saving Zaid's life—which causes the wraith to smile adoringly in my direction. I talk about my quest to find answers and my fear that I'll be whisked away and forced back into that damn room. I tell her about the dagger and the way it merged with my flesh, becoming a tattoo. I mention our brief meeting with Aphrodite.

Rafe interrupts then, claiming he traveled back to the goddess's apartment during an orgy and discovered a sketchbook belonging to Athena.

A sketchbook that held images of the runes etched on my dagger.

I didn't know he did that, and all I can think is—the fucker went to an orgy?! He better not have participated, or so help me god—

"This is...very concerning." Athena's brows pull low over glowering eyes.

"You recognize the runes on the dagger, don't you?" Zaid presses.

She stares sullenly ahead, her gaze unseeing, before she nods once. "Of course I do. I... I created them. Or at least, the one that's causing Thea's current predicament."

The outcry is instantaneous.

Krystian's bow materializes in his hands, and Everett's hands tighten around my ankles, the hold almost bruising. Rafe has gone very, very still. Too still. A predator hiding in a bush, waiting to strike. Only Zaid appears unperturbed, keeping his curious gaze fixed on Athena.

The goddess absently brushes a curl behind her ear. "Don't look at me like that. I'm not the one who put the rune on the dagger."

"What does it do?" I ask quickly, trying to get the conversation back on track.

I don't know if the guys are capable of killing a goddess, and I really, really don't want to find out.

I've become a little attached to them, dammit, and I refuse to lose them now.

Athena's long, perfectly manicured fingers tap against her thigh. "It... It holds souls."

"Holds souls?" Everett repeats, incredulous.

"Anywhere from one soul to...a million. A couple million."

An uneasy feeling snakes through me, making the acid in my stomach sluice uncomfortably.

"Are you saying that when I reap a soul, their soul is trapped in the dagger?" I whisper.

"That rune you described...the one on the pedestal..." Athena stands suddenly and moves towards a bookshelf beside her bed. She peruses the titles before evidently finding the one she's looking for, pulling it free with a satisfied hum. She returns to us while flipping through the pages. "Is this what it looks like?"

She thrusts the book in front of me, and I peer at the intricately drawn rune on the page.

I nod stiffly. "That's it. But there are hundreds of that rune etched across the pedestal."

Athena nods as if she expected as much, but her face has drained of all color. She swallows convulsively and all but falls into the armchair once more.

"Fuck," she breathes.

"What does this rune mean?" Krystian demands, his tone impatient.

"It's... It's a way to transfer power."

"What are you saying?" I ask, though I already know.

"I'm saying that every time you use that dagger to reap a soul, that soul—and consequently its energy—transfers to it. And every time you place that dagger on the pedestal, the energy of the soul relocates to the one who placed the runes in the first place, while the soul remains trapped in the dagger."

Athena turns to stare at me, fear brimming in her dark eyes. "Someone is collecting power. A *lot* of power. More power than maybe even Zeus has. And I can think of only one reason someone would do that."

She swallows again, her hand shaking slightly. "We are so fucked."

CHAPTER THIRTY-ONE

THEA

"So someone is using me to steal souls and harness their powers," I surmise, an angry flush crawling up my cheeks. "And because of that, the souls are trapped in my dagger with no hope of escape?"

My entire life, I thought I had a purpose, and while I hated the cage I was put in, I deluded myself into thinking I was helping the souls. Allowing them to cross over to a better place.

But that was all a lie.

I jerk upright on the couch, dislodging Rafe's and Everett's hands, and fold my arms over my chest.

"Who the fuck is behind this?" I growl, an almost incandescent anger welling up inside of me.

Athena shakes her head. "I don't know."

"You're the Goddess of Wisdom, and you don't know?" I stare at her incredulously.

She turns away, her lips pursed. "I haven't been around in quite a while."

"Because your team died, right?" Krystian says bluntly—oblivious to the pain creasing Athena's beautiful face.

Athena's gaze flickers towards the photograph once more.

"They were more than just my team," she says softly, standing and moving towards the frame. She grabs it tenderly—almost reverently—and a single tear cascades down her cheek. "They were my everything."

She returns to us and passes me the photograph. I take it, unsurprised to see a smiling Athena in the center of the photo. Surrounding her are five men, all various shapes and sizes but all undeniably handsome.

The pose is eerily similar to what I saw before I blacked out—Athena, surrounded by five hazy silhouettes.

Could those have been...? No. No.

I stare harder at the picture, noting the birthmark on the tallest man's cheek, the blemish somehow adding to his appeal. That birthmark...

A memory slams into me, so sudden and startling that I gasp and drop the picture. Only Everett's quick reflexes keep it from shattering.

"Thea!" Everett says, focusing on me even as he passes the framed photo back to the goddess.

But all I can picture are five men on a bloody battlefield, hundreds and hundreds of feral vampires advancing on them. Tearing them apart while they screamed for mercy.

I remember the vampire uprising—or at least, the number of deaths associated with it.

Over one hundred years ago, a group of vampire extremists, totaling one thousand strong, decided they'd had enough of hunting from the shadows. They wanted to be at the top of the food chain. They went on a killing spree, murdering humans and supernaturals indiscriminately.

"I know these men," I whisper brokenly, turning towards Athena. My heart cracks down the center. "I... I reaped them."

Athena freezes, her head still lowered as she stares at the picture of her beloveds.

"You...what?" Her voice is mechanical. Impassive, almost.

"Athena...I'm so sorry." That's all I can think to say, but even those words don't feel adequate enough.

"Do you know what happens to a soul that can't cross over? A soul that has no energy?" She's still speaking softly, but there's a sharp edge to it I've never heard before. The sound causes Zaid to shift imperceptibly closer to me and Krystian to grab his bow once more. "The soul becomes insane. Desperate. Monstrous."

A lump forms in my throat, and a prickling burn erupts behind my eyes.

I've reaped thousands and thousands of souls.

And to know that all of them are trapped in the damn dagger...

Unable to move on because they have no energy or power...

"That's what's making Thea insane," Zaid breathes in understanding. He turns towards us. "Every time she reaps a soul, the energy of the newly departed gives the other souls enough juice to make themselves known."

"But they're so fucking insane they make Thea insane," Everett growls.

"Exactly." Zaid nods once.

"And when she places the dagger on the pedestal, the energy is drained from it," Krystian says. "Which stops all of the hallucinations and voices because the souls no longer have power."

"So do we use the rune to drain the excess energy from Thea now?" Everett asks, his brows furrowing together.

Athena hasn't looked away from the picture, pain

slicing across her face, but at his words, she shakes her head minutely. "No."

"No?" Rafe growls, his hand clamping down on my thigh and tightening.

"She's right," Zaid agrees with a shaky exhale, running a hand through his hair. "The runes on the dagger are linked to the runes on the pedestal. It won't work any other way."

"And we can't give the bastard behind this any more power," Athena growls, a thunderous expression darkening her face.

God, how do I even begin to apologize for what I've done? I know it wasn't my fault, but still. The men she loves are trapped in the dagger currently tattooed into my skin. She probably was comforted by the fact that they moved on and found peace. But to know that they're trapped? Insane? Because of me?

"We need to find a way to free all the souls," I say, keeping my gaze trained on Athena and allowing her to see the sincerity in my eyes.

"That won't stop the person behind this," Zaid points out, oblivious to the internal exchange between me and the goddess. "We need to find a way to drain him or her of all of this excess energy. All of this unnatural power."

"And we will," I insist. "But we also need to find a

way to save all of these souls. To remove them from the dagger."

Athena nods slowly, cautiously, her mouth molded in a frown.

"I'll help you." The hand not holding the picture frame curls into a tight fist. "I don't know who's behind this, but he or she just made me an enemy."

"So what do we do?" Krystian asks. "What's our next step? Do you have any idea who's behind this?"

"Probably the god in charge of souls themselves. The god who is always battling against Poseidon and Zeus for the crown." Athena finally flicks her gaze up and spears us all with an indecipherable look.

"You mean Hades?" I squeak.

King of the Underworld? Ruthless killer?

"We can't just go and confront him," Everett snarls. "If he is behind this, and he discovers Thea escaped, then he'll lock her away again."

"I'm not saying to confront Hades," Athena says slowly, her keen gaze fixed on the shifter beside me. "But there's someone you can talk to who knows everything there is to know about the Underworld and reapers. If anyone has heard an inkling of Hades's plan, it'll be him."

Everett, if it's even possible, becomes even stiffer beside me, a statue hewn from marble.

"Who are you talking about?" I ask, volleying my gaze between Athena and Everett.

"Cerberus," Krystian responds tiredly, ruffling his golden hair. "She's talking about Cerberus."

Everett's scowl deepens, painting cavernous lines on his face. "Otherwise known as my father."

CHAPTER THIRTY-TWO

EVERETT

"Remember," Athena says a short while later, as we all gather around her to be transported back to the safe house. Her unnervingly penetrating stare is fixed on Thea. "I put a bandage on the issue, but it's fragile. *You're* fragile. One more reaped soul will blow it open."

She whirls to face the four of us surrounding her. "Do *not* kill anyone around her. I don't know how the magic inside of her works—not yet, anyway—but I do know she will have no choice but to reap. She won't be able to stop herself."

I nod solemnly, as do my brothers. We will do whatever it takes to save Thea from herself.

The reaper absently twirls a strand of golden hair, her expression contemplative. "But aren't we going to encounter a shit ton of souls in the Underworld? Should I be worried then?"

Athena's lips twitch slightly before straightening out. "Those souls have already been reaped. They should be no problem for you."

"Oh." Thea's shoulders sag in physical relief, and Zaid wraps an arm around her from the side, pulling her in close.

The sight makes my heart pound even faster.

I want to be the one to fucking comfort her.

God, what did this girl do to me?

"I'll do some research here and will contact you once I discover something," Athena continues.

Once, not if. I have to admire the goddess's confidence. Then again, she is the Goddess of Wisdom. I imagine there's very little she won't be able to solve if she sets her mind to it.

And she's highly motivated.

I find my gaze wandering towards the framed photo once more on her nightstand. Once upon a time, she loved those five men fiercely and then lost them. She probably hoped or believed they were safe in Elysium, but to know that they've been trapped in Thea's dagger this entire time? Slowly losing their minds? I can't help but feel sympathy for the goddess.

Though she'll probably smite me if she discovered the truth.

"Good luck, young reaper," Athena says gravely. "I wish you well on your travels."

Then she waves her hand in the air, and a white light engulfs us instantly. I squint, my eyes burning, and the cavern fades away, replaced by familiar furniture.

The safe house.

All of us release a collective breath, and Thea plops down on the couch, her head lolling back.

"We need to come up with a plan for tomorrow," Zaid says, pacing.

He chews on his thumbnail, his dark gaze flicking between the four of us.

"Not right now." Krystian moves towards the television—and the newest PlayStation underneath it. He grabs two controllers and returns to the couch, sitting beside Thea. "Right now, we're going to play video games."

Thea's brows furrow adorably. "Video games?"

"You promised you'd play with me," Krystian points out. "And there's this new two-player action game I think you'll really like."

Thea seems uncertain, her gaze moving from the controller held out in front of her to our faces. When her eyes lock on mine, I try for a reassuring smile that probably makes me look like I'm seizing.

"I want to watch," I say simply, moving to sit on her other side.

We're so close that I can feel each graze of her thigh against my own, the heat her body emits almost palpable. It warms me from the inside out.

"I guess we can use a break," Zaid says, attempting to smile for Thea's sake.

But I can tell my brother is still stressed, still worried about tomorrow and what the future will hold.

Rafe simply positions himself against the wall, his arms crossed over his chest and his eyes fixed on the screen. After a moment, Zaid claims the armchair.

An hour later, Thea and Krystian are attempting to take on a horde of zombies, their combined laughter filling the room. I've left for a short while to make some homemade pizzas, and the evidence of my hard work lies scattered on the coffee table, nothing but crust and crumbs.

"Push X," Krystian instructs as he slices at the zombie with his sword.

"I am pushing X," Thea insists.

On screen, her character crouches, rises, crouches, rises, and then crouches again.

"That's O."

"Oh...okay." Thea begins pushing more buttons, and her character walks repeatedly into a wall.

A zombie sneaks up behind her, and Krystian stealthily kills it.

"What the fuck are you doing, love?" Krystian chuckles.

"I don't know!" Thea's tongue sticks out of her mouth in concentration as she wiggles the joystick, causing her character to turn in a circle.

Two zombies burst out of the house she's in front of and advance on her.

"Krystian! Help! I'm under attack!" She pushes more buttons, and her gun appears in her hand. Then it disappears, replaced by a stick. Then that disappears as well, and she begins karate chopping the zombies. "Am I doing it? Am I killing them?"

"Yes, sweetheart. You're killing them," Zaid says from the armchair, laughter evident in his voice.

And that may be true, but they're also simultaneously killing her. Her character falls to the floor, dead.

"I broke the game," she deadpans, frowning.

Krystian laughs. "You can't break the game."

"I just did."

"Push X to respawn," Zaid tells her.

Thea pushes a button at random.

"That's O," Rafe murmurs from his spot against the wall.

Krystian leans towards her to press the correct

button, and then her character reappears on the screen, though a far distance away from Krystian's.

"Where did all my supplies go?" She stares at Krystian incredulously.

"When you died, they died with you. Now come on. Start collecting loot. I'll meet up with you. Hopefully, we'll be able to take on the zombies in the north sector next," Krystian says.

"Aren't they the hardest enemies?"

Krystian arches a brow. "Will that be a problem?"

Thea's face scrunches in fierce determination, and she narrows her eyes at the screen. "Bring it on, bitches."

I settle back against the couch, a tentative smile on my face. My eyes drift shut as Thea's laughter swirls in the air around me. I've never noticed it before. Not like this—the way it fills the space. The warmth of it.

I fade away with Thea's name on my lips.

"AGAIN," Cerberus growls, his deep voice vibrating through the air.

He's in his shifted form, and he's a terrifying sight to behold. His three heads—each with a varying expression ranging from stern, to calculating, to angry—stare down at me from above. His numerous eyes are relentless, his presence suffocating.

"Focus," one head snaps.

"You're not trying hard enough," another bites out.

I raise my fists to block the next strike, but I mess up. I don't even know what happened. One second, I'm peering up at his three snarling faces, and the next, I'm sprawled on the ground, my knees scraped and bloodied and the taste of dirt filling my mouth.

"Pathetic," a head snarls.

I push myself to my feet, glaring at the ground as my hands tremble.

Cerberus—I stopped calling him Father a year ago, when a training session left me with bruised ribs and a broken wrist—has made it clear that he thinks the gods made a mistake.

I'm weak, according to him.

A failure.

It's why Hades didn't choose me as a member of his team.

"Again," Cerberus's center head barks, his tone like stone. "You don't stop until you do it right."

My head aches, but I know complaining will only get me lashes across the back.

I try again, forcing my body to move, but I'm not

fast enough. Not strong enough. Not fucking good enough.

Then, without warning, the air shifts. A chill careens down my spine, and the ground under my feet seems to tremble with unencumbered power. A shadow falls over me, and I hesitantly look up.

The sight of him... It shakes me. His presence is so overwhelming and domineering that my chest tightens. He's tall, his form draped in shadows, his handsome features sharp and unyielding. His eyes burn like hell-fire, molten and intense.

Hades.

I know it's him, even before Cerberus's heads turn in unison, his demeanor shifting. One head dips in submission, while the others grow still. And I realize then that my father—this terrifying, monstrous being—is not the ultimate authority. Not truly. There's someone far more powerful out there.

Someone like this god.

"Leave the boy," Hades drawls lazily, waving a hand in my direction. "We have much to discuss."

I glance up at my father, my heart hammering in the general vicinity of my throat.

Cerberus has never allowed us to end a training session early. He has made me fight with broken bones and bruises and gaping wounds.

But no one can say no to Hades, not even my father.

"Understood." Then, without another word to me, he turns and follows Hades, leaving me alone and confused.

I stagger the rest of the way to my feet, trying to catch my breath.

My father never gave me comfort before. He didn't hold me when I fell or praise me when I did something right. All I ever saw in him was that cold, indifferent face he wore like a mask. My entire life, I thought he was the biggest, baddest monster of them all. That he was invincible.

But there's something out there much, much worse.

The raw power Hades exuded...

The malevolent glint in those inhuman eyes...

The darkness he seemed to wear like a cloak...

He wasn't a man who simply lived in the shadows; he commanded them.

It makes sense that Hades's right-hand man would grow to be just as cold, just as angry.

I pray I won't end up like them.

That eternity won't wither away my softness the way it did theirs.

Swallowing heavily, I move my fists into position again. Cerberus may not be here, but that doesn't mean I can't train.

I need to be the best, and to do that, I need to practice.

So I do it alone.

I WAKE with something soft wrapped around me, cocooning me in warmth.

I blink groggily, wondering which of my brothers placed a blanket on me. But then someone shifts beside me, and I know it wasn't any of them.

It was Thea.

Beautiful, irritating Thea.

There's something about her that hits me like a soft wind. It doesn't blow me off my feet, but it's a constant presence, a perpetual awareness I feel in the marrow of my bones. She has slowly and surely slipped past my defenses one witty retort or innate rambling at a time.

She sits beside me now, her legs curled up beneath her. Her expression as she gazes at me is soft and tender. I could stare at her like this for hours, taking in every diminutive detail I've never noticed before. Like the darker streaks in her blonde hair. Or the way her perfect nose is slightly turned up at the tip. Or the pink flush on her cheeks. Or the way her lips part just slightly...

"Sorry. I didn't mean to stare at you like such a creeper," she says when our eyes clash.

Most girls would be embarrassed at being caught watching me sleep, but not Thea.

"It's okay," I grumble, sitting upright.

The television is off, and the room is dark. Farther down the hall, I can hear the steady snores of most of my brothers.

"How long have I been asleep?"

"Not too long. We stopped playing shortly after you fell asleep. And I was going to wake you, but you just looked so peaceful..." She absently runs her fingers over the blanket surrounding her. "Well, you needed your sleep. You're always grumpy without it."

I smirk and roll out my neck, trying to alleviate the stiffness there. "I'm grumpy with it."

"So I just can't win, can I?" Her eyes sparkle impishly, then dim, turning subdued. She focuses once more on the blanket. "Are you anxious about seeing your father again tomorrow?" She risks peeking up at me through her fringe of sooty lashes, gauging my reaction. "I have a feeling—based on your reaction to hearing his name—that you two don't get along well."

The part of me that pushed people away my entire life wants to snap at her to mind her own business.

But I'm done hiding. Done building up impenetrable walls.

"It's hard," I admit. "He was always tough on me. Never thought I was good enough."

I glance away, unable to bear seeing the emotions in her eyes. I don't want her to pity me. I would fucking die before I allowed that to happen.

"He knew from my birth that I was fated to join Ares's team, and he was pissed. He didn't understand why Ares chose me and not Hades, his boss. I feel like, because of that, he thought I wasn't good enough. Like, if Hades didn't pick me, there was obviously a reason."

Fuck, I'm saying too much. These are words I've never spoken out loud—not to anyone, not even my brothers—but I can't stop the verbal freight train now that it's left the station.

"You don't have to visit him if you don't want to." Thea leans towards me, her expression open and earnest. "We can find another way. We can..."

Her breath hitches, and she drops her gaze to her hand—which is held in mine now.

I rub my thumb over her knuckles absently, focusing on the sensation of her hand in mine and the current of electricity rippling between us.

"I thought you hated me," she whispers, her voice trembling slightly.

I swallow. "I've never hated you. Maybe, at first, I didn't trust you, but can you blame me? You material-ized out of thin air and started spewing crazy-ass shit.

But even then, I didn't hate you. How could I? You're warm and vibrant and real..." I look away, my throat clogged. "I admit, when I first met you, I tried to push you away. I don't want to say I was afraid, because I wasn't, but—"

"You totally were afraid." Thea's brows lift in surprise. "But why? Did you think I would hurt you or the team?"

Yes, but not in the way she seems to believe. Not physically.

We've all been alone for so long, only having each other, that the thought of someone infiltrating our group terrified me. But I've been fighting against myself for too damn long. Fighting the way I feel when she's around. Fighting the way she makes me think of things I've never considered before.

"I'm done fighting," I say.

Done being afraid.

Before I even realize what I'm doing, I lean forward and kiss her.

And it feels inherently right—the quiet storm between us finally stilling.

CHAPTER THIRTY-THREE

THEA

Everett is kissing me.

Gruff, antagonistic Everett is kissing me.

On the mouth.

With lips.

And tongue.

Oh my god.

I come to my senses—albeit slowly—and place my hands on his chest, giving him a slight push. On my own, I'm not strong enough to move him, but he parts from me without complaint, his hazel eyes hooded with desire. The unbridled heat in his gaze makes my stomach curdle.

"Everett, you need to speak clearly. What do you want from me?" I can't help the vulnerability that seeps into my voice.

I don't think I can handle him pulling me in and

then pushing me away again. My poor heart has been abused and beaten and stomped on; it's understandably fragile, and I'm terrified the wrong word will break it completely.

"I...I want a chance, Thea. That's all." His fingertips graze my cheek, leaving tingles in their wake.

Everett has pushed me away from the very first day, yet he continually looked after me in his own subtle way. He fed me, bought me clothes, protected me. Beneath his cantankerous exterior is a total teddy bear.

Before I can lose my nerve, I lean forward and kiss him once more. I hold perfectly still, simply breathing him in, and then his lips begin to move underneath mine. Slowly. Seriously. It feels as if he's savoring the kiss, savoring me.

A giddy, euphoric feeling bubbles in my chest as I deepen the kiss, reaching out to run my fingers through his shaggy, blond-brown hair. The strands feel soft to the touch, and when I tug on them, he growls low in his throat. The sound sends a rippling wave of heat straight through me.

I push both of our blankets aside and move until I'm straddling his lap. His hard cock presses against me, straining against the denim of his jeans.

Holy fuck.

I didn't expect kissing Everett to be like this. He

consumes me, one swipe of his tongue at a time. My entire body transforms into one giant goose bump, and wave after wave of fire rushes through my veins.

Everett gently pushes me away, his lips slightly puffy and a dazed expression on his face.

"Thea..." He says my name like a prayer, his face scrunching together in what appears to be pain.

"Everett," I say.

"We need to stop." Even as he says this, he thrusts his hips upwards, his cock brushing against me oh so deliciously through the material of his pants.

"Umm..." Instinctively, I rock against him, and he moans low in his throat. "You don't really seem like you want to stop."

"Want to?" He chuckles wickedly. "No. Need to?" He lowers his hands to my waist and then lifts me up as if I weigh nothing. He deposits me onto the couch beside him once more. "I'm not going to fuck you today, baby."

"But...why?"

Do I whine? Yes. I have absolutely no shame. Apparently, my time on this earth has transformed me into a shameless hussy.

A dark, ravishing smile tugs up his lips. "Because I want to be worthy of you before I fuck you. I want to earn every moan you give me, every plea for more. And when I finally take you to bed, there will be no going back for either of us. You will be mine."

His eyes ensnare mine, burning with possession. "So let me woo you. Let me be worthy of you. Then I'll rip your clothes apart, spread your creamy thighs, and fuck you until you're screaming my name for everyone to hear."

I gulp as liquid heat rushes through me.

Is it hot in here?

I absently bring my hand up to fan my cheeks, hoping that will help alleviate the fire in them.

Everett smirks cockily, as if he knows exactly where my mind has gone, and leans forward to kiss my forehead. "Go to bed, baby. We have a busy day ahead of us."

I attempt to swallow around the ball of daggers in my throat. "A-are you going to bed?"

"I think I'm going to take a shower first. A long, cold shower." With that, he stands, and I automatically flick my gaze to the massive bulge in his pants.

Warmth envelops me instantly.

"Yeah. A shower... A shower sounds good. Make sure to use soap and water," I ramble as he walks away, his husky laugh drifting back to me.

Fuck.

Deciding that Everett has the right idea, I hurry towards the bedroom they deemed as mine and dart into the en suite bathroom. I really wish I'd showered earlier, before the stench of death and engine grease and mold permeated the air. Ugh. I'm sooo not used to showering.

I like it, though.

There's something refreshing about the warm water pelting me from above, washing away the worries and fears of the day.

When I step out of the shower twenty minutes later, I feel infinitely lighter, like the weight of the world has been washed away.

I pad back into my room in only a towel...and nearly jump a foot in the air at the sight of the familiar blood fae reclining against the stack of pillows.

Rafe's dressed for bed, wearing a black T-shirt and shorts. I've never seen him like this before. It's not as if he dresses fancy normally, but he's usually never showing so much skin. Every time I've seen him before, he's been wearing long pants and an oversized hoodie.

A knot forms in my throat as I drift my gaze over his muscular arms and legs, the latter covered with thousands and thousands of tiny cuts and scars.

Concern knits my brows together, and I hurry forward, momentarily forgetting I'm only in a towel.

"What happened here?" I kneel beside him and gently trace one of the ragged lines on his calf.

He shivers slightly, his hooded eyes fixed on my own. "You know how I get my magic."

I do. He...cuts himself.

I've never thought too much about it before—hell, I even thought it was beautiful—but to see the evidence firsthand...

"Why didn't they heal?" I whisper, lifting my fingers to another scar, this one just above his knee. "I've seen you cut your palm numerous times, but there are no scars there."

"These healed once upon a time," Rafe confesses with a shrug. "Until they didn't. Soon, it'll be the same for my palms. Then when those become too scarred, I'll move to my wrists and arms."

He says all this nonchalantly, not knowing that every word is a whip that slashes at my skin.

"I don't like the thought of you hurting yourself," I whisper.

He stills nearly imperceptibly, his muscles locking together. "I have to."

"I know, but..." I gently trace a third scar, this one on his thigh. "I just don't like seeing you hurt."

He tilts his head to the side, studying me curiously. I can't quite read the emotions percolating in his dark, fathomless gaze.

When he speaks next, his voice is a mere husk. "I've never cared about being hurt before."

"Well, I'll care enough for the both of us," I say.

Before I can touch a fourth scar, he grabs my wrist, his fingers digging into my skin hard enough to bruise. His touch is a startling contrast to Everett's, who treated me like I was fragile.

"I can heal from almost everything," he rasps out. "We all can. But repeated injuries can be lasting on fae, which is why my body is covered in scars. Is it...?" His brows clench together. "Is it ugly?"

"Of course not." Nothing about Rafe—or any of the guys, for that matter—is ugly.

It's incredibly unfair.

A dark, sinful smile tugs up his lips, and a shiver ripples down my spine at the sight. "I heard what happened out in the living room." He leans forward until his lips graze the shell of my ear. "Everett left you needy, didn't he?"

The reminder sends heat gushing through me. A whimper escapes me.

"You're aching, aren't you, little bird?" His voice is a raspy, seductive pull that tugs at me, propelling me towards him. "You want my touch. My lips. My cock. Do you want me to give them to you?"

I rub my thighs together instinctively, but I don't answer. I can't. I'm incapable of speech.

Everett doused me in gasoline, and Rafe just lit the match.

Abruptly, the blood fae grabs a fistful of my hair, pulling my head back.

"Use your words," he growls.

"Yes," I pant out. "Yes, I want you to touch me. Kiss me. Fuck me."

His smile broadens, and the sight has wetness coating my thighs.

"Good answer." He lowers his gaze to the towel still wrapped around me. "Get rid of the towel."

"But..."

"Now, little bird." He tugs harder on my hair, eliciting a gasp.

Quickly—and somewhat awkwardly considering, I'm still kneeling on the bed with a portion of the towel underneath me—I untie it and let it fall to the ground.

Rafe's hungry gaze trails over me, the desperation in his eyes making my core pulse.

"You're so beautiful, Thea," he rasps, his fingers moving to my aching nipples and pulling tightly.

I gasp and instinctively arch my back, pushing my breasts farther into his groping hands.

"And you're mine, aren't you?" He tugs my nipples harshly and then releases them. "Say you're mine."

Those words are a dark, insidious threat that shouldn't make me as wet as I am.

But I've come to realize I'm a little fucked up, especially when it comes to these men.

"I'm yours," I breathe, wilting towards him.

I want him to kiss me. Would his kisses be playful and passionate like Krystian's and Krys's? Would they be soft but possessive like Everett's?

"Good girl," he praises, bringing his hands back to my tender breasts to play with them. "Now, what I want to do to you might be a little scary, but I promise you that you're safe. Everything I do is for your pleasure only."

My heart begins to pound even faster, fear and intrigue mingling in my chest. "What do you want to do to me?"

His hands leave my breasts and trail down my arms, stopping when they reach my wrists.

"I'll tie you here." He releases my wrists and moves his hands down my stomach, my thighs, my calves... and finally land on my ankles, extended behind me. "And here."

"You want to tie me up?" I ask, my stomach tightening.

"I want to spread you out like my own personal feast." His voice is a dark, seductive promise.

I bite down on my lower lip. "Will it hurt?"

"Maybe at times," he confesses. "But that pain will only help amplify your pleasure."

I consider, trailing my gaze across his painfully handsome face.

"Okay," I decide on at last. "I trust you."

Pride shines in his eyes at hearing those words. "Good girl." He runs his finger up and down my cheek. "But you'll need a safe word before we go any further."

I frown. "Can't we just use the word stop?"

He smirks slightly before becoming serious. "How often do you say the word stop without actually meaning it? If you say stop, I might slow down, but if you use your safe word, I'll stop everything I'm doing, regardless of the situation."

Oh. That makes sense.

Heat dusts my cheeks as I think. "Umm...maybe watermelon?"

There's no way in hell I would be chanting out watermelon during sex.

"Watermelon," Rafe repeats, his expression considerate. Then he nods. "Okay. Watermelon it is."

"So...what's next? What's going to— Oh!" I let out a cry of alarm as a burst of magic pushes me onto my back on the bed and then spreads my arms and legs.

Rafe moves to stand beside the bed, a wickedly sinful smirk on his face. He reaches behind him for a dagger he must've kept in the waistband of his shorts and creates a shallow cut on his palm. Red magic swirls through the air and coils around first one of my wrists, then the other, tying them to the bedpost. They solidify seconds later, creating impenetrable bindings.

I struggle futilely against them, but I don't actually want to break free. There's something heady, intoxicating, about being Rafe's prisoner.

When Rafe does the same things to my ankles, pulling my legs apart, a flush dusts my chest. This new position makes me feel oddly vulnerable. I'm keenly aware that Rafe can see everything from this angle.

Is it normal for me to be this wet already?

I wiggle slightly as Rafe moves around the bed to stand at the foot.

"You look so beautiful splayed out for me like this. Such a good, perfect little slut." He keeps his eyes fixed on my pussy as he lowers himself to his knees on the floor. He leans in close and inhales, his lashes fluttering shut. "You smell like ambrosia."

I jolt when his tongue teases my clit in a light circle.

"Holy fuck!" I cry, thrusting my hips up.

"You taste better than I imagined. Fuck, you're such a good girl for me. Such a good slut."

And then he stops talking as he devours me.

My god, I didn't know my blood fae had such a wicked, decadent tongue. He laps and groans, feasting on me like I'm the only meal he needs. His tongue delves deeper than I thought would be possible, demanding everything. When he sucks on my clit, I come undone, screaming my release for the entire house to hear.

"That's orgasm number one," he rasps, then he dives back in.

"Rafe, please. Fuck me. I want you to fuck me." My legs begin to shake as his talented, ethereal tongue circles my throbbing pussy.

His teeth graze my clit once again.

It's almost embarrassing how fast I come a second time.

"That's two." He grins up at me, his lips wet and his pupils dilated.

"Rafe, please," I beg.

I want to feel his cock inside of me. Stretching me.

"You want me to fuck you, little bird?" As he speaks, he slips his fingers inside of my cunt, pistoning them in and out in slow, shallow thrusts.

I gasp and moan and shake, tears blurring my vision.

"Yes!" I strain against the bindings, wanting to reach for him. To touch him. To run my fingers through that midnight-black hair with colorful undertones.

I can feel myself reaching that precipice yet again, but before I can fall over the edge, Rafe pulls his hands and mouth away. I'm left trembling and shaking, sweat dripping down my cheeks and chest.

"W-what?" I blink at him dazedly, confused as to why he wouldn't let me come.

His features are grave, his eyes stony.

"You want to come?" He rises to his feet and slowly begins removing his clothes.

First is his shirt, revealing a sculpted torso littered with shallow cuts. Then it's his shorts and boxer briefs. His cock springs free, hard and veiny and already dripping in precum.

"I want you to fuck me," I correct, whimpering at the predatorial intensity in his gaze.

He slowly climbs onto the bed and begins to crawl up my body.

"You don't tell me what to do," he snaps, reaching up to slap my breast.

It sways slightly, and I gasp at the sharp, biting sensation. It...hurt. I don't understand why I become even wetter, my pussy throbbing.

Is this what he meant about pain contributing to my pleasure? Amplifying it?

"You'll take what I give you," he continues, slapping my other tit. "Now normally, I would make you suck my cock until you're desperate for breath, but in this position, I'm afraid you might gag." Despite his harsh words, his hands are unexpectedly gentle as he brushes strands of hair away from my face. "So instead, I'm going to fuck your perfect pussy, but you're not allowed to come until I give you permission. Do you understand?"

I whimper and nod.

He slaps my tit a third time, the pale skin turning slightly red.

"I thought I told you to use your words."

"Yes. Yes, I understand," I cry out.

"Good girl." He palms my tit, his touch gentling. "You're being such a good slut for me. When I finally give you permission to come, you're going to fucking explode around my shaft."

My pussy throbs at the thought.

Keeping his gaze trained on me, he lines himself up with my slick folds. He meets little resistance as he slips inside, my body already wet and primed for him.

He's thicker than Krystian but not as long, his cock stretching me in an entirely new way. My pussy reflexively flutters around him, squeezing him.

He shudders and closes his eyes briefly. "Goddammit, Thea. Stay the fuck still."

I do as instructed, waiting until he's finished pushing in the last few inches.

God, I feel so stuffed. So full. So...consumed.

"I'm going to fuck you now, Thea. Remember—you can't come until I give you permission."

He doesn't give me the chance to respond as he

pulls his hips back and then thrusts them forward, his cock dragging against me deliciously.

"Oh my god!" I scream as he fucks me roughly.

Savagely. Possessively.

His tongue traces the side of my neck, and I roll my hips instinctively, chasing him.

"Yes, Rafe! Yes!" I cry out, struggling against the restraints.

I want to touch him. I'm almost desperate. I want to know what his skin feels like under my fingers—if it's soft or rough from all the scars. Would he like it if I dragged my nails down his spine, the way I did with Krystian?

I can feel my release fast approaching, but I bite down on my lip, refusing to come until he gives me permission. I don't know what punishment he plans to dish out if I come before he says so, but I have a feeling I won't like it.

"So fucking perfect. Your pussy is so goddamn tight." His thrusts turn jerky. "I don't know how much longer I can last. Fuck. Fuck. Fuck."

"Yes, Rafe. Just like that. *Yes*."

Abruptly, a devious smile crosses his face.

"I have an idea," he says, and the magic holding my ankles and wrists hostage disappears.

But before I can reach for him, touch him, run my fingers over his skin the way I crave, he flips me.

"Hands and knees, little bird."

I do as he says and feel his cock line up with my cunt from behind. He slowly pushes in once more, and I moan, pleasure arcing through me.

It's at that moment I realize we're not alone.

Someone is watching us.

My eyes meet Zaid's from where he stands in the open doorway, a tiny blush painting his cheeks. He bites down on his lower lip and lowers his gaze to my breasts, which sway with each brutal thrust of Rafe's hips.

"Your wraith has been watching for quite a while," Rafe murmurs huskily from behind. "But he's too shy to come inside. Maybe he needs a formal invitation."

Zaid's blush deepens, and my desire amplifies.

The thought of Zaid watching...

Fuck.

"You want me to ask him to join?" I ask, moaning yet again when Rafe's cock hits a spot deep inside of me.

Absently, I distribute my weight to one hand and use the other to fondle my dangling tits. Zaid's gaze zeros in on my fingers squeezing and twisting first one nipple and then the next.

"Suck his cock while I fuck you from behind. I know you want to. I can feel the way your pussy flutters around my cock at just the thought. You're a greedy little slut, aren't you?"

Fuck, yes.

I attempt to give Zaid come-hither eyes, but I'm not sure I have the effect I'm going for. Either way, his eyes flare with desire, and he takes a hesitant step forward.

"Thea, are you sure? You don't have to..." He trails off when I use one hand to clumsily reach for him, desperate to free his cock. "Fuck."

He helps me push down his shorts just enough for his shaft to spring free, bouncing against his stomach.

I lower my hand back to the bed and lean forward, parting my lips so I can take him in my mouth.

I've never given a guy a blowjob before, and despite knowing what one is, I have no idea what I'm doing. I hollow my cheeks and take him in deep, remembering to breathe out of my nose.

"Holy fuck. Your mouth is amazing, Thea. You're amazing. Oh, *fuck*." Zaid's fingers rake through my sweaty hair.

"Such a good girl, Thea. Our good girl," Rafe coos as he sweeps a hand down my spine.

At some point—probably when I first started sucking Zaid—he stopped moving. I wiggle my ass encouragingly, and he chuckles, his palm smacking my ass cheek.

"Greedy, desperate girl."

And then he resumes fucking me, each thrust of his hips pushing me farther onto Zaid's cock. Tears burn in my eyes, and saliva drizzles down my chin. But I don't stop. I can't. I'm as desperate for these men as they are for me.

Pleasure sears through my entire body, but I remember Rafe's threat and hold it back, focusing instead on getting Zaid to come.

I use my tongue to trace the vein on his dick and then balance on one hand to fondle his balls.

"Fuck. Fuck. Fuck." He thrusts his hips forward, inarticulate praises leaving his lips, and then ropes of silky cum rain down my throat.

I try to swallow as much of it as I can, though a good amount runs down my chin and onto the bed.

Zaid pulls out of me with a muffled curse. His eyes are glazed with desire.

"Come for me, Thea," Rafe whispers huskily, and I feel a burst of magic directly over my clit.

Pleasure hits me so hard, I can't breathe. Can't think. Can't do anything but cry out as I tumble head over heels off the steepest cliff side I've ever felt. My heart pounds, and emotions I can't quite name bombard me from all directions. I shake and tremble, my legs giving out as I collapse onto my belly on the bed.

Rafe thrusts into me two more times, his fingers

biting into the skin of my hips, and then he explodes as well. I can feel his warm cum deep inside of me and drizzling down my thighs.

I don't really know what happens next. I'm too out of it—too consumed by pleasure—to think straight. One second, I'm lying on my belly, and the next, hands are carrying me to the center of the bed. Someone washes my chin, breasts, and pussy with a warm washcloth.

"You're okay, my little bird," a raspy voice coos, stroking my hair. "You're okay."

A warm body snuggles into me from the other side, wrapping an arm around me.

Zaid.

"Sleep, sweetheart," he says.

"We'll be here," vows Rafe from my other side.

I try to think of something to say—anything that will express my gratitude and affection—but the words dry up. Instead, I curl up between the two of them and allow exhaustion to pull me away.

CHAPTER THIRTY-FOUR

THEA

The entrance to the Underworld is in...an amusement park.

An abandoned one, to be exact, located about one hundred miles south of Chicago.

"I never knew this place existed," I murmur, staring up at the dilapidated sign reading *Frankie's Fun Zone*.

Krystian snorts from beside me. "You didn't know a lot of places existed. Hell, you thought McDonald's was an actual clown and not a fast-food restaurant until this morning."

"He *is* a clown," I declare adamantly.

"The McDonald's mascot may be a clown, but I don't think that's his name," Krystian says.

I arch a brow. "You sure about that?"

He opens his mouth, closes it, and then opens it

again. Finally, he concedes with a sigh, absently scratching at the back of his neck. "Okay, okay. Point taken."

I fist pump the air, and he rolls his eyes at me.

"You're such a dork."

"So where exactly in this park are we going?" Everett asks, scowling.

He stands at the front of the group but turns to stare at us over his shoulder.

Zaid, who's behind me, says, "The Hall of Mirrors. At least, that's what Athena said."

Apparently, Athena's been texting Zaid. Yup, they're texting buddies now. I'm not sure how I feel about that. Yes, I know Athena's in love with dead men and Zaid has feelings for me, but still. The little green monster inside of me refuses to calm down.

The only thing that settles the beast is the reminder of what we got up to last night. A warm flush spreads through me at the memory of his cock in my mouth, his hands in my hair. He stared at me with nothing short of reverence, like I was the goddess he chose to worship, not Athena.

I bite my lip and glance over my shoulder at Zaid and Rafe, who both meet my gaze with hooded looks.

Yeah. I suppose I don't have anything to be jealous about.

"Come on." Everett gestures for us to follow him.

The air's thick with the scent of decay and mold as we move through the entrance gate, which is now nothing but a crumbling structure overrun with weeds and ivy.

"What happened to this place? Why is it abandoned?" I ask, lifting my legs to step over a rotted piece of wood.

"Owner must've fallen on hard times," Krystian answers, his lips pursing as he studies our surroundings. "They probably had no choice but to put it up for sale. When no one bought it, they shut it down and allowed it to wither away. No point in upkeeping a closed business."

We step cautiously over cracked pavement, the sound of our footsteps echoing eerily in the empty space.

The towering Ferris wheel looms in the distance, its once-bright colors now faded and chipped. Some of the seats sway slightly in the breeze, creating a ghostly, haunting rhythm.

Roller coaster tracks thrust overhead like a massive skeletal hand, reaching towards the sky but suspended in time, forgotten. A dilapidated funhouse with peeling paint and boarded-up windows stands nearby, its mirrors cracked, distorting the faint reflections of us as we pass.

Krystian pauses, studying the mirror curiously.

"Is that where we have to go?" I ask, stopping beside him.

"No, this is the funhouse, not the mirror maze. It's just..." A frown tugs at his lips, and he shakes his head ruefully. "It's nothing."

"It's obviously something," I counter.

The others have moved slightly ahead, granting us a semblance of privacy, which I'm grateful for. Something is obviously bothering Krystian. It has been since this morning. He tries to act like his usual jovial self, but there's a heaviness to him that hasn't been there prior.

"What's going on?" I press, nudging him slightly with my elbow.

"It's just..." He bites down on his lip, debating, before blurting out, "It's Krys."

I frown. "What about him?"

"Do you remember when we were in the maze? And we were staring into the loom?"

How could I forget? I saw image after image of some of the more memorable souls I reaped.

The old man holding his wife's hand.

The little girl lying on a hospital bed.

The young woman who had just been beaten, raped, and left for dead on the side of the road.

"Well, I saw things that didn't make sense," Krystian continues. "The memories I saw... They weren't mine. At least, I didn't think they were until I started looking closer. I realized that they were Krys's memories."

He takes a shuddering breath, but I don't speak to fill the silence—which is a miracle, because I love speaking. However, I can tell he needs to gather his thoughts before he's capable of continuing the story.

"I saw some of the things Krys did—some of the people he hurt and killed—and at first, I was horrified. But then some of his thoughts drifted to me, and I realized how horrible these people were. They were murderers. Rapists. The scum of the earth. Take the motorcycle club you two visited. Every person in that bar was involved in an underground trafficking ring."

He turns to stare at me, confusion swarming in his eyes. "The people he kills aren't all that different from the ones *I* kill."

"Krys isn't some sort of evil monster," I tell him gently, rubbing his arm. "He's you. And yes, he may have darker urges and a lack of inhibition, but he's not the bad guy. At least, he isn't in your story."

"Last night..." He ruffles a strand of his white-gold hair. "Last night was the first time I remembered everything that happened. I didn't wake up confused and disoriented, wondering where I was and how I'd gotten there."

"Maybe it's because you're finally accepting that part of yourself?" I suggest.

"Yeah. Maybe." He rubs a hand down his face with a ragged sigh. Then he forces a smile, that single dimple appearing on his cheek. "But enough of this depressing shit. We have the Underworld to get to."

"Krystian..." I don't want to leave this conversation if the issue is still bothering him.

His smile turns more genuine. "Later," he promises, grabbing my hand and giving it a squeeze. "I promise."

I nod to show him I understand. Now isn't the time.

We meet with the others, who are watching us curiously. Everett levels an unreadable glance at Krystian and cocks an eyebrow.

"We good?" the shifter asks.

Krystian nods. "Yeah. We're good."

The five of us continue to walk once more, past a carousel with horses frozen in mid-gallop, cloaked in shadows. Past game stalls with dirty bears dangling from the ceiling, pieces of their bodies missing and stuffing protruding from their bellies.

We wander deeper, our breaths visible in the cold. We don't speak again, as if any noise will shatter the illusion of serenity.

"This is it," Everett tells us gruffly, pulling to a stop in front of a huge purple building.

The sign above reads *Hall of Mirrors* in bright, peeling paint.

"So the portal is just...inside?" I bring my thumb to my lip and chew on the nail, my nerves frolicking in my belly.

"According to Athena, yes," Zaid answers. "Hades hid one here years ago. Apparently, he made a deal with the owner."

My nose wrinkles. "Why would anyone make a deal with the God of the Dead?"

"The owner was probably promised a permanent spot in Elysium," Zaid explains. He frowns and studies the crumbling building. "But one thing Athena stressed in her message—only one of us can enter the building at a time. We must wait at least five seconds, and then the next can enter."

"What?" Everett's scowl deepens.

"Not happening," Rafe agrees, lazily spinning a knife in the air.

Zaid's lips firm. "If we don't follow her instructions, then we're dead."

An uneasy silence permeates the air until Everett breaks it. "All right. I'll go first. Krystian, you follow. Then Thea. Then Zaid. Then Rafe. Everybody in agreement?"

Krystian, Zaid, and I say, "Yes."

Rafe simply mutters, "No," and shoots a dark glance at the windowless building.

Everett ignores him and steps forward. He stops suddenly, whirls around, and halts before me. He grips my cheeks tightly, possessively, and guides my lips to his.

It's a fleeting kiss, but it makes my insides light up like a thousand fireworks.

"Ohh. Everett and Thea kissing in a tree. K-I-S-S-I-N-G," Krystian sings, stopping only when Rafe hits him across the back of the head.

"Be safe," I tell Everett.

I know he's going first to scout for any threats. He always puts himself in harm's way to protect us. It's infuriating.

"Always." He flashes me a cocky grin and then spins towards the maze of mirrors. He disappears through the entrance seconds later.

"One. Two. Three. Four. Five," Zaid counts. He turns towards Krystian. "Your turn."

Krystian smirks and turns towards me, playfully tapping at his lips. "Kiss for good luck?"

I pretend to think about it, then I lean forward and plant a chaste kiss to his cheek. Before I can pull away, he grips the back of my neck and brings my lips to his.

"Naughty, naughty girl," he growls playfully,

nipping at my lower lip. Energy fires up my spine in a series of sporadic explosions.

What would he do if I deepen the kiss?

Bite him back?

Tug at his hair?

He pulls away, albeit reluctantly, and turns towards the others, effectively obliterating all of my naughty thoughts.

"See you on the other side." He salutes them then bounces up the steps.

The door opens, and he disappears inside of it.

Five more seconds pass.

"I don't understand why we have to do this," I murmur, shifting uncomfortably. "Is it because the door is a portal? Is the portal inside? Why the five-second rule? It's not like this is food that's been dropped on the ground, you know?"

I'm rambling. I know I am.

But I can't seem to stop.

Fear has twisted my stomach into tight knots.

"You'll be okay," Zaid reassures me, pulling me in for a hug. His arms wrap around me, safe and comforting. "Everett and Krystian will be waiting for you. Rafe and I won't be far behind."

I meet Rafe's gaze over Zaid's shoulder, and he nods solemnly, reiterating everything Zaid just told me.

"Okay." I reluctantly untangle myself from Zaid's embrace. "Let's do this."

Steeling my spine, I stalk up the stone steps and through the front door.

The first thing I notice is that Everett and Krystian are nowhere to be seen.

The next thing is that I'm not yet in the Underworld.

The air is thick with a chill that seems to wrap around my skin. Darkness stretches endlessly, only broken by the eerie glow of mirrors standing erect in the black void.

Each one reflects me, but not as I am. They're all twisted versions of myself. They stare back at me, their faces contorted into demented grins, their eyes wild and hollow. Their smile... It's wrong. It's like I'm looking at someone else, someone evil. The kind of innate evil that chills you to your core.

I turn away quickly, but everywhere I look, those reflections are there, mocking me with their monstrous expressions. Some smile wider, their eyes glinting with a sinister light, while others point, their fingers rigid and accusing. They all seem to be pointing in the same direction, to the far end of the maze.

I hesitate, my heart pounding in my chest, but I can't ignore them. They want me to go that way. I have no choice but to follow.

I walk, my footsteps deafeningly loud, and with each step, the twisted reflections grin wider, their eyes burning with an unsettling anger.

The mirrors around me start to distort even more, their edges bending and flickering like broken television screens.

I blindly move through the maze, following the direction of their fingers. Left, right, left, right, right, left. At one point, I accidentally brush against one of the mirrors, and a sharp, icy sensation crawls up my arm. I flinch automatically, backing away from the reflection that is now laughing uproariously.

Finally, after what feels like hours, I reach the end.

There's a stand but no mirror, just an empty frame.

My breath catches.

Something pulls at my insides, a gut-wrenching sensation.

In the middle of the frame is a void, a black hole, so deep and fathomless it looks like the fabric of reality itself has been torn open. It's so dark that I can't see anything beyond it.

A part of me screams to turn back, to find another way, but I know that this is where I'm supposed to go.

The portal to the Underworld.

Beyond it, Krystian and Everett are waiting for me.

This maze of mirrors is obviously some type of test.

It wouldn't surprise me if Athena herself designed it, given her penchant for mazes.

I take a step forward, and then another, until I'm standing in front of it. My mind is screaming at me to stop and turn away, but my feet move of their own accord.

And before I can even suck in a full breath, I'm falling into the darkness.

CHAPTER THIRTY-FIVE

ZAID

Most people believe that wraiths are synonymous with spirits. Ghosts. Poltergeists. That's a common misconception that started centuries earlier, before the humans learned the truth of the supernatural's existence.

But we're not dead, despite popular belief. I think the legend stemmed from the way we can make our bodies incorporeal and shadowy.

I've never stepped foot in the Underworld before.

I hope I never will again—at least, not for a few hundred more years.

It's beautiful—but in the way a storm on the horizon is beautiful, or a field of poppies grown from spilled blood. The sky above is a dome of smoldering onyx, speckled with dim, unmoving stars. The ground shimmers faintly, veined with lines of silver and ghost light, and pale flowers bloom from cracks in the stone—lilies that release no scent, but turn ever so slightly to follow our steps.

The other three are already there when I step through the portal, Everett and Krystian standing protectively around Thea.

A second later, a rift opens in the middle of the air, and Rafe steps through, looking entirely unbothered by the horror show he no doubt witnessed in the Hall of Mirrors. Then again, nothing seems to ruffle the psychotic blood fae.

Excluding Thea, of course.

"Who knew the Underworld would be so cold?" Thea absently rubs at her bare arms, her gaze flicking in both directions rapidly.

Before I can remove my sweatshirt, Everett does so, passing it her way. She takes it gratefully and puts it on, the material dwarfing her much smaller frame.

"You look fucking adorable," Krystian says, poking her nose.

She swats him away irritatedly.

"I'm not adorable. I'm a terrifying menace," she counters, her lips puckering.

"See?" Krystian turns towards us, jabbing his thumb in her direction. "Adorable."

"Where to next?" Rafe asks darkly, a blade already extended and clutched tightly in his hand.

I point. "There."

Before us, the River Styx coils like a black serpent, its waters glowing with a blueish gleam. A rickety wooden boat rocks gently at the bank, waiting, its master cloaked in silence, his eyes unreadable beneath his hood.

Charon. The ferryman for the dead.

Trepidation crawls up my spine, and my tongue turns to cotton in my mouth.

"We need to pay the ferryman's toll," I whisper to the others as we regard the lone figure.

I can't distinguish any of his features—not with his hood casting shadows over his face—but he has a slightly hunched back. The hand holding the lantern is pale and covered in wrinkles.

"What is his toll?" Everett folds his arms over his chest.

"And where are all the other souls? Shouldn't there be, like, a line?" Thea queries, her eyes darting in all directions.

I can't help but agree with her. The silence here is...eerie. Unnatural. It makes my senses heighten and the hairs on the back of my neck stand on end.

Is it possible that Thea has reaped so many souls

that the Underworld has no new arrivals? No...that can't be true. She hasn't reaped a soul—excluding the oracle—in days. There should be hundreds of thousands here.

"Stay close," I warn the others, taking the lead.

Everett may be in charge of all things physical, but I know where my talents lie. Bartering? Making deals? That's my domain.

As we approach the boat, Charon turns towards us, his eyes glowing an eerie shade of purple beneath his hood.

"You must pay the toll for admittance." His voice is a deep, booming baritone, surprisingly youthful considering his frail appearance.

Charon considers us. His unnerving gaze jumps from face to face, lingering on Thea for a longer moment than necessary.

"One memory," he decides on at last.

"No," Rafe snarls.

"Absolutely fucking not!" exclaims Krystian.

"You may choose the memory," Charon continues, ignoring my brothers' outbursts. "But it must be important to you. The River will know if you lie."

An important memory?

I swallow down the nail that got hammered down my throat.

I have an entire childhood of memories, and more from my time at the compound training—though those are few and far between, due to the deep sleep I was put in. The most important memories, however? The ones that took place over the last couple of days. I refuse to give any of those up.

"All right," I agree for the group, ignoring the withering glares the guys throw my way.

Only Thea appears unperturbed, her hands fiddling with the bottom of Everett's hoodie.

"I'm not doing it," Rafe snaps.

"You are," I counter easily. "For Thea, you are."

I level him with a serious look, reminding him of everything we have at stake. Namely, her.

"You don't have to," Thea cuts in quickly. "I can go on my own."

"Not fucking happening," Everett snaps, scowling.

"It doesn't have to be a current memory or even the most important one," I tell the others. "Think of something from your past. A dinner with your family that made you feel safe. One of the times we played a board game during training."

"The memory doesn't have to be happy either," Thea points out, her voice uncharacteristically subdued. "Sometimes the most important memories can be ones you want to forget."

I wonder if she's thinking of something in particular, and the thought causes my breath to hitch.

The guys all exchange solemn looks and then step forward.

"Perfect," Charon says.

I can't see his face, but I have the distinct impression he's smiling beneath his hood.

He turns to me with a wrinkled finger extended. "Think of a memory, but be very, very careful. Whatever you think of is what I'll steal."

I nod to show him I understand and tune out the rest of the world. In my head, I envision our first battle after we awoke from our comatose states. The first man I ever killed.

Charon places his finger against my forehead, and his eyes glow with a strange, preternatural light, the color luminescent in the monochromatic world. He slowly pulls his finger away, and a tiny sliver of light follows, resembling a worm on a hook. He tosses the light into the River, where it disappears.

And I have no idea what I just lost.

"The River feeds on the memories of the lost," Charon says, turning to Thea. "Now it's your turn, darling."

I nearly lose my shit when he touches Thea—and I'm considered the level-headed one. Rafe grips his blade so tightly that his knuckles turn white, and Everett continually growls. Krystian merely narrows his eyes at the spot Charon touches our reaper, as if he's mentally obliterating the finger in his mind.

Then, one by one, Charon repeats the process for the rest of us.

"Five memories. Five tolls. You may enter the boat." Charon steps back to allow us to board, which we do so.

The tiny boat rocks and sways at our combined weight but holds.

Thea sits down, and I immediately claim the spot beside her, tingles spreading through me where our bodies meet.

We don't say a word as Charon aims the lantern straight ahead, the simple movement somehow propelling the boat forward.

At first, it's quiet. Unnaturally so.

Then ghastly, guttural moans slice through the air.

"What the fuck?" Thea whispers, peering over the edge.

I follow the direction of her gaze and go still.

Within the River's murky depths, countless souls writhe in agony—half seen, half formed, their translucent faces twisted in eternal torment.

They reach upward with skeletal hands, their voices a chorus of anguish, rising in shrill, wordless screams that echo through the cavernous gloom. Their cries for help are lost in the endless churning of the river, swallowed by the current that offers no mercy and no escape. Each soul is a fragment of a life once lived, now condemned to drift in the cold, slow-moving waters of oblivion.

"Is this what happens to a soul once they die?" Thea whispers in horror.

I shake my head wordlessly, struggling to speak. "No," I say at last. "Only souls too terrified to face Hades and receive judgment. Over time, the souls become...trapped."

"Some prefer this over being sentenced to Tartarus," Krystian adds from in front of us, swiveling on his bench.

"Tartarus?" Thea asks.

It's sometimes easy to forget how little she knows of this world.

"Over there." I point to the right of us.

From a distant ridge, the pit of Tartarus yawns like a wound in the skin of the world. The edges are black and jagged, seared as though fire has licked them for centuries without rest. Foul vapors drift up in slow, curling tendrils, each one carrying whispers no ear should catch—too soft to understand, yet heavy with malice. A faint red glow pulses deep within, not like firelight but like the heartbeat of something slumbering and hateful.

Even from afar, the air tastes of ash and iron, thick with despair.

And the screams...

God, the screams...

They'll haunt me, even knowing the majority of the people trapped inside of it deserve their fate.

"It's an eternity of torture and suffering," Everett deadpans, his gaze fixed straight ahead.

"Probably where I'm going to go when I die," Rafe adds casually.

Thea whirls on him. "Don't fucking say that."

"But isn't it the truth, little bird? I did some fucked-up things over the years." He shrugs one shoulder, exuding nonchalance.

Thea's fists clench, and her face turns red. "You did those things to people who deserve it—just like the souls in the pit. You deserve nothing but good things, Rafe, and if you ever say shit like that again, I'll...I'll..."

She can't seem to come up with a scary enough threat.

"You'll what?" Rafe's lips twitch, even as his eyes glimmer with something soft.

"You don't want to find out," she says at last, huffing.

And I have a feeling that's the truth. Thea can be terrifying when she wants to be.

The boat glides through the water for a few more minutes, the pit disappearing behind us.

"You see over there?" I point to the left of Thea. "That's the Asphodel Meadow."

Vast fields stretch before us, the grass whispering as if breathing. Souls drift through, gray and flickering like candlelight in the wind, their faces calm and vacant.

"This is where all the unremarkable, ordinary souls go," Krystian chirps. Then, because he can't help himself, he tacks on, "Like Everett."

"Fuck off." The shifter flips him off.

"It's said that the souls here drift in a mindless state, with no memories of their human life and unable to create ones in their afterlife," I add.

The five of us all turn to stare at the millions and millions of souls spreading as far as the eye can see. They're all so close together, they practically collide, though not one expression shifts, caught in a perpetual indifference.

"If this is what the afterlife holds, maybe it's a blessing that those souls are trapped in the dagger," Thea says, keeping her voice soft so Charon won't overhear—though the ferryman seems completely oblivious to any of our conversations, his gaze intent on some unseen destination ahead.

"You don't mean that," I tell her.

"Their choices are either torture trapped in the River, torture in the pit, or torture as a zombie," she says seriously.

"And going insane is better?" I query—not judging her but genuinely trying to understand her thought process.

"No. Yes. Fuck, I don't know." She throws her hands up in the air. "Isn't there somewhere nice in the Underworld? Paradise?"

"Elysium," Rafe answers.

"It's said to be located behind Hades's palace. Only the best souls are allowed access, though," I add, eager, as always, to show off my extensive knowledge.

"The gods are seriously gatekeeping the afterlife?" Thea asks, incredulous. "That's so wrong. Let me guess —only those who worship them are allowed entry, right? It doesn't matter how good of a person you are, only how much money you spend to please the gods."

Rafe's lips twitch. "Touché."

Everett suddenly goes still, his gaze fixed straight ahead. "We're here."

Towering before us is the palace of Hades, carved into the very bones of the world. It shimmers with obsidian and gold, its spires like teeth, its gates currently closed. The air grows colder the closer we get, but it isn't the cold of wind or winter—it's the cold of permanence. The cold of endings.

There are gardens here, impossibly lush—strange trees heavy with jeweled fruit, vines that move while no wind stirs, flowers that open to reveal eyes at their center. I always heard that Hades's wife, Persephone, had a green thumb. She somehow demoted the Underworld from terrifying to approachable.

"Krystian will cast another glamour on you to hide you from Cerberus," Everett instructs, easily taking over the leadership role now that a battle is approaching. "I'll talk to him first. Only engage if we have no other choice."

He directs the last statement at me, Krystian, and Rafe.

We nod. Well, Krystian and I nod. Rafe simply slices his palm in preparation.

"We have arrived," Charon booms, the boat slowing to a stop directly in front of Hades's palace, which is half obscured by towering gates.

Charon stands perfectly immobile, a statue made of flesh, as the five of us exit the boat. Only when the last of us steps foot on land does the ferryman steer the boat away, disappearing into the gloom.

"Let's do this," Everett says gravely, stalking forward.

Directly towards the beast guarding Hades's palace.

Cerberus stands sentinel at the edge of shadows, a

hulking mass of muscle and malice coiled tight with purpose. Three heads rise from his broad shoulders like dark monuments—each one a snarl of teeth and unnaturally glowing eyes. His growl rumbles like boulders grinding in a deep, forgotten chasm.

His middle head—alert, commanding—surveys his surroundings with cold intelligence. The left turns quickly, always watchful, nostrils flaring for the scent of trespassers. The right twitches erratically, jaws snapping as if there are phantoms only he can see surrounding him. Around his paws, the earth lies scorched and dead, as though life itself dares not take root near him.

A serpent coils in place of a tail, flicking its tongue in the air, its gaze just as piercing and cruel.

The gates of Hades's palace rise behind him, carved in bone and obsidian.

All three heads turn in our direction as we approach.

"Hello, Father," Everett greets coldly, and I know he hates using that name for the monster before him.

He hasn't been a father to Everett in a long time.

"Son," the middle head says.

Then, to my surprise, Cerberus's form ripples and distorts, his arms and legs shortening and his tail retreating into his body. His three heads merge into one, and he stands on human legs.

Where before I was staring at a three-headed monster, I'm now looking at a man who looks eerily similar to Everett. Same light-brown hair. Same sharp jawline. Same hazel eyes.

The man smiles coldly. "I see you brought your team. And..." He trains his gaze with unerring accuracy on Thea, who should be invisible thanks to Krystian's glamour. "I see you brought a friend." His lips lift even farther. "Did you really think your tricks would work down here? All powers of the living are dampened in the Underworld. You know that, Everett."

He chuckles, but the noise is a cold, malevolent sound. "So tell me, son. Why are you here? And why are you trying to hide this pretty reaper from me?"

CHAPTER THIRTY-SIX

THEA

"I don't know what you're talking about," Everett says, shifting slightly so he's blocking me from view.

Cerberus laughs, but the sound is devoid of any humor. "Don't play with me, boy." He bares his teeth and takes a step closer. "Right now, I'm merely amused. But my amusement can morph into anger very, very quickly. You don't want to see me lose my temper."

"Guys, it's okay," I whisper.

Rafe and Krystian both whirl to glare at me, but I ignore them and step around Everett. I don't feel any different, but I can tell the glamour has been lowered when Cerberus's bright, penetrating eyes lock onto mine. He arches an eyebrow.

"You're a reaper," he says simply.

Captain Obvious over here.

"Yes, we've established as much," I say, wringing my hands together as nerves tangle in my belly.

It's not simply because this man is intimidating—though that certainly plays a part in it.

It's because this is Everett's dad, who never thought Everett was good enough.

Righteous indignation fills me at just the thought.

How could he possibly think that? Isn't he aware that Everett grew to be one of the most protective men I know? One of the best?

Cerberus begins to circle me, his hands clasped behind his back and his chin lifted haughtily in the air. He practically exudes arrogance, which isn't all that different from Everett, now that I think about it. But Everett has every right to be cocky, while Cerberus... doesn't. He's nothing but a damn watchdog whose entire existence revolves around Hades.

"But you're not any reaper who's currently active," Cerberus continues, his shrewd eyes narrowed. He returns to his spot in front of me. "You must meet with Hades at once."

"No way in hell," Rafe growls, moving to stand beside me.

Cerberus ignores him and extends a hand towards me. "Come, darling. Hades needs to know—"

He's shoved aside by a snarling, half-rabid Everett.

"Don't fucking touch her," the shifter hisses, his eyes glinting with a strange, primordial energy.

Cerberus growls. "Boy…"

"I'm not a fucking boy."

And then Everett shifts.

Oh my god.

He's just as big and terrifying as his father—a three-headed beast, though Everett's fur is a dark shade of blue streaked with white and gray.

I stand frozen, my feet glued to the ground and my breath caught in my throat. It feels like the world is closing in on me, the air thick with anger and fear.

Everett is going to fight his father.

For me.

Fuck.

"Everett!" I scream, taking an automatic step forward—quite stupidly, I might add.

I know it'll be a horrible idea to get between the two of them, though Cerberus has yet to shift.

Rafe and Zaid each grab one of my arms and tug me back, while Krystian keeps his arrow locked on Cerberus's side, though he doesn't pull back the string. I don't know if it's because he's afraid of what his arrows will do in the Underworld or if he's terrified of accidentally killing Hades's right-hand man.

"I won't let you take her." Everett's voice is a low growl, barely recognizable as his.

He's practically vibrating with fury. I know this rage—it's familiar to me—but now it's twisted and demented, honed from years of suppressed anger. This isn't just about me. This is about him—him and his father.

Cerberus doesn't hesitate. He shifts too, his hulking form rising up like a living shadow, his fur thick and dark, and his eyes glowing with an ancient malice. Everett's and his father's eyes are the same...but they're not. One is filled with a protective kind of rage; the other with something far darker.

The ground trembles beneath their combined weight as they circle each other, snarling and snapping.

"You're a fool, Everett," Cerberus growls, his layered voice seeming to vibrate in my chest. "You always have been, but I assumed your training over the years would've changed you."

Everett growls fiercely and stalks closer, his huge paws kicking up black rock and sooty dirt. "Fuck you."

"She's a reaper, son. She belongs to death, not to you."

The words hit me like a slap, sending a wave of cold dread through me.

She belongs to death, not to you.

Belongs to death.

Oh...hell no. I belong to no one and nothing. Not

ever again. Cerberus can take his assumptions and shove them right up his ass where they belong.

Everett lunges at Cerberus, snapping all three of his jaws, but Cerberus sidesteps easily. That doesn't stop Everett, though, who pounces on his back with another guttural roar. They roll onto the ground, and I can't tell who's winning. The sound of their teeth grinding against each other is sickening, the kind of noise that makes my skin crawl.

My heart hammers in my chest, terror twisting my gut as I watch them fight.

Please, Everett. Please.

You don't want to do this.

You don't want to hurt your father.

"We need to get Thea the fuck out of here," Krystian says, his eyes flicking in all directions rapidly.

"How?" Zaid demands. "There's no boat."

"Then we fucking swim!"

"And have the souls of the dead pull her deep into the River's depth?" Zaid asks scathingly, frustration evident in his taut posture. He rakes a hand through his hair. "Fuck." He pauses like an idea has occurred to him and then turns towards Rafe, who's scanning our surroundings with a clinical detachment. "Rafe, can you portal us out of here?"

Rafe's lips thin as he answers simply, "No."

As the guys continue to discuss their options, I turn

my attention back to Everett and his father, still engaged in a fierce battle.

Blood stains Everett's side, but I don't know if it's from him or Cerberus. That disgusting red liquid speckles them both, and the latter appears to be missing an eye from its left head.

My heart aches at the sight of my shifter, at the way he's fighting—fighting his own father. His father, who should've been protecting and supporting him instead of constantly putting him down. Who should've offered to help his son instead of trying to take me away.

I don't know what hurts more—the fact that I'm powerless to stop them, or the terrifying realization that this is all because of me. Maybe not entirely, but I'm certainly the catalyst.

The fight continues, blood mixing with dirt and dust as their two forms collide. All I can do is stand here, desperation arcing through my veins and fear coiling in my belly like a nest of venomous snakes.

Shadows converge in front of me, and Zaid immediately tugs me behind him, protecting me with his body. Rafe and Krystian move on either side of me.

At first, I think that this is a wraith like Zaid or even a spirit. But as the darkness solidifies, and I sense the ancient power crackling through the air, I realize that this isn't just a normal supernatural.

It's a god.

Hades.

An olive complexion, made all the more striking against his rich, ebony hair. Cold, unnerving gray eyes. A dark scowl. An aura of danger.

Before any of us can even blink, Hades's hand thrusts out and wraps around my throat. His hold isn't tight—I can still breathe—but it's enough to make my guys stop moving. Hell, I'm not even sure they're breathing.

"Stop fighting, young Everett, or I'll snap the reaper's neck." Hades's voice is a dark, insidious promise.

I can't see much with Hades in front of me, consuming my vision, but the sound of growls and cries ceases. When Hades finally removes his hand from my throat and steps aside, I see Everett on his belly with Cerberus looming over him, though I know my proud shifter was winning only a few minutes earlier. Yet he doesn't hesitate now to bare his throat, to surrender.

For me.

"I'm sorry," I mouth as all three of Everett's heads turn to stare at me intently, searching me for injuries.

Hades once again reclaims my vision, his head tilted to the side in contemplation. I feel like a butterfly pinned between two glass slides and positioned beneath a microscope. His gaze is assessing, curious, confused.

He snaps his fingers in the air, and creatures of all shapes and sizes materialize seemingly out of thin air. I spot a minotaur—seriously, another one?—with a furry head and strong legs, carrying an ax the size of my body. Beside him stands a creature that appears to be a cross between a lion and an eagle. Another creature is nothing but a skeleton bedecked in heavy armor.

"Guards," Hades says, his gaze never leaving mine. "Take our...*guests* to the throne room. I need to have a word with them."

CHAPTER THIRTY-SEVEN

THEA

Hades's palace looms like a monument to the Underworld itself—massive, unyielding, and carved from the very bones of the earth. The walls are a tapestry of black stone, polished to a smooth sheen, and etched with intricate, swirling patterns—images of death, decay, and forgotten souls. They're so detailed they seem to pulse with life.

As we maneuver through the bustling halls, I can't help but note the lack of warmth. Only a pervasive chill that sinks deep into my bones, as though the very air is touched by the cold embrace of the dead.

The floor beneath me is smooth, like glass, but with veins of gold running through it, twisting like rivers of frozen ichor. It reflects the dim, flickering light that emanates from the torches lining the hallway and the sconces embedded in the walls.

The ceiling above is an endless, starless black—an abyss that feels too vast for anyone to ever truly comprehend. It's dotted with faint, shifting points of light, but the lights seem very far away. Distant. Unreachable.

Like the souls trapped in the Underworld itself.

At times, I think I see something move in the shadows, but I dare not look too closely.

"In here," the minotaur snaps in a gruff voice, pushing my shoulder.

Everett growls, Krystian shouts my name, and Zaid asks if I'm okay. Rafe remains quiet—suspiciously so—and when I glance at him over my shoulder, his gaze is fixed on the minotaur, his eyes flaring with a deadly promise.

I try to give him a smile, but the minotaur shoves me again, and my smile shifts into a grimace.

Fuck. Ow.

We finally enter what appears to be a throne room, and I can't help but gawk, momentarily forgetting the shit show we've found ourselves starring in.

"Woah."

It's vast, more of an arena than a room, with ornate pillars spread an equal distance apart along the walls. The throne itself is an enormous, unsettling work of beauty. The seat appears as if it were crafted from a stone pulled from the depths of the River Styx—black, glimmering, and oddly liquid in its form.

The back of the throne arches up impossibly high, crowned with jagged spires that resemble the peaks of a mountain lost in eternal darkness. Bones and skulls surround the throne, though I'm not sure if they're merely for cosmetic sake or if there's a reason for their intricate arrangement. Vines of withered, blackened roses crawl up the sides, their petals frozen in perpetual decay.

Hades sits on his throne, his presence dominating the room. His form is cloaked in shadows—the flickering light never fully illuminating him—yet his molten gray eyes seem to pierce through the dark like the steel of two swords. The power he radiates is suffocating, a constant, pressing force that makes it impossible to look away.

"Kneel," he instructs, and the minotaur shoves on my shoulders, forcing me to my knees.

On either side of me, my guys are forced down as well.

Hades watches us calmly from his seat on the throne, his long fingers tapping against his armrest that I'm pretty sure is actually a femur bone.

"I could ask you five why you thought it would be a good idea to sneak into my realm," Hades begins, his tone almost conversational despite the sharpness in his eyes. "Or why you decided to attack my loyal guard."

This is directed at Everett, who doesn't look the least bit repentant. Behind him, Cerberus growls and slams a hand down on Everett's shoulder, hard enough that Everett grimaces.

"But I have a far more important question to ask..." Hades's head swivels in my direction. "How are you alive?"

Out of everything I expected him to say, it wasn't that.

I blink at him, certain I heard him wrong, but Hades's impassive gaze doesn't waver. I can't help but compare him to...Rafe.

And that's fucking terrifying.

Rafe may be a psychopath, but I know he's on my side, always.

Hades?

A shiver of fear ripples down my spine.

"I-I don't know what you mean," I say, frowning.

Hades's fingers repeatedly tap against the armrests of his throne. "How." Tap. "Are you." Tap, tap. "Alive?" Tap.

Everett snarls. "I won't let you fucking hurt her."

"We won't let you lock her away again," tacks on Krystian, baring his teeth.

Hades blinks—the only outward sign of his confusion. "Excuse me?"

"We know what you did," Krystian presses on, ignoring Zaid's warning look. "We know that you trapped her and forced her to reap souls for you and—"

"Enough." Hades doesn't yell the word, but he doesn't need to. He could whisper it, and the entire world would drop to their knees in reverence.

Hades waits until the throne room is utterly silent before he speaks again. "I have no idea what you're talking about, elf." His upper lip curls away from his teeth. "All I know is that this reaper here disappeared over four hundred years ago. She was presumed dead."

"Thea," I interrupt, my heart hammering in my chest.

Hades arches a brow, seemingly stunned by my audacity to speak directly to him.

Well, fuck him. I refuse to be known as "this reaper" or "that reaper."

"Excuse me?"

"My name is Thea," I say, hefting my chin in the air and emulating a confidence I don't truly feel.

"Thea." His mouth twists downwards in what appears to be distaste, his hands clenching on the armrests of the chair. "How...cute."

He uses that term as if it's synonymous with disgusting—which for him, it probably is.

"Did you know me? Before I went missing, I mean?" I venture tentatively, unable to hold his gaze for longer than a second or two at a time.

He really is one of the most powerful gods, isn't he? I didn't feel this way around Athena or Aphrodite. I wasn't drowning in their power.

"Of course I did." His fingers resume their impatient tapping. "I...created you, after all."

"You created me?" I ask, blinking.

Hades scoffs. "Of course I did. I created every reaper that has walked this earth, every one that currently does, and I'll continue to create them long after you expire."

A muscle in his jaw twitches, and he turns away momentarily, seemingly lost in thought.

When he returns his attention to me, the coldness in his gaze siphons the breath from my lungs. "Now tell me...where were you?"

"As if you don't know," Krystian snaps, seemingly unable to help himself.

That big mouth is going to get him killed one of these days.

Hades slowly flicks his eyes in Krystian's direction. "If you accuse me of harming the reaper one more time, I will skin you alive," he threatens.

Krystian bares his teeth but wisely keeps quiet.

Thank fuck. I really, really don't think I'll be

capable of killing a god—but if he harms one of my guys, I'll certainly try.

"What do you remember before you got...taken?" Hades asks, studying me intently.

"Nothing," I confess.

My very first memory was waking up in that room, with the inherent knowledge that my one job in life was to reap souls. It was never strange to me that I arrived with the ability to read, write, and communicate. I just thought those were...perks of the job, so to speak.

"What about you four?" Hades asks, swiveling his head to address my guys.

"What?" Zaid's frown deepens.

"What do you mean?" Everett demands.

Hades waves a hand flippantly in the air, appearing bored with this entire conversation, his eyes languorous and his lips firm.

"I take it that means you four remember nothing," he says, reclining in his throne.

"They weren't a part of my life until a few days ago," I tell Hades, wondering if I should explain the entire situation to him.

It's not as if I trust him, but at the same time...I don't believe he was behind my disappearance. He's difficult to read, but I swear that was genuine surprise in his eyes when we confronted him. And for a man as ancient and icy as Hades to be surprised, even for a second...

He didn't know about me.

"So none of you remember," Hades murmurs, sounding confused.

He tilts his head to the side, a strand of obsidian hair catching in the torchlight and giving it blue undertones.

"Umm...?" I simply stare at him, silently urging him to continue.

Hades sighs heavily. "Hundreds of years ago, the five of you grew up together. Trained together. You, my dear reaper, were the fifth and final member of their team."

CHAPTER THIRTY-EIGHT

THEA

I can't seem to wrap my head around what I just heard. Maybe the minotaur pushed me a little too hard and I hit my head. Could I be concussed? Perhaps the "bandage" Athena placed on me ripped and I'm hallucinating again. Hearing things.

Because there's no way in hell Hades is telling me I was once a member of an elite team of supernatural warriors.

That would mean I trained with them. Knew them. Cared for them. Maybe even...

I swallow, though it's immensely difficult to do with the knot in my throat.

"How is that possible?" Krystian barks.

"We would've remembered her," adds Zaid, though his expression is bleak.

"No," Rafe simply says, that one word a low, guttural growl.

But Everett, surprisingly, is quiet. There's a tiny crease between the shifter's brows.

"We don't remember a lot of things from our training," he says softly, his eyes narrowing. "What if one of the memories we lost...was of her?"

"No." Zaid shakes his head adamantly. "I have memories of the four of us training. Doing drills. Playing card games. Thea doesn't make an appearance once."

"Unless someone fucked with our memory of her. For all we know, she could've been with us during all of those events, and we just don't remember," Everett points out.

"Fuck." Krystian's face drains of color, his skin turning almost as white as his hair.

I want to demand answers, ask if there's a way to receive missing memories, but my tongue feels like a huge, wet cotton ball in my mouth. I can't speak. I'm paralyzed, a plethora of emotions I can't name holding me hostage.

"I'll give you some time to...digest this information," Hades says, his lips firming. "But tomorrow, I will receive answers."

He levels a cold, penetrating glare in my direction. I would've assumed that the God of the Underworld would have red eyes, like hell fire, or black, like the rocks in the River Styx. The molten silver is somehow more unnerving than anything I've seen. They're so... simplistic. Normal, almost.

Which makes the coldness emanating from them exponentially more terrifying.

"Guards!" Hades snaps his fingers together. "Show them to their rooms for the night." To us, he says, "We'll reconvene in the morning. And you *will* tell me the truth."

It's a threat and a warning combined. If we choose to disobey him...

Well...

I imagine we won't be walking out of this palace alive.

The guys still seem stunned, so I agree for all of us, nodding sharply.

Hades stands and walks gracefully away, moving towards a door directly behind his throne. Before he can reach it, however, it opens, and a petite woman steps through.

While Hades appears as if he's in his mid-thirties, early forties, this newcomer can't be older than twenty-five. Despite her youthful appearance, there's an ancientness in her forest-green gaze, a primitive intensity.

Her rosy cheeks are flushed—almost as if she just

ran a mile to get here—and her blonde curls cascade loosely around her shoulders, the top strands braided into an intricate crown that wraps around her head. She wears a violet dress that hugs her curves, flaring at the waist in a poof of tulle. She's beautiful and elegant and staring at the five of us intently.

I narrow my eyes at her.

If this bitch even thinks of making a move on my men...

"Hades." Her voice is soft. Sweet. Lyrical.

She places a hand on his arm to capture his attention.

Am I mistaken, or do his features soften when he stares down at her? Somehow, that's even more terrifying to behold.

"Yes, my beloved." He lifts a hand to rub the backs of his fingers against her cheek in the softest of grazes.

"Let me show our...guests to their rooms," she says, her voice a near plea. She places her hand over his. "Please."

Hades hesitates, his eyes searching hers intensely, before he concedes with a nod and a sigh. "All right. You know I can't resist you."

She beams and pushes up on her tiptoes to kiss his lips. "Thank you, thank you, thank you."

Ah. This must be Persephone, Hades's wife.

What did I hear about her?

That Hades fell in love with her and kidnapped her from her mother, Demeter. Demeter's grief at losing her daughter is what brought upon the four seasons. Persephone lives with Hades in the Underworld but is able to visit her mother every few months.

The little green monster that always makes an appearance when these beautiful, sexy, flawless goddesses are around my men is appeased, albeit slightly. But if this bitch tries anything...

"Hello! Welcome!" Persephone hurries towards us, her smile widening and tears glittering in her eyes.

I awkwardly wave. "Um. Hello. I'm Thea, and—"

She pulls me into her arms, smelling of orchids and freshly cut grass.

I hold perfectly still, my hands loose by my sides, and she sniffles then pulls away, holding me at arm's length. Her verdant gaze sweeps over me, more tears welling.

"Hi! It's so nice to...meet you!" Persephone gushes.

"Likewise?" It comes out as a question.

"Come, come. Let me show you to the guest rooms." She links her arm with mine and pulls me out of the room with single-minded determination.

I glance helplessly at the guys as we pass them, wordlessly asking, *"What the fuck?"*

They don't have a response for me as they trail along behind us, all seemingly lost in thought. Well, except for Rafe. The psychotic bastard is focused on where Persephone's arm is linked with mine, his eyes narrowing ever so slightly.

Over my shoulder, I mouth, *"Behave."*

He frowns and mouths back, *"Make me."*

Umm...yes please. Especially if it involves ropes again.

I turn to face forward as Persephone rattles off random facts about the creation of Hades's castle and her relationship with him. She seems...nervous. Or maybe she doesn't know how to talk to a living being. My guess is the latter. Spending so much time down here, with only men like Hades and Cerberus for company, would make any person insane.

I tune her out when she starts discussing the difference between thread counts and instead think through Hades's shocking revelation.

I...was once a member of the guys' team.

I knew them.

What was life for us like back then? Were we friends? Lovers? Did I get along with all of them? Did Everett push every single button I possess? Did Krystian continue to struggle with his identity? Was Zaid still shy and sweet, always knowing what I needed before I did? Was Rafe psychotic even back then?

How different would my life—my immortality—be if I'd stayed there?

Sadness wraps around me like a weighted blanket, impossibly heavy.

Whoever is behind this stole not only my future away but the guys' futures too.

"We need to speak to Ares," Krystian is saying behind me, his tone uncharacteristically harsh.

"You don't think he's behind this, do you?" Zaid asks.

"If he knew about Thea, why wouldn't he tell us about her?" Everett demands.

"Maybe he got his memories erased too?" Zaid suggests, though he doesn't sound certain.

"He wasn't put to sleep like the rest of us," Krystian points out.

"Unless we lost our memories of Thea before we were put to sleep..." Rafe suggests, his tone low and dangerous.

"Here we are!" Persephone trills, either oblivious to our conversation or choosing to ignore it. She stops between two doors. "I figured you guys would want to remain close together. There's a door inside that connects the two rooms as well."

She claps her hands together and rocks back on her heels. I wait for her to say more or retreat, but she simply stands there, watching us with wide, guileless eyes.

The lights are on, but there's no one home.

Definitely insane.

"Thank you, Persephone," I tell her gently.

How do I tell a goddess—Hades's wife, to be exact—to fuck off? Kindly, of course. To *kindly* fuck off.

"Do you need anything?" She keeps her gaze trained on me. "Pillows? More blankets? Towels?"

"We're good," Everett grunts, shoving around her to enter the door on her right.

The others follow, though Zaid lingers behind, unwilling to leave me alone with her. We don't trust anyone at the moment.

"Oh." Persephone's face falls slightly. "It's just... It's just been so long since I've been around a living person, you know? But... But I'll leave you to it. Please let me know if you need anything. The guards will come to collect you right away in the morning, so be prepared." She stares at me again, her eyes strangely beseeching, but when I don't say anything to that, she blows out a breath. "Well, I suppose I'll see you later."

She seems reluctant to leave, her feet dragging against the carpeted floor. A forlorn sigh escapes her as she disappears around the corner.

I watch her go with a strange pinch in my heart.

"What's that look for?" Zaid asks softly, brushing his hand down my arm.

"I just feel bad for her," I confess. "She seems so... lonely." Then, in a quieter voice, I add, "I know what that feels like."

Zaid's expression creases in sympathy, and he wraps an arm around my waist, pulling me against him.

He presses his lips against my temple. "Not anymore, you don't. You will never be lonely again, Thea. Not if I have anything to say about it."

My heart warms at his proclamation, even as familiar tendrils of terror coil around my heart, squeezing it like barbed wire.

"But what if—" I start to ask, wanting to voice one of my deepest fears.

Zaid places a finger against my parted lips. "You. Will. Not. Be. Alone. Wherever you go, we will find you. Can you believe that? Can you believe *me?*"

I take in his beautiful face—pale skin, dark eyes, and midnight-colored hair—and find myself nodding.

Yes, I believe him.

How could I not, when he's staring at me like he'll pluck the stars from the sky if I asked him to?

And I realize, then, that all the guys would, in their own way.

Zaid would make a deal with Zeus, if that's what it took.

Krystian would shoot the stars down, refusing to leave my side.

Everett would threaten the gods. And if that didn't work, he would sneak up to the stars and steal them straight from the sky.

And Rafe? He would torture every god and goddess until they have no choice but to declare me Goddess of Stars. One star wouldn't be enough for my psychotic blood fae.

The knowledge of what they would do for me isn't just a revelation; it's a damn homecoming.

Is it possible to fall in love in the span of days? Maybe. Or maybe it's the emotions we felt for each other hundreds of years ago—the emotions that have been eradicated from existence—making an emergence, clawing their way out of the grave.

I...love these men.

At least, I think I do.

Lust bleeds through the longer I stare up at Zaid, taking in the smooth column of his neck. His high cheekbones. The sweep of hair across his forehead that doesn't seem to want to settle.

"Thea..." Zaid whispers, taking a step closer.

And then we're meeting in the middle in a flurry of tangled lips, gnashing teeth, and battling tongues.

"What the fuck are you two doing... Oh fuck,"

Everett says, but we ignore him as we burst through the door of the empty bedroom.

Zaid kicks it shut behind us, his lips still on mine, his hands roaming my body. His touch is fiercely possessive, burning my skin.

I gasp and whimper, arching my neck to grant him better access. He swipes his tongue across the skin there, a guttural, sexy moan building in the back of his throat.

"Fuck, Thea. I don't think you know how badly I want you. How badly I need you."

"Show me," I whisper, already reaching for my top and pulling it over my head.

We hungrily rip at each other's clothes and throw them on the ground behind us. I crash onto the bed, Zaid looming over me, his touch lighting my skin on fire. His hand trails down my stomach to find that sweet spot between my legs. I gasp against his lips as he curls one finger deep inside of me.

"Fuck, you're so wet already, sweetheart," he whispers, the words slightly muffled since his lips are still pressed to mine.

I kiss him ravenously, desperately, raking my fingers down his back.

When a second finger joins the first, I rip my lips away from his to gasp, pleasure coursing through me in liquid waves.

"Zaid…" I whimper.

"I know, sweetheart. I know," he soothes, continuing his relentless assault on my pussy.

He lowers his head to kiss my breast, his tongue flicking my aching nipple repeatedly.

Fissions of electricity ripple across my skin as I convulse around his fingers, screaming out his name—a benediction and a cry for mercy all at once.

"Fuck, Thea." Zaid continues to finger me through the aftershocks of my orgasm, his pupils dilated with lust.

"Zaid…" I whisper, gently grabbing his arm to pull his fingers away from my wet cunt.

He watches me in confusion, frown lines knitted between his eyes, and I feel a zing of excitement sizzle along my nerves.

Slowly, I move onto my knees and straddle his body.

"Let me make you feel good too," I whisper, kissing the hollow of his throat.

His right pec.

His left pec.

His toned stomach.

His inner thigh.

"Holy fuck." His cock jerks against his stomach, and I smirk at him before licking at the precum gathered on the tip.

I take my time with his cock, memorizing every inch of it with my tongue. The slit on the top. The vein on the right side. I lick every last inch of him as he moans and begs for more.

"Please, Thea. Please. Fuck." His hips gyrate upwards.

Fuck, I like it when he begs.

Really, really like it.

I wrap my hand around the thick girth of his cock and begin to stroke him as I suck on his balls. I have no idea what I'm doing, but he seems to like it, if his breathy moans and pleas for mercy are any indication.

"Thea, you need to stop, sweetheart. Fuck, you need to stop."

I slowly pull my mouth away from his dick, his steely shaft brushing against my cheek as I grin at him.

"Do you really want me to stop?" I ask, remembering Rafe's words from the other night.

"No, but...I won't be able to last much longer, and I want to fuck you. I need to. I haven't done this, and..."

He swallows convulsively, his hooded eyes trailing across my face with a worshipful reverence.

"You haven't...had sex?" I whisper, my heart thundering.

A blush stains my wraith's cheeks. "Maybe I did before I was put to sleep, but I don't remember it."

He gives me a pointed look, letting me know he

believes that we may have had sex hundreds of years ago.

The thought makes my stomach flutter and my heart pick up speed.

"But since I've been awake, I haven't... I haven't felt the need." The excitement in his eyes lightens the blue-gray to a cerulean color.

Beautiful.

Intoxicating.

Mine.

Zaid is truly a handsome man, though his looks are different from the others.

Krystian is traditionally beautiful, with perfect features and long, thick lashes.

Everett encompasses an unmerciful kind of beauty I've only ever seen in predators before. He's a lion waiting to pounce and tear through the unsuspecting zebra entering his domain.

Rafe is sexy in a rugged, dangerous type of way. One glance into his fathomless dark eyes would have you running and screaming in the opposite direction. However, a twisted part of you wants to know him, save him, banish the demons in his eyes.

Zaid, on the other hand, is softer than his counter-parts. Smaller too, though not by much. His features may appear unassuming at first glance, but then he smiles at you, and you wonder why you ever thought this man was ordinary.

Lust curls through my veins like flames at the knowledge that...at least subconsciously...he waited for me. I don't judge the other guys for their past, but it's nice to know that at least one of them doesn't have a body count a mile long—and I'm not talking about dead bodies.

"Say something," Zaid pleads. "Is it weird? Fuck, it's weird, isn't it? I know I shouldn't have—"

I shut him up with a kiss.

When I pull away, I'm smiling. "You waited for me."

"I did," he agrees, his hands moving to my hips. "Maybe I didn't consciously know about you, but a part of me realized that other women couldn't add up to the woman in my head. A woman I now realize is...you."

The warmth in his eyes is a blazing beacon that calls to my soul.

"I think... I think I love you," I confess in a rush, my heart damn near close to bursting.

Zaid's eyes light up, and a breathtaking smile overtakes his face. Beautiful. So fucking beautiful. "I think I love you too."

He flips us then, so I'm underneath him and the length of his body is overtop of mine. He uses one hand to grab the base of his cock and line it up with my entrance.

"Is this okay?" he asks hesitantly, his hand still wrapped around his throbbing dick.

"Fuck me, Zaid," I plead.

He bites down on his lower lip hard enough to draw blood as he pushes inside of me.

"Yes. Fuck, yes," he whispers, his cock twitching inside of me. But my sweet wraith cares more about my pleasure and comfort than his. Instead of moving his hips, he pauses, his fingers digging into my waist. "Is this okay?"

I nod again.

Zaid begins to move his hips—slowly at first, like he's gauging my reaction—and then faster. Harder. Each thrust hits that spot deep inside me that makes me see stars.

"Yes, Zaid. *Yes.*"

Zaid uses one hand to grab both of my wrists and pin them above my head, forcing my breasts into the air and closer to his face. He wastes no time licking and sucking at my nipples.

His pace increases, and dark spots speckle my vision as I feel my orgasm approach.

And when his free hand lowers between our bodies to strum my clit? I detonate.

I come with a scream, but Zaid doesn't let up,

continually flicking my clit to extend my orgasm and steal my breath away.

It isn't long until he comes as well, thrusting deep inside of me—so deep that my vision tinges red and gold—and roaring his release. He grabs my tit in a punishing grip, holding on for dear life.

He collapses on top of me, both of us breathing heavily, then shifts us so I'm nestled on his chest with his arm coiled around my waist.

For a moment, we lie in silence, and love for him coils through me. I absently trace patterns on his chest as I struggle to find my breath again.

"So...do you think the others know what we were up to?" I ask lightly.

His husky chuckle causes me to vibrate. "I think they may have an idea or two."

"And they didn't want to join in?" I ask, only halfway teasing. A quarter teasing.

Zaid freezes underneath me, and his gaze sharpens on my face. "Is that something you'd be interested in?"

I don't blush often, but right now, heat seeps into my cheeks and crawls down my neck.

"I mean, as you know from before, I wouldn't be opposed..."

I half expect the door connecting the two rooms to burst open and the men to file inside. After all, I know

Everett can hear just about everything we're saying with his enhanced hearing.

Then again, maybe he doesn't want his first time with me to be in a group. Maybe he's waiting until we're alone.

A flush spreads through me once more—but this time for an entirely different reason.

"It's something we can talk about," Zaid says, chuckling. He kisses my temple. "I don't think any of us would be opposed either."

"Have any of you...shared a girl before?" I ask, unsure if I actually want the answer to that question. "Besides yesterday, I mean."

"You already know I didn't," Zaid says, his hand smoothing up and down my arm. "And as for the others? I'm not sure, but I honestly don't think so. Actually, I'm ninety-nine percent positive they've never even considered it."

A thrill shoots through me.

Is it wrong that I feel pride at being the first one they would be willing to share? That I want to find all their past lovers, give them the middle finger, and scream, "Suck it," at the top of my lungs?

Zaid continues to hold me as I process that revelation.

"So..." Zaid begins.

"So?" I tilt my head to stare up at him.

"What are your thoughts on what Hades said? About you being the final member of our team?"

I anxiously lick my lips. "I...I don't know how I feel about it, to be honest. None of us have any memories of all this time we apparently had together. How can I miss what I don't remember? But at the same time, it pisses me the fuck off. Whoever is behind this hurt not only me, but also you guys. We could've had a life together, and it was just...stolen."

I take a deep breath, struggling to speak. "Then I wonder if this is all secretly a blessing in disguise. What if we hated each other before I went missing? What if we were only friends, or you guys had girl-friends, or I had a boyfriend, or—"

Zaid cuts off my ramblings with a heated, passionate kiss I feel all the way in the marrow of my bones, imprinted on my very soul.

"None of us have memories of that time," he begins, his voice raspy. "But I can promise you that all of us were in love with you. I know it, they know it, and I think you know it too. I refuse to believe there was ever a timeline we weren't all ardently devoted to you. We loved you then, we love you now, and we'll love you in the next life. Don't you feel it? We're... connected. Our souls are tethered together. It's why you were drawn to us in the first place—and I don't think it was to reap my soul. You're ours, Thea, and we're yours. Always."

The vehemence of his statement brings an unexpected lump to my throat and tears to my eyes. It's impossible to disagree with him when he's staring at me like that—like I own him, heart, body, and soul.

"Always," I agree, snuggling against him.

It's the only thing I can think to say.

Always.

Always.

Always.

CHAPTER THIRTY-NINE

KRYSTIAN

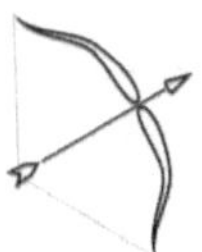

Something is different when I wake up the next morning.

I...remember.

I remember everything that happened the night before, when I was Krys.

Holy fuck.

That has never happened to me before.

I remember discussing the plan for today with Everett and Rafe, before all of us went silent, transfixed by the cries and moans drifting through the door. I remember stalking forward, placing my hand on the knob, and preparing to barge inside. But...something stopped me.

Zaid's whispered confession about this being his first time.

I remember the shame that filled me when I

thought about my own sordid past and the flings with girls I used and discarded. Then, I remember thinking —why not let Zaid have his moment?

It took considerable self-restraint, but I returned to the queen-sized bed and sat down stiffly, my cock feeling like granite in my pants.

Krys showed...restraint.

I showed restraint.

Fuck.

The other two guys are still sleeping—Everett awkwardly draped in one of the armchairs, his body too big for the minuscule piece of furniture. Rafe sleeps like a damn vampire in the bed beside mine, his body perfectly still and his hands folded on his chest.

I shakily run a hand through my hair, my thoughts whirling.

How is this possible? How do I remember everything that happened last night? How is it that Krys showed restraint when he lacks the ability to?

Unless...

I swallow the lump in my throat and pad on silent feet to the bathroom, slipping inside and closing the door behind me. I place my hands on the granite countertop and take a deep, shuddering breath.

I know the others have been claiming for years that Krys and I are the same, yet I haven't believed them. I always considered us two entirely separate entities—a Jekyll and Hyde case scenario.

But...

But they're right.

Thea is right.

Taking another deep breath, I finally lift my head and take in my reflection.

A gasp lodges in my throat.

I'm...me. But I also look different.

My eyes are darker, the cerulean blue appearing almost indigo in the bathroom light. And my hair... My hair is darker too, the white strands underscored with black streaks.

"What the fuck?" I whisper, bringing a trembling hand to my face.

Those are definitely my features. I can feel the pressure of my fingers against my jawline.

Is it possible that Thea was right about more than just Krys and me being the same? Have we finally...merged?

I catalogue myself, my emotions, wondering if I feel differently.

I still feel like me, but...more confident. There's a part of me that wants to march into Hades's throne room and demand answers. That same part wants to crawl into bed with Thea, part her creamy thighs, and lap at her slit until she's crying my name.

And since the first idea will get me killed...

I slip out of the bathroom and move towards the connecting door. Rafe and Everett are still asleep, which surprises me. Then again, we did have a stressful few days. I can't imagine either of them has slept more than a wink since Thea materialized in our lives. I wonder if they took comfort in the fact they could hear her—her breathy moans, her pleas for more, her ragged breaths.

My cock stirs to life, as it always does at just the thought of her.

I slip into the second bedroom and pause to admire my beautiful sleeping reaper. It's strange to watch her like this, unencumbered. With her lashes shut, she looks soft and vulnerable. Normally, there's a combative glint in her blue eyes that never fails to rile me up.

Zaid is curled around her, also naked, his hand cupping her perfect tit in his sleep.

Lucky bastard.

I move to her side of the bed and kneel before her, taking in the flawless perfection that is her face.

"Thea," I whisper, keeping my voice soft to not disturb Zaid. "Thea, love."

Her lashes flutter, confusion creasing her brow. She blinks repeatedly before her hooded eyes settle on me.

"Krys?" She blinks again, rubs at her face, and then frowns. "Krystian?"

I can't stop the small smile from unfurling on my lips.

Krys...

Krystian.

I suppose either will work.

"It's me, shortstack," I say, tenderly brushing a strand of golden hair behind her ear.

She gawks in surprise, moving to sit up. Zaid's hand falls on the bed with an audible thump.

I lick my lips as I admire her naked upper body. God, those tits... I could lick and suck on them for hours. I wonder what they would look like with my cock between them.

"You called me shortstack," she whispers, stunned.

I frown. "I...did." Where does that nickname come from? Is it...Krys's for her? "Are you okay with that?"

"Of course." She tenderly cups my cheek, and I allow my eyes to shut as I lean in to her touch. Warmth migrates from her palm and spreads through me like wildfire. "I love whatever name you call me." Her thumb absently brushes just underneath my right eye. "Your eyes are darker."

"They are," I concede easily.

She swallows. "And your hair..."

"Something happened last night," I confess, grabbing her wrist to pull her hand off my face. I absently begin to play with her fingers as I struggle to find the right words. "I...I remember what Krys did."

Her brows scrunch together. "This is the first time that's ever happened, right?"

I nod. "Right. But the last few days, I started thinking of Krys differently. Like he was a part of me, instead of someone else entirely. You were right, Thea. Of course you were right. Krys is me. He may be loud and obnoxious and pigheaded, but he wouldn't do anything I wouldn't do."

A wide, beatific smile spreads across her face, and I don't think I've ever seen anything more beautiful.

"I had a feeling for a while that Krys remembered everything you did during the day, that he accepted you. All you needed to do was accept him in return," she confesses, twisting our combined hands so she's the one playing with my fingers instead. A shiver runs through me at her feather-like touch. "Do you feel different?"

"Not overly," I say with a shrug. "Maybe a little more confident and daring."

"I'm... I'm happy for you, Krystian. Proud of you. I know you struggled with the two facets of your person-ality." A tiny blush heats her cheeks, and she lowers her head, focusing on our fingers.

"You helped me," I whisper, leaning towards her.

"I never would've gotten to this point without your encouragement."

Her brows lower. "I didn't do anything."

"You did everything," I assure her.

I kiss her before she can argue.

Thea melts against me instantly, her hands trailing up my arms to curl around my neck. Her bare breasts press against my shirt, and all I can think is that I want her. Again and again and again.

I want every piece of her, the good and the bad. The parts that she tries to hide and the parts she happily embraces. Her anger and jealousy. Her happiness and joy. Her sadness. And if she gives herself to me, I'll treasure every piece of her until the day I die.

We already lost so much damn time together. I refuse to waste even another second.

I pull away just enough to rasp out, "I wanted to wake you up with my tongue between your pretty thighs, lapping at your sweet pussy, but I need your permission first. Can I wake you up like that, love? With you shaking and panting and crying my name as I fucking devour you?"

Her chest heaves, lust darkening her eyes. "Yes... god, yes."

I smirk and tug her back into my arms. "Good answer."

I kiss her again—each swipe of my tongue against

hers a possessive claim—and she suddenly goes still. I grin wickedly when I see Zaid behind her, his lips nibbling on the skin of her neck.

Goose bumps pebble on her skin, and Zaid moans huskily.

"Fuck, you're so responsive, sweetheart."

"If I shove my fingers between your thighs, will you be wet?" I ask, desperate to do just that.

"So wet," she whimpers.

I grin and exchange a sly glance with Zaid. Our reaper isn't ready for double penetration yet—we'll have to ease her into it with butt plugs and fingers—but that doesn't mean there aren't other things we can all do together.

Maybe she can ride my cock while sucking off Zaid, or vice versa.

Maybe she can wrap her tiny hands around both of our shafts, and we can paint her perfect tits in our cum.

Maybe she can alternate sucking on us, her head swiveling as she licks up and down our dicks.

Maybe she can—

"Get dressed!" Everett barks, pounding his fist against the door connecting the two rooms.

All three of us freeze.

"Hades's goddamn minions are here!" Everett snarls. "They're taking us to him, and so help me god, if any of these fuckers hear a single moan from Thea, I'll go on a murder spree."

"I already did," Rafe murmurs...from directly behind us.

We all spin, Zaid and I moving instinctively to block Thea from view.

Rafe stands at the foot of the bed wearing his favorite leather jacket, his black hair hanging loose and disheveled around his face. In his hand is...a minotaur horn.

Holy fuck.

Rafe throws it into the air carelessly and catches it, his eyes trained on Thea between Zaid and me.

"I'll have to add it to your bouquet of fingers," he says simply—like the goddamn psychopath he is.

Though...I am happy he murdered the minotaur who thought he could push around our girl. I'm also grateful Rafe chose to do it away from us, so as not to trigger Thea's reaping frenzy.

"You kept my finger bouquet?" Thea asks with hearts in her eyes.

"Of course." Rafe offers her a droll look, as if she's silly for thinking otherwise. "I have it displayed in my bedroom, though we'll have to move it when we return home. Perhaps to the dining room table?"

"No way in hell," Everett snaps from the other side of the door, obviously listening in.

Thea simply swoons, her lashes fluttering as if she's envisioning jumping the crazy blood fae right then and there.

I wouldn't be entirely averse to that idea.

But then I remember we have a bunch of armed, dangerous guards right outside the door, and my cock softens instantly.

"Fucking cockblocking god," I murmur, moving back to the other room to get dressed.

I want to kill the God of the Underworld.

Then, I want to fuck Thea senseless while my brothers watch.

For now, I need to shower and change.

A long, *cold* shower.

Fucking Hades.

CHAPTER FORTY

The dining room is just as grand and extravagant as the throne room. A large table that's easily able to seat twenty dominates the space, constructed out of rich mahogany wood. A three-tiered chandelier dangles from the ceiling, but on closer inspection, it appears to be made of bones. The skull in the center emanates a radiant white light.

Only two of the twenty seats are occupied. Hades, of course, sits at the head, with Persephone in the seat to the right of him.

"Oh! You're here!" Persephone's hands flutter to her throat as she stares at me. "How did you sleep? Were the beds comfortable?"

Instinctively, I snap my gaze in Zaid's direction, feeling a blush heat my cheeks.

"It was...great," I say, forcing my attention back on Persephone.

She appears pleased, her smile broadening. "Fantastic! Do you want it to be your permanent room here? We can add some color to it, if you want! Maybe some nice blinds? Blankets? Decorations? What do you think about—"

"Seph!" Hades admonishes, though he doesn't even flick his eyes her way.

His features remain entirely impassive as he sips what appears to be coffee.

Do the gods even need to eat and drink? I suppose I never really thought about it before, but now I wonder—

"Sit." Hades waves a hand in the air, and five chairs are pulled away from the table simultaneously.

I exchange a glance with my guys, steely determination bolstering me, and sit in the seat beside Hades, opposite Persephone. Everett glares at me, obviously not pleased with my choice, but I stick my tongue out at him.

Yes, my disappearance impacted all of us, but I was the one locked away for hundreds of years. Tortured, if you think about it. I have questions, and Hades may be the only one who can answer them.

Before I can even begin to voice one of the thousands of thoughts percolating in my head, Hades snaps his fingers. Seven servants hurry into the room, each carrying a silver tray. Plates of the fluffiest-looking pancakes I've ever seen are placed in front of us, followed by scrambled eggs and strips of bacon.

"We can't have this conversation on empty stomachs," Persephone explains, though she doesn't lift a hand to eat her own food. She just continues watching me, her eyes abnormally wide and doe-like.

It's...unnerving. A little freaky.

Before I can dig into my breakfast, Zaid stops me, placing a hand on my knee.

"Don't," he warns, his voice quiet but his eyes sharp.

But...pancakes.

I must give him a pathetic, puppy-dog look because he sighs heavily. "Certain foods eaten in the Underworld can make it impossible for you to leave."

Hades scoffs and gracefully cuts off a piece of his pancake. It's so strange to see. He's a terrifying, powerful guy, yet this makes him seem almost...normal. Domesticated.

Even if he does eat like a goddamn horse, his teeth nibbling at each bite he brings to his lips.

"As if I want you five here longer than necessary," he says, his tone carefully apathetic.

"It's perfectly safe," Persephone is quick to reassure.

"Isn't food how Hades trapped you here to begin with?" I ask, narrowing my eyes suspiciously as I recount the legend of her entrapment.

I feel a little shitty when her face falls, her eyes misting.

"Enough!" Hades slams his fist down on the table, causing it to rattle.

He spears me with a penetrating glare that makes fear snake down my spine.

How could I ever think he was normal?

I can practically feel the raw, unencumbered power radiating off him in malevolent waves. The delicate hairs on my arms stand straight up, as if the air is alive with electricity. Every instinct demands that I run away—and run far.

And the most terrifying part of all of this?

I don't think Hades is truly mad. Irritated, yes, and undoubtedly annoyed.

But mad? No.

I can't imagine what he would be like if he released all of that festering rage inside of him. I don't think the world would survive his wrath.

"You do not come into my home and insult my wife," Hades continues, his tone scathing.

"Our apologies," Zaid says quickly—ever the diplomat. "We meant no disrespect."

"Of course you didn't mean disrespect," Persephone pipes in, waving her hands at her eyes as if she hopes to dry up her tears. "I'm just sensitive. But I'm fine. It's fine. Everything's fine."

She offers her husband a timid, shaky smile, and he seems to physically deflate.

He may be the most powerful god in existence, but she definitely wears the pants in that relationship. She has him wrapped around her dainty finger, and he doesn't even seem to realize it. It makes me a little sad to know that his love for her is unreciprocated—at least if the rumors are true.

But at the same time, he did kidnap her and force her into marriage, so fuck him.

"Now," Hades continues, and the power permeating the room seems to dissipate, at least slightly. I can finally breathe. "Tell me everything."

I exchange glances with my guys, debating. But at the end of the day, we came here for answers. Like with Athena, we have no choice. Keeping secrets won't help us in this situation.

Everett nods, and Krystian grins encouragingly. Zaid gives my thigh another squeeze. Rafe doesn't acknowledge me, keeping his glare fixed on Hades, as if waiting for him to make any sudden movements.

Taking a deep breath, I tell Hades everything.

He listens without interruption, his features carefully blank except for the nearly imperceptible tightening of his eyes. At one point, Persephone cries out, her eyes wide with horror. She places a trembling hand against her mouth as tears stream down her cheeks.

When I'm done, silence permeates the air, stiff with an acrimonious type of tension.

Hades's long fingers tap against the tabletop.

"This...is concerning." A frown tugs at his lips. "This could explain the soul imbalance over the last couple hundred years."

"Soul imbalance?" I ask, confused.

Hades seems surprised, blinking slightly, and I realize he didn't mean to let that little tidbit slip.

He tilts his head to the side, contemplating me, before seeming to come to some sort of conclusion.

Settling back in his chair, he folds his arms over his chest. "What I'm about to tell you five cannot leave this room. Do you understand?"

There's an unstated threat in that question, one that promises pain, misery, and death if we don't agree.

"We understand," I say, answering for us all.

Hades studies us for another long moment, his eyes piercing, before he blows out a haggard breath, that one sound rife with an eternity of responsibility and pain.

"The Underworld is different from the realm above. The gods created it, yes, but we don't maintain it. Up above, every god and goddess has a purpose to keep the world running. Poseidon is in charge of the sea and the creatures in it. Zeus took the sky. Demeter allows things to grow. Apollo is in charge of the sun. I could go on and on. It takes an entire pantheon of gods to run the living world. But the Underworld? It's only me, and it's just as grand as the world above—if not grander. It needs more than just my power to thrive."

"The power of souls," Zaid breathes, shock splaying across his face.

Hades nods gravely. "That's correct. When a new soul joins the Underworld, a tiny sliver of their power goes towards the upkeep of the land. Not enough to make the soul go insane, but enough that the...lights are powered, so to speak." He turns towards Persephone. "Did I say that right, my dear?"

She beams, her beautiful face spotlighting every insecurity I've ever had. Ugh.

"You did perfect," she coos.

"But I haven't reaped enough souls to make that big of a difference," I insist. "How many people die every single day? One hundred thousand? I reap, at most, one thousand a day."

"One thousand?" Krystian interrupts, incredulous.

Zaid gives me a pained expression, his brows tugged low over his somber eyes.

I know they're thinking of my...condition.

What they don't understand is that I've grown used to it. At my prime, I could reap over one hundred souls before I would need to place the dagger on the pedestal, alleviating the effects of insanity.

I don't need their pity. Not for this. Not for something I survived and will continue to survive, regardless of what's thrown my way.

"That makes a bigger difference than you think," Hades says gravely. "At first, I believed the imbalance stemmed from modern medicine and treatments. Humans found ways to defy the will of the gods." His upper lip curls away from his teeth. "But that didn't explain why the Underworld seemed to...rebel. Now it makes sense. The Underworld knew souls were being stolen from it, and it became pissed."

Krystian tentatively lifts his hand in the air but doesn't wait to be called upon. "You're speaking as if the Underworld is sentient. As if it's...alive."

Pretty ironic, because it's the realm of the dead.

"Isn't it?" Hades quirks a single eyebrow. "The world above is alive, is it not? It has grass and trees and flowers. Is it impossible to believe that the Underworld is too, in its own unique way?"

Errr...

I don't have an answer to that, mainly because my mind hurts just thinking about it for longer than a few seconds.

"My brain hurts," Krystian moans, rubbing at his temples.

We truly are soulmates.

"Same," I agree. "I'm happy I'm not the only stupid one here."

Zaid, of course, lights up and leans forward. "I think I understand."

"Of course you do," Krystian mutters, exchanging a tiny, conspiratorial smile with me.

"Is this why there are no new souls?" I ask, piecing everything together.

Maybe I'm not the dumbest one of the group. Yay!

"You noticed that," Hades says.

"Kind of hard to miss," Everett deadpans.

"This power imbalance..." Hades grabs his napkin and dabs at his lips, his gaze far away and distant. "It's worse than you can possibly imagine. The Underworld is refusing to admit new souls."

A boulder drops in my stomach. "What does that mean?"

"It's been steadily getting worse over the last two hundred years, but we reached the breaking point a few weeks ago," Hades continues.

"A breaking point?" I question.

"One of my reapers was sent to a battlefield. Hundreds and hundreds of souls to reap. But when he tried, it... It didn't work." He drops his napkin back onto the table and lowers his gaze.

I can't quite read the emotion in his eyes.

"The souls couldn't get reaped?" I ask.

"They got reaped," Hades corrects, confusing me further. "But they didn't end up here."

Ice travels down my spine. "What happened to them?"

"They just...disappeared. Ceased to exist." Hades's voice is glacial, his eyes tight. "After that, I sent my reapers out on a few more test runs. It was all the same. So...I forced the reapers to stop."

"To stop reaping souls?" Everett sounds horrified, and I can't blame him.

If that's the case, then there are millions of souls currently wandering the earth, confused and lost and desperate. I wouldn't be surprised if the humans experienced an increase in hauntings and poltergeist attacks.

"What else was there to do?" Hades explodes, grabbing his coffee cup and throwing it at the wall. It shatters, black liquid raining down like rivulets of tar. "I didn't really have a choice, did I?"

His shoulders shake as he struggles to get his emotions under control.

Persephone rubs his back soothingly.

It seems to help because he takes a deep breath, his fingers flexing around the edge of the table, and then he slowly reclines back in his seat.

We all watch him warily, realizing he's a faulty

bomb seconds from exploding. None of us want to be in range when he detonates.

"You said the power of the souls transferred to another god or goddess, correct?" Hades says, his voice significantly calmer than it was seconds earlier.

"That's what we believe," I say hesitantly.

The last thing I want to do is set Hades off again.

"We need to get the power back into the Underworld," Hades continues. "It's the only way to save all of the souls—both here and on earth."

"How do you suppose we do that?" Everett demands, his jaw clenching.

Hades levels the shifter with a cold, unreadable look. "Figure it the fuck out."

"Hades!" Persephone admonishes, swatting at his shoulder. "Don't be an ass."

I imagine she's the only person alive—or dead— who can get away with talking to him like that. If I tried, he'd cut me into tiny pieces and feed me to Cerberus.

"We'll figure it out," I rush to reassure him, desperate to appease his volatile temper. "Athena's helping us. She will know what to do."

"Athena..." Hades's lips firm. "Yes. She's intelligent. If anyone has a solution, it'll be her."

Relieved that the dangerous god's temper tantrum

is apparently over, I ask the question that's been gnawing at me.

"The souls trapped in the dagger...the ones without any power... Is there a way to free them?" I ask tentatively, lowering my hand to my hip.

Something akin to sympathy flashes in Hades's eyes. Sympathy...or pity. I can't tell which. Either way, the sight has a lump manifesting in my throat.

"Only the power of a god can free them now. *All* of the power. There are too many for even my magic to work," he tells me.

"I don't understand. You said that it takes the power of a god—"

"In this case," Hades interrupts me. "I'm speaking of the life force of a god. The power of a god's soul." He must see the shock on my face because his lips twitch upwards microscopically. "Yes, gods' souls hold immense power too. And you'll need that level of power to free the souls in that dagger."

"So even if we restore the Underworld's power..." I swallow.

"The souls in the dagger will still be trapped. I'm sorry, child. There's nothing we can do for them."

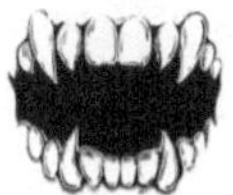

CHAPTER FORTY-ONE

We unanimously agree that our next stop will be the compound.

It's time to visit Ares and demand answers.

I'm not as...attached to the God of War as my brethren are. Then again, I don't truly care for anyone except for my brothers and Thea.

Zaid may think of Ares as a father figure, but I know the truth.

He's nothing but our owner, and it's about time we fought back.

I wonder how easy it would be to torture a god. Would he scream if I cut off each of his fingers, or would they grow back right away? What is his tolerance for pain? I know ordinary measures won't kill him, but if I discover he's behind what happened to my little bird, I'll find a way. I'll scour every book I can get my hands on, speak to every contact I possess, try every method I have at my disposal. Something will stick. I'll make sure of it.

"Are you sure you guys can't stay one more day?" Persephone asks, staring up at us with wide, creepy-ass eyes.

"No, sorry." Thea winces, her features creasing with sympathy as she regards the Goddess of...Spring, maybe?

Fuck if I know.

Persephone's face falls. "Oh."

"But maybe we can come visit in the future," Thea tacks on tentatively.

I turn to stare at my girl, incredulous.

Willingly visit the Underworld? Fuck no.

But when Persephone's face lights up, and Thea gifts her a smile in return, I understand.

Thea sees herself in Persephone. Someone who's trapped and alone. Who knows what the fuck Hades does to Persephone when no one's around to stop him?

"I packed you some sandwiches for the road," Persephone says, thrusting a basket into Thea's hands.

"Oh, thank you." Thea puts aside the picnic basket, a frown drawing her brows together.

"Please. Let us know if you need anything. Hades and I will both help you. He may seem like a grumpy bastard, but he's a big teddy bear underneath it all," Persephone continues earnestly.

"A teddy bear from a horror movie, maybe," Krystian murmurs from beside me.

I snort in agreement.

Thea still seems hesitant, but she promises to get in touch if we run into any issues. I don't know how the fuck she expects to do that, but then again, I don't care. Not my problem.

"Be safe!" Persephone chirps, pulling my little bird into a tight hug.

I growl and take a threatening step forward, seconds away from cutting the goddess's arms from her body, but Thea is already untangling herself, her smile tight.

"It was nice meeting you, Persephone."

Tears cascade down the goddess's cheeks as she sniffles. "Please return."

Conversation ceases as we step up to the portal that should take us to the mortal realm.

Persephone begins to goddamn wail as we step through one at a time. I always suspected the goddess had a few screws loose, but this confirms it.

Like recognizes like, after all.

I step through last, feeling the air shift and distort around me. The Underworld fades away, and in its place is a familiar building—the compound.

"This is where you grew up?" Thea asks, peering up at the unassuming structure with its gray walls and vaulted blue roof.

"Where *we* grew up," Everett corrects quietly, and Thea's expression twists.

It's still goddamn insane to realize that we grew up with Thea. Knew her. Cared for her. Probably loved her, if I'm being completely honest. Yet all of those memories were stolen from us. Was it the sleep that caused it? Ares? The god or goddess behind this entire fucked-up situation?

I want answers.

And blood.

Do gods bleed red like the humans and supernaturals they look after? Or is their blood golden? Silver? Black?

I'm certain I'll find out.

"Remember, we don't know if Ares knows anything about what happened to Thea," Zaid says, obviously trying to think the best of his "daddy."

"But if he does..." I warn.

I need Zaid to be okay with what I'm about to do. I need them all to be okay with it.

A bloated storm cloud ripples across Zaid's face, darkening his features. "Then we take care of him."

A smile tugs up my lips instinctively. I fucking love it when my brothers embrace their dark sides. They're just as twisted as me sometimes, though they'll never admit it.

"Krystian, put the glamour on Thea," Everett instructs.

Krystian salutes the shifter and then turns towards our reaper. He concentrates for a long moment, his eyebrows drawn together, before he nods and turns away.

"Done." A cold smile unfurls on the elf's face—one of the many indications that Krys is present as well.

Krystian would be a little more hesitant about spilling a god's blood, but Krys? He'll relish the opportunity, especially if the bastard hurt our girl. Krystian finally came to terms with who he is—*what* he is—and we have Thea to thank for that.

She saved him, just like she saved the rest of us, and now we'll burn the world down if that's what it takes to keep her safe.

"So it'll be like it was with Aphrodite? You guys will be able to hear and see me, but Ares won't?" Thea asks.

"That's the plan," Krystian says.

"But what if it fails like it did in the Underworld?" She nibbles on her lower lip.

"It won't," Krystian assures her. "I should've taken into account that the magic down there is different from up here. Weaker. But my glamour will hold up perfectly, at least for a couple of hours."

"Let's go," I snarl, anger flooding my veins, dark and caustic.

I want to rip Ares apart limb from limb.

Gouge his eyes out.

Slice off his tongue.

Castrate him.

The list is endless.

I try to remind myself that Zaid is right—he could be innocent in this mess—but my gut says something different. And I've learned to always trust my intuition.

After all, it's what declared Thea as mine from the very first meeting.

I kick open the door and stalk forward, trembles reverberating through my body.

Ares is sitting behind a desk in the far corner, a pile of envelopes in front of him.

He glances up when we enter, surprise on his face, which quickly morphs into anger.

"There you guys are! It's been days without a single word!" He stands, seven entire feet full of rippling muscles and malevolent energy. "We have hundreds of cases lined up, so get your asses over here for a debriefing."

"Remember. We need to be subtle," Zaid whispers.

But fuck subtlety.

"What the hell did you do to Thea?" I demand, the words a guttural growl.

Ares stares at us in shock. "Who?"

"The reaper," Krystian interjects angrily. "Blonde hair. Perfect body. Perfect face. Perfect everything."

"Awww," Thea coos from where she has moved to stand off to the side, watching the exchange.

"Thea?" Ares's brows draw tight together, and then a look of realization dawns on his face. His cheeks drain of color, and he stumbles backwards. "Do you mean...Winnifred?"

"Winnifred?" Thea pops her hip to the side, aghast. "What type of name is that? Was my name seriously *Winnifred* once upon a time?"

Krystian turns towards her, seemingly forgetting she's supposed to be invisible to Ares. "Thea isn't your real name?"

"Of course not." She throws her hands up in the air. "I didn't have a name, so I gave myself one. Thea was one of the first souls I reaped, so I stole the name for myself. I thought it was pretty."

"Winnifred..." I murmur, and flashes of images barrage me.

They occur too quickly for me to analyze them, but I see a flash of golden hair and plump pink lips.

Winnie.

"You know, maybe it's good you have no memories of me from before. If one of you mumbled Winnifred in your sleep or during sex, I probably would've murdered you," Thea says seriously.

"Even now that we know it's you?" Krystian asks, amused.

"What can I say? I'm a jealous, petty bitch, even of myself."

He snorts and looks away, but I can tell he's charmed by her. We all fucking are.

Fortunately, Ares is too lost in his own thoughts to realize Krystian is having a conversation with someone who isn't there.

"It's impossible," Ares whispers, dropping his face into his hands. "She's dead. Winnie's dead."

"What the fuck do you mean by that?" Everett demands, stalking closer. "What the fuck did you do, Ares?"

"I didn't hurt her!" Ares insists, whipping his head up. "I would *never* hurt her. I loved her."

Stunned silence settles over us all. Thea is staring at Ares in shock, her eyes wide and her lips slightly parted.

Did we...? Did we get it all wrong?

Was Thea in a relationship with Ares, not us? There's no way she was with all five of us. Ares doesn't share.

"Krystian, drop the glamour," Thea instructs, her voice unexpectedly hard.

Krystian shakes his head wordlessly, his eyes not leaving Ares's forlorn, devastated face.

"Krystian..." Thea warns.

He finally peels his gaze away from the god and turns towards our reaper, his eyes subdued.

Thea takes a step closer and grips his hand. "Trust me."

He hesitates, indecision swarming in his dark-blue eyes, before he nods once. "All right."

I can tell the exact moment the glamour hiding Thea dissipates.

Ares's head whips up, and shock widens his eyes. He looks like he's just seen a ghost.

Or...a reaper.

"Winnie." His tone is soft. Reverent.

I want to fucking kill him.

And when he stands and steps towards her, his arms extended? I decide that I'm going to. Fuck the consequences. I'll find a way to move him far away from my little bird, then I'll cut out his heart. He may not die from it, but it'll make me feel better.

"Winnie, it's you." Disbelief makes his voice low and husky.

Or maybe that's just the lust emanating from his normally cold eyes.

He grabs at her arm.

And Thea abruptly tenses and seizes up, her eyes glazing slightly.

I lose my goddamn shit.

CHAPTER FORTY-TWO

THEA

The gate shuts behind me with a heavy clang that echoes down my spine.

I glance over my shoulder once—at the life I left behind—and then back to the compound in front of me. Stone buildings, looming walls, and training fields dotted with bodies moving in synchronized violence. It doesn't look like a school.

It looks like a war waiting to happen.

An unfamiliar woman leads me through a courtyard and stops beside a shaded patch of grass.

"Your team," she says, nodding towards a group of boys admiring a wall of weapons.

They look up when I approach, four pairs of eyes landing on me like I'm some exotic animal they weren't expecting to see.

I absently bring my hand to my hip, where my birthmark rests.

The birthmark indicating I belong to Ares.

The one who speaks first is tall and already broadshouldered. His sandy blond hair falls haphazardly into sharp, penetrating eyes.

"This is who we're paired with?" He folds his arms over his chest with a scoff. "She's tiny."

"Everett," the dark-haired stranger beside him reprimands.

The boy—Everett—scowls but shuts up, though his glare never leaves my face.

The boy on his other side grins so wide it lights up his whole face.

"I'm Krystian," he says, bouncing on the balls of his feet like he's raw energy contained in a tiny body. "You're Winnie, right? Pretty name."

I offer a timid smile in return. "Thanks."

"I'm Zaid," greets the boy who defended me, his voice barely louder than a whisper.

He ducks his head, his cheeks tinting pink, and offers me a shy wave.

The last boy says nothing. He simply stares, his gaze almost unsettling. It reminds of an impromptu storm— no warning and capable of decimating entire cities.

A tendril of fear curls around my heart, tightening.

"That's Rafe," Krystian introduces, nudging him.

"Don't mind him. He stares at everyone. I think he was dropped on his head one too many times as a baby."

"Does he talk?" I ask, frowning.

"Sometimes." Zaid shrugs. "When it matters."

Rafe doesn't even blink, his unnerving gaze trained on me.

Everett grunts and turns back to the weapons, studying them as intently as Rafe's studying me. "Whatever. You're one of us now, so that means we got your back. Do you know how to use any weapons?"

Krystian throws an arm around my shoulders like we're already best friends. "Yeah. We'll look out for you."

"We're your boys now," Zaid agrees, then blushes when he realizes how his words could be construed.

Heat enters my own cheeks.

Your boys.

Why do I like the sound of that?

I've never had anyone look after me before or care about me. I know my parents do, in their own way, but this...feels different. More permanent.

Rafe says nothing, but when I meet his eyes, he dips his chin once in the smallest of acknowledgments. Not a greeting. A promise.

I straighten my spine. "Good. Because I'm not here to be protected. I'm here to fight."

Everett snorts. "We'll see."

Krystian whistles low, a wide smile blossoming on his face. "I like her already."

Good.

Because I like you four already as well.

MY PALM SLAMS into Everett's chest, and I twist, using his momentum against him.

He hits the mat hard enough to rattle the floor beneath us.

"Damn," he breathes, flat on his back.

I drop into a crouch beside him, grinning through the sweat dripping into my eyes. "Told you I could kick your ass without my dagger."

He exhales a laugh, rough and disbelieving. "Yeah, yeah, yeah. Whatever. You just got lucky."

"No luck involved." I shrug nonchalantly. "I'm just better than you."

"Brat," he playfully growls.

"Always."

Everett props himself up on his elbows, his hair sticking to his forehead and his mouth curved in something halfway between pride and irritation. "You've gotten mean in your old age."

"You're mean at any age," I counter, playfully swatting at his shoulder.

We're close—closer than we probably should be. The air between us tightens, the tension in it sharper than any sword we've trained with. His hazel gaze lingers on me, steady and unreadable in a way it never used to be when we were kids.

I'm about to say something—something dumb, probably, or reckless—when the hairs on the back of my neck lift.

I turn my head slowly, my heart already beating faster for reasons that have nothing to do with the spar.

Ares stands at the edge of the training floor, his arms crossed over his broad chest as he watches. He's been doing that more and more often—watching us.

Watching me.

His presence is always accompanied by a prickle of awareness and a dozen alarm bells. I know I shouldn't be afraid—this is Ares, for fuck's sake, who's practically our foster father—but still.

I move away from Everett like I've been caught doing something wrong.

Ares doesn't speak. Doesn't move. His eyes are as unreadable as they've always been—steel behind glass.

Everett follows my gaze, his eyes narrowing. "How long has he been standing there?"

"No idea." I climb to my feet and brush off my pants, my pulse still thrumming.

Fuck, I need to stop being so paranoid. Ares is probably just gauging my progress, as all the gods and goddesses are doing. He wants to make sure I don't drag the team down.

It's been ten years since I started training with them all, and he still doesn't trust me.

"Come on," Everett whispers, jumping to his feet. "Let's continue training."

"Yeah," I respond shakily.

I glance over my shoulder, but Ares is gone.

If Everett didn't see him as well, I would've thought I imagined him in the first place.

"YOU WANTED TO SEE ME?" I ask, knocking on the door to Ares's office.

It's my twenty-first birthday, and the guys told me they have something planned for tonight. I want to get this meeting over with as quickly as possible.

"Yes, come in," he calls, his voice slightly breathless.

I step inside, my hands clasped behind my back.

"*Did something happen—*" I cut myself off as I take in the sight before me.

Ares sits on his office chair, his hand wrapped around his erect dick as he strokes himself.

My eyes widen, and I release a strangled, choking sound.

A wicked grin curves up Ares's lips, and he begins to move his hand even faster. "You like this? Fuck. All I can think about is how good your pussy would feel wrapped around my cock. Goddamn."

Horror and disgust mingle in my stomach, but I can't look away. It's as if I'm watching two trains approaching from opposite directions and am helpless to stop the inevitable collision.

"Touch your tits, Winnie. Let me see you."

I just stand there, gawking, and Ares explodes with a roar, ropes of cum covering his shirt.

It's only then that I get the courage to spin around and race out of the room.

"HE WON'T COME *near you again,*" Everett vows vehemently.

"Never," Krystian agrees, kissing my neck.

Zaid's hand tightens around my own. "Fuck, I can't believe this. How could he?" He shakes his head with a look of disgust. "He watched you grow up. Practically raised you."

"He goddamn groomed her," Everett snarls.

"We need to kill him," Rafe says softly, his voice a deadly purr.

"No." I shake my head, still trembling from what I just witnessed. I immediately returned to the bunkhouse and told the guys what Ares did. A part of me was worried they wouldn't believe me, but of course, I needn't have worried. "If we hurt Ares, the other gods and goddesses will retaliate. They'll kill us."

And the thought terrifies me.

I'm not worried for myself, though, but my guys. I refuse to allow anything to happen to them, especially defending me. The best thing for all of us is keeping our distance from Ares and pretending that it didn't happen.

"We'll do it your way," Everett agrees, his voice a soft rumble. "But if he tries anything again..."

"Nothing will stop us from killing him," Rafe finishes.

THE NEXT YEAR PASSES UNEVENTFULLY.

We train, we fight, and we fuck.

Somewhere along the way, our friendship transitions into a beautiful relationship.

I love these men with the entirety of my being, and I know they feel the same for me.

"Yes, love. Look how beautiful you are riding my cock," Krystian praises, his fingers digging into my hips hard enough to leave bruises.

Behind me, Everett kisses my neck.

"She's perfection, isn't she?" Zaid says from the armchair, where he strokes his cock.

"Perfection," Rafe agrees.

He stands against the far wall, his arms crossed over his chest and his cock contained within his pants, despite the obvious bulge. I think my blood fae may be a little bit of a masochist. Just a smidge.

I smirk and begin to ride Krystian harder, my breasts bouncing. I rake my nails down my elf's chest as my orgasm fast approaches.

"Fuck, yes," I say, lifting my hips and dropping them back down.

And that's when I feel a weight that's always

accompanied by someone's eyes on me. The air turns stale and sticky, getting stuck in my throat. My stomach twists painfully, and I slowly peel my eyes away from Krystian's face.

Ares watches from the doorway, stroking himself.

I gasp, stilling. "What the fuck?"

"Huh?" Krystian's brows crease, and he tilts his head back to follow the direction of my gaze.

I can tell the exact moment he sees Ares because an incandescent anger—the likes of which I've never seen before—crosses his face.

"Motherfucker!"

Everett immediately attempts to cover me with his body, and Rafe stalks towards the door, magic sparking in his palms.

But Ares has already left.

Zaid tucks his now limp dick back in his pants, his expression wild. "We need to leave. Now."

I SHOULD'VE KNOWN *Ares would never let us go.*

A sob catches in my throat as I stare at the unconscious bodies of my lovers. They didn't stand a chance against the God of War. They're young. Untrained. Inexperienced.

"Did you really think I would let you leave me?" Ares demands, his hand twisting in my hair. Pain explodes from my scalp, and I cry out, futilely attempting to free myself from his impenetrable hold. *"I allowed you to fuck around with those...those inferior men, even knowing that you belong to me. But no more."*

Roughly, he grabs the front of my shirt and rips it. His free hand immediately begins to grope my bare breast, roughly twisting my nipple.

"Why can't you just let me love you?" he rasps in my ear as I sob. *"YOU STUPID BITCH!"*

He pulls my hair even harder and then pushes me away. Before I can even get to my feet, he punches me across the face.

I fall to the ground, blood filling my mouth and tears staining my cheeks.

He straddles me from above and roughly pushes my breasts together.

"You are mine, Winnifred. MINE!" He brings his lips to mine, but it's not a kiss. His teeth bite down on my lower lip and tug, causing me to cry out. *"I chose you. Even before you were born, I knew you were mine."*

As he speaks, his thumbs absently flick my nipples.

And then I say the words that seal my fate once and for all.

"I'll never be yours."

The next hour is the worst of my life.

Every punch, every kick, every scratch... I feel it all. Unconsciousness doesn't claim me, despite how desperately I plead for it to.

"You'll always be mine, Winnie," Ares growls, staring hungrily down at my beaten, broken body. His fingers roughly thrust into my pussy, making me scream at the unwelcome intrusion. "Always."

I SNAP out of the memories with a gasp. I'm cold everywhere. Can't think. Can't breathe. Terror coils around my heart like a venomous snake.

I stare up at the face of my stalker, my tormentor, my murderer.

"Y-you killed me," I whisper, feeling as if I'm speaking around a thousand tiny knives in my throat.

Slowly, I back away from him, though he doesn't make a move to follow me, seemingly frozen, shock splayed across his face.

"What?" Everett bellows.

All of my guys move closer, surrounding me, enveloping me in their warmth—though it does very little to thaw my frozen body.

"When he touched me...I...I remembered pieces of my past. Meeting you four. Falling in love. And..." God, I can't speak. I'm going to be sick. Bile claws at my throat like acid-tipped talons. "Ares became obsessed with me. He stalked me. He..." A sob catches in my throat. "He did things to me and then..."

And then left me for dead.

Hell, he was probably the one to trap me in that room. It wouldn't surprise me. He was desperate to possess me, own me, make me his.

Zaid's expression has gone carefully blank. "Thea, are you saying that he...?"

He can't seem to finish his question.

"He's going to die," Rafe vows.

And then everything happens really, really fast.

Everett's body cracks as it contorts. The shift takes less than five seconds. His skin rips, fur explodes outwards, and three monstrous heads rise from his shoulders—a blue version of Cerberus in all his wrathful glory. Three sets of eyes lock on Ares like he's dinner.

Rafe slices his palm open with clean precision. Blood streams down his fingers.

Krystian notches an arrow and aims it at the God of War's chest.

Zaid fades into incorporeal smoke, his shadowy form racing behind Ares.

All of this takes place in less than a few seconds, but I can barely process it all. I'm paralyzed where I stand, fear and anger running amok in my chest.

I can't look away from Ares.

The monster who watched me while I slept.

Who breathed down my neck from the shadows.

Who whispered my name like a promise and a curse.

Who attacked me.

Who brutalized me.

Who no doubt locked me away for hundreds of years, erasing my memories of my guys and theirs of me.

Did the deep sleep my guys were put under truly cause their memory loss, or was that just a lie Ares told them to hide his wicked deeds?

Now I realize that...I'm angry.

Yes, the fear is still there, potent and stifling, but the rage flooding through my veins eclipses it. Shivers reverberate through me, and something solidifies in my hand.

My dagger.

The same dagger previously tattooed on my skin.

I sprint towards Ares, blade low, body fluid.

He's fast—but I'm faster. My rage makes me so.

I feign left and drive the dagger towards his ribs. He blocks, but I twist and slide past him, carving a line across his back. He hisses, stumbling.

Krystian fires.

Ares deflects the first arrow, but the second finds a home in his thigh—and the magic goes to work immediately, eating at his flesh with a wet hiss.

Ares grits his teeth and raises a blade of violet flame. It seems to have materialized out of thin air.

I duck just as he swings, heat slashing the air above my head.

"Thea, move!" Rafe grunts, and I roll to the side just as my fae hurls a spear of hardened blood into Ares's side, momentarily pinning him to the wall behind him.

Everett charges, all three jaws opened wide, and slams into Ares with enough force to break every bone of a mortal.

The wall behind Ares crumbles away, and the two of them fall onto the grassy field outside, nothing but a tangle of limbs.

One of Everett's heads clamps onto Ares's shoulder while the other two snap at his arms, holding him still.

Zaid appears beside me, solid again.

"Thea," he breathes, pulling me into his arms.

"I need to finish this," I whisper, pulling away and moving towards Ares.

He tortured me.

Assaulted me.

Kidnapped me.

He'll pay with his life.

"Thea, no," Zaid tries again, grabbing my arm. "You can't use your dagger on him. Fuck, you know you can't. Sweetheart, stop."

Everett, Rafe, and Krystian have Ares contained, but I have no idea how long that'll last. Ares is a god, and even three of the most powerful supernaturals are no match for him.

It's now or never.

I don't look back at Zaid as I move towards a prone Ares, still lying on his back.

"Thea," Krystian exclaims, alarmed.

"No!" Everett barks.

I lunge at the God of War.

Ares gasps beneath me, the tip of my dagger hovering just above his heart. He's bleeding from half a dozen wounds—Krystian's flesh-eating arrows, Rafe's blood-forged spikes, Everett's monstrous mauling, and Zaid's claws—but it's me he looks at now.

Good.

I want him to see the end coming from the person he thought was the weakest.

"Winnifred... Thea..." he whispers, blood drizzling from his parted lips.

Behind me, my guys seem to be holding their breaths, terrified of making any sudden movements.

"You don't get to say my name. Either of them," I whisper, pressing the blade deeper.

Not a killing blow, though. Not yet.

He spits out blood, laughing weakly. "You think you've won?"

A feral grin unfurls on my lips. "No. This isn't a win. This is justice."

The dagger burns hot in my hand—hotter than ever before, as if it can sense the enormity of the god's power ripe for the taking. The hilt hums against my skin, channeling something cold and righteous inside of me. The earth beneath us shakes, and the sky above turns still.

I apply a little more pressure, digging the blade in—

Krystian grabs my wrist, his eyes wild. "Thea, no."

I snap my head towards him, but he continues to beseech me with his gaze to listen.

"Who knows what the fuck killing him will do to you? Can the dagger handle that much power? Can *you*? What about his soul? Will it consume you? Thea, please. Don't. Please." Tears begin to stream down his cheeks. "I love you, Thea. I love you. Please don't do this."

A tremble works its way through me.

One of Everett's three heads swivels and pierces me with an unreadable look.

"Don't," he growls, his voice a booming baritone.

But if I don't, then Ares is going to be set free. The guys don't know how to kill him, and even if they did, they wouldn't risk angering the gods.

I need to do this.

For them.

For me.

For the past that was stolen from us.

And then the ground groans.

The air tightens, as if it's being sucked from the world, and goose bumps pebble on my arms.

A void opens directly in front of me—ripping reality apart at the seams—and *he* steps through.

Hades.

He doesn't speak at first, but then again, he doesn't have to. His presence says enough. Everything in nature recoils from him—leaves shrivel, the sunlight dims, and even the clouds seem to float away.

Hades tilts his head slightly as he stares at me. There's something behind his eyes I've never seen before, at least from him. Respect, maybe? Pride?

Whatever it is disappears before I can analyze it further, replaced by his impassive mask once more.

His gaze drops to Ares, who moans at his feet.

"So," Hades says, his voice like stone tumbling down a mountain, "this is what's become of the God of War."

"He's behind all of this," Krystian snaps, tears forming in his eyes as he glares down at Ares. "He stalked her. Assaulted her. He..."

He looks away with a choked sound, his hand tightening around his bow.

"He called it love," Rafe adds, disgust curling his lip.

He hasn't peeled his eyes away from Ares once since we took him down. My blood fae is seconds from losing the remnants of his sanity.

Hades turns towards me, his expression unreadable. "And you? What do you call it?"

"Violation. Control. Obsession." I glare down at the pathetic waste of space.

Fuck, I want to stab him. End him. I'm not even sure if my dagger is capable of such a thing, but if it is... I want to be the one to do it.

"If he's the one behind your imprisonment, then we need to figure out a way to drain the power out of him," Hades says calmly.

Too calmly.

But there's something in his eyes that makes me pause.

I mentioned before that I've never seen Hades angry before.

I think that's about to change.

"I don't know what the fuck you're talking about," Ares snaps, snarling. "The little bitch is lying—"

Hades lifts one hand, and shadows erupt from the earth like writhing chains. They wrap around Ares's body, hauling him into the air. I stagger backwards—landing against Everett, who has shifted back into his human form—as Ares floats in the air, thrashing against the restraints.

"You are no longer fit to walk amongst the living," Hades says simply, his cold, malevolent gaze fixed on Ares. "You've dishonored Olympus, your name, and yourself."

The chains tighten, binding Ares like a fly in a web.

"I will place him in Tartarus," Hades says to us. "Where time forgets. Where screams echo without end. He will not touch you or your world again."

Ares's eyes widen in panic. "You can't do this! Zeus will never let you!"

A smile slashes across Hades's face. "You damn well know Zeus won't stop me."

His words hold some sort of meaning that I don't understand, but Ares obviously does.

"Hades, please. Please. I didn't mean to. Please."

With a ripple in the air, the earth swallows Ares whole—him and the shadows and his screams of terror.

Silence returns.

Hades stands where he is, his expression carefully blank, his gaze trained on where Ares disappeared.

He's...gone.

Ares is gone.

I collapse to my knees as relief fills me. The dagger falls from my hand and disappears from sight once more—no doubt becoming a tattoo on my skin yet again.

"Thank you," I whisper to Hades through numb lips, knowing he just saved my life.

Because if he hadn't imprisoned Ares, I would've killed him. I know I would have.

Hades turns his piercing silver gaze in my direction. "You're...welcome."

"Why did you come? Why did you help us?" I ask, tears staining my cheeks.

Hades hesitates and then says simply, "Because I created you, which makes you my responsibility."

And then in a blink of darkness and ash, he's gone.

The five of us are left alone beside the shattered wall of the compound. Panting. Bloody. Bruised.

But alive.

Krystian slings his bow back over his shoulder, and it instantly dematerializes.

"Let's go home," he says, sounding exhausted.

"Yes," Rafe agrees.

Everett holds me tighter, his arms the only thing keeping me from falling to the ground.

I can't peel my gaze away from the scorched earth where Ares disappeared.

He's gone. He's really, truly gone.

Does that mean this is over?

Or has it only just begun?

CHAPTER FORTY-THREE

THEA

"res has to have been the one behind all of this," Krystian insists as we sit around the dining room table hours later.

Everett has prepared a feast of filet mignon, mashed potatoes, green beans, and a chocolate lava cake for dessert.

It looks delicious, but...

But I can't even think about eating.

"Ares didn't attack us as if he had the power of millions of souls at his beck and call," Zaid points out, moving the contents of his plate around without eating a single bite.

"This has to be over." Krystian turns desperate eyes onto me. "Please let this be over."

Everett, who has remained silent up until now, stands abruptly.

"All right, everyone but Thea out," he barks.

The guys blink at him.

"Ex-fucking-cuse me?" Krystian asks.

"I want you three to do a perimeter check," Everett instructs. "Until we know for certain this is over, we need to be on our guard twenty-four seven."

Zaid, Rafe, and Krystian all exchange an indecipherable look before they nod and stand. One by one, they stop where I sit, kissing whatever part of me they can reach—my head, temple, and cheek.

"We'll be back soon," Zaid says, grabbing his coat off the hanger.

The other two nod and follow him outside.

Leaving me alone with a hulking, surly beast.

I push food around with my fork, heaving out a breath. "I know you sent them away so you can get me alone."

"We need to talk." Everett folds his arms over his chest and jerks his chin towards the living room. "Let's move somewhere more comfortable. We both know you're not eating that."

I agree easily and shuffle towards the living room, my feet dragging. I feel...different. I have memories of my past now, but I'm not sure I even want them. They paint a picture that's nothing but jagged lines and bloody strokes.

God, why couldn't my past have been beautiful

and loving? Why does it need to be a double-edged sword that stabs and slices?

I move onto the couch and place my legs underneath me. Everett sits opposite me, his expression for once unguarded but no less intense.

"What do you need from us, Thea?" He leans forward, as if to take my hands in his, but pulls back before he can make contact.

But fuck that. I want him to touch me. I want them all to. The last thing I need is for them to treat me like I'm made of glass. At one point, they saw me as their equal, a warrior just like them.

I capture his hands in mine, holding tight.

"I...I don't know," I confess, exhaling raggedly.

"Do you want to talk about what you saw in the vision? Talk to a therapist? Do you want us to slow down with you, give you space?"

"No!" I say quickly. Then, working to lower my voice, I repeat, "No, I don't want space."

Everett swallows. "I don't have memories of you before we met a few days ago. None of us do, but I wish I did. I wish you didn't have to carry this burden alone."

My heart swells then meets resistance against the barbed wire surrounding it. "I don't want you four to remember everything. It's not... It doesn't have a happy ending."

"But we must've had good times as well, right?" A surprisingly vulnerable expression crosses his face.

My lips twitch. "We did."

"Tell me about the good times. If you want."

So I do.

Everett chuckles when he realizes even his younger self was an ass to me, then he glows with pride when I describe how I bested him in the training ring. I don't mention Ares once as I describe the very few memories I have of us all together.

Somehow, I find myself leaning against him on the couch, my back flush to his chest and his arms coiled around mine.

"You know, when we first met, I never would've thought we'd end up here," I say, tilting my head back to smile up at him. "Who knew you were just a big teddy bear underneath that gruff exterior?"

Everett playfully snaps his teeth in my face. "Take that back."

"Make me," I say, grinning.

The smile slowly slips from his face, replaced by something softer. Warmer.

"Thea..." He caresses my cheek with the backs of his fingers. "You said that you never would've believed we'd end up here, but I knew we would."

I lift my brows. "You hated me."

"I told you I didn't. I never have." He swallows, a

look of indecision crossing his face before he blurts out, "I love you."

My heart begins to pound even faster. "I...I love you too."

And I do. I love them all, even if I haven't admitted it to anyone other than Zaid. They have somehow permanently imprinted themselves on my soul. It'll be impossible to untangle myself from them.

I don't believe in fate or soulmates or anything as ridiculous as that, but if I did, they'd be mine. We found each other in my first life, then again in my next. And I have no doubt we'll be drawn to each other in death too.

"Thea..." Everett's gaze flicks to my lips, his eyes heating. Turning molten. But then he grits his teeth together and turns away. "Fuck, I'm sorry, baby."

"No," I say quickly, guiding his face back to mine. "Don't be sorry. I... I want you, Everett."

He closes his eyes and grimaces, as if in immense pain.

"I want you too, baby, but I don't want our first time to be because you've just been traumatized by god-awful memories." His fingers flex on my cheek sporadically.

"I promise you, Everett. That's not why I want to do this." I allow my gaze to trail over his ruggedly hand-some face, noting the scruff on his jawline that has begun to grow out, resembling a beard. "Was what happened to me—to us—awful? Of course. I'll probably have nightmares for years to come. But that doesn't change the fact that I love you, that I'm in love with you. And right now, I want nothing more than to know that you're here with me and that I'm free."

I crane my neck to plant a chaste, gentle kiss on his jawline, which ripples with tension. "Please, Everett. I need this. I need you."

He trembles, his arms around me flexing, but his restraint is crumbling. He wants me just as badly.

His hands slide up my waist, pulling me closer. His unique, woodsy scent surrounds me, and I breathe him in, wondering what he would taste like on my lips. I want to kiss him. I'm desperate to.

I twist my neck, and our mouths meet, his lips parting.

I shift on the couch so I'm now straddling him, our tongues tangling in a desperate, sultry dance, his hands roaming my body.

I expected him to be domineering in the bedroom like Rafe, but he's...gentle. Passionate. I don't know if he's always like this or if this is a side of him reserved solely for me, but I appreciate it more than I care to admit.

I want to feel loved and cherished. I need to know that he's here, that he loves me, that he'll protect me.

His hands trail down my back and cup my ass, squeezing.

"Everett..." I moan, kissing him again.

"Take those clothes off, baby. Let me see you."

It takes less than a second for me to stand and rid myself of my clothes and undergarments, tossing them aside. He quickly chucks off his own T-shirt and jeans, but before I can admire him, he grabs my arm and hauls me back onto his lap.

"You're beautiful," he whispers, cupping my aching breasts and tweaking my hyper-sensitive nipples.

Heat rushes to my core instantly, and I moan, rocking slightly.

His tongue traces the seam of my lips in a slow, sensual pathway before trailing down my neck. I arch for him, granting him better access, and he uses the opportunity to bite and suck on my skin. A part of me wants him to do it even harder—to leave a mark behind. I want the world to know that I belong to him and he belongs to me.

He arches his hips slightly, and that's when I feel it —the prominent bulge resting thick and hard against my most sensitive area.

He's big. Bigger than any of the others, and that's saying something. Of course, I should've expected him to be big, considering his size, but to have the evidence quite literally brushing against me—

Everett must've felt me freeze, because he tenses up, his hazel eyes locking on my own.

"Are you okay? Is it a flashback?" He places his hands on my hips, as if he means to lift me off of him, but I clutch at his shoulders desperately.

"No, it's not that." I kiss his cheek, his bottom lip, his upper one. "It's just..."

"It's just?"

"You're...huge." I gesture towards his erection, wondering if he's oblivious to the lethal weapon between his legs or choosing to ignore it.

His eyes widen in surprise...and then a shit-eating grin spreads across his face.

"Huge?"

"Fucking massive," I agree with a nod.

He chuckles and resumes kissing and nipping at my neck. "Fuck, do you have any idea what you do to me? Hearing you talk about my dick like that makes me hard as steel. God, I want nothing more than to worship you like the goddess you are. I want to lap at your sweet, perfect pussy until my name is the only one you remember. I want your wetness coating my tongue and lips for the rest of my life. Do you know I can smell when you're aroused? It's the best fucking smell in the world."

He inhales deeply, and my pussy gushes, heat rushing through my veins.

"I want you more than I've ever wanted anyone in my life." One of his hands slips between my legs, his large fingers curling in my wet folds.

I gasp and rock my hips, helping him find a rhythm.

"Yes. Just like that, baby. Just like that. Ride my hand." A sexy grin stretches his lips as he focuses on where he touches me, his fingers swallowed by my clenching pussy.

One of his fingers circles my core while the other teases my clit.

"Everett," I moan, leaning forward to kiss him once more and trapping his hand between our bodies.

He chuckles against my lips. "Yes, baby?"

"More," I breathe huskily, desperately jerking my hips forward to meet each thrust of his fingers.

"More?" His fingers slide deeper inside of me, curling up as they move back and forth. My eyelids flutter as sensations overwhelm me. "How about another finger?"

"Fuck, Everett." I gasp as another finger joins the first two, eliciting moan after moan from my parted lips.

My hips rock as if they have a mind of their own, meeting each of his thrusts as I chase my release. I'm right on the edge, and any second I'll teeter over that cliff side.

Faster. I need him to go faster.

He grips my chin with his free hand, his fingers bruising, and kisses me once more. Below, he begins to move his hand even faster, his digits curling deep inside of me as I cry out.

A smug grin splits his cheeks as he slowly pulls his wet fingers out of my cunt, bringing them to his lips to taste one after the other. I watch, transfixed, my chest heaving, as he sensually licks first one huge finger and then the next.

"Fucking divine," he growls.

"Everett," I moan, running my hands down his broad shoulders and corded forearms.

"Yes, baby?"

"Fuck me," I whisper, kissing his chin.

He grunts, his hips jerking upwards. "What's the magic word?"

"Now," I snap.

A strangled noise—something between a moan and a laugh—escapes him, and the next thing I know, I'm on my back with him hovering over me. He keeps all of his weight on his arms so as to not crush me.

"Are you sure, baby?" he whispers, staring intently down at my face, gauging my reaction for any signs of discomfort or regret.

But I want him.

I love him.

I cup his face and meet his lips in a kiss so fiery and passionate, I wouldn't be surprised if the couch we're on explodes into flames.

"I'm sure," I whisper.

He nods once, his eyes searching mine, and reaches between our bodies for his massive dick.

"I'll go slow," he promises, and the tip of him enters me, one inch at a time.

My breath hitches at the intrusion, because gods above, he's huge. Somehow, he feels even bigger inside of me, both in width and length.

"You're okay, Thea. You're okay," Everett soothes, pausing to allow me time to adjust. When I nod, encouraging him to continue, he pushes another inch inside of me. "Look at how well you're taking my cock. You look so goddamn beautiful like this."

Inch after painful inch, he enters me. And when he's finally all the way inside of me, he pauses, lowering his forehead to mine.

"Are you okay, baby?" He kisses away first one tear and then the next.

When did I start crying?

But I am okay, despite the initial pain.

He may not have rewritten my past—none of the guys are capable of doing that—but he's replacing a horrible memory with a better one. Now, when I think of the battle with Ares, I'll remember this moment, with him.

"I'm perfect," I promise. Then, in a more hesitant voice, I add, "But go slow at first."

Everett's eyes heat as he nods, kissing my lips chastely before I force him to deepen it, my tongue tangling with his. I may want him to go slow, but that doesn't mean I want him to hold back. Not with me. Never with me.

I survived things no one should ever have to go through, and I emerged on the other side of it stronger than anyone can possibly imagine. I can handle everything Everett throws at me—all of his anger and passion.

Everett begins to move his hips—but slowly at first. Allowing me to get used to him. He slides a hand down my belly to stroke the sensitive bundle of nerves.

"Yes, Everett," I cry out, wrapping my legs around his waist and digging my heels into the toned muscles of his ass. "Faster."

"Are you sure?"

"Yes."

He grins slightly—devilishly—before picking up the pace, his balls slapping against me with every forward thrust. The sensation of being stretched and filled by him is like nothing I've ever felt before. As he fucks me, he continues to play with my clit, stroking and thrumming it with ruthless abandon.

My body arches as my climax rampages through me, stealing my breath and all coherent thoughts. All I'm capable of doing is chanting his name. A feeling of rightness, of belonging, cascades through me as Everett's hips turn jerky and he roars out his own release.

This is where I belong.

With him.

With them.

Our breathing is shallow as we stare at each other, both of us lost in the moment. Lost in each other. I can't look away from his eyes, which seem to be speckled with gold.

"I love you so damn much, Thea," Everett whispers, his eyes sparking with adoration.

He leans down to brush his nose against mine, the cute gesture doing just as much to me as those words.

"I love you too," I whisper, maintaining eye contact.

I want him to see my sincerity, to know that he owns me, heart, body, and soul.

An expression I would almost describe as giddy lights up Everett's face. He shifts us slightly so I'm nestled in the crook of his arm, my back against the couch. He absently strokes my bare skin.

"The others are going to be here soon," he tells me, though he makes no room to move or get up.

I grin up at him. "Are you suggesting we turn this two-way into a five-way?"

I have the great pleasure of seeing red creep into his cheeks as he sputters and coughs. When I laugh, he playfully snarls.

"Brat." He swats at my ass, and I giggle, attempting to arch away.

"You act like that's a bad thing, but you know you love it," I tease, smiling up at him.

And then my smile fades as I'm wracked by pain so intense that my breath leaves me.

"Thea?" Everett's eyes instantly shadow with concern, and he shifts us so we're both sitting upright. "Baby? What's going on?"

"No...No...No," I whisper as my chest seems to crack down the middle, my internal organs rearranging themselves.

Behind Everett, the walls begin to drip steadily, blood raining down. A shadowy monster materializes from around the corner, grinning malevolently.

"Thea! Answer me! What's happening?" Everett's eyes are frantic as they search my own.

But I can't speak past the pain twisting up my insides.

The bandage Athena put on me... It broke.

It finally snapped, just like she said it would. I don't know if it's because of the excess of souls on earth or something else, but I know that this is it. I can feel it in my bones.

The end.

"Everett." Tears cascade down my cheeks as I stare into his ruggedly handsome face, knowing it will be the last time I'll ever see it. "I love you. I love the others. Tell them."

His eyes widen. "Thea, no. Please—"

But before he can finish his sentence, I'm yanked away.

I must black out for a second, because when I reopen my eyes, I'm no longer with Everett in the safe house.

I'm back in my little room, with the dagger of souls clenched tightly in my hand.

CHAPTER FORTY-FOUR

THEA

I'm...back.

In my bedroom.

My prison.

My personal hell.

However you want to look at it.

I'm back, and the voices are screaming at me, and the walls are oozing tar, and shadowy monsters are crawling towards me, and a frog is hopping on my easel. At least I'm dressed, though I have no idea how that happened. Better than being butt-ass naked, though.

And there, directly in front of me, is the pedestal that will end this all. The madness. The hallucinations. The incessant voices. The pain.

How is this even possible?

I haven't reaped a soul that I know of. Or maybe I

did and haven't even realized it. Maybe souls were attracted to the tattoo on my hip wherever I went and only Athena's spell blocked the effects.

Tears prick my eyes.

I want this to stop, but doing so will be giving the bastard exactly what he or she wants—more power.

"No!" I scream, knowing no one will hear me. "No more!"

I refuse to be an unwitting pawn in this scheme a second longer.

Is it Ares, attempting to use this power to free himself from the Underworld?

"You're not getting any more power," I growl at no one in particular.

And so, for the first time in my life, I don't drop the dagger onto the pedestal. I keep it held firmly in my hand, ignoring the burning, prickling sensation spreading up my arm. God, it feels like it's on fire. Like *I'm* on fire.

"Stupid bitch!"

"Die!"

"Did you really think you could escape us?"

"You're meant to be alone."

"SHUT UP!" I scream, placing my hands over my ears.

They're wrong. I'm not meant to be alone. I have the guys, and I know that they're searching for me right now. They won't rest until they find me. I just have to be patient. I just have to—

No. Fuck that. I'm not some pretty princess who needs to be saved. I'll find my own way out of here, regardless of the consequences.

"There's no escape."

"You're trapped here forever."

"Forever."

"Forever."

"Forever."

"Shut the fuck up!" I bellow, slamming my dagger in the general direction of one of the voices.

But of course, it goes through nothing but air... before slamming into the wall.

And cutting through it.

For a moment, shock holds me immobile, rooting my feet to the ground. Then I'm moving, grabbing my fallen dagger and slicing at the stone in front of me.

"What the fuck?" I whisper.

It cuts through the wall like butter.

"No fucking way," I breathe, tears pricking my eyes, though I'm not sure if they're from horror or relief.

Never in my life have I used the dagger outside of work. When I wasn't reaping souls, the dagger sat on the pedestal. A part of me always associated it with madness and pain. I didn't want to put myself through that any longer than necessary, so as soon as I released the dagger, I promptly ignored it until my next call.

So, to discover that I could have escaped hundreds of years ago? It's a slap to the face.

The dagger is power. Raw, unfettered power.

And right now, it may just be the thing that will set me free.

I ignore the voices, the pain, the monsters that slash and claw at me, the screaming in my head. Gritting my teeth together, I cut at the wall, creating a rectangular shape large enough for me to squeeze through. When my creation is completed, I shove at it, pushing it back.

"Fuck," I whisper, whirling around.

I'm not leaving this room without Potty the Cactus. Fuck that.

I grab the cactus and hug her against my chest, but of course the prickly bitch doesn't even thank me for freeing her.

With my heart hammering in my chest, I race through the hole.

And enter a very, very familiar apartment.

"No fucking way," I breathe.

From the bed, Aphrodite turns to stare at me, the slightest widening of her eyes the only sign of her surprise at my appearance. But then a cold, malevolent grin unfurls on her perfect lips as she stands gracefully, dressed from head to toe in black fighting leathers.

"To be completely honest, I didn't expect you to find your way out," she says casually, brushing her manicured hand over the mantel of her fireplace. "You didn't in over four centuries, yet you managed to escape in less than ten minutes now."

"I didn't have motivation before," I hiss, trying to ignore the cockroach crawling out of the goddess's ear.

If she isn't reacting to it, then that means it probably isn't real. Or she just has a really strange fetish.

"You mean those...teammates of yours?" Her lips quirk up. "I was actually just about to go see them. Offer my help in tracking you down. Of course I would offer them a shoulder to cry on when they need it." Her smile grows, turning malicious and wicked. "And a tight pussy when they decide they're done waiting for you."

I slowly lower Potty to the ground, never taking my eyes off the Goddess of Bitchy. "You bitch."

Aphrodite throws her head back in lilting laughter, the sound as beautiful as it is dangerous. "*I'm* the bitch. Me?" She sneers, her perfect face distorting into something I would almost describe as grotesque. "You're the one who stole Ares from me."

Her accusation actually takes me by surprise.

I gawk at her. "What?!"

"He became obsessed with you," she says, her lips curling in a sneer. "He was devastated when he hurt you." She tsks her tongue disapprovingly. "Did you know that I was the one who stumbled upon your broken, naked body?" A mirthless chuckle escapes her. "You begged me to help you, to save you, but all I could see was the piece of trash my lover fucked. I wanted to leave you to die, but then I came up with another solution for you."

"You... You trapped me. Used me to collect the power from souls." Horror fills me as I finally see Aphrodite as she truly is.

Her beautiful face belies something much more hideous.

She's a monster. No amount of makeup can hide the vile woman underneath it.

"It was Athena's idea, actually, though I'm sure she didn't intend for me to do what I did." She wets her lips, a devious smirk on her face. "You see, people always forget that I'm more than just the Goddess of Beauty. I'm also the Goddess of Love. When Athena lost her lovers, she came to me for advice. I hinted that there could be a way for her to tie their souls to hers so she could be with them always. Athena, of course, ran with the idea and created the first rune—the one designed to hold souls.

"She decided not to use it, but me? Well, I've always been an opportunist." She absently glances at her manicured fingernails, buffing them on the edge of her shirt like a walking, talking mean-girl cliché. "It's about time a woman runs this male-dominated world, wouldn't you say?"

"If that woman is anyone but you, then yes," I deadpan, taking great satisfaction in the way her eyes flare with anger.

Good. I want her to be angry. She seems to be more willing to tell me her nefarious schemes that way.

"I found the second rune in an ancient tome," Aphrodite continues. "This was designed to transfer power from one being to another. I wanted to see if it would work with souls, and it did." A giddy, euphoric giggle escapes her, making me cringe. "It was quite simple to wipe your memories. After that, it was easy—almost too easy, if you ask me. Whenever you reaped a soul, you did it for me, not Hades."

Something bitter crosses her face then. "Every god and goddess always underestimated me. They thought I was a vapid, shallow bitch just because I specialized in love and beauty. But there's more to me than meets the eyes."

I mean, I can understand her being pissed that she's looked down upon by the other gods. But does that really justify all of the evil acts she committed to gain more power? Yeah...no. I'm all for girl power, but this bitch is simply delusional.

"I thank you for helping me realize my full potential," Aphrodite says, smiling. But then her lips curl downwards and her eyes narrow. "But I have no more use for a self-aware, repulsive brat."

The air shivers around me, electric and thick with tension.

I tighten my fingers around the hilt of the dagger, even as another wave of agony ripples through me.

"You're out of your depth, reaper," Aphrodite says in a singsong voice.

I meet her gaze, unflinching. "You've taken what doesn't belong to you. All of those souls you destroyed? All of that power you took? Yeah...I'm going to need that back."

I lower myself into a defensible stance—the way I remember doing in my past training.

A flicker of amusement crosses her face at my defiance before her lips curl. "Magic flows through all things, Thea. It's my right—just as love is. I simply... take what's mine."

She raises her hand, a deceptively casual gesture, and the world around us warps. The air hums and crackles, and my breath hitches in my chest as a pulse of pure energy rips through me—too much, too fast. My heart skips then hammers in my chest, but I hold my ground.

I've dealt with pain all my life. This is nothing.

I can feel it now—the way her power infiltrates my

mind, wrapping around every thought, every instinct. It's not just the magic. It's *her*. The essence of love, the tenderness, the hunger, the need to drop my weapon and give in to her.

I grit my teeth, trying to shove it aside.

Aphrodite tilts her head, watching me struggle. Her eyes glow with wicked delight. "Do you feel it, my dear? The rush of creation, of devotion, of obsession? It courses through your veins now. This is what it is to hold true power. You're mine to do with as I wish."

I don't want to feel it, but I do. God help me, I do. The magic surges in me, flooding my senses—sweet and intoxicating. I can't escape it. Aphrodite must've been holding back the last time we visited her. This... This is like nothing I've ever felt before. I can feel her power everywhere, crackling through the air like waves of electricity. It's pure and intense and not hers.

I think of my guys.

That's true love. Not...this. Not this twisted, demented emotion she's attempting to make me feel. Fuck her.

I tighten my grip on the dagger, and despite the hallucinations and voices and agonizing pain...my mind is clearer than before.

I won't let her control me.

Aphrodite laughs softly, a sound that chills me to the bone. "You think you can resist? You think you can stop me? You are nothing but a shadow, a whisper against the storm of desire."

Does she hear herself? My god. Who talks like that in real life?

She's probably the type who thinks she's far more educated and posh than she truly is. She attends book clubs after reading the summaries on Wikipedia.

Bitch.

With a roar, I dive at her with my dagger, the blade slicing through the air with an audible hiss.

But she's fast—too fast. She swirls away with a jovial laugh, her magic surging again. It wraps around my limbs, squeezing, suffocating. I gasp for air, but it's like my body's pinned by invisible hands.

My thoughts start to blur as her magic pokes and prods at my brain, whispering seductive promises, but I fight against it.

You love the guys.

You love the guys.

I love the guys.

I gather my strength and pull myself free, ripping through the magic by sheer force of will. Aphrodite's eyes flash with surprise and then begrudging admiration.

"I can see why Ares loved you so much," she muses, her power swirling around us like a tempest.

"Do you know what that fucker did to me?" I

scream. "He hurt me. Beat me. Assaulted me. Left me for dead. He's a monster."

If I expected the Goddess of Love and Beauty to be sympathetic to me, I was sorely mistaken. She simply waves an errant hand in the air, her nostrils flaring.

"I don't want to talk about that cheating, lying bastard a second longer. You're lucky I didn't kill you the second I found you, like the whore you are." She raises her hand again, and this time, the earth beneath my feet cracks open, sending waves of molten energy rushing at me.

I leap to the side, my heart pounding and adrenaline coursing through me.

There's no time to hesitate.

This time, there will be no second chances.

I had a life as Winnifred that ended horribly, and I refuse to allow that same fate to happen to Thea.

"Fuck you, bitch," I hiss, charging at her again, my dagger a blur of silver in the air.

The magic crackles as the blade cuts through the pulse of energy she sends out, splintering the attack.

The goddess's expression darkens. "You fight like you have nothing left to lose. But you do, Thea. You have everything to lose. Do you really think I'll allow this slight to stand? If you give up now, I'll leave your precious men alone, but if you don't..."

She steps forward, her lips curling into a predatory

smile. "I'll fuck them until they forget you even exist. Then, when they're so consumed by love for me, I'll slit their fucking throats."

A roar of rage bursts free.

She can threaten me all she wants, but the second she mentions my men? Yeah, the gloves have come off. She'll fucking die.

I swipe at her repeatedly, forcing her back step after step—and straight onto my cactus.

She screams in pain, flicking her gaze towards the plant.

"What the fuck?" She lifts a foot to kick it away, but I slash at her before she can, cutting the fabric of her shirt.

No one is allowed to hurt Potty.

"Enough playing, you insolent bitch!" She lifts her arms in the air—

Just as the door to her apartment is kicked open, my guys spilling inside, followed by a panting Athena.

"Thea!" Everett calls, relief overtaking his features.

They're here.

My guys are here.

They found me.

I knew they would—that they wouldn't stop—but to see the evidence firsthand...

Everything around me fades away.

The voices go silent, as if they're holding their

collective breaths. The blood dripping from the wall freezes, as do the shadowy monsters advancing in my direction.

A few things become painfully clear.

My men came for me, as they promised they would.

Aphrodite is a threat that needs to be stopped.

I'm the only one capable of doing that.

The goddess is currently distracted, her gaze homing in on my men, whom she deems the biggest threat.

Her mistake.

I don't think, don't give myself a chance to second-guess my decision.

I bring the dagger down into Aphrodite's heart.

For a moment, nothing happens. We simply stand there, her eyes slightly narrowed and her lips parted. But then the ground beneath us begins to shake and a wild wind whips through the apartment. Furniture goes flying, and even Athena is knocked off her feet, slamming into the wall with an audible thump.

Spirit after spirit leaves the dagger in glittering silver orbs that fill the air like a million shooting stars.

Free. They're free.

"No!" Aphrodite screams, twisting, blood foaming in her mouth.

Cracks materialize on her beautiful face like stone that has been dropped on concrete one too many times.

"The only thing capable of killing you is the same power you stole," I whisper, my hands shaking from exertion. But I force myself to hold on, force myself to stare into her wide, terrified eyes. "Goodbye, Aphrodite. I hope you enjoy an eternity in Tartarus with Ares."

My legs tremble and then give out. I drop to my knees, tears spilling down my cheeks.

"Someone stop her!" Athena yells. "This is killing her."

But I can't stop. I won't. Not until all of the souls are free and Aphrodite is gone from this earth for good.

One final soul...

"Thea, baby, please. Stop," Everett begs.

"Thea!" Krystian cries out.

Someone else is crying beside me.

Rafe.

I'm not sure he has ever cried before in his life.

"Sweetheart, stop. It's over. Please," Zaid pleads.

I can feel myself fading, dark splotches erupting across my vision.

And then Aphrodite shatters into a thousand pieces like a boulder that just exploded.

I fall, only to immediately be captured by strong arms.

Four faces surround me, peering down at me as if I'm their entire world.

I'm sorry, I want to say.

Please forgive me.

But I don't have time for all of that. So instead, I say the only thing I can think of.

"I love you."

And then I die.

CHAPTER FORTY-FIVE

Death is painful.

Who would've thought?

At first, I'm tumbling head over heels in a fathomless abyss of darkness. It feels like it lasts for an eternity but is probably more like five minutes.

Then I see a blinding flash—the light at the end of the tunnel?—and I find myself drifting towards it.

Floating.

Buoyant.

Free.

I know that there's something I need to remember —or someone—but whenever I try to grasp a hold of the thought, it eludes me.

Then I fall through a portal and land on my knees, the impact rattling my teeth.

What the...?

It all comes rushing back to me.

The guys.

Ares.

The guys.

Aphrodite.

The guys.

The fight.

The guys.

The guys.

My guys.

I peer around my surroundings, momentarily surprised to find myself in Hades's throne room. The God of Death himself stands before me, his expression unreadable.

"You killed a goddess," he says, his tone carefully impassive.

I can't quite tell how he feels about that.

Am I going to be punished?

The thought of spending my afterlife trapped in Tartarus with the very people who tortured me in life...

A chill slithers down my spine.

"I'm...dead," I whisper, the revelation settling over me like a heavy cloak, weighing me down.

"Yes," Hades answers simply.

I swallow.

Fuck.

My guys...

They're probably devastated. They've just opened themselves to love after years of fighting against it. Will they ever find someone now that they've lost me again? A selfish part of me rebels at the thought of them with another woman, the little green monster inside of me rearing her ugly head. But at the end of the day... I just want them to be happy.

Even if it's not with me.

Hades's next words shock me speechless.

"But you don't have to be."

"What?"

His piercing silver eyes rest on my own. "I want to offer you a deal, young reaper. As you know, your... teammates have been granted immortality by Ares, and though Ares is locked away, he's still alive. They will live as long as they don't do anything reckless. I'm willing to offer you immortality as well, but only if you do something for me."

This sounds too good to be true—which usually means it is. But I'm desperate. I would do anything, give up anything, to be with my men.

"Tell me what you need," I say, my words tumbling over themselves in their haste to escape.

"I want you to be my reaper," Hades says simply. "My personal reaper, who works directly alongside me. There are thousands and thousands of reapers out in the world, but their lifespans are only slightly longer than that of a human. With the immortality I'll grant you, you can help train the new reapers, as well as reap souls that have...captured my interest, so to speak. There are a lot of souls roaming this earth, and now that the Underworld has been balanced, I'm going to need all the help I can get reaping them."

A ball of tension forms in my throat as I gape at him.

"W-why me?" I whisper. "You could have asked any reaper to do this. Why did you choose me?"

I know it's not because of my sparkly personality.

Hades regards me indifferently for a long moment, his head tilted to one side, before he blows out a breath. "I told you. I created you."

"You create all reapers," I point out.

"Not in the way I created you," Hades says. Then, his voice softer than I've ever heard before, at least directed at me, he adds, "Persephone always wanted a child. I agreed to give her one. You were the result."

Shock wraps its spindly fingers around my throat and squeezes. I suck in a sharp, shuddering breath.

"*What?*"

"You're not my biological daughter." Hades focuses on something in the distance, something only he can see, his lips compressing into a perfectly straight line. "But you're also not a normal reaper. You were chosen as a baby to be our child. Our Winnie. We knew you would have potential to be strong—after all, Ares chose you as his champion—and we wanted you for ourselves. Your birth mother died during childbirth, and your birth father was no longer in the picture. So... we took you. Raised you. Treated you as our own since neither of us can have children."

I can't even begin to wrap my head around this revelation.

Hades and Persephone were my...adoptive parents? What the hell?

Later. I'll dissect this discovery later, when I have the brain capacity to do more than gawk.

"Did you...?" I suddenly can't ask the question. It gets trapped in my throat, corrugating into a huge ball. But the words need to be said, despite my trepidation. "Did you look for me? When I went missing, I mean? Did you look for me?"

Hades's eyes sharpen, and he purses his lips, considering. At first, I think he's not going to answer, but then he rasps out, "Yes, I looked for you. I tore the whole damn world—and the Underworld—apart to find you. Ares reported you as missing, and I was foolish enough to take his word at face value. To believe him. If I would've known what he did...that Aphrodite had you right underneath our noses this entire time..."

He hisses out a breath, his hand forming a fist by

his side. Then he takes a deep, calming breath and forces his fingers to relax. "But alas, hindsight is...how do they say it? A bitch. I'm going to be honest, Thea.

"I don't know how to be a father to you. I didn't when you were a child, either. Persephone seems to believe there's something wrong with me, and that may be true, but I *will* protect you. You're my...responsibility." He clears his throat, his gruff countenance dropping for just a second. "So accept my offer. Become my reaper. Stay with your men. It's the best I can offer you."

Unexpected tears fill my eyes. Maybe he doesn't love me, and that's okay. But he's offering me the chance to spend eternity with men who do. I'll be forever grateful for that.

"I accept," I whisper, my heart thundering in my chest.

Hades clears his throat, appearing uncomfortable with my tears. "Good. Now I'm going to send you back and—"

"Wait!" a feminine voice shouts, and Persephone runs into the throne room, breathing raggedly.

She throws herself at me in a bruising hug, but this time, I return it.

My...mother.

Fuck, that's weird to even think in my head, especially since she looks only a few years older than me.

"Please promise you'll return," she whispers brokenly, her tears wetting my shoulder.

I meet Hades's steely eyes, and he nods slightly, letting me know he'll find a way to make that happen.

"I promise," I tell her.

This time, I actually mean it.

Persephone pulls away and sniffles. "Good." A wobbly smile spreads on her face. She cups my cheeks, her touch incredibly gentle. "I'm so, so proud of you, my darling girl. And I'm so, so sorry we couldn't save you the first time around."

"You're allowing me to return to my men," I tell her. "I can forgive you both for just about anything because of that."

A single tear cascades down Persephone's blotchy face, though she doesn't lift a finger to brush it away.

"Go. Return to your loves. We'll be here when you need us." She gives my cheeks one final squeeze and then releases me, stepping away.

I turn to face Hades—my father.

"I'm ready," I tell him. "Bring me to my men."

CHAPTER FORTY-SIX

THEA

One thing is certain. I am most definitely not a fan of dying and coming back to life. It fucking hurts.

Hades couldn't have healed me when he brought me back to the land of the living? Even a little bit?

Dad of the year.

Awareness returns to me in stages. First, I become aware of an incandescent burning sensation in my chest, like my heart has been physically removed from my body and stomped on. Then my hands and feet begin to tingle. A pounding headache erupts behind my eyelids, drowning out all other sounds.

Finally, I hear the voices.

Their voices.

Rafe. Everett. Krystian. Zaid.

My blood fae. My shifter. My elf. My wraith.

It feels like I'm swimming through sticky black tar that clings to my skin. I'm desperate to escape it, desperate to get to them, but the darkness holds me back.

Let. Me. Go.

With one final burst of strength, I lunge to the surface, coughing and sputtering.

"Thea!"

Four faces hover around me, their expressions ranging from shocked to disbelieving. Hope and pain battle for dominance in their eyes.

Fuck, my chest hurts. And my head. And my face. And my arms. And my legs. And my—

Can I just say everything hurts?

Dying sucks.

Arms are around me instantly, though I can't tell which pair belongs to which guy. What I do know is that I'm in Aphrodite's destroyed apartment, lying on a bed that smells fresh, like the sheets have been cleaned recently.

"See? I told you she'll be fine," a familiar voice retorts dryly from somewhere over their shoulder.

Athena?

"Don't you ever fucking do that shit again," Krystian reprimands me, pulling back just enough to stare at me intently. Tears glisten in his dark-blue eyes. "Don't you dare fucking die again."

I manage a weak smile. "Wasn't planning on it."

"What the fuck were you thinking?" Everett roars, his arms tightening around me.

He lowers his head so he can inhale my hair—which probably smells retched, if I'm being completely honest. Ugh.

"Athena told us you were making a deal with Hades to come back to us, but when you didn't wake up..." Zaid's voice breaks.

I flick my gaze in Athena's direction, only to find her watching me, her gaze keen and knowing.

"What happened?" I ask, my mind racing. "How did you guys get to me? How did you know where I was?"

"Athena pieced it together," Krystian responds, though he still doesn't sound like his usual jovial self. When I glance at him, he offers me a tentative, wobbly smile, his eyes glossy. "She told us that Aphrodite was more than likely behind your disappearance. We came here straight away."

"Aphrodite was the one who convinced me to create the rune in the first place, years before my lovers were killed, while they were still training. She told me it was the only way to keep them safe, to keep them with me, even when death tried to rip us apart," Athena pipes up, her tone solemn. "Once she gave you the dagger etched with runes, you were no longer reaping for the Underworld. You were reaping for *her*. She had been stronger the past century or two, though the change had been so subtle I'd barely paid attention to it. More crimes of passion. More sexual scandals. More affairs. It wasn't hard to put two and two together and realize she was the one behind all of this. She would've wanted you close, so I told your men that she's keeping you somewhere near her apartment."

"Of course you managed to break free without our help," Zaid says, a tiny sliver of amusement entering his voice. "Then..."

"Then you fucking died," Rafe snaps.

I tilt my head back to stare into his dark, arresting eyes, currently locked on me and brimming with unbridled anger.

"You died, and there was nothing we could do."

"We would've lost our shit completely if Athena hadn't told us you would come back," Everett says severely.

Once again, I glance at Athena, who's sitting in an armchair in a living room that has otherwise been torn apart.

The Goddess of Wisdom has certainly lived up to her name.

"You knew, didn't you? About my parents?" I ask her softly, though I already know the answer.

"I suspected," Athena says, her gaze distant. "Hades's reaction to Ares's attack only confirmed it."

"Your parents?" Krystian asks, a frown marring his perfect face.

"Hades and Persephone. They're my adoptive parents, apparently," I say.

Quickly, I explain what they told me and about the deal I made to remain with my guys.

"You'll be...immortal," Zaid repeats, sounding dazed. "Like us."

"And all I'll need to do is reap souls for Hades," I say.

Everett's perpetual scowl deepens. "Do you know what that will entail?"

I know he's thinking about the centuries of torture I endured reaping souls for Aphrodite. The insanity. The excruciating pain.

"It won't be like that," Athena interjects, sounding tired. "There will be no side effects reaping souls for the Underworld. And I doubt you'll reap much, anyway. Hades has thousands and thousands of reapers to do his bidding. I suspect he only offered Thea the position as a way to keep her around."

"Thea..." Krystian regards me curiously. "Should we even call you that anymore? Or should we start referring to you as Winnie?"

I wrinkle my nose in distaste. "Thea works, thank you very much."

It was the name I chose for myself, the name I earned. Winnifred died centuries ago, when she was abused and broken and left for dead. I don't want to remember that life. Maybe, in time, I'll find a way to regain my lost memories. It'll be nice to see how I fell in love with the guys the first time around.

But that's then. This is now.

A new story.

A new beginning.

Emotions I can't quite articulate clog my throat, making it hard to breathe. I reach forward instinctively, not even caring which guy I'm holding on to. I need them all.

Over their shoulders, Athena stands gracefully and nods in my direction.

"Thank you," she whispers, and I know her gratitude extends far beyond stopping Aphrodite and Ares.

I may not have been able to give her back her lovers, but I freed them. That's the next best thing.

I nod, and for a moment, we stare at each other in silent solidarity. Then she smiles weakly and slides out the door, shutting it gently behind her.

Leaving me alone with my guys.

I hug them all to me—even Rafe, who I suspect

would rather stab his eye out than engage in group cuddles. But I need to feel them against me. Their hearts pounding in tandem to mine. Their heat enveloping me.

They're alive. I'm alive. We're alive.

Even my pain is dissipating. I can't help but wonder if Hades had a part to play in that. I almost feel...normal.

"Is this real?" I ask no one in particular, belatedly aware of hands caressing my back, hair, and face.

"It better fucking be real," Krystian snaps. "Or so help me god—errr gods—I'll burn the world down."

"You're ours, Thea. Now and forever," Everett says solemnly.

"You were ours then, and you're ours now," Zaid agrees.

Rafe simply says, "Ours."

Their possessive ownership of me sends heat careening down my back.

I...want them.

Need them.

I defied death to get this chance with them. Not even a second chance but a third one. I'll be damned if I waste even a single moment of our time together.

I reach for Zaid first since he's closest to me and claim his lips with mine. It's a ravenous kiss saying everything that I don't dare say out loud. I put all of my feelings and emotions into it, refusing to hold back. Not now. Not ever again.

Zaid deepens the kiss, his hands tangling in my hair and tugging gently. Someone else moves behind me and slides their tongue across my throat.

Krystian.

A needy, desperate sound escapes me. I instinctively arch my neck, granting the elf better access. His lips skate across my skin, and goose bumps flutter on both of my arms.

I reach for Everett to the right of me and tug on the waistband of his pants, urging him closer.

He chuckles, the sound low and spine-tingling. "Greedy little thing, aren't you?"

He hasn't even begun to see greedy.

I wrench my lips away from Zaid's just long enough to exclaim, "I died, you know. And if that doesn't deserve a sexy five-way, then I don't know what does. Dying is actually quite painful. Zero out of ten, wouldn't recommend. Seriously, fuck death. And fuck Aphrodite while we're at it too. So yeah. Dying. It sucks. I think I deserve—"

Everett cuts off my rant with another possessive kiss, one I feel from the roots of my hair to the tips of my toes. His mouth moves over mine fiercely, angrily, the scruff on his face providing a delicious amount of friction.

When he pulls away, his eyes burn with an indecipherable emotion—an emotion that looks a lot like anger.

"Don't fucking talk about that," he rasps out, his large chest heaving.

"Talk about what?" I furrow my brows. "Dying?"

All four of my men flinch.

"Yeah…maybe we can discuss this in a few hundred years. Or maybe never," Krystian says with a one-shoulder shrug.

He distractedly runs a hand through his dark-blond locks.

"That was the worst moment of my life, Thea," Rafe whispers. His dark, penetrating gaze homes in on my face. "I can't even think about it without…"

He clenches his jaw and balls his hands into fists.

"We lost you." Zaid grabs my hands and holds them in his. "Not once, but twice. I'm not sure how any of us can survive that."

A huge boulder drops in my stomach. "I'm here now. And I'm not going anywhere. Pinkie promise."

Everett snorts, some of the pain I saw before dissipating from his eyes. "Pinkie promise? You're weird."

"Not weird enough to keep you away," I quip.

"Never."

Then we're kissing again. Honestly, I'm not sure who reaches for whom. All I know is I find myself pulling away from the others to straddle his lap, my fingers buried in his sandy-colored hair.

He pulls away to press his forehead against mine. "I lost you, Thea."

"I know. We talked about this—"

"No," he interrupts, a tiny bit of a growl seeping into his tone. "I. Lost. You. You were with me, under my protection, when you were taken by Aphrodite just now."

I'm stunned to see a misting of tears in his normally combative hazel eyes.

"I'm so fucking sorry, baby." His voice breaks. "So sorry."

My heart aches for him, for the pain and guilt he feels. I want to tell him that it's not his fault at all. That he couldn't have prevented what happened. That everything worked out in the end.

But I know my words will provide little comfort right now. Instead, I need to show him that I'm not mad—and that there's no reason for him to apologize.

I slowly move off his lap and drop to my knees before him, staring at him through heavily lidded eyes.

"What are you doing, baby?" He arches an eyebrow, though molten heat enters his gaze.

I drag my nails up and down his thighs. "If it's not blatantly obvious, then I need to rethink my life choices."

"And what life choices are those?" Krystian asks, amused.

"Being a slut for the four of you," I answer honestly, and all of them groan.

I reach for the button of Everett's jeans and pop it open, then take my sweet damn time sliding the denim down his toned legs. His cock strains against his boxer briefs, the tip visible at the top. It presses against his stomach.

"Thea, you don't have to. For fuck's sake, you just died—"

"Shhh." I plant a kiss to his throbbing cock through the material of his boxers. "Let me do this. I want to do this."

I slowly inch the fabric of his underwear down until his massive cock springs free, already dripping with precum and desperate for my mouth.

"God, you're so fucking big," I praise, running the pad of my thumb over the slit at the tip. "I want to put my mouth on you, Everett. Can I?"

I bat my lashes up at him innocently, but I know he'll say yes. There's nothing but unbridled desire and possession in his gaze as he stares down at me. He'll give me whatever I ask for.

Fortunately, all I want is him.

Them.

"Fuck, yes. Baby. God." He throws his head back

with a muffled curse as I lower my head to his shaft and take him in deep, making sure to hollow my cheeks so I won't gag.

Behind me, I hear shuffling then feel hands on my pants, tugging them down. My panties follow next. Warm breath ghosts over my pussy, eliciting a moan from me.

"Yes, baby. Just like that. God, you suck my cock so good. You look so beautiful with saliva dripping down your chin and tears in your eyes. Fuck, there's nothing more perfect than you impaled on my cock."

Everett's dirty talk encourages me to move even faster, bobbing my head up and down his shaft with ruthless abandon.

A wet tongue glides across my pussy lips, and I gyrate my hips automatically, seeking more friction.

Krystian's low, throaty chuckle echoes from between my legs.

"You want more, sweetheart?" He kisses my slit.

"Does she deserve more?" Rafe demands from the side of me.

A second later, rough hands grab my shirt and yank it in half, tossing it aside. Much more gentle hands—Zaid's—unhook my bra, allowing my breasts to spill free.

Rafe angrily begins to palm them, his fingers

tweaking my nipples. "She fucking left us. I'm not sure she deserves anything."

I whimper and shake my hips, wordlessly encouraging Krystian to continue.

"That's not really her fault," Zaid reasons.

My sweet, gentle wraith.

"She *did* come back to us," Krystian points out.

"I don't fucking care what we decide, but for fuck's sake, I need her to move or I'm going to combust," Everett growls, his hands tightening in my hair.

Rafe moves until he's standing over Everett's shoulder, peering down at me with hard, unrelenting eyes.

"What do you say, little bird? Do you deserve to come?" He arches an eyebrow at me, not waiting for me to respond. Not that I even can, considering my mouth is otherwise occupied. "How about this? Why don't you suck Everett off like a good slut, then maybe I'll consider letting you come. Can you do that? Can you be my good girl and get Everett off?"

His taunting words are a challenge, and I've never been one to back down.

I resume sucking Everett's cock like my life depends on it, taking him in as deep as I can without gagging. Everett fucks my face ruthlessly, not holding back, his hands tangled in my disheveled hair.

Beneath me, Krystian occasionally nips and sucks

at my pussy, completely ignoring the sensitive bundle of nerves demanding his attention.

"Fuck." Everett pulls my mouth away from his dick with a guttural growl. Before I can ask him what's wrong, he picks me up and drags me onto him. We both groan as his cock slides into my wet, sensitive pussy. "I love the shit out of you, Thea. You know that, right?"

"I love you too," I whisper, pulling his lips to mine as I begin to ride him.

"Holy fuck," Krystian exclaims from behind. "God, that's hot."

"Why don't you join in?" Rafe suggests, a devilish glint in his dark eyes from where he watches me from behind Everett.

All I hear behind me is the shuffling of clothes, and then Krystian and Zaid move to stand on either side of me, both of them completely naked.

Fuck yes.

Still riding Everett, I reach for each of my men and grip their shafts tightly, beginning to stroke them. Krystian throws his head back with a muffled curse, while Zaid reverently strokes my cheeks.

"You're beautiful, sweetheart," Zaid says.

"Fucking divine," Krystian agrees.

"I'm close," Everett warns, grabbing one of my bouncing breasts and squeezing.

My own orgasm is fast approaching, and I close my eyes, preparing myself for the inevitable explosion.

But just before I can detonate, Rafe's raspy voice snaps out, "Don't let her come!"

Everett's grip tightens on my breast as he explodes inside of me, a guttural roar escaping him. His cock spasms inside of my pussy, and he drops his forehead to my shoulder, breathing hard.

I gape at him. "What...? Why...?"

Everett slowly slides out of me, an uncharacteristic impish smirk on his face. "Sorry, baby. I was just obeying the rules."

"But you're the boss!" I protest, feeling petulant.

Just as Everett deposits me back on my feet, I feel someone approach me from behind. I don't even have time to turn before Rafe is slapping my ass.

"Don't be a brat," Rafe warns—though his tone suggests that's exactly what he wants me to be.

However, I know that resisting will only lead to a lack of orgasms, which will make me really, really sad.

"I won't," I promise Rafe, spinning around.

I reach for him somewhat desperately, but he steps back with a disapproving tsking sound.

"Prove it," he purrs, then he flicks his gaze towards Krystian and Zaid. A wicked gleam ignites in his eyes. "Have you ever tried taking two at once?"

My heart begins to pound even faster, crashing against my breastbone.

"Like...DP?" I ask tentatively. "Double penetration."

Krystian moans and grabs his shaft, fisting it. "Fuck, just hearing you say that makes me want to bust a nut."

"Real romantic, Krys," Zaid says.

I'm not even sure he notices he instinctively used the nickname for Krystian's nighttime counterpart.

Krystian simply grins. "That's what all the girls say."

"All the girls, eh?" I place a hand on my hip and arch an eyebrow. "How many girls are you busting a nut with?"

His face drains of all color, and he offers me a sheepish smile. "Just you, my love. Forever just you."

"Damn right it's just me."

Maybe it's hypocritical to have the four of them share me yet not allow them to be with anyone else, but I'm a possessive bitch. These men are mine. Only mine.

"God, I love it when you get possessive of us," Rafe murmurs in my ear, then he punctuates the words with a teasing nip to my lobe.

I shiver. "Are you going to let me come now?"

"Not yet." He gives my behind a playful swat. "Now go to your men."

Everett slowly heaves himself off the armchair and moves towards the shelves against the far wall.

"What are you looking for?" I ask.

Everett grins impishly and then returns his attention to the shelf. A second later, he must find what he's looking for because he grabs a small bottle off the shelf and waves it triumphantly in the air.

"This!" He tosses the bottle to Krystian, who grins like the cat that got the cream.

When he catches me looking, he holds it up for me to inspect. "Lube."

"We need to warm you up first, sweetheart," Zaid explains gently. He turns towards Krystian. "Maybe start with a finger or two?"

"A finger?" Up my ass? Um...

Trepidation curdles low in my stomach, but it's tempered by something else. Something stronger.

Lust.

"Will that be okay, Thea?" Krystian brushes my hair over one shoulder and kisses my cheek. "We don't have to do anything if you don't feel comfortable."

"I want... I want to try." Does my voice come out embarrassingly high-pitched? Yes. Yes, it does.

Krystian pours a generous amount of lube on his hands and then moves towards me.

"Bend, darling," he instructs.

Oh, I can do one better.

With an impish smirk, I lower myself to all fours and give my ass a tiny shake.

"It might hurt a little bit at first," Krystian warns from behind me, sounding breathless.

"Just do it," I tell him, and a second later, his lubricated finger presses against my ass crack.

"Is this okay?" He sounds hesitant, and I realize he's scared of hurting me.

And after multiple lifetimes of nonstop pain, having someone care for me like this feels...amazing.

"Yes. A little strange, but not horrible."

"Good. I'm going to press in a little farther, okay?" His finger breaches the tight hole, finding resistance.

I wince instinctively at the initial stab of pain. It's not awful, but I can't imagine anything bigger than a finger inside of me. Even with lube, everything feels too tight.

"Another finger," Rafe instructs gruffly.

I can instantly tell when Krystian obliges. The stretch becomes even more intense.

Krystian begins to move his fingers slowly—in and out, in and out. My eyes roll into the back of my head as sensations overwhelm me.

"Do you think you can handle me in your ass,

shortstack?" Krystian rasps in my ear, sounding just as breathless and hoarse as me.

To be completely honest, I'm not sure. I've never given anal much thought before, but the thought of having two of my lovers at the same time...

A thrill cascades down my spine, heating my stomach. A flush crawls up my cheeks.

"Yes. Fuck, yes," I breathe, twisting my head to kiss him sloppily.

"I love you so damn much, Thea," Krystian tells me, removing his fingers. "You're my entire world."

I shudder in anticipation as the hard length of his cock presses against my stretched ass.

"Lube," Krystian instructs, and Rafe pours more lube on my ass and Krystian's cock.

His shaft teases my entrance, but he doesn't enter me. Not yet. I can tell he's still unsure, still worried about hurting me.

"Are you okay, sweetheart?" Zaid asks worriedly from in front of me.

I reach for him, pulling myself onto my knees in the process.

"I'm one hundred percent perfect," I assure him. "And I want you both. Now."

"Fucking hell," Krystian rasps.

Zaid simply stares at me, awe and love mingling in his dark, fathomless eyes.

My wraith doesn't ask me if I'm sure. He must see it in my eyes. Instead, he reaches for my shoulders, lines himself up with my wet pussy, and thrusts deep inside of me.

We both groan.

God, I feel so stuffed, so full, already. What will it be like with Krystian in my ass?

Zaid falls onto his back, and I shift myself until I'm straddling him, Krystian still teasing my ass.

Zaid reaches up to pinch my nipple, though his touch is gentler than Everett's. He begins to thrust his hips upwards, and I moan and throw my head back.

"Fuck, you look perfect," Krystian rasps from behind, inching his hips forward.

I gasp at the stretch, the fullness.

Definitely thicker than two fingers.

Zaid slows, allowing Krystian to enter me fully.

It hurts. It feels strange, but it also feels really fucking good. Holy fuck.

Zaid curses and tightens his grip on my tit, staring up at me like I'm the center of his existence.

A flush creeps into my cheeks at the ardent adoration in his gaze.

"I love you, Thea," he whispers.

"I love you too."

Just as those words leave my lips, Krystian thrusts

all the way inside of me, forcing me farther onto Zaid. He jolts and swears, lowering his grip to my hips.

"Look how perfect she looks between them," Rafe growls.

"Like a fucking goddess," Everett agrees.

It isn't long until my men find a rhythm. Krystian pulls out as Zaid pushes in, then they switch, the two of them fucking me in tandem. I can do nothing but whimper and cry as they work my body like it's their own personal toy to play with. All I can focus on is the sensation of their cocks sliding against each other, only a tiny sliver of skin separating them.

I feel full—too full. But it still isn't enough.

Lust streaks through me, and I can feel my orgasm fast approaching. I lower a hand between my body, prepared to strum my clit, when Rafe grabs ahold of my hand, stopping me.

"No," he growls, his eyes ensnaring mine and refusing to release them.

I swallow convulsively, shakes reverberating through my body, but refuse to look away. I'm still holding Rafe's penetrating gaze when Krystian groans and comes inside of my ass, which causes Zaid to explode inside of me with a shout.

Rafe doesn't wait until they slide out of me. Instead, he picks me up and pushes me against the wall. I instinctively wrap my legs around him and dig my heels into his ass.

"You're still dressed," I point out, breathless.

His expression doesn't change. "I am."

"How are you supposed to fuck me with pants on?" I give him a bratty eyebrow raise that I know will drive him insane.

He growls, the noise ricocheting through my body in a flood of liquid heat, and then presses his lips to mine.

Rafe is...kissing me.

Our first kiss.

It occurs to me then that he didn't kiss me during our first time together. Not once. He kissed my body, my breasts, my pussy...but not my lips. Never my lips.

I think I can die like this—with Rafe's lips melded to mine, his stubble dragging enticingly against my cheeks and chin. When his tongue prods the seam of my lips, demanding entrance, I grant it to him eagerly. We kiss and kiss and kiss—until I'm worried I may pass out from lack of oxygen.

Is that even possible for me? Dying again? I'll have to ask Hades about it later.

Though the last thing I want to think about right now is my father.

Rafe pulls away with a ragged gasp and presses his forehead against my own. His breathing is uneven as he stares at me, and for once, his eyes are swarming with a plethora of emotions.

"I love you, Thea. So much."

Unexpected tears burn my eyes at his confession. I know he does—he's shown it in all the ways that count—but out of all my guys, he's the least likely to admit it.

"I love you too."

Rafe doesn't even bother undressing. Instead, he uses one hand to free his throbbing cock while the other helps support my weight against the wall. He jerks his hips up and enters me in one thrust, his cock stretching me impossibly wide.

He fucks me ruthlessly, harshly, possessively. His eyes never leave my own.

"Promise you won't leave us again," he growls out.

"I promise," I pant out. I would say just about anything at the moment. I'm practically putty in his skilled hands. "And if I do leave you, I'll always come back."

Always.

Each strike of Rafe's hips against my own is almost painful, but I wouldn't want it any other way. I'm almost desperate for the bruises I know he's going to leave behind.

A sign of ownership.

Of claiming.

Of possession.

"Rafe..." I whimper, curling my fingers in his dark hair.

"Come for me, my goddess," he whispers, kissing me once more. "I want you to milk my cock like the good little slut I know you are."

I don't think I could stop my orgasm from coming even if he asked me to. I'm too pent-up, too needy, too desperate.

I explode around his shaft with a scream, stars blotting out my vision. I can't breathe, can't think, can't do anything but ride out wave after wave of lust.

I collapse against Rafe, feeling sweaty and sated and utterly spent.

And loved. So, so loved.

I don't know what's going to happen in the future, but I do know it won't be like the past. History won't repeat itself this time around.

I have my guys, immortality, and lifetimes upon lifetimes to perfect our happily ever after.

And nothing will stand in my way.

"I just don't want you to be disappointed." Krystian ruffles his hair, a frown marring his perfect lips.

"I won't be," I assure him as anticipation thrums through my veins.

I lick my lips, practically salivating at this point.

Rafe and Everett exchange amused looks before refocusing on me.

"You're so cute sometimes," Everett says with a rueful chuckle and a head shake.

"All the time." Rafe's grin broadens when I stick my tongue out at him.

He's been doing that more often—smiling. It's... magical to see, the way it completely transforms his face.

I'd like to think my presence in their lives brought

about that change, but I don't think it's the only factor. With Ares imprisoned, Aphrodite dead, and the gods in disarray, no one argued with us reopening the compound to volunteers willing to fight with us. So far, we have over one hundred teams that have trained to protect the innocents from the supernatural world.

Fuck the gods and their bets.

Maybe, in time, we'll be able to wake the other sleeping teams. There are dozens of them hidden away deep within the compound—a discovery that still makes me squeamish to this day. For now, this will have to do.

My guys still help when they can, but usually, they're spending their time training the recruits.

Which means lots and lots of free time.

Surprisingly, Athena agreed to also teach at the makeshift academy we created in the ruins of the old compound. It makes sense that the Goddess of Wisdom will have a class on war strategies.

"Come on," I whine, pouting. "I want it in my mouth."

Zaid coughs to hide his laugh, a red flush on his cheeks.

"Fighting words, shortstack." Krystian finally reaches into the popcorn bucket. "I'm going to throw it."

"Ready." I automatically open my mouth, waiting.

"You know, I have a better idea of what you can put in that sweet mouth of yours..." Rafe suggests with a dark smirk.

Without breaking eye contact with Krystian, I swat at my blood fae.

No one will ruin this moment for me.

"You ready?" Krystian arches an eyebrow.

"Ready," I respond.

Or at least, I try to, but it's kind of difficult with my mouth already open.

Krystian winds up dramatically and then tosses the buttery piece of popcorn at my mouth. I shift slightly in order to catch it and feel a deep sense of accomplishment when I do. Triumphantly, I raise both fists in the air.

Popcorn is *amazing*. Seriously, is this what I've been missing out on when I was imprisoned? Fuck that Goddess of Love and Beauty. Seriously, fuck her.

"So? What do you think?" Zaid queries, his eyes glimmering with something akin to adoration.

In lieu of a verbal answer, I moan obscenely, the noise eliciting growls from my four men.

I love popcorn. I do, but I love my men's cocks more. I want nothing more than to drop to my knees, free their straining erections, and—

A familiar tingle reverberates through me, and I inwardly curse Hades's horrible timing. Cock block.

My scythe materializes in my hand. It's strange to use this weapon after reaping souls with my dagger for so long, but I have to admit that I don't hate it. The handle feels like an extension of myself.

Everett releases a guttural rumbling sound. "Hades?"

"Yup." I pop the P.

A flicker of panic crosses Rafe's face as he takes a step closer. "Right now?"

It's been six months, and all of my men lose their shit whenever I get called away to reap a soul. I think they're afraid that one of these days, I won't return.

Fortunately, these missions only take a few minutes at a time, and they've become less and less frequent since we're finally caught up on reaping souls. Usually, my "duties" as Hades's official reaper is venturing into the Underworld for meetings with the King of the Dead.

I think this is just his excuse to spend time with me, though the grumpy bastard will never admit it.

"I love you all," I tell my men as I feel myself fade away.

"We love you too," they respond simultaneously.

And then I'm gone, the taste of death on my tongue and my scythe glimmering like molten moonlight in my hand.

There's no pain, no insanity, no incessant voices

screaming at me. Only...peace. Security. An innate knowledge that this is what I am meant to do.

Now invisible, I give my men a two-fingered salute that they can't even see before allowing the tides of death to pull me away.

A tiny smile curls up my lips.

Another day, another soul.

A reaper's job is never done.

I defied death, and then I became it.

And I wouldn't have it any other way.

AFTERWORD

Thank you so much for reading! As some of you know, this project started while I was on vacation and was *supposed* to be resting. I had just finished the first rough draft of Mated by Fire 3.

However, once I started writing, I found I couldn't stop. These characters consumed me. I decided to challenge myself. Am I capable of writing a book in a week? I worked every day as soon as I woke up until my hands started cramping. It was a series of long, emotional days. I fell asleep dreaming about these characters.

The result? Six days. It took me six days to complete the first rough draft of this story. Of course, it had to go through extensive self-edits, beta edits, and final edits. But I'm super proud of the story and world I created!

Maybe in the future, I can revisit these characters! Thank you so much for reading.

ACKNOWLEDGMENTS

Thank you to my alpha team—Mae, Tami, Rachel, and Ash. This book wouldn't have been possible without your feedback.

Thank you to my editor Lindsey and my cover designer Sanja.

A huge thank you to my Hot Pitches! Love all of you ladies.

And finally, I would like to thank you, my reader, for taking a chance on this story and world. I hope you enjoyed!

ABOUT THE AUTHOR

Katie May is a reverse harem author, a KDP All-Star winner, and an *USA Today* Bestselling Author. She lives in West Michigan with her family, cat, and adorable puppy. When not writing, she can be found reading a good book, listening to broadway musicals, or playing games. Join Katie's Gang to stay updated on all her releases! And did you know she has a TikTok? Yeah, me neither. Follow her here! But be warned... she's an awkward noodle.

Together We Fall (Apocalyptic Reverse Harem, COMPLETED)

1. The Darkness We Crave

2. The Light We Seek

3. The Storm We Face

4. The Monsters We Hunt

Beyond the Shadows (Horror Reverse Harem, COMPLETED)

1. Gangs and Ghosts

2. Guns and Graveyards

3. Gallows and Ghouls

Out of Sight (Prison Reverse Harem, COMPLETED)

1. Blindly Indicted

2. Blindly Acquitted

Kingdom of Wolves (Shifter Reverse Harem Duet, COMPLETED)

1. Torn to Bits

2. Ripped to Shreds

Tory's School for the Trouble (Bully Horror Academy Reverse Harem, COMPLETED)

1. Between

2. Beyond

3. Beneath

The Damning (Fantasy Paranormal Reverse Harem, COMPLETED)

1. Greed

2. Envy

3. Gluttony

4. Sloth

5. Pride

6. Lust

7. Wrath

Prodigium Academy (Horror Comedy Academy Reverse Harem, COMPLETED)

1. Monsters

2. Roaring

3. Venom

4. Fangs

5. Blood

Kings of Grove Academy (Contemporary Academy Reverse Harem)

1. Mania

2. Psychotic

3. Pandemonium

4. Delirium

The Death Whisper (Fantasy Reverse Harem)

1. Of Rain and Wrath

2. Of Heat and Obsession

3. Of Wind and Terror

Supernaturalette (Interactive Reverse Harem)

1. Introductions

2. First Dates

3. Group Outing

4. Game Night

5. Exes

6. Truth or Dare

7. Scavenger Hunt

8. Reveals

CO-WRITES

Afterworld Academy with Loxley Savage (Academy Fantasy Reverse Harem, COMPLETED)

1. Dearly Departed

2. Darkness Deceives

3. Defying Destiny

Darkest Flames with Ann Denton (Paranormal Reverse Harem, COMPLETED)

1. Demon Kissed

1.5. Demon Stalked

2. Demon Loved

3. Demon Sworn

Darkest Queen with Ann Denton (Paranormal Reverse Harem)

1. For Whom the Bell Tolls

Dark Temptations with Ann Denton (Monster Reverse Harem, COMPLETED)

1. Ravaged by Monsters

2. Devoured by Monsters

3. Worshipped by Monsters

Fae Revealed with Quinn Arthurs (Paranormal Reverse Harem)

1. Courting Darkness

2. Seducing Shadows

3. Loving Demons

STAND-ALONES

Toxicity (Contemporary Reverse Harem)

Not All Heroes Wear Capes (Just Dresses) (Short Comedic Reverse Harem)

Charming Devils (Bully/Revenge Reverse Harem)

Goddess of Pain (Fantasy Reverse Harem)

Demon's Joy (Holiday Reverse Harem)

Broken Howl (Wolf Shifter Reverse Harem)

Dark Paradise (Paranormal Motorcycle Club Reverse Harm)

Ruthless as a Cheetah (Paranormal Romantic Comedy Reverse Harem)

BOXSETS

Together We Fall